Henry James

Henry James OM (15 April 1843 – 28 February 1916) was an American-British author regarded as a key transitional figure between literary realism and literary modernism, and is considered by many to be among the greatest novelists in the English language. He was the son of Henry James Sr. and the brother of renowned philosopher and psychologist William James and diarist Alice James.

He is best known for a number of novels dealing with the social and marital interplay between émigré Americans, English people, and continental Europeans. Examples of such novels include The Portrait of a Lady, The Ambassadors, and The Wings of the Dove. His later works were increasingly experimental. In describing the internal states of mind and social dynamics of his characters, James often made use of a style in which ambiguous or contradictory motives and impressions were overlaid or juxtaposed in the discussion of a character's psyche.(Source: Wikipedia)

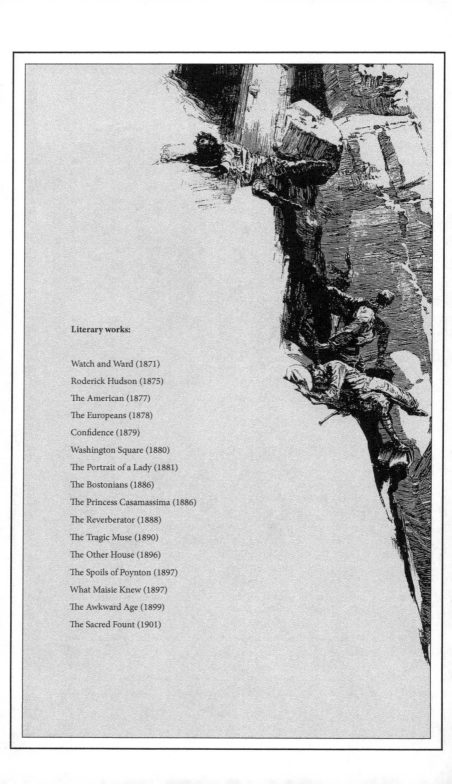

Literary works:

Watch and Ward (1871)

Roderick Hudson (1875)

The American (1877)

The Europeans (1878)

Confidence (1879)

Washington Square (1880)

The Portrait of a Lady (1881)

The Bostonians (1886)

The Princess Casamassima (1886)

The Reverberator (1888)

The Tragic Muse (1890)

The Other House (1896)

The Spoils of Poynton (1897)

What Maisie Knew (1897)

The Awkward Age (1899)

The Sacred Fount (1901)

Moon
CLASSICS

THE
WORKS
OF
HENRY JAMES

VOL. 03 (OF 24)

CONFIDENCE

DAISY MILLER

EMBARRASSMENTS

An Imprint of Moon Classics LLC

A Wholly Owned Subsidiary of Queenior LLC

A Melodragon Company

First Printing: 2020

ISBN 978-1-6627-1624-9 (Paperback)

ISBN 978-1-6627-1625-6 (Hardcover)

Published by Moon Classics

www.moonclassics.com

Contents

CONFIDENCE   **13**

CHAPTER I   15

CHAPTER II   26

CHAPTER III   30

CHAPTER IV   38

CHAPTER V   43

CHAPTER VI   48

CHAPTER VII   53

CHAPTER VIII   59

CHAPTER IX   67

CHAPTER X   73

CHAPTER XI   83

CHAPTER XII   91

CHAPTER XIII   99

CHAPTER XIV   104

CHAPTER XV   113

CHAPTER XVI   120

CHAPTER XVII   130

CHAPTER XVIII   138

CHAPTER XIX   140

CHAPTER XX   149

CHAPTER XXI   156

CHAPTER XXII   163

CHAPTER XXIII   168

CHAPTER XXIV   179

CHAPTER XXV   187

CHAPTER XXVI   196

CHAPTER XXVII   206

CHAPTER XXVIII   215

CHAPTER XXIX   225

CHAPTER XXX   234

DAISY MILLER 241

PART I 243

PART II 272

EMBARRASSMENTS 307

THE FIGURE IN THE CARPET 309

I 309

II 311

III. 315

IV 320

V 324

VI 327

VII 331

VIII 334

IX 337

X 339

XI 342

GLASSES 347

I 347

II 349

III 353

IV 357

V 361

VI 364

VII 366

VIII 370

IX   373

X   377

XI   381

XII   385

XIII   388

THE NEXT TIME   **394**

I   397

II   404

III   410

IV   418

V   424

THE WAY IT CAME   **433**

I   433

II   436

III   439

IV   442

V   444

VI   449

VII   454

About Author   **461**

NOTABLE WORKS   **479**

THE
WORKS
OF
HENRY JAMES
VOL. 03 (OF 24)

CONFIDENCE

CHAPTER I

It was in the early days of April; Bernard Longueville had been spending the winter in Rome. He had travelled northward with the consciousness of several social duties that appealed to him from the further side of the Alps, but he was under the charm of the Italian spring, and he made a pretext for lingering. He had spent five days at Siena, where he had intended to spend but two, and still it was impossible to continue his journey. He was a young man of a contemplative and speculative turn, and this was his first visit to Italy, so that if he dallied by the way he should not be harshly judged. He had a fancy for sketching, and it was on his conscience to take a few pictorial notes. There were two old inns at Siena, both of them very shabby and very dirty. The one at which Longueville had taken up his abode was entered by a dark, pestiferous arch-way, surmounted by a sign which at a distance might have been read by the travellers as the Dantean injunction to renounce all hope. The other was not far off, and the day after his arrival, as he passed it, he saw two ladies going in who evidently belonged to the large fraternity of Anglo-Saxon tourists, and one of whom was young and carried herself very well. Longueville had his share—or more than his share—of gallantry, and this incident awakened a regret. If he had gone to the other inn he might have had charming company: at his own establishment there was no one but an aesthetic German who smoked bad tobacco in the dining-room. He remarked to himself that this was always his luck, and the remark was characteristic of the man; it was charged with the feeling of the moment, but it was not absolutely just; it was the result of an acute impression made by the particular occasion; but it failed in appreciation of a providence which had sprinkled Longueville's career with happy accidents—accidents, especially, in which his characteristic gallantry was not allowed to rust for want of exercise. He lounged, however, contentedly enough through these bright, still days of a Tuscan April, drawing much entertainment from the high picturesqueness of the things about him. Siena, a few years since, was a flawless gift of the Middle Ages to the modern imagination. No other Italian city could have been more interesting to an observer fond of reconstructing obsolete manners. This was a taste of Bernard Longueville's, who had a relish for serious literature, and at one time had made several lively excursions into mediaeval history. His friends thought him very clever, and at the same time had an easy feeling about him which was a tribute to his freedom from pedantry. He was clever indeed, and an excellent companion; but the real measure of his brilliancy was in the success with which he entertained himself. He was much addicted to conversing with his own wit, and he greatly enjoyed his own society. Clever as he often was in talking with his friends, I am not sure that his best things, as the phrase is, were not for his own ears. And this was not on account of any cynical contempt for the understanding of his fellow-creatures: it was simply because what I have called his own society was more of a stimulus than that of most other people. And yet he was not for this reason fond of solitude; he was, on the contrary, a very sociable animal. It must be admitted at the outset that he had a nature which seemed at several points to contradict itself, as will probably be perceived in the course of this narration.

He entertained himself greatly with his reflections and meditations upon Sienese architecture and early Tuscan art, upon Italian street-life and the geological idiosyncrasies of the Apennines. If he had only gone to the other inn, that nice-looking girl whom he had seen passing under the dusky portal with her face turned away from him might have broken bread with him at this intellectual banquet. Then came a day, however, when it seemed for a moment that if she were disposed she might gather up the crumbs of the feast. Longueville, every morning after breakfast, took a turn in the great square of Siena—the vast piazza, shaped like a horse-shoe, where the market is held beneath the windows of that crenellated palace from whose overhanging cornice a tall, straight tower springs up with a movement as light as that of a single plume in the bonnet of a captain. Here he strolled about, watching a brown contadino disembarrass his donkey, noting the progress of half an hour's chaffer over a bundle of carrots, wishing a young girl with eyes like animated agates would let him sketch her, and gazing up at intervals at the beautiful, slim tower, as it played at contrasts with the large blue air. After he had spent the greater part of a week in these grave considerations, he made up his mind to leave Siena. But he was not content with what he had done for his portfolio. Siena was eminently sketchable, but he had not been industrious. On the last morning of his visit, as he stood staring about him in the crowded piazza, and feeling that, in spite of its picturesqueness, this was an awkward place for setting up an easel, he bethought himself, by contrast, of a quiet corner in another part of the town, which he had chanced upon in one of his first walks—an angle of a lonely terrace that abutted upon the city-wall, where three or four superannuated objects seemed to slumber in the sunshine—the open door of an empty church, with a faded fresco exposed to the air in the arch above it, and an ancient beggar-woman sitting beside it on a three-legged stool. The little terrace had an old polished parapet, about as high as a man's breast, above which was a view of strange, sad-colored hills. Outside, to the left, the wall of the town made an outward bend, and exposed its rugged and rusty complexion. There was a smooth stone bench set into the wall of the church, on which Longueville had rested for an hour, observing the composition of the little picture of which I have indicated the elements, and of which the parapet of the terrace would form the foreground. The thing was what painters call a subject, and he had promised himself to come back with his utensils. This morning he returned to the inn and took possession of them, and then he made his way through a labyrinth of empty streets, lying on the edge of the town, within the wall, like the superfluous folds of a garment whose wearer has shrunken with old age. He reached his little grass-grown terrace, and found it as sunny and as private as before. The old mendicant was mumbling petitions, sacred and profane, at the church door; but save for this the stillness was unbroken. The yellow sunshine warmed the brown surface of the city-wall, and lighted the hollows of the Etruscan hills. Longueville settled himself on the empty bench, and, arranging his little portable apparatus, began to ply his brushes. He worked for some time smoothly and rapidly, with an agreeable sense of the absence of obstacles. It seemed almost an interruption when, in the silent air, he heard a distant bell in the town strike noon. Shortly after this, there was another interruption. The sound of a soft footstep caused him to look up; whereupon he saw a young woman standing there and bending her eyes upon the graceful artist. A second glance assured him that she was that nice girl whom he had seen going into the other inn with her mother, and suggested that she had just emerged from the little church. He suspected, however—I hardly know why—that she had been looking at him for some moments before he perceived her. It would perhaps be impertinent to inquire what she thought of him; but Longueville, in the space of an instant, made two or three reflections upon the young lady. One of them was to the effect that she was a handsome creature, but that she looked rather bold; the burden of the other was that—yes, decidedly—she was a compatriot. She turned away almost as soon as she met his eyes; he had hardly time to raise his hat, as, after a moment's hesitation, he proceeded to do. She herself appeared to feel a certain hesitation; she glanced back at the church door, as if under the impulse to retrace her steps. She stood there a moment longer—long enough to let him see that she was a person of easy attitudes—and then she walked away slowly to the parapet of the terrace. Here she stationed herself, leaning her arms upon the high stone ledge, presenting her back to Longueville, and gazing at rural Italy. Longueville went on with his sketch, but less attentively than before. He wondered what this young lady was doing there alone, and then it occurred to him that her companion—her mother, presumably—was in the church. The two ladies had been in the church when he arrived; women liked to sit in churches; they had been there more than half an hour, and the mother had not enough of it even yet. The young lady, however, at present preferred the view that Longueville was painting; he became aware that she had placed herself in the very centre of his foreground. His first feeling was that she would spoil it; his second was that she would improve it. Little by little she turned more into profile, leaning only one arm upon the parapet, while the other hand, holding her folded parasol, hung down at her side. She was motionless; it was almost as if she were standing there on purpose to be drawn. Yes, certainly she improved the picture. Her profile, delicate and thin, defined itself against the sky, in the clear shadow of a coquettish hat; her figure was light; she bent and leaned easily; she wore a gray dress, fastened up as was then the fashion, and displaying the broad edge of a crimson petticoat. She kept her position; she seemed absorbed in the view. "Is she posing—is she attitudinizing for my benefit?" Longueville asked of himself. And then it seemed to him that this was a needless assumption, for the prospect was quite beautiful enough to be looked at for itself, and there was nothing impossible in a pretty girl having a love of fine landscape. "But posing or not," he went on, "I will put her into my sketch. She has simply put herself in. It will give it a human interest. There is nothing like having a human interest." So, with the ready skill that he possessed, he introduced the young girl's figure into his foreground, and at the end of ten minutes he had almost made something that had the form of a likeness. "If she will only be quiet for another ten minutes," he said, "the thing will really be a picture." Unfortunately, the young lady was not quiet; she had apparently had enough of her attitude and her view. She turned away, facing Longueville again, and slowly came back, as if to re-enter the church. To do so she had to pass near him, and as she approached he instinctively got up, holding his drawing in one hand. She looked at him again, with that expression that he had mentally characterized as "bold," a few minutes before—with dark, intelligent eyes. Her hair was dark and dense; she was a strikingly handsome girl.

"I am so sorry you moved," he said, confidently, in English. "You were so—so beautiful."

She stopped, looking at him more directly than ever; and she looked at his sketch, which he held out toward her. At the sketch, however, she only glanced, whereas there was observation in the eye that she bent upon Longueville. He never knew whether she had blushed; he afterward thought she might have been frightened. Nevertheless, it was not exactly terror that appeared to dictate her answer to Longueville's speech.

"I am much obliged to you. Don't you think you have looked at me enough?"

"By no means. I should like so much to finish my drawing."

"I am not a professional model," said the young lady.

"No. That's my difficulty," Longueville answered, laughing. "I can't propose to remunerate you."

The young lady seemed to think this joke in indifferent taste. She turned away in silence; but something in her expression, in his feeling at the time, in the situation, incited Longueville to higher play. He felt a lively need of carrying his point.

"You see it will be pure kindness," he went on,—"a simple act of charity. Five minutes will be enough. Treat me as an Italian beggar."

She had laid down his sketch and had stepped forward. He stood there, obsequious, clasping his hands and smiling.

His interruptress stopped and looked at him again, as if she thought him a very odd person; but she seemed amused. Now, at any rate, she was not frightened. She seemed even disposed to provoke him a little.

"I wish to go to my mother," she said.

"Where is your mother?" the young man asked.

"In the church, of course. I did n't come here alone!"

"Of course not; but you may be sure that your mother is very contented. I have been in that little church. It is charming. She is just resting there; she is probably tired. If you will kindly give me five minutes more, she will come out to you."

"Five minutes?" the young girl asked.

"Five minutes will do. I shall be eternally grateful." Longueville was amused at himself as he said this. He cared infinitely less for his sketch than the words appeared to imply; but, somehow, he cared greatly that this graceful stranger should do what he had proposed.

The graceful stranger dropped an eye on the sketch again.

"Is your picture so good as that?" she asked.

"I have a great deal of talent," he answered, laughing. "You shall see for yourself, when it is finished."

She turned slowly toward the terrace again.

"You certainly have a great deal of talent, to induce me to do what you ask." And she walked to where she had stood before. Longueville made a movement to go with her, as if to show her the attitude he meant; but, pointing with decision to his easel, she said—

"You have only five minutes." He immediately went back to his work, and she made a vague attempt to take up her position. "You must tell me if this will do," she added, in a moment.

"It will do beautifully," Longueville answered, in a happy tone, looking at her and plying his brush. "It is immensely good of you to take so much trouble."

For a moment she made no rejoinder, but presently she said—

"Of course if I pose at all I wish to pose well."

"You pose admirably," said Longueville.

After this she said nothing, and for several minutes he painted rapidly and in silence. He felt a certain excitement, and the movement of his thoughts kept pace with that of his brush. It was very true that she posed admirably; she was a fine creature to paint. Her prettiness inspired him, and also her audacity, as he was content to regard it for the moment. He wondered about her—who she was, and what she was—perceiving that the so-called audacity was not vulgar boldness, but the play of an original and probably interesting character. It was obvious that she was a perfect lady, but it was equally obvious that she was irregularly clever. Longueville's little figure was a success—a charming success, he thought, as he put on the last touches. While he was doing this, his model's companion came into view. She came out of the church, pausing a moment as she looked from her daughter to the young man in the corner of the terrace; then she walked straight over to the young girl. She was a delicate little gentlewoman, with a light, quick step.

Longueville's five minutes were up; so, leaving his place, he approached the two ladies, sketch in hand. The elder one, who had passed her hand into her daughter's arm, looked up at him with clear, surprised eyes; she was a charming old woman. Her eyes were very pretty, and on either side of them, above a pair of fine dark brows, was a band of silvery hair, rather coquettishly arranged.

"It is my portrait," said her daughter, as Longueville drew near. "This gentleman has been sketching me."

"Sketching you, dearest?" murmured her mother. "Was n't it rather sudden?"

"Very sudden—very abrupt!" exclaimed the young girl with a laugh.

"Considering all that, it 's very good," said Longueville, offering his picture to the elder lady, who took it and began to examine it. "I can't tell you how much I thank you," he said to his model.

"It 's very well for you to thank me now," she replied. "You really had no right to begin."

"The temptation was so great."

"We should resist temptation. And you should have asked my leave."

"I was afraid you would refuse it; and you stood there, just in my line of vision."

"You should have asked me to get out of it."

"I should have been very sorry. Besides, it would have been extremely rude."

The young girl looked at him a moment.

"Yes, I think it would. But what you have done is ruder."

"It is a hard case!" said Longueville. "What could I have done, then, decently?"

"It 's a beautiful drawing," murmured the elder lady, handing the thing back to Longueville. Her daughter, meanwhile, had not even glanced at it.

"You might have waited till I should go away," this argumentative young person continued.

Longueville shook his head.

"I never lose opportunities!"

"You might have sketched me afterwards, from memory."

Longueville looked at her, smiling.

"Judge how much better my memory will be now!"

She also smiled a little, but instantly became serious.

"For myself, it 's an episode I shall try to forget. I don't like the part I have played in it."

"May you never play a less becoming one!" cried Longueville. "I hope that your mother, at least, will accept a memento of the occasion." And he turned again with his sketch to her companion, who had been listening to the girl's conversation with this enterprising stranger, and looking from one to the other with an air of earnest confusion. "Won't you do me the honor of keeping my sketch?" he said. "I think it really looks like your daughter."

"Oh, thank you, thank you; I hardly dare," murmured the lady, with a deprecating gesture.

"It will serve as a kind of amends for the liberty I have taken," Longueville added; and he began to remove the drawing from its paper block.

"It makes it worse for you to give it to us," said the young girl.

"Oh, my dear, I am sure it 's lovely!" exclaimed her mother. "It 's wonderfully like you."

"I think that also makes it worse!"

Longueville was at last nettled. The young lady's perversity was perhaps not exactly malignant; but it was certainly ungracious. She seemed to desire to present herself as a beautiful tormentress.

"How does it make it worse?" he asked, with a frown.

He believed she was clever, and she was certainly ready. Now, however, she reflected a moment before answering.

"That you should give us your sketch," she said at last.

"It was to your mother I offered it," Longueville observed.

23

But this observation, the fruit of his irritation, appeared to have no effect upon the young girl.

"Is n't it what painters call a study?" she went on. "A study is of use to the painter himself. Your justification would be that you should keep your sketch, and that it might be of use to you."

"My daughter is a study, sir, you will say," said the elder lady in a little, light, conciliating voice, and graciously accepting the drawing again.

"I will admit," said Longueville, "that I am very inconsistent. Set it down to my esteem, madam," he added, looking at the mother.

"That 's for you, mamma," said his model, disengaging her arm from her mother's hand and turning away.

The mamma stood looking at the sketch with a smile which seemed to express a tender desire to reconcile all accidents.

"It 's extremely beautiful," she murmured, "and if you insist on my taking it—"

"I shall regard it as a great honor."

"Very well, then; with many thanks, I will keep it." She looked at the young man a moment, while her daughter walked away. Longueville thought her a delightful little person; she struck him as a sort of transfigured Quakeress—a mystic with a practical side. "I am sure you think she 's a strange girl," she said.

"She is extremely pretty."

"She is very clever," said the mother.

"She is wonderfully graceful."

"Ah, but she 's good!" cried the old lady.

"I am sure she comes honestly by that," said Longueville, expressively, while his companion, returning his salutation with a certain scrupulous grace of her own, hurried after her daughter.

Longueville remained there staring at the view but not especially seeing it. He felt as if he had at once enjoyed and lost an opportunity. After a while he tried to make a sketch of the old beggar-woman who sat there in a sort of palsied immobility, like a rickety statue at a church-door. But his attempt to reproduce her features was not gratifying, and he suddenly laid down his brush. She was not pretty enough—she had a bad profile.

CHAPTER II

Two months later Bernard Longueville was at Venice, still under the impression that he was leaving Italy. He was not a man who made plans and held to them. He made them, indeed—few men made more—but he made them as a basis for variation. He had gone to Venice to spend a fortnight, and his fortnight had taken the form of eight enchanting weeks. He had still a sort of conviction that he was carrying out his plans; for it must be confessed that where his pleasure was concerned he had considerable skill in accommodating his theory to his practice. His enjoyment of Venice was extreme, but he was roused from it by a summons he was indisposed to resist. This consisted of a letter from an intimate friend who was living in Germany—a friend whose name was Gordon Wright. He had been spending the winter in Dresden, but his letter bore the date of Baden-Baden. As it was not long, I may give it entire.

"I wish very much that you would come to this place. I think you have been here before, so that you know how pretty it is, and how amusing. I shall probably be here the rest of the summer. There are some people I know and whom I want you to know. Be so good as to arrive. Then I will thank you properly for your various Italian rhapsodies. I can't reply on the same scale—I have n't the time. Do you know what I am doing? I am making love. I find it a most absorbing occupation. That is literally why I have not written to you before. I have been making love ever since the last of May. It takes an immense amount of time, and everything else has got terribly behindhand. I don't mean to say that the experiment itself has gone on very fast; but I am trying to push it forward. I have n't yet had time to test its success; but in this I want your help. You know we great physicists never make an experiment without an 'assistant'—a humble individual who burns his fingers and stains his clothes in the cause of science, but whose interest in the problem is only indirect. I want you to be my assistant, and I will guarantee that your burns and stains shall not be dangerous. She is an extremely interesting girl, and I really want you to see her—I want to know what you think of her. She wants to know you, too, for I have talked a good deal about you. There you have it, if gratified vanity will help you on the way. Seriously, this is a real request. I want your opinion, your impression. I want to see how she will affect you. I don't say I ask for your advice; that, of course, you will not undertake to give. But I desire a definition, a characterization; you know you toss off those things. I don't see why I should n't tell you all this—I have always told you everything. I have never pretended to know anything about women, but I have always supposed that you knew everything. You certainly have always had the tone of that sort of omniscience. So come here as soon as possible and let me see that you are not a humbug. She 's a very handsome girl."

Longueville was so much amused with this appeal that he very soon started for Germany. In the reader, Gordon Wright's letter will, perhaps, excite surprise rather than hilarity; but Longueville thought it highly characteristic of his friend. What it especially pointed to was Gordon's want of imagination—a deficiency which was a matter of common jocular allusion between the two young men, each of whom kept a collection of acknowledged oddities as a playground for the other's wit. Bernard had often spoken of his comrade's want of imagination as a bottomless pit, into which Gordon was perpetually inviting him to lower himself. "My dear fellow," Bernard said, "you must really excuse me; I cannot take these subterranean excursions. I should lose my breath down there; I should never come up alive. You know I have dropped things down—little jokes and metaphors, little fantasies and paradoxes—and I have never heard them touch bottom!" This was an epigram on the part of a young man who had a lively play of fancy; but it was none the less true that Gordon Wright had a firmly-treading, rather than a winged, intellect. Every phrase in his letter seemed, to Bernard, to march in stout-soled walking-boots, and nothing could better express his attachment to the process of reasoning things out than this proposal that his friend should come and make a chemical analysis—a geometrical survey—of the lady of his love. "That I shall have any difficulty in forming an opinion, and any difficulty in expressing it when formed—of this he has as little idea as that he shall have any difficulty in accepting it when expressed." So Bernard reflected, as he rolled in the train to Munich. "Gordon's mind," he went on, "has no atmosphere; his intellectual process goes on in the void. There are no currents and eddies to affect it, no high winds nor hot suns, no changes of season and temperature. His premises are neatly arranged, and his conclusions are perfectly calculable."

Yet for the man on whose character he so freely exercised his wit Bernard Longueville had a strong affection. It is nothing against the validity of a friendship that the parties to it have not a mutual resemblance. There must be a basis of agreement, but the structure reared upon it may contain a thousand disparities. These two young men had formed an alliance of old, in college days, and the bond between them had been strengthened by the simple fact of its having survived the sentimental revolutions of early life. Its strongest link was a sort of mutual respect. Their tastes, their pursuits were different; but each of them had a high esteem for the other's character. It may be said that they were easily pleased; for it is certain that neither of them had performed any very conspicuous action. They were highly civilized young Americans, born to an easy fortune and a tranquil destiny, and unfamiliar with the glitter of golden opportunities. If I did not shrink from disparaging the constitution of their native land for their own credit, I should say that it had never been very definitely proposed to these young gentlemen to distinguish themselves. On reaching manhood, they had each come into property sufficient to make violent exertion superfluous. Gordon Wright, indeed, had inherited a large estate. Their wants being tolerably modest, they had not been tempted to strive for the glory of building up commercial fortunes—the most obvious career open to young Americans. They had, indeed, embraced no career at all, and if summoned to give an account of themselves would, perhaps, have found it hard to tell any very impressive story. Gordon Wright was much interested in physical science, and had ideas of his own on what is called the endowment of research. His ideas had taken a practical shape, and he had distributed money very freely among the investigating classes, after which he had gone to spend a couple of years in Germany, supposing it to be the land of laboratories. Here we find him at present, cultivating relations with several learned bodies and promoting the study of various tough branches of human knowledge, by paying the expenses of difficult experiments. The experiments, it must be added, were often of his own making, and he must have the honor of whatever brilliancy attaches, in the estimation of the world, to such pursuits. It was not, indeed, a brilliancy that dazzled Bernard Longueville, who, however, was not easily dazzled by anything. It was because he regarded him in so plain and direct a fashion, that Bernard had an affection for his friend—an affection to which it would perhaps be difficult to assign a definite cause. Personal sympathies are doubtless caused by something; but the causes are remote, mysterious to our daily vision, like those of the particular state of the weather. We content ourselves with remarking that it is fine or that it rains, and the enjoyment of our likes and dislikes is by no means apt to borrow its edge from the keenness of our analysis. Longueville had a relish for fine quality—superior savour; and he was sensible of this merit in the simple, candid, manly, affectionate nature of his comrade, which seemed to him an excellent thing of its kind. Gordon Wright had a tender heart and a strong will—a combination which, when the understanding is not too limited, is often the motive of admirable actions. There might sometimes be a question whether Gordon's understanding were sufficiently unlimited, but the impulses of a generous temper often play a useful part in filling up the gaps of an incomplete imagination, and the general impression that Wright produced was certainly that of intelligent good-nature. The reasons for appreciating Bernard Longueville were much more manifest. He pleased superficially, as well as fundamentally. Nature had sent him into the world with an armful of good gifts. He was very good-looking—tall, dark, agile, perfectly finished, so good-looking that he might have been a fool and yet be forgiven. As has already been intimated, however, he was far from being a fool. He had a number of talents, which, during three or four years that followed his leaving college, had received the discipline of the study of the law. He had not made much of the law; but he had made something of his talents. He was almost always spoken of as "accomplished;" people asked why he did n't do something. This question was never satisfactorily answered, the feeling being that Longueville did more than many people in causing it to be asked. Moreover, there was one thing he did constantly—he enjoyed himself. This is manifestly not a career, and it has been said at the outset that he was not attached to any of the recognized professions. But without going into details, he was a charming fellow—clever, urbane, free-handed, and with that fortunate quality in his appearance which is known as distinction.

CHAPTER III

He had not specified, in writing to Gordon Wright, the day on which he should arrive at Baden-Baden; it must be confessed that he was not addicted to specifying days. He came to his journey's end in the evening, and, on presenting himself at the hotel from which his friend had dated his letter, he learned that Gordon Wright had betaken himself after dinner, according to the custom of Baden-Baden, to the grounds of the Conversation-house. It was eight o'clock, and Longueville, after removing the stains of travel, sat down to dine. His first impulse had been to send for Gordon to come and keep him company at his repast; but on second thought he determined to make it as brief as possible. Having brought it to a close, he took his way to the Kursaal. The great German watering-place is one of the prettiest nooks in Europe, and of a summer evening in the gaming days, five-and-twenty years ago, it was one of the most brilliant scenes. The lighted windows of the great temple of hazard (of as chaste an architecture as if it had been devoted to a much purer divinity) opened wide upon the gardens and groves; the little river that issues from the bosky mountains of the Black Forest flowed, with an air of brook-like innocence, past the expensive hotels and lodging-houses; the orchestra, in a high pavilion on the terrace of the Kursaal, played a discreet accompaniment to the conversation of the ladies and gentlemen who, scattered over the large expanse on a thousand little chairs, preferred for the time the beauties of nature to the shuffle of coin and the calculation of chance; while the faint summer stars, twinkling above the vague black hills and woods, looked down at the indifferent groups without venturing to drop their light upon them.

Longueville, noting all this, went straight into the gaming-rooms; he was curious to see whether his friend, being fond of experiments, was trying combinations at roulette. But he was not to be found in any of the gilded chambers, among the crowd that pressed in silence about the tables; so that Bernard presently came and began to wander about the lamp-lit terrace, where innumerable groups, seated and strolling, made the place a gigantic conversazione. It seemed to him very agreeable and amusing, and he remarked to himself that, for a man who was supposed not to take especially the Epicurean view of life, Gordon Wright, in coming to Baden, had certainly made himself comfortable. Longueville went his way, glancing from one cluster of talkers to another; and at last he saw a face which brought him to a stop. He stood a moment looking at it; he knew he had seen it before. He had an excellent memory for faces; but it was some time before he was able to attach an identity to this one. Where had he seen a little elderly lady with an expression of timorous vigilance, and a band of hair as softly white as a dove's wing? The answer to the question presently came—Where but in a grass-grown corner of an old Italian town? The lady was the mother of his inconsequent model, so that this mysterious personage was probably herself not far off. Before Longueville had time to verify this induction, he found his eyes resting upon the broad back of a gentleman seated close to the old lady, and who, turning away from her, was talking to a young girl. It was nothing but the back of this gentleman that he saw, but nevertheless, with the instinct of true friendship, he recognized in this featureless expanse the robust personality of Gordon Wright. In a moment he had stepped forward and laid his hand upon Wright's shoulder.

His friend looked round, and then sprang up with a joyous exclamation and grasp of the hand.

"My dear fellow—my dear Bernard! What on earth—when did you arrive?"

While Bernard answered and explained a little, he glanced from his friend's good, gratified face at the young girl with whom Wright had been talking, and then at the lady on the other side, who was giving him a bright little stare. He raised his hat to her and to the young girl, and he became conscious, as regards the latter, of a certain disappointment. She was very pretty; she was looking at him; but she was not the heroine of the little incident of the terrace at Siena.

"It 's just like Longueville, you know," Gordon Wright went on; "he always comes at you from behind; he 's so awfully fond of surprises." He was laughing; he was greatly pleased; he introduced Bernard to the two ladies. "You must know Mrs. Vivian; you must know Miss Blanche Evers."

Bernard took his place in the little circle; he wondered whether he ought to venture upon a special recognition of Mrs. Vivian. Then it seemed to him that he should leave the option of this step with the lady, especially as he had detected recognition in her eye. But Mrs. Vivian ventured upon nothing special; she contented herself with soft generalities—with remarking that she always liked to know when people would arrive; that, for herself, she never enjoyed surprises.

"And yet I imagine you have had your share," said Longueville, with a smile. He thought this might remind her of the moment when she came out of the little church at Siena and found her daughter posturing to an unknown painter.

But Mrs. Vivian, turning her benignant head about, gave but a superficial reply.

"Oh, I have had my share of everything, good and bad. I don't complain of anything." And she gave a little deprecating laugh.

Gordon Wright shook hands with Bernard again; he seemed really very glad to see him. Longueville, remembering that Gordon had written to him that he had been "making love," began to seek in his countenance for the ravages of passion. For the moment, however, they were not apparent; the excellent, honest fellow looked placid and contented. Gordon Wright had a clear gray eye, short, straight, flaxen hair, and a healthy diffusion of color. His features were thick and rather irregular; but his countenance—in addition to the merit of its expression—derived a certain grace from a powerful yellow moustache, to which its wearer occasionally gave a martial twist. Gordon Wright was not tall, but he was strong, and in his whole person there was something well-planted and sturdy. He almost always dressed in light-colored garments, and he wore round his neck an eternal blue cravat. When he was agitated he grew very red. While he questioned Longueville about his journey and his health, his whereabouts and his intentions, the latter, among his own replies, endeavored to read in Wright's eyes some account of his present situation. Was that pretty girl at his side the ambiguous object of his adoration, and, in that case, what was the function of the elder lady, and what had become of her argumentative daughter? Perhaps this was another, a younger daughter, though, indeed, she bore no resemblance to either of Longueville's friends. Gordon Wright, in spite of Bernard's interrogative glances, indulged in no optical confidences. He had too much to tell. He would keep his story till they should be alone together. It was impossible that they should adjourn just yet to social solitude; the two ladies were under Gordon's protection. Mrs. Vivian—Bernard felt a satisfaction in learning her name; it was as if a curtain, half pulled up and stopped by a hitch, had suddenly been raised altogether—Mrs. Vivian sat looking up and down the terrace at the crowd of loungers and talkers with an air of tender expectation. She was probably looking for her elder daughter, and Longueville could not help wishing also that this young lady would arrive. Meanwhile, he saw that the young girl to whom Gordon had been devoting himself was extremely pretty, and appeared eminently approachable. Longueville had some talk with her, reflecting that if she were the person concerning whom Gordon had written him, it behooved him to appear to take an interest in her. This view of the case was confirmed by Gordon Wright's presently turning away to talk with Mrs. Vivian, so that his friend might be at liberty to make acquaintance with their companion.

Though she had not been with the others at Siena, it seemed to Longueville, with regard to her, too, that this was not the first time he had seen her. She was simply the American pretty girl, whom he had seen a thousand times. It was a numerous sisterhood, pervaded by a strong family likeness. This young lady had charming eyes (of the color of Gordon's cravats), which looked everywhere at once and yet found time to linger in some places, where Longueville's own eyes frequently met them. She had soft brown hair, with a silky-golden thread in it, beautifully arranged and crowned by a smart little hat that savoured of Paris. She had also a slender little figure, neatly rounded, and delicate, narrow hands, prettily gloved. She moved about a great deal in her place, twisted her little flexible body and tossed her head, fingered her hair and examined the ornaments of her dress. She had a great deal of conversation, Longueville speedily learned, and she expressed herself with extreme frankness and decision. He asked her, to begin with, if she had been long at Baden, but the impetus of this question was all she required. Turning her charming, conscious, coquettish little face upon him, she instantly began to chatter.

"I have been here about four weeks. I don't know whether you call that long. It does n't seem long to me; I have had such a lovely time. I have met ever so many people here I know—every day some one turns up. Now you have turned up to-day."

"Ah, but you don't know me," said Longueville, laughing.

"Well, I have heard a great deal about you!" cried the young girl, with a pretty little stare of contradiction. "I think you know a great friend of mine, Miss Ella Maclane, of Baltimore. She 's travelling in Europe now." Longueville's memory did not instantly respond to this signal, but he expressed that rapturous assent which the occasion demanded, and even risked the observation that the young lady from Baltimore was very pretty. "She 's far too lovely," his companion went on. "I have often heard her speak of you. I think you know her sister rather better than you know her. She has not been out very long. She is just as interesting as she can be. Her hair comes down to her feet. She 's travelling in Norway. She has been everywhere you can think of, and she 's going to finish off with Finland. You can't go any further than that, can you? That 's one comfort; she will have to turn round and come back. I want her dreadfully to come to Baden-Baden."

"I wish she would," said Longueville. "Is she travelling alone?"

"Oh, no. They 've got some Englishman. They say he 's devoted to Ella. Every one seems to have an Englishman, now. We 've got one here, Captain Lovelock, the Honourable Augustus Lovelock. Well, they 're awfully handsome. Ella Maclane is dying to come to Baden-Baden. I wish you 'd write to her. Her father and mother have got some idea in their heads; they think it 's improper—what do you call it?—immoral. I wish you would write to her and tell her it is n't. I wonder if they think that Mrs. Vivian would come to a place that 's immoral. Mrs. Vivian says she would take her in a moment; she does n't seem to care how many she has. I declare, she 's only too kind. You know I 'm in Mrs. Vivian's care. My mother 's gone to Marienbad. She would let me go with Mrs. Vivian anywhere, on account of the influence—she thinks so much of Mrs. Vivian's influence. I have always heard a great deal about it, have n't you? I must say it 's lovely; it 's had a wonderful effect upon me. I don't want to praise myself, but it has. You ask Mrs. Vivian if I have n't been good. I have been just as good as I can be. I have been so peaceful, I have just sat here this way. Do you call this immoral? You 're not obliged to gamble if you don't want to. Ella Maclane's father seems to think you get drawn in. I 'm sure I have n't been drawn in. I know what you 're going to say—you 're going to say I have been drawn out. Well, I have, to-night. We just sit here so quietly—there 's nothing to do but to talk. We make a little party by ourselves—are you going to belong to our party? Two of us are missing—Miss Vivian and Captain Lovelock. Captain Lovelock has gone with her into the rooms to explain the gambling—Miss Vivian always wants everything explained. I am sure I understood it the first time I looked at the tables. Have you ever seen Miss Vivian? She 's very much admired, she 's so very unusual. Black hair 's so uncommon—I see you have got it too—but I mean for young ladies. I am sure one sees everything here. There 's a woman that comes to the tables—a Portuguese countess—who has hair that is positively blue. I can't say I admire it when it comes to that shade. Blue 's my favorite color, but I prefer it in the eyes," continued Longueville's companion, resting upon him her own two brilliant little specimens of the tint.

He listened with that expression of clear amusement which is not always an indication of high esteem, but which even pretty chatterers, who are not the reverse of estimable, often prefer to masculine inattention; and while he listened Bernard, according to his wont, made his reflections. He said to himself that there were two kinds of pretty girls—the acutely conscious and the finely unconscious. Mrs. Vivian's protege was a member of the former category; she belonged to the genus coquette. We all have our conception of the indispensable, and the indispensable, to this young lady, was a spectator; almost any male biped would serve the purpose. To her spectator she addressed, for the moment, the whole volume of her being—addressed it in her glances, her attitudes, her exclamations, in a hundred little experiments of tone and gesture and position. And these rustling artifices were so innocent and obvious that the directness of her desire to be well with her observer became in itself a grace; it led Bernard afterward to say to himself that the natural vocation and metier of little girls for whom existence was but a shimmering surface, was to prattle and ruffle their plumage; their view of life and its duties was as simple and superficial as that of an Oriental bayadere. It surely could not be with regard to this transparent little flirt that Gordon Wright desired advice; you could literally see the daylight—or rather the Baden gaslight—on the other side of her. She sat there for a minute, turning her little empty head to and fro, and catching Bernard's eye every time she moved; she had for the instant the air of having exhausted all topics. Just then a young lady, with a gentleman at her side, drew near to the little group, and Longueville, perceiving her, instantly got up from his chair.

"There 's a beauty of the unconscious class!" he said to himself. He knew her face very well; he had spent half an hour in copying it.

"Here comes Miss Vivian!" said Gordon Wright, also getting up, as if to make room for the daughter near the mother.

She stopped in front of them, smiling slightly, and then she rested her eyes upon Longueville. Their gaze at first was full and direct, but it expressed nothing more than civil curiosity. This was immediately followed, however, by the light of recognition—recognition embarrassed, and signalling itself by a blush.

Miss Vivian's companion was a powerful, handsome fellow, with a remarkable auburn beard, who struck the observer immediately as being uncommonly well dressed. He carried his hands in the pockets of a little jacket, the button-hole of which was adorned with a blooming rose. He approached Blanche Evers, smiling and dandling his body a little, and making her two or three jocular bows.

"Well, I hope you have lost every penny you put on the table!" said the young girl, by way of response to his obeisances.

He began to laugh and repeat them.

"I don't care what I lose, so long—so long—"

"So long as what, pray?"

"So long as you let me sit down by you!" And he dropped, very gallantly, into a chair on the other side of her.

"I wish you would lose all your property!" she replied, glancing at Bernard.

"It would be a very small stake," said Captain Lovelock. "Would you really like to see me reduced to misery?"

While this graceful dialogue rapidly established itself, Miss Vivian removed her eyes from Longueville's face and turned toward her mother. But Gordon Wright checked this movement by laying his hand on Longueville's shoulder and proceeding to introduce his friend.

"This is the accomplished creature, Mr. Bernard Longueville, of whom you have heard me speak. One of his accomplishments, as you see, is to drop down from the moon."

"No, I don't drop from the moon," said Bernard, laughing. "I drop from—Siena!" He offered his hand to Miss Vivian, who for an appreciable instant hesitated to extend her own. Then she returned his salutation, without any response to his allusion to Siena.

She declined to take a seat, and said she was tired and preferred to go home. With this suggestion her mother immediately complied, and the two ladies appealed to the indulgence of little Miss Evers, who was obliged to renounce the society of Captain Lovelock. She enjoyed this luxury, however, on the way to Mrs. Vivian's lodgings, toward which they all slowly strolled, in the sociable Baden fashion. Longueville might naturally have found himself next Miss Vivian, but he received an impression that she avoided him. She walked in front, and Gordon Wright strolled beside her, though Longueville noticed that they appeared to exchange but few words. He himself offered his arm to Mrs. Vivian, who paced along with a little lightly-wavering step, making observations upon the beauties of Baden and the respective merits of the hotels.

CHAPTER IV

"Which of them is it?" asked Longueville of his friend, after they had bidden good-night to the three ladies and to Captain Lovelock, who went off to begin, as he said, the evening. They stood, when they had turned away from the door of Mrs. Vivian's lodgings, in the little, rough-paved German street.

"Which of them is what?" Gordon asked, staring at his companion.

"Oh, come," said Longueville, "you are not going to begin to play at modesty at this hour! Did n't you write to me that you had been making violent love?"

"Violent? No."

"The more shame to you! Has your love-making been feeble?"

His friend looked at him a moment rather soberly.

"I suppose you thought it a queer document—that letter I wrote you."

"I thought it characteristic," said Longueville smiling.

"Is n't that the same thing?"

"Not in the least. I have never thought you a man of oddities." Gordon stood there looking at him with a serious eye, half appealing, half questioning; but at these last words he glanced away. Even a very modest man may wince a little at hearing himself denied the distinction of a few variations from the common type. Longueville made this reflection, and it struck him, also, that his companion was in a graver mood than he had expected; though why, after all, should he have been in a state of exhilaration? "Your letter was a very natural, interesting one," Bernard added.

"Well, you see," said Gordon, facing his companion again, "I have been a good deal preoccupied."

"Obviously, my dear fellow!"

"I want very much to marry."

"It 's a capital idea," said Longueville.

"I think almost as well of it," his friend declared, "as if I had invented it. It has struck me for the first time."

These words were uttered with a mild simplicity which provoked Longueville to violent laughter.

"My dear fellow," he exclaimed, "you have, after all, your little oddities."

Singularly enough, however, Gordon Wright failed to appear flattered by this concession.

"I did n't send for you to laugh at me," he said.

"Ah, but I have n't travelled three hundred miles to cry! Seriously, solemnly, then, it is one of these young ladies that has put marriage into your head?"

"Not at all. I had it in my head."

"Having a desire to marry, you proceeded to fall in love."

"I am not in love!" said Gordon Wright, with some energy.

"Ah, then, my dear fellow, why did you send for me?"

Wright looked at him an instant in silence.

"Because I thought you were a good fellow, as well as a clever one."

"A good fellow!" repeated Longueville. "I don't understand your confounded scientific nomenclature. But excuse me; I won't laugh. I am not a clever fellow; but I am a good one." He paused a moment, and then laid his hand on his companion's shoulder. "My dear Gordon, it 's no use; you are in love."

"Well, I don't want to be," said Wright.

"Heavens, what a horrible sentiment!"

"I want to marry with my eyes open. I want to know my wife. You don't know people when you are in love with them. Your impressions are colored."

"They are supposed to be, slightly. And you object to color?"

"Well, as I say, I want to know the woman I marry, as I should know any one else. I want to see her as clearly."

"Depend upon it, you have too great an appetite for knowledge; you set too high an esteem upon the dry light of science."

"Ah!" said Gordon promptly; "of course I want to be fond of her."

Bernard, in spite of his protest, began to laugh again.

"My dear Gordon, you are better than your theories. Your passionate heart contradicts your frigid intellect. I repeat it—you are in love."

"Please don't repeat it again," said Wright.

Bernard took his arm, and they walked along.

"What shall I call it, then? You are engaged in making studies for matrimony."

"I don't in the least object to your calling it that. My studies are of extreme interest."

"And one of those young ladies is the fair volume that contains the precious lesson," said Longueville. "Or perhaps your text-book is in two volumes?"

"No; there is one of them I am not studying at all. I never could do two things at once."

"That proves you are in love. One can't be in love with two women at once, but one may perfectly have two of them—or as many as you please— up for a competitive examination. However, as I asked you before, which of these young ladies is it that you have selected?"

Gordon Wright stopped abruptly, eying his friend.

"Which should you say?"

"Ah, that 's not a fair question," Bernard urged. "It would be invidious for me to name one rather than the other, and if I were to mention the wrong one, I should feel as if I had been guilty of a rudeness towards the other. Don't you see?"

Gordon saw, perhaps, but he held to his idea of making his companion commit himself.

"Never mind the rudeness. I will do the same by you some day, to make it up. Which of them should you think me likely to have taken a fancy to? On general grounds, now, from what you know of me?" He proposed this problem with an animated eye.

"You forget," his friend said, "that though I know, thank heaven, a good deal of you, I know very little of either of those girls. I have had too little evidence."

"Yes, but you are a man who notices. That 's why I wanted you to come."

"I spoke only to Miss Evers."

"Yes, I know you have never spoken to Miss Vivian." Gordon Wright stood looking at Bernard and urging his point as he pronounced these words. Bernard felt peculiarly conscious of his gaze. The words represented an illusion, and Longueville asked himself quickly whether it were not his duty to dispel it. The answer came more slowly than the question, but still it came, in the shape of a negative. The illusion was but a trifling one, and it was not for him, after all, to let his friend know that he had already met Miss Vivian. It was for the young girl herself, and since she had not done so—although she had the opportunity—Longueville said to himself that he was bound in honor not to speak. These reflections were very soon made, but in the midst of them our young man, thanks to a great agility of mind, found time to observe, tacitly, that it was odd, just there, to see his "honor" thrusting in its nose. Miss Vivian, in her own good time, would doubtless mention to

Gordon the little incident of Siena. It was Bernard's fancy, for a moment, that he already knew it, and that the remark he had just uttered had an ironical accent; but this impression was completely dissipated by the tone in which he added—"All the same, you noticed her."

"Oh, yes; she is very noticeable."

"Well, then," said Gordon, "you will see. I should like you to make it out. Of course, if I am really giving my attention to one to the exclusion of the other, it will be easy to discover."

Longueville was half amused, half irritated by his friend's own relish of his little puzzle. "'The exclusion of the other' has an awkward sound," he answered, as they walked on. "Am I to notice that you are very rude to one of the young ladies?"

"Oh dear, no. Do you think there is a danger of that?"

"Well," said Longueville, "I have already guessed."

Gordon Wright remonstrated. "Don't guess yet—wait a few days. I won't tell you now."

"Let us see if he does n't tell me," said Bernard, privately. And he meditated a moment. "When I presented myself, you were sitting very close to Miss Evers and talking very earnestly. Your head was bent toward her—it was very lover-like. Decidedly, Miss Evers is the object!"

For a single instant Gordon Wright hesitated, and then—"I hope I have n't seemed rude to Miss Vivian!" he exclaimed.

Bernard broke into a light laugh. "My dear Gordon, you are very much in love!" he remarked, as they arrived at their hotel.

CHAPTER V

Life at Baden-Baden proved a very sociable affair, and Bernard Longueville perceived that he should not lack opportunity for the exercise of those gifts of intelligence to which Gordon Wright had appealed. The two friends took long walks through the woods and over the mountains, and they mingled with human life in the crowded precincts of the Conversation-house. They engaged in a ramble on the morning after Bernard's arrival, and wandered far away, over hill and dale. The Baden forests are superb, and the composition of the landscape is most effective. There is always a bosky dell in the foreground, and a purple crag embellished with a ruined tower at a proper angle. A little timber-and-plaster village peeps out from a tangle of plum-trees, and a way-side tavern, in comfortable recurrence, solicits concessions to the national custom of frequent refreshment. Gordon Wright, who was a dogged pedestrian, always enjoyed doing his ten miles, and Longueville, who was an incorrigible stroller, felt a keen relish for the picturesqueness of the country. But it was not, on this occasion, of the charms of the landscape or the pleasures of locomotion that they chiefly discoursed. Their talk took a more closely personal turn. It was a year since they had met, and there were many questions to ask and answer, many arrears of gossip to make up. As they stretched themselves on the grass on a sun-warmed hill-side, beneath a great German oak whose arms were quiet in the blue summer air, there was a lively exchange of impressions, opinions, speculations, anecdotes. Gordon Wright was surely an excellent friend. He took an interest in you. He asked no idle questions and made no vague professions; but he entered into your situation, he examined it in detail, and what he learned he never forgot. Months afterwards, he asked you about things which you yourself had forgotten. He was not a man of whom it would be generally said that he had the gift of sympathy; but he gave his attention to a friend's circumstances with a conscientious fixedness which was at least very far removed from indifference. Bernard had the gift of sympathy—or at least he was supposed to have it; but even he, familiar as he must therefore have been with the practice of this charming virtue, was at times so struck with his friend's fine faculty of taking other people's affairs seriously that he constantly exclaimed to himself, "The excellent fellow—the admirable nature!"

Bernard had two or three questions to ask about the three persons who appeared to have formed for some time his companion's principal society, but he was indisposed to press them. He felt that he should see for himself, and at a prospect of entertainment of this kind, his fancy always kindled. Gordon was, moreover, at first rather shy of confidences, though after they had lain on the grass ten minutes there was a good deal said.

"Now what do you think of her face?" Gordon asked, after staring a while at the sky through the oak-boughs.

"Of course, in future," said Longueville, "whenever you make use of the personal pronoun feminine, I am to understand that Miss Vivian is indicated."

"Her name is Angela," said Gordon; "but of course I can scarcely call her that."

"It 's a beautiful name," Longueville rejoined; "but I may say, in answer to your question, that I am not struck with the fact that her face corresponds to it."

"You don't think her face beautiful, then?"

"I don't think it angelic. But how can I tell? I have only had a glimpse of her."

"Wait till she looks at you and speaks—wait till she smiles," said Gordon.

"I don't think I saw her smile—at least, not at me, directly. I hope she will!" Longueville went on. "But who is she—this beautiful girl with the beautiful name?"

"She is her mother's daughter," said Gordon Wright. "I don't really know a great deal more about her than that."

"And who is her mother?"

"A delightful little woman, devoted to Miss Vivian. She is a widow, and Angela is her only child. They have lived a great deal in Europe; they have but a modest income. Over here, Mrs. Vivian says, they can get a lot of things for their money that they can't get at home. So they stay, you see. When they are at home they live in New York. They know some of my people there. When they are in Europe they live about in different places. They are fond of Italy. They are extremely nice; it 's impossible to be nicer. They are very fond of books, fond of music, and art, and all that. They always read in the morning. They only come out rather late in the day."

"I see they are very superior people," said Bernard. "And little Miss Evers—what does she do in the morning? I know what she does in the evening!"

"I don't know what her regular habits are. I have n't paid much attention to her. She is very pretty."

"Wunderschon!" said Bernard. "But you were certainly talking to her last evening."

"Of course I talk to her sometimes. She is totally different from Angela Vivian—not nearly so cultivated; but she seems very charming."

"A little silly, eh?" Bernard suggested.

"She certainly is not so wise as Miss Vivian."

"That would be too much to ask, eh? But the Vivians, as kind as they are wise, have taken her under their protection."

"Yes," said Gordon, "they are to keep her another month or two. Her mother has gone to Marienbad, which I believe is thought a dull place for a young girl; so that, as they were coming here, they offered to bring her with them. Mrs. Evers is an old friend of Mrs. Vivian, who, on leaving Italy, had come up to Dresden to be with her. They spent a month there together; Mrs. Evers had been there since the winter. I think Mrs. Vivian really came to Baden-Baden—she would have preferred a less expensive place—to bring Blanche Evers. Her mother wanted her so much to come."

"And was it for her sake that Captain Lovelock came, too?" Bernard asked.

Gordon Wright stared a moment.

"I 'm sure I don't know!"

"Of course you can't be interested in that," said Bernard smiling. "Who is Captain Lovelock?"

"He is an Englishman. I believe he is what 's called aristocratically connected—the younger brother of a lord, or something of that sort."

"Is he a clever man?"

"I have n't talked with him much, but I doubt it. He is rather rakish; he plays a great deal."

"But is that considered here a proof of rakishness?" asked Bernard. "Have n't you played a little yourself?"

Gordon hesitated a moment.

"Yes, I have played a little. I wanted to try some experiments. I had made some arithmetical calculations of probabilities, which I wished to test."

Bernard gave a long laugh.

"I am delighted with the reasons you give for amusing yourself! Arithmetical calculations!"

"I assure you they are the real reasons!" said Gordon, blushing a little.

"That 's just the beauty of it. You were not afraid of being 'drawn in,' as little Miss Evers says?"

"I am never drawn in, whatever the thing may be. I go in, or I stay out; but I am not drawn," said Gordon Wright.

"You were not drawn into coming with Mrs. Vivian and her daughter from Dresden to this place?"

"I did n't come with them; I came a week later."

"My dear fellow," said Bernard, "that distinction is unworthy of your habitual candor."

"Well, I was not fascinated; I was not overmastered. I wanted to come to Baden."

"I have no doubt you did. Had you become very intimate with your friends in Dresden?"

"I had only seen them three times."

"After which you followed them to this place? Ah, don't say you were not fascinated!" cried Bernard, laughing and springing to his feet.

CHAPTER VI

That evening, in the gardens of the Kursaal, he renewed acquaintance with Angela Vivian. Her mother came, as usual, to sit and listen to the music, accompanied by Blanche Evers, who was in turn attended by Captain Lovelock. This little party found privacy in the crowd; they seated themselves in a quiet corner in an angle of one of the barriers of the terrace, while the movement of the brilliant Baden world went on around them. Gordon Wright engaged in conversation with Mrs. Vivian, while Bernard enjoyed an interview with her daughter. This young lady continued to ignore the fact of their previous meeting, and our hero said to himself that all he wished was to know what she preferred—he would rigidly conform to it. He conformed to her present programme; he had ventured to pronounce the word Siena the evening before, but he was careful not to pronounce it again. She had her reasons for her own reserve; he wondered what they were, and it gave him a certain pleasure to wonder. He enjoyed the consciousness of their having a secret together, and it became a kind of entertaining suspense to see how long she would continue to keep it. For himself, he was in no hurry to let the daylight in; the little incident at Siena had been, in itself, a charming affair; but Miss Vivian's present attitude gave it a sort of mystic consecration. He thought she carried it off very well—the theory that she had not seen him before; last evening she had been slightly confused, but now she was as self-possessed as if the line she had taken were a matter of conscience. Why should it be a matter of conscience? Was she in love with Gordon Wright, and did she wish, in consequence, to forget—and wish him not to suspect—that she had ever received an expression of admiration from another man? This was not likely; it was not likely, at least, that Miss Vivian wished to pass for a prodigy of innocence; for if to be admired is to pay a tribute to corruption, it was perfectly obvious that so handsome a girl must have tasted of the tree of knowledge. As for her being in love with Gordon Wright, that of course was another affair, and Bernard did not pretend, as yet, to have an opinion on this point, beyond hoping very much that she might be.

He was not wrong in the impression of her good looks that he had carried away from the short interview at Siena. She had a charmingly chiselled face, with a free, pure outline, a clear, fair complexion, and the eyes and hair of a dusky beauty. Her features had a firmness which suggested tranquillity, and yet her expression was light and quick, a combination—or a contradiction— which gave an original stamp to her beauty. Bernard remembered that he had thought it a trifle "bold"; but he now perceived that this had been but a vulgar misreading of her dark, direct, observant eye. The eye was a charming one; Bernard discovered in it, little by little, all sorts of things; and Miss Vivian was, for the present, simply a handsome, intelligent, smiling girl. He gave her an opportunity to make an allusion to Siena; he said to her that his friend told him that she and her mother had been spending the winter in Italy.

"Oh yes," said Angela Vivian; "we were in the far south; we were five months at Sorrento."

"And nowhere else?"

"We spent a few days in Rome. We usually prefer the quiet places; that is my mother's taste."

"It was not your mother's taste, then," said Bernard, "that brought you to Baden?"

She looked at him a moment.

"You mean that Baden is not quiet?"

Longueville glanced about at the moving, murmuring crowd, at the lighted windows of the Conversation-house, at the great orchestra perched up in its pagoda.

"This is not my idea of absolute tranquillity."

"Nor mine, either," said Miss Vivian. "I am not fond of absolute tranquillity."

"How do you arrange it, then, with your mother?"

Again she looked at him a moment, with her clever, slightly mocking smile.

"As you see. By making her come where I wish."

"You have a strong will," said Bernard. "I see that."

"No. I have simply a weak mother. But I make sacrifices too, sometimes."

"What do you call sacrifices?"

"Well, spending the winter at Sorrento."

Bernard began to laugh, and then he told her she must have had a very happy life—"to call a winter at Sorrento a sacrifice."

"It depends upon what one gives up," said Miss Vivian.

"What did you give up?"

She touched him with her mocking smile again.

"That is not a very civil question, asked in that way."

"You mean that I seem to doubt your abnegation?"

"You seem to insinuate that I had nothing to renounce. I gave up—I gave up—" and she looked about her, considering a little—"I gave up society."

"I am glad you remember what it was," said Bernard. "If I have seemed uncivil, let me make it up. When a woman speaks of giving up society, what she means is giving up admiration. You can never have given up that—you can never have escaped from it. You must have found it even at Sorrento."

"It may have been there, but I never found it. It was very respectful—it never expressed itself."

"That is the deepest kind," said Bernard.

"I prefer the shallower varieties," the young girl answered.

"Well," said Bernard, "you must remember that although shallow admiration expresses itself, all the admiration that expresses itself is not shallow."

Miss Vivian hesitated a moment.

"Some of it is impertinent," she said, looking straight at him, rather gravely.

Bernard hesitated about as long.

"When it is impertinent it is shallow. That comes to the same thing."

The young girl frowned a little.

"I am not sure that I understand—I am rather stupid. But you see how right I am in my taste for such places as this. I have to come here to hear such ingenious remarks."

"You should add that my coming, as well, has something to do with it."

"Everything!" said Miss Vivian.

"Everything? Does no one else make ingenious remarks? Does n't my friend Wright?"

"Mr. Wright says excellent things, but I should not exactly call them ingenious remarks."

"It is not what Wright says; it 's what he does. That 's the charm!" said Bernard.

His companion was silent for a moment. "That 's not usually a charm; good conduct is not thought pleasing."

"It surely is not thought the reverse!" Bernard exclaimed.

"It does n't rank—in the opinion of most people—among the things that make men agreeable."

"It depends upon what you call agreeable."

"Exactly so," said Miss Vivian. "It all depends on that."

"But the agreeable," Bernard went on—"it is n't after all, fortunately, such a subtle idea! The world certainly is agreed to think that virtue is a beautiful thing."

Miss Vivian dropped her eyes a moment, and then, looking up,

"Is it a charm?" she asked.

"For me there is no charm without it," Bernard declared.

"I am afraid that for me there is," said the young girl.

Bernard was puzzled—he who was not often puzzled. His companion struck him as altogether too clever to be likely to indulge in a silly affectation of cynicism. And yet, without this, how could one account for her sneering at virtue?

"You talk as if you had sounded the depths of vice!" he said, laughing. "What do you know about other than virtuous charms?"

"I know, of course, nothing about vice; but I have known virtue when it was very tiresome."

"Ah, then it was a poor affair. It was poor virtue. The best virtue is never tiresome."

Miss Vivian looked at him a little, with her fine discriminating eye.

"What a dreadful thing to have to think any virtue poor!"

This was a touching reflection, and it might have gone further had not the conversation been interrupted by Mrs. Vivian's appealing to her daughter to aid a defective recollection of a story about a Spanish family they had met at Biarritz, with which she had undertaken to entertain Gordon Wright. After this, the little circle was joined by a party of American friends who were spending a week at Baden, and the conversation became general.

CHAPTER VII

But on the following evening, Bernard again found himself seated in friendly colloquy with this interesting girl, while Gordon Wright discoursed with her mother on one side, and little Blanche Evers chattered to the admiring eyes of Captain Lovelock on the other.

"You and your mother are very kind to that little girl," our hero said; "you must be a great advantage to her."

Angela Vivian directed her eyes to her neighbors, and let them rest a while on the young girl's little fidgeting figure and her fresh, coquettish face. For some moments she said nothing, and to Longueville, turning over several things in his mind, and watching her, it seemed that her glance was one of disfavor. He divined, he scarcely knew how, that her esteem for her pretty companion was small.

"I don't know that I am very kind," said Miss Vivian. "I have done nothing in particular for her."

"Mr. Wright tells me you came to this place mainly on her account."

"I came for myself," said Miss Vivian. "The consideration you speak of perhaps had weight with my mother."

"You are not an easy person to say appreciative things to," Bernard rejoined. "One is tempted to say them; but you don't take them."

The young girl colored as she listened to this observation.

"I don't think you know," she murmured, looking away. Then, "Set it down to modesty," she added.

"That, of course, is what I have done. To what else could one possibly attribute an indifference to compliments?"

"There is something else. One might be proud."

"There you are again!" Bernard exclaimed. "You won't even let me praise your modesty."

"I would rather you should rebuke my pride."

"That is so humble a speech that it leaves no room for rebuke."

For a moment Miss Vivian said nothing.

"Men are singularly base," she declared presently, with a little smile. "They don't care in the least to say things that might help a person. They only care to say things that may seem effective and agreeable."

"I see: you think that to say agreeable things is a great misdemeanor."

"It comes from their vanity," Miss Vivian went on, as if she had not heard him. "They wish to appear agreeable and get credit for cleverness and tendresse, no matter how silly it would be for another person to believe them."

Bernard was a good deal amused, and a little nettled.

"Women, then," he said, "have rather a fondness for producing a bad impression—they like to appear disagreeable?"

His companion bent her eyes upon her fan for a moment as she opened and closed it.

"They are capable of resigning themselves to it—for a purpose."

Bernard was moved to extreme merriment.

"For what purpose?"

"I don't know that I mean for a purpose," said Miss Vivian; "but for a necessity."

"Ah, what an odious necessity!"

"Necessities usually are odious. But women meet them. Men evade them and shirk them."

"I contest your proposition. Women are themselves necessities; but they are not odious ones!" And Bernard added, in a moment, "One could n't evade them, if they were!"

"I object to being called a necessity," said Angela Vivian. "It diminishes one's merit."

"Ah, but it enhances the charm of life!"

"For men, doubtless!"

"The charm of life is very great," Bernard went on, looking up at the dusky hills and the summer stars, seen through a sort of mist of music and talk, and of powdery light projected from the softly lurid windows of the gaming-rooms. "The charm of life is extreme. I am unacquainted with odious necessities. I object to nothing!"

Angela Vivian looked about her as he had done—looked perhaps a moment longer at the summer stars; and if she had not already proved herself a young lady of a contradictory turn, it might have been supposed she was just then tacitly admitting the charm of life to be considerable.

"Do you suppose Miss Evers often resigns herself to being disagreeable—for a purpose?" asked Longueville, who had glanced at Captain Lovelock's companion again.

"She can't be disagreeable; she is too gentle, too soft."

"Do you mean too silly?"

"I don't know that I call her silly. She is not very wise; but she has no pretensions—absolutely none—so that one is not struck with anything incongruous."

"What a terrible description! I suppose one ought to have a few pretensions."

"You see one comes off more easily without them," said Miss Vivian.

"Do you call that coming off easily?"

She looked at him a moment gravely.

"I am very fond of Blanche," she said.

"Captain Lovelock is rather fond of her," Bernard went on.

The girl assented.

"He is completely fascinated—he is very much in love with her."

"And do they mean to make an international match?"

"I hope not; my mother and I are greatly troubled."

"Is n't he a good fellow?"

"He is a good fellow; but he is a mere trifler. He has n't a penny, I believe, and he has very expensive habits. He gambles a great deal. We don't know what to do."

"You should send for the young lady's mother."

"We have written to her pressingly. She answers that Blanche can take care of herself, and that she must stay at Marienbad to finish her cure. She has just begun a new one."

"Ah well," said Bernard, "doubtless Blanche can take care of herself."

For a moment his companion said nothing; then she exclaimed—

"It 's what a girl ought to be able to do!"

"I am sure you are!" said Bernard.

She met his eyes, and she was going to make some rejoinder; but before she had time to speak, her mother's little, clear, conciliatory voice interposed. Mrs. Vivian appealed to her daughter, as she had done the night before.

"Dear Angela, what was the name of the gentleman who delivered that delightful course of lectures that we heard in Geneva, on—what was the title?—'The Redeeming Features of the Pagan Morality.'"

Angela flushed a little.

"I have quite forgotten his name, mamma," she said, without looking round.

"Come and sit by me, my dear, and we will talk them over. I wish Mr. Wright to hear about them," Mrs. Vivian went on.

"Do you wish to convert him to paganism?" Bernard asked.

"The lectures were very dull; they had no redeeming features," said Angela, getting up, but turning away from her mother. She stood looking at Bernard Longueville; he saw she was annoyed at her mother's interference. "Every now and then," she said, "I take a turn through the gaming-rooms. The last time, Captain Lovelock went with me. Will you come to-night?"

Bernard assented with expressive alacrity; he was charmed with her not wishing to break off her conversation with him.

"Ah, we 'll all go!" said Mrs. Vivian, who had been listening, and she invited the others to accompany her to the Kursaal.

They left their places, but Angela went first, with Bernard Longueville by her side; and the idea of her having publicly braved her mother, as it were, for the sake of his society, lent for the moment an almost ecstatic energy to his tread. If he had been tempted to presume upon his triumph, however, he would have found a check in the fact that the young girl herself tasted very soberly of the sweets of defiance. She was silent and grave; she had a manner which took the edge from the wantonness of filial independence. Yet, for all this, Bernard was pleased with his position; and, as he walked with her through the lighted and crowded rooms, where they soon detached themselves from their companions, he felt that peculiar satisfaction which best expresses itself in silence. Angela looked a while at the rows of still, attentive faces, fixed upon the luminous green circle, across which little heaps of louis d'or were being pushed to and fro, and she continued to say nothing. Then at last she exclaimed simply, "Come away!" They turned away and passed into another chamber, in which there was no gambling. It was an immense apartment, apparently a ball-room; but at present it was quite unoccupied. There were green velvet benches all around it, and a great polished floor stretched away, shining in the light of chandeliers adorned with innumerable glass drops. Miss Vivian stood a moment on the threshold; then she passed in, and they stopped in the middle of the place, facing each other, and with their figures reflected as if they had been standing on a sheet of ice. There was no one in the room; they were entirely alone.

"Why don't you recognize me?" Bernard murmured quickly.

"Recognize you?"

"Why do you seem to forget our meeting at Siena?"

She might have answered if she had answered immediately; but she hesitated, and while she did so something happened at the other end of the room which caused her to shift her glance. A green velvet portiere suspended in one of the door-ways—not that through which our friends had passed—was lifted, and Gordon Wright stood there, holding it up, and looking at them. His companions were behind him.

"Ah, here they are!" cried Gordon, in his loud, clear voice.

This appeared to strike Angela Vivian as an interruption, and Bernard saw it very much in the same light.

CHAPTER VIII

He forbore to ask her his question again—she might tell him at her convenience. But the days passed by, and she never told him—she had her own reasons. Bernard talked with her very often; conversation formed indeed the chief entertainment of the quiet little circle of which he was a member. They sat on the terrace and talked in the mingled starlight and lamplight, and they strolled in the deep green forests and wound along the side of the gentle Baden hills, under the influence of colloquial tendencies. The Black Forest is a country of almost unbroken shade, and in the still days of midsummer the whole place was covered with a motionless canopy of verdure. Our friends were not extravagant or audacious people, and they looked at Baden life very much from the outside—they sat aloof from the brightly lighted drama of professional revelry. Among themselves as well, however, a little drama went forward in which each member of the company had a part to play. Bernard Longueville had been surprised at first at what he would have called Miss Vivian's approachableness—at the frequency with which he encountered opportunities for sitting near her and entering into conversation. He had expected that Gordon Wright would deem himself to have established an anticipatory claim upon the young lady's attention, and that, in pursuance of this claim, he would occupy a recognized place at her side. Gordon was, after all, wooing her; it was very natural he should seek her society. In fact, he was never very far off; but Bernard, for three or four days, had the anomalous consciousness of being still nearer. Presently, however, he perceived that he owed this privilege simply to his friend's desire that he should become acquainted with Miss Vivian—should receive a vivid impression of a person in whom Gordon was so deeply interested. After this result might have been supposed to be attained, Gordon Wright stepped back into his usual place and showed her those small civilities which were the only homage that the quiet conditions of their life rendered possible—walked with her, talked with her, brought her a book to read, a chair to sit upon, a couple of flowers to place in the bosom of her gown, treated her, in a word, with a sober but by no means inexpressive gallantry. He had not been making violent love, as he told Longueville, and these demonstrations were certainly not violent. Bernard said to himself that if he were not in the secret, a spectator would scarcely make the discovery that Gordon cherished an even very safely tended flame. Angela Vivian, on her side, was not strikingly responsive. There was nothing in her deportment to indicate that she was in love with her systematic suitor. She was perfectly gracious and civil. She smiled in his face when he shook hands with her; she looked at him and listened when he talked; she let him stroll beside her in the Lichtenthal Alley; she read, or appeared to read, the books he lent her, and she decorated herself with the flowers he offered. She seemed neither bored nor embarrassed, neither irritated nor oppressed. But it was Bernard's belief that she took no more pleasure in his attentions than a pretty girl must always take in any recognition of her charms. "If she 's not indifferent," he said to himself, "she is, at any rate, impartial—profoundly impartial."

It was not till the end of a week that Gordon Wright told him exactly how his business stood with Miss Vivian and what he had reason to expect and hope—a week during which their relations had been of the happiest and most comfortable cast, and during which Bernard, rejoicing in their long walks and talks, in the charming weather, in the beauty and entertainment of the place, and in other things besides, had not ceased to congratulate himself on coming to Baden. Bernard, after the first day, had asked his friend no questions. He had a great respect for opportunity, coming either to others or to himself, and he left Gordon to turn his lantern as fitfully as might be upon the subject which was tacitly open between them, but of which as yet only the mere edges had emerged into light. Gordon, on his side, seemed content for the moment with having his clever friend under his hand; he reserved him for final appeal or for some other mysterious use.

"You can't tell me you don't know her now," he said, one evening as the two young men strolled along the Lichtenthal Alley—"now that you have had a whole week's observation of her."

"What is a week's observation of a singularly clever and complicated woman?" Bernard asked.

"Ah, your week has been of some use. You have found out she is complicated!" Gordon rejoined.

"My dear Gordon," Longueville exclaimed, "I don't see what it signifies to you that I should find Miss Vivian out! When a man 's in love, what need he care what other people think of the loved object?"

"It would certainly be a pity to care too much. But there is some excuse for him in the loved object being, as you say, complicated."

"Nonsense! That 's no excuse. The loved object is always complicated."

Gordon walked on in silence a moment.

"Well, then, I don't care a button what you think!"

"Bravo! That 's the way a man should talk," cried Longueville.

Gordon indulged in another fit of meditation, and then he said—

"Now that leaves you at liberty to say what you please."

"Ah, my dear fellow, you are ridiculous!" said Bernard.

"That 's precisely what I want you to say. You always think me too reasonable."

"Well, I go back to my first assertion. I don't know Miss Vivian—I mean I don't know her to have opinions about her. I don't suppose you wish me to string you off a dozen mere banalites—'She 's a charming girl—evidently a superior person—has a great deal of style.'"

"Oh no," said Gordon; "I know all that. But, at any rate," he added, "you like her, eh?"

"I do more," said Longueville. "I admire her."

"Is that doing more?" asked Gordon, reflectively.

"Well, the greater, whichever it is, includes the less."

"You won't commit yourself," said Gordon. "My dear Bernard," he added, "I thought you knew such an immense deal about women!"

Gordon Wright was of so kindly and candid a nature that it is hardly conceivable that this remark should have been framed to make Bernard commit himself by putting him on his mettle. Such a view would imply indeed on Gordon's part a greater familiarity with the uses of irony than he had ever possessed, as well as a livelier conviction of the irritable nature of his friend's vanity. In fact, however, it may be confided to the reader that Bernard was pricked in a tender place, though the resentment of vanity was not visible in his answer.

"You were quite wrong," he simply said. "I am as ignorant of women as a monk in his cloister."

"You try to prove too much. You don't think her sympathetic!" And as regards this last remark, Gordon Wright must be credited with a certain ironical impulse.

Bernard stopped impatiently.

"I ask you again, what does it matter to you what I think of her?"

"It matters in this sense—that she has refused me."

"Refused you? Then it is all over, and nothing matters."

"No, it is n't over," said Gordon, with a positive head-shake. "Don't you see it is n't over?"

Bernard smiled, laid his hand on his friend's shoulder and patted it a little.

"Your attitude might almost pass for that of resignation."

"I 'm not resigned!" said Gordon Wright.

"Of course not. But when were you refused?"

Gordon stood a minute with his eyes fixed on the ground. Then, at last looking up,

"Three weeks ago—a fortnight before you came. But let us walk along," he said, "and I will tell you all about it."

"I proposed to her three weeks ago," said Gordon, as they walked along. "My heart was very much set upon it. I was very hard hit—I was deeply smitten. She had been very kind to me—she had been charming—I thought she liked me. Then I thought her mother was pleased, and would have liked it. Mrs. Vivian, in fact, told me as much; for of course I spoke to her first. Well, Angela does like me—or at least she did—and I see no reason to suppose she has changed. Only she did n't like me enough. She said the friendliest and pleasantest things to me, but she thought that she knew me too little, and that I knew her even less. She made a great point of that—that I had no right, as yet, to trust her. I told her that if she would trust me, I was perfectly willing to trust her; but she answered that this was poor reasoning. She said that I was trustworthy and that she was not, and—in short, all sorts of nonsense. She abused herself roundly—accused herself of no end of defects."

"What defects, for instance?"

"Oh, I have n't remembered them. She said she had a bad temper—that she led her mother a dreadful life. Now, poor Mrs. Vivian says she is an angel."

"Ah yes," Bernard observed; "Mrs. Vivian says that, very freely."

"Angela declared that she was jealous, ungenerous, unforgiving—all sorts of things. I remember she said 'I am very false,' and I think she remarked that she was cruel."

"But this did n't put you off," said Bernard.

"Not at all. She was making up."

"She makes up very well!" Bernard exclaimed, laughing.

"Do you call that well?"

"I mean it was very clever."

"It was not clever from the point of view of wishing to discourage me."

"Possibly. But I am sure," said Bernard, "that if I had been present at your interview—excuse the impudence of the hypothesis—I should have been struck with the young lady's—" and he paused a moment.

"With her what?"

"With her ability."

"Well, her ability was not sufficient to induce me to give up my idea. She told me that after I had known her six months I should detest her."

"I have no doubt she could make you do it if she should try. That 's what I mean by her ability."

"She calls herself cruel," said Gordon, "but she has not had the cruelty to try. She has been very reasonable—she has been perfect. I agreed with her that I would drop the subject for a while, and that meanwhile we should be good friends. We should take time to know each other better and act in accordance with further knowledge. There was no hurry, since we trusted each other—wrong as my trust might be. She had no wish that I should go away. I was not in the least disagreeable to her; she liked me extremely, and I was perfectly free to try and please her. Only I should drop my proposal, and be free to take it up again or leave it alone, later, as I should choose. If she felt differently then, I should have the benefit of it, and if I myself felt differently, I should also have the benefit of it."

"That 's a very comfortable arrangement. And that 's your present situation?" asked Bernard.

Gordon hesitated a moment.

"More or less, but not exactly."

"Miss Vivian feels differently?" said Bernard.

"Not that I know of."

Gordon's companion, with a laugh, clapped him on the shoulder again.

"Admirable youth, you are a capital match!"

"Are you alluding to my money?"

"To your money and to your modesty. There is as much of one as of the other—which is saying a great deal."

64

"Well," said Gordon, "in spite of that enviable combination, I am not happy."

"I thought you seemed pensive!" Bernard exclaimed. "It 's you, then, who feel differently."

Gordon gave a sigh.

"To say that is to say too much."

"What shall we say, then?" his companion asked, kindly.

Gordon stopped again; he stood there looking up at a certain particularly lustrous star which twinkled—the night was cloudy—in an open patch of sky, and the vague brightness shone down on his honest and serious visage.

"I don't understand her," he said.

"Oh, I 'll say that with you any day!" cried Bernard. "I can't help you there."

"You must help me;" and Gordon Wright deserted his star. "You must keep me in good humor."

"Please to walk on, then. I don't in the least pity you; she is very charming with you."

"True enough; but insisting on that is not the way to keep me in good humor—when I feel as I do."

"How is it you feel?"

"Puzzled to death—bewildered—depressed!"

This was but the beginning of Gordon Wright's list; he went on to say that though he "thought as highly" of Miss Vivian as he had ever done, he felt less at his ease with her than in the first weeks of their acquaintance, and this condition made him uncomfortable and unhappy.

"I don't know what 's the matter," said poor Gordon. "I don't know what has come between us. It is n't her fault—I don't make her responsible for it. I began to notice it about a fortnight ago—before you came; shortly after that talk I had with her that I have just described to you. Her manner has n't changed and I have no reason to suppose that she likes me any the less; but she makes a strange impression on me—she makes me uneasy. It 's only her nature coming out, I suppose—what you might call her originality. She 's thoroughly original—she 's a kind of mysterious creature. I suppose that what I feel is a sort of fascination; but that is just what I don't like. Hang it, I don't want to be fascinated—I object to being fascinated!"

This little story had taken some time in the telling, so that the two young men had now reached their hotel.

"Ah, my dear Gordon," said Bernard, "we speak a different language. If you don't want to be fascinated, what is one to say to you? 'Object to being fascinated!' There 's a man easy to satisfy! Raffiné, va!"

"Well, see here now," said Gordon, stopping in the door-way of the inn; "when it comes to the point, do you like it yourself?"

"When it comes to the point?" Bernard exclaimed. "I assure you I don't wait till then. I like the beginning—I delight in the approach of it—I revel in the prospect."

"That's just what I did. But now that the thing has come—I don't revel. To be fascinated is to be mystified. Damn it, I like my liberty—I like my judgment!"

"So do I—like yours," said Bernard, laughing, as they took their bedroom candles.

CHAPTER IX

Bernard talked of this matter rather theoretically, inasmuch as to his own sense, he was in a state neither of incipient nor of absorbed fascination. He got on very easily, however, with Angela Vivian, and felt none of the mysterious discomfort alluded to by his friend. The element of mystery attached itself rather to the young lady's mother, who gave him the impression that for undiscoverable reasons she avoided his society. He regretted her evasive deportment, for he found something agreeable in this shy and scrupulous little woman, who struck him as a curious specimen of a society of which he had once been very fond. He learned that she was of old New England stock, but he had not needed this information to perceive that Mrs. Vivian was animated by the genius of Boston. "She has the Boston temperament," he said, using a phrase with which he had become familiar and which evoked a train of associations. But then he immediately added that if Mrs. Vivian was a daughter of the Puritans, the Puritan strain in her disposition had been mingled with another element. "It is the Boston temperament sophisticated," he said; "perverted a little—perhaps even corrupted. It is the local east-wind with an infusion from climates less tonic." It seemed to him that Mrs. Vivian was a Puritan grown worldly—a Bostonian relaxed; and this impression, oddly enough, contributed to his wish to know more of her. He felt like going up to her very politely and saying, "Dear lady and most honored compatriot, what in the world have I done to displease you? You don't approve of me, and I am dying to know the reason why. I should be so happy to exert myself to be agreeable to you. It 's no use; you give me the cold shoulder. When I speak to you, you look the other way; it is only when I speak to your daughter that you look at me. It is true that at those times you look at me very hard, and if I am not greatly mistaken, you are not gratified by what you see. You count the words I address to your beautiful Angela—you time our harmless little interviews. You interrupt them indeed whenever you can; you call her away—you appeal to her; you cut across the conversation. You are always laying plots to keep us apart. Why can't you leave me alone? I assure you I am the most innocent of men. Your beautiful Angela can't possibly be injured by my conversation, and I have no designs whatever upon her peace of mind. What on earth have I done to offend you?"

These observations Bernard Longueville was disposed to make, and one afternoon, the opportunity offering, they rose to his lips and came very near passing them. In fact, however, at the last moment, his eloquence took another turn. It was the custom of the orchestra at the Kursaal to play in the afternoon, and as the music was often good, a great many people assembled under the trees, at three o'clock, to listen to it. This was not, as a regular thing, an hour of re-union for the little group in which we are especially interested; Miss Vivian, in particular, unless an excursion of some sort had been agreed upon the day before, was usually not to be seen in the precincts of the Conversation-house until the evening. Bernard, one afternoon, at three o'clock, directed his steps to this small world-centre of Baden, and, passing along the terrace, soon encountered little Blanche Evers strolling there under a pink parasol and accompanied by Captain Lovelock. This young lady was always extremely sociable; it was quite in accordance with her habitual geniality that she should stop and say how d' ye do to our hero.

"Mr. Longueville is growing very frivolous," she said, "coming to the Kursaal at all sorts of hours."

"There is nothing frivolous in coming here with the hope of finding you," the young man answered. "That is very serious."

"It would be more serious to lose Miss Evers than to find her," remarked Captain Lovelock, with gallant jocosity.

"I wish you would lose me!" cried the young girl. "I think I should like to be lost. I might have all kinds of adventures."

"I 'guess' so!" said Captain Lovelock, hilariously.

"Oh, I should find my way. I can take care of myself!" Blanche went on.

"Mrs. Vivian does n't think so," said Bernard, who had just perceived this lady, seated under a tree with a book, over the top of which she was observing her pretty protege. Blanche looked toward her and gave her a little nod and a smile. Then chattering on to the young men—

"She 's awfully careful. I never saw any one so careful. But I suppose she is right. She promised my mother she would be tremendously particular; but I don't know what she thinks I would do."

"That is n't flattering to me," said Captain Lovelock. "Mrs. Vivian does n't approve of me—she wishes me in Jamaica. What does she think me capable of?"

"And me, now?" Bernard asked. "She likes me least of all, and I, on my side, think she 's so nice."

"Can't say I 'm very sweet on her," said the Captain. "She strikes me as feline."

Blanche Evers gave a little cry of horror.

"Stop, sir, this instant! I won't have you talk that way about a lady who has been so kind to me."

"She is n't so kind to you. She would like to lock you up where I can never see you."

"I 'm sure I should n't mind that!" cried the young girl, with a little laugh and a toss of her head. "Mrs. Vivian has the most perfect character— that 's why my mother wanted me to come with her. And if she promised my mother she would be careful, is n't she right to keep her promise? She 's a great deal more careful than mamma ever was, and that 's just what mamma wanted. She would never take the trouble herself. And then she was always scolding me. Mrs. Vivian never scolds me. She only watches me, but I don't mind that."

"I wish she would watch you a little less and scold you a little more," said Captain Lovelock.

"I have no doubt you wish a great many horrid things," his companion rejoined, with delightful asperity.

"Ah, unfortunately I never have anything I wish!" sighed Lovelock.

"Your wishes must be comprehensive," said Bernard. "It seems to me you have a good deal."

The Englishman gave a shrug.

"It 's less than you might think. She is watching us more furiously than ever," he added, in a moment, looking at Mrs. Vivian. "Mr. Gordon Wright is the only man she likes. She is awfully fond of Mr. Gordon Wright."

"Ah, Mrs. Vivian shows her wisdom!" said Bernard.

"He is certainly very handsome," murmured Blanche Evers, glancing several times, with a very pretty aggressiveness, at Captain Lovelock. "I must say I like Mr. Gordon Wright. Why in the world did you come here without him?" she went on, addressing herself to Bernard. "You two are so awfully inseparable. I don't think I ever saw you alone before."

"Oh, I have often seen Mr. Gordon Wright alone," said Captain Lovelock—"that is, alone with Miss Vivian. That 's what the old lady likes; she can't have too much of that."

The young girl, poised for an instant in one of her pretty attitudes, looked at him from head to foot.

"Well, I call that scandalous! Do you mean that she wants to make a match?"

"I mean that the young man has six thousand a year."

"It 's no matter what he has—six thousand a year is n't much! And we don't do things in that way in our country. We have n't those horrid match-making arrangements that you have in your dreadful country. American mothers are not like English mothers."

"Oh, any one can see, of course," said Captain Lovelock, "that Mr. Gordon Wright is dying of love for Miss Vivian."

"I can't see it!" cried Blanche.

"He dies easier than I, eh?"

"I wish you would die!" said Blanche. "At any rate, Angela is not dying of love for Mr. Wright."

"Well, she will marry him all the same," Lovelock declared.

Blanche Evers glanced at Bernard.

"Why don't you contradict that?" she asked. "Why don't you speak up for your friend?"

"I am quite ready to speak for my friend," said Bernard, "but I am not ready to speak for Miss Vivian."

"Well, I am," Blanche declared. "She won't marry him."

"If she does n't, I 'll eat my hat!" said Captain Lovelock. "What do you mean," he went on, "by saying that in America a pretty girl's mother does n't care for a young fellow's property?"

"Well, they don't—we consider that dreadful. Why don't you say so, Mr. Longueville?" Blanche demanded. "I never saw any one take things so quietly. Have n't you got any patriotism?"

"My patriotism is modified by an indisposition to generalize," said Bernard, laughing. "On this point permit me not to generalize. I am interested in the particular case—in ascertaining whether Mrs. Vivian thinks very often of Gordon Wright's income."

Miss Evers gave a little toss of disgust.

"If you are so awfully impartial, you had better go and ask her."

"That 's a good idea—I think I will go and ask her," said Bernard.

Captain Lovelock returned to his argument.

"Do you mean to say that your mother would be indifferent to the fact that I have n't a shilling in the world?"

"Indifferent?" Blanche demanded. "Oh no, she would be sorry for you. She is very charitable—she would give you a shilling!"

"She would n't let you marry me," said Lovelock.

"She would n't have much trouble to prevent it!" cried the young girl.

Bernard had had enough of this intellectual fencing.

"Yes, I will go and ask Mrs. Vivian," he repeated. And he left his companions to resume their walk.

CHAPTER X

It had seemed to him a good idea to interrogate Mrs. Vivian; but there are a great many good ideas that are never put into execution. As he approached her with a smile and a salutation, and, with the air of asking leave to take a liberty, seated himself in the empty chair beside her, he felt a humorous relish of her own probable dismay which relaxed the investigating impulse. His impulse was now simply to prove to her that he was the most unobjectionable fellow in the world—a proposition which resolved itself into several ingenious observations upon the weather, the music, the charms and the drawbacks of Baden, the merits of the volume that she held in her lap. If Mrs. Vivian should be annoyed, should be fluttered, Bernard would feel very sorry for her; there was nothing in the world that he respected more than the moral consciousness of a little Boston woman whose view of life was serious and whose imagination was subject to alarms. He held it to be a temple of delicacy, where one should walk on tiptoe, and he wished to exhibit to Mrs. Vivian the possible lightness of his own step. She herself was incapable of being rude or ungracious, and now that she was fairly confronted with the plausible object of her mistrust, she composed herself to her usual attitude of refined liberality. Her book was a volume of Victor Cousin.

"You must have an extraordinary power of abstracting your mind," Bernard said to her, observing it. "Studying philosophy at the Baden Kursaal strikes me as a real intellectual feat."

"Don't you think we need a little philosophy here?"

"By all means—what we bring with us. But I should n't attempt the use of the text-book on the spot."

"You should n't speak of yourself as if you were not clever," said Mrs. Vivian. "Every one says you are so very clever."

Longueville stared; there was an unexpectedness in the speech and an incongruity in Mrs. Vivian's beginning to flatter him. He needed to remind himself that if she was a Bostonian, she was a Bostonian perverted.

"Ah, my dear madam, every one is no one," he said, laughing.

"It was Mr. Wright, in particular," she rejoined. "He has always told us that."

"He is blinded by friendship."

"Ah yes, we know about your friendship," said Mrs. Vivian. "He has told us about that."

"You are making him out a terrible talker!"

"We think he talks so well—we are so very fond of his conversation."

"It 's usually excellent," said Bernard. "But it depends a good deal on the subject."

"Oh," rejoined Mrs. Vivian, "we always let him choose his subjects." And dropping her eyes as if in sudden reflection, she began to smooth down the crumpled corner of her volume.

It occurred to Bernard that—by some mysterious impulse—she was suddenly presenting him with a chance to ask her the question that Blanche Evers had just suggested. Two or three other things as well occurred to him. Captain Lovelock had been struck with the fact that she favored Gordon Wright's addresses to her daughter, and Captain Lovelock had a grotesque theory that she had set her heart upon seeing this young lady come into six thousand a year. Miss Evers's devoted swain had never struck Bernard as a brilliant reasoner, but our friend suddenly found himself regarding him as one of the inspired. The form of depravity into which the New England conscience had lapsed on Mrs. Vivian's part was an undue appreciation of a possible son-in-law's income! In this illuminating discovery everything else became clear. Mrs. Vivian disliked her humble servant because he had not thirty thousand dollars a year, and because at a moment when it was Angela's prime duty to concentrate her thoughts upon Gordon Wright's great advantages, a clever young man of paltry fortune was a superfluous diversion.

"When you say clever, everything is relative," he presently observed. "Now, there is Captain Lovelock; he has a certain kind of cleverness; he is very observant."

Mrs. Vivian glanced up with a preoccupied air.

"We don't like Captain Lovelock," she said.

"I have heard him say capital things," Bernard answered.

"We think him brutal," said Mrs. Vivian. "Please don't praise Captain Lovelock."

"Oh, I only want to be just."

Mrs. Vivian for a moment said nothing.

"Do you want very much to be just?" she presently asked.

"It 's my most ardent desire."

"I 'm glad to hear that—and I can easily believe it," said Mrs. Vivian.

Bernard gave her a grateful smile, but while he smiled, he asked himself a serious question. "Why the deuce does she go on flattering me?—You have always been very kind to me," he said aloud.

"It 's on Mr. Wright's account," she answered demurely.

In speaking the words I have just quoted, Bernard Longueville had felt himself, with a certain compunction, to be skirting the edge of clever impudence; but Mrs. Vivian's quiet little reply suggested to him that her cleverness, if not her impudence, was almost equal to his own. He remarked to himself that he had not yet done her justice.

"You bring everything back to Gordon Wright," he said, continuing to smile.

Mrs. Vivian blushed a little.

"It is because he is really at the foundation of everything that is pleasant for us here. When we first came we had some very disagreeable rooms, and as soon as he arrived he found us some excellent ones—that were less expensive. And then, Mr. Longueville," she added, with a soft, sweet emphasis which should properly have contradicted the idea of audacity, but which, to

Bernard's awakened sense, seemed really to impart a vivid color to it, "he was also the cause of your joining our little party."

"Oh, among his services that should never be forgotten. You should set up a tablet to commemorate it, in the wall of the Kursaal!—The wicked little woman!" Bernard mentally subjoined.

Mrs. Vivian appeared quite unruffled by his sportive sarcasm, and she continued to enumerate her obligations to Gordon Wright.

"There are so many ways in which a gentleman can be of assistance to three poor lonely women, especially when he is at the same time so friendly and so delicate as Mr. Wright. I don't know what we should have done without him, and I feel as if every one ought to know it. He seems like a very old friend. My daughter and I quite worship him. I will not conceal from you that when I saw you coming through the grounds a short time ago without him I was very much disappointed. I hope he is not ill."

Bernard sat listening, with his eyes on the ground.

"Oh no, he is simply at home writing letters."

Mrs. Vivian was silent a moment.

"I suppose he has a very large correspondence."

"I really don't know. Just now that I am with him he has a smaller one than usual."

"Ah yes. When you are separated I suppose you write volumes to each other. But he must have a great many business letters."

"It is very likely," said Bernard. "And if he has, you may be sure he writes them."

"Order and method!" Mrs. Vivian exclaimed. "With his immense property those virtues are necessary."

Bernard glanced at her a moment.

"My dear Lovelock," he said to himself, "you are not such a fool as you seem.—Gordon's virtues are always necessary, doubtless," he went on. "But should you say his property was immense?"

Mrs. Vivian made a delicate little movement of deprecation. "Oh, don't ask me to say! I know nothing about it; I only supposed he was rich."

"He is rich; but he is not a Croesus."

"Oh, you fashionable young men have a standard of luxury!" said Mrs. Vivian, with a little laugh. "To a poverty-stricken widow such a fortune as Mr. Wright's seems magnificent."

"Don't call me such horrible names!" exclaimed Bernard. "Our friend has certainly money enough and to spare."

"That was all I meant. He once had occasion to allude to his property, but he was so modest, so reserved in the tone he took about it, that one hardly knew what to think."

"He is ashamed of being rich," said Bernard. "He would be sure to represent everything unfavorably."

"That 's just what I thought!" This ejaculation was more eager than Mrs. Vivian might have intended, but even had it been less so, Bernard was in a mood to appreciate it. "I felt that we should make allowances for his modesty. But it was in very good taste," Mrs. Vivian added.

"He 's a fortunate man," said Bernard. "He gets credit for his good taste—and he gets credit for the full figure of his income as well!"

"Ah," murmured Mrs. Vivian, rising lightly, as if to make her words appear more casual, "I don't know the full figure of his income."

She was turning away, and Bernard, as he raised his hat and separated from her, felt that it was rather cruel that he should let her go without enlightening her ignorance. But he said to himself that she knew quite enough. Indeed, he took a walk along the Lichtenthal Alley and carried out this line of reflection. Whether or no Miss Vivian were in love with Gordon

Wright, her mother was enamored of Gordon's fortune, and it had suddenly occurred to her that instead of treating the friend of her daughter's suitor with civil mistrust, she would help her case better by giving him a hint of her state of mind and appealing to his sense of propriety. Nothing could be more natural than that Mrs. Vivian should suppose that Bernard desired his friend's success; for, as our thoughtful hero said to himself, what she had hitherto taken it into her head to fear was not that Bernard should fall in love with her daughter, but that her daughter should fall in love with him. Watering-place life is notoriously conducive to idleness of mind, and Bernard strolled for half an hour along the overarched avenue, glancing alternately at these two insupposable cases.

A few days afterward, late in the evening, Gordon Wright came to his room at the hotel.

"I have just received a letter from my sister," he said. "I am afraid I shall have to go away."

"Ah, I 'm sorry for that," said Bernard, who was so well pleased with the actual that he desired no mutation.

"I mean only for a short time," Gordon explained. "My poor sister writes from England, telling me that my brother-in-law is suddenly obliged to go home. She has decided not to remain behind, and they are to sail a fortnight hence. She wants very much to see me before she goes, and as I don't know when I shall see her again, I feel as if I ought to join her immediately and spend the interval with her. That will take about a fortnight."

"I appreciate the sanctity of family ties and I project myself into your situation," said Bernard. "On the other hand, I don't envy you a breathless journey from Baden to Folkestone."

"It 's the coming back that will be breathless," exclaimed Gordon, smiling.

"You will certainly come back, then?"

"Most certainly. Mrs. Vivian is to be here another month."

"I understand. Well, we shall miss you very much."

Gordon Wright looked for a moment at his companion.

"You will stay here, then? I am so glad of that."

"I was taking it for granted; but on reflection—what do you recommend?"

"I recommend you to stay."

"My dear fellow, your word is law," said Bernard.

"I want you to take care of those ladies," his friend went on. "I don't like to leave them alone."

"You are joking!" cried Bernard. "When did you ever hear of my 'taking care' of any one? It 's as much as I can do to take care of myself."

"This is very easy," said Gordon. "I simply want to feel that they have a man about them."

"They will have a man at any rate—they have the devoted Lovelock."

"That 's just why I want them to have another. He has only an eye to Miss Evers, who, by the way, is extremely bored with him. You look after the others. You have made yourself very agreeable to them, and they like you extremely."

"Ah," said Bernard, laughing, "if you are going to be coarse and flattering, I collapse. If you are going to titillate my vanity, I succumb."

"It won't be so disagreeable," Gordon observed, with an intention vaguely humorous.

"Oh no, it won't be disagreeable. I will go to Mrs. Vivian every morning, hat in hand, for my orders."

Gordon Wright, with his hands in his pockets and a meditative expression, took several turns about the room.

"It will be a capital chance," he said, at last, stopping in front of his companion.

"A chance for what?"

"A chance to arrive at a conclusion about my young friend."

Bernard gave a gentle groan.

"Are you coming back to that? Did n't I arrive at a conclusion long ago? Did n't I tell you she was a delightful girl?"

"Do you call that a conclusion? The first comer could tell me that at the end of an hour."

"Do you want me to invent something different?" Bernard asked. "I can't invent anything better."

"I don't want you to invent anything. I only want you to observe her—to study her in complete independence. You will have her to yourself—my absence will leave you at liberty. Hang it, sir," Gordon declared, "I should think you would like it!"

"Damn it, sir, you 're delicious!" Bernard answered; and he broke into an irrepressible laugh. "I don't suppose it 's for my pleasure that you suggest the arrangement."

Gordon took a turn about the room again.

"No, it 's for mine. At least, it 's for my benefit."

"For your benefit?"

"I have got all sorts of ideas—I told you the other day. They are all mixed up together and I want a fresh impression."

"My impressions are never fresh," Bernard replied.

"They would be if you had a little good-will—if you entered a little into my dilemma." The note of reproach was so distinct in these words that Bernard stood staring. "You never take anything seriously," his companion went on.

Bernard tried to answer as seriously as possible.

"Your dilemma seems to me of all dilemmas the strangest."

"That may be; but different people take things differently. Don't you see," Gordon went on with a sudden outbreak of passion—"don't you see that I am horribly divided in mind? I care immensely for Angela Vivian—and yet—and yet—I am afraid of her."

"Afraid of her?"

"I am afraid she 's cleverer than I—that she would be a difficult wife; that she might do strange things."

"What sort of things?"

"Well, that she might flirt, for instance."

"That 's not a thing for a man to fear."

"Not when he supposes his wife to be fond of him—no. But I don't suppose that—I have given that up. If I should induce Angela Vivian to accept me she would do it on grounds purely reasonable. She would think it best, simply. That would give her a chance to repent."

Bernard sat for some time looking at his friend.

"You say she is cleverer than you. It 's impossible to be cleverer than you."

"Oh, come, Longueville!" said Gordon, angrily.

"I am speaking very seriously. You have done a remarkably clever thing. You have impressed me with the reality, and with—what shall I term it?—the estimable character of what you call your dilemma. Now this fresh impression of mine—what do you propose to do with it when you get it?"

"Such things are always useful. It will be a good thing to have."

"I am much obliged to you; but do you propose to let anything depend upon it? Do you propose to take or to leave Miss Vivian—that is, to return to the charge or to give up trying—in consequence of my fresh impression?"

Gordon seemed perfectly unembarrassed by this question, in spite of the ironical light which it projected upon his sentimental perplexity.

"I propose to do what I choose!" he said.

"That 's a relief to me," Bernard rejoined. "This idea of yours is, after all, only the play of the scientific mind."

"I shall contradict you flat if I choose," Gordon went on.

"Ah, it 's well to warn me of that," said Bernard, laughing. "Even the most sincere judgment in the world likes to be notified a little of the danger of being contradicted."

"Is yours the most sincere judgment in the world?" Gordon demanded.

"That 's a very pertinent question. Does n't it occur to you that you may have reason to be jealous—leaving me alone, with an open field, with the woman of your choice?"

"I wish to heaven I could be jealous!" Gordon exclaimed. "That would simplify the thing—that would give me a lift."

And the next day, after some more talk, it seemed really with a hope of this contingency—though, indeed, he laughed about it—that he started for England.

CHAPTER XI

For the three or four days that followed Gordon Wright's departure, Bernard saw nothing of the ladies who had been committed to his charge. They chose to remain in seclusion, and he was at liberty to interpret this fact as an expression of regret at the loss of Gordon's good offices. He knew other people at Baden, and he went to see them and endeavored, by cultivating their society, to await in patience the re-appearance of Mrs. Vivian and her companions. But on the fourth day he became conscious that other people were much less interesting than the trio of American ladies who had lodgings above the confectioner's, and he made bold to go and knock at their door. He had been asked to take care of them, and this function presupposed contact. He had met Captain Lovelock the day before, wandering about with a rather crest-fallen aspect, and the young Englishman had questioned him eagerly as to the whereabouts of Mrs. Vivian.

"Gad, I believe they 've left the place—left the place without giving a fellow warning!" cried Lovelock.

"Oh no, I think they are here still," said Bernard. "My friend Wright has gone away for a week or two, but I suspect the ladies are simply staying at home."

"Gad, I was afraid your friend Wright had taken them away with him; he seems to keep them all in his pocket. I was afraid he had given them marching orders; they 'd have been sure to go—they 're so awfully fond of his pocket! I went to look them up yesterday—upon my word I did. They live at a baker's in a little back-street; people do live in rum places when they come abroad! But I assure you, when I got there, I 'm damned if I could make out whether they were there or not. I don't speak a word of German, and there was no one there but the baker's wife. She was a low brute of a woman—she could n't understand a word I said, though she gave me plenty of her own tongue. I had to give it up. They were not at home, but whether they had left Baden or not—that was beyond my finding out. If they are here, why the deuce don't they show? Fancy coming to Baden-Baden to sit moping at a pastry-cook's!"

Captain Lovelock was evidently irritated, and it was Bernard's impression that the turn of luck over yonder where the gold-pieces were chinking had something to do with the state of his temper. But more fortunate himself, he ascertained from the baker's wife that though Mrs. Vivian and her daughter had gone out, their companion, "the youngest lady—the little young lady"— was above in the sitting-room.

Blanche Evers was sitting at the window with a book, but she relinquished the volume with an alacrity that showed it had not been absorbing, and began to chatter with her customary frankness.

"Well, I must say I am glad to see some one!" cried the young girl, passing before the mirror and giving a touch to her charming tresses.

"Even if it 's only me," Bernard exclaimed, laughing.

"I did n't mean that. I am sure I am very glad to see you—I should think you would have found out that by this time. I mean I 'm glad to see any one—especially a man. I suppose it 's improper for me to say that—especially to you! There—you see I do think more of you than of some gentlemen. Why especially to you? Well, because you always seem to me to want to take advantage. I did n't say a base advantage; I did n't accuse you of anything dreadful. I 'm sure I want to take advantage, too—I take it whenever I can. You see I take advantage of your being here—I 've got so many things to say. I have n't spoken a word in three days, and I 'm sure it is a pleasant change—a gentleman's visit. All of a sudden we have gone into mourning; I 'm sure I don't know who 's dead. Is it Mr. Gordon Wright? It 's some idea of Mrs. Vivian's—I 'm sure it is n't mine. She thinks we have been often enough to the Kursaal. I don't know whether she thinks it 's wicked, or what. If it 's wicked the harm 's already done; I can't be any worse than I am now. I have seen all the improper people and I have learnt all their names; Captain Lovelock has told me their names, plenty of times. I don't see what good it does me to be shut up here with all those names running in my ears. I must say I do prefer society. We have n't been to the Kursaal for four days—we have only gone out for a drive. We have taken the most interminable drives. I do believe we have seen every old ruin in the whole country. Mrs. Vivian and Angela are so awfully fond of scenery—they talk about it by the half-hour. They talk about the mountains and trees as if they were people they knew—as if they were gentlemen! I mean as if the mountains and trees were gentlemen. Of course scenery 's lovely, but you can't walk about with a tree. At any rate, that has been all our society—foliage! Foliage and women; but I suppose women are a sort of foliage. They are always rustling about and dropping off. That 's why I could n't make up my mind to go out with them this afternoon. They 've gone to see the Waterworths—the Waterworths arrived yesterday and are staying at some hotel. Five daughters—all unmarried! I don't know what kind of foliage they are; some peculiar kind—they don't drop off. I thought I had had about enough ladies' society—three women all sticking together! I don't think it 's good for a young girl to have nothing but ladies' society—it 's so awfully limited. I suppose I ought to stand up for my own sex and tell you that when we are alone together we want for nothing. But we want for everything, as it happens! Women's talk is limited—every one knows that. That 's just what mamma did n't want when she asked Mrs. Vivian to take charge of me. Now, Mr. Longueville, what are you laughing at?—you are always laughing at me. She wanted me to be unlimited—is that what you say? Well, she did n't want me to be narrowed down; she wanted me to have plenty of conversation. She wanted me to be fitted for society—that 's what mamma wanted. She wanted me to have ease of manner; she thinks that if you don't acquire it when you are young you never have it at all. She was so happy to think I should come to Baden; but she would n't approve of the life I 've been leading the last four days. That 's no way to acquire ease of manner—sitting all day in a small parlor with two persons of one's own sex! Of course Mrs. Vivian's influence— that 's the great thing. Mamma said it was like the odor of a flower. But you don't want to keep smelling a flower all day, even the sweetest; that 's the shortest way to get a headache. Apropos of flowers, do you happen to have heard whether Captain Lovelock is alive or dead? Do I call him a flower? No; I call him a flower-pot. He always has some fine young plant in his button-hole. He has n't been near me these ten years—I never heard of anything so rude!"

Captain Lovelock came on the morrow, Bernard finding him in Mrs. Vivian's little sitting-room on paying a second visit. On this occasion the two other ladies were at home and Bernard was not exclusively indebted to Miss Evers for entertainment. It was to this source of hospitality, however, that Lovelock mainly appealed, following the young girl out upon the little balcony that was suspended above the confectioner's window. Mrs. Vivian sat writing at one of the windows of the sitting-room, and Bernard addressed his conversation to Angela.

"Wright requested me to keep an eye on you," he said; "but you seem very much inclined to keep out of my jurisdiction."

"I supposed you had gone away," she answered—"now that your friend is gone."

"By no means. Gordon is a charming fellow, but he is by no means the only attraction of Baden. Besides, I have promised him to look after you—to take care of you."

The girl looked at him a moment in silence—a little askance.

"I thought you had probably undertaken something of that sort," she presently said.

"It was of course a very natural request for Gordon to make."

Angela got up and turned away; she wandered about the room and went and stood at one of the windows. Bernard found the movement abrupt and not particularly gracious; but the young man was not easy to snub. He followed her, and they stood at the second window—the long window that opened upon the balcony. Miss Evers and Captain Lovelock were leaning on the railing, looking into the street and apparently amusing themselves highly with what they saw.

"I am not sure it was a natural request for him to make," said Angela.

"What could have been more so—devoted as he is to you?"

She hesitated a moment; then with a little laugh—

"He ought to have locked us up and said nothing about it."

"It's not so easy to lock you up," said Bernard. "I know Wright has great influence with you, but you are after all independent beings."

"I am not an independent being. If my mother and Mr. Wright were to agree together to put me out of harm's way they could easily manage it."

"You seem to have been trying something of that sort," said Bernard. "You have been so terribly invisible."

"It was because I thought you had designs upon us; that you were watching for us—to take care of us."

"You contradict yourself! You said just now that you believed I had left Baden."

"That was an artificial—a conventional speech. Isn't a lady always supposed to say something of that sort to a visitor by way of pretending to have noticed that she has not seen him?"

"You know I would never have left Baden without coming to bid you good-bye," said Bernard.

The girl made no rejoinder; she stood looking out at the little sunny, slanting, rough-paved German street.

"Are you taking care of us now?" she asked in a moment. "Has the operation begun? Have you heard the news, mamma?" she went on. "Do you know that Mr. Wright has made us over to Mr. Longueville, to be kept till called for? Suppose Mr. Wright should never call for us!"

Mrs. Vivian left her writing-table and came toward Bernard, smiling at him and pressing her hands together.

"There is no fear of that, I think," she said. "I am sure I am very glad we have a gentleman near us. I think you will be a very good care-taker, Mr. Longueville, and I recommend my daughter to put great faith in your judgment." And Mrs. Vivian gave him an intense—a pleading, almost affecting—little smile.

"I am greatly touched by your confidence and I shall do everything I can think of to merit it," said the young man.

"Ah, mamma's confidence is wonderful!" Angela exclaimed. "There was never anything like mamma's confidence. I am very different; I have no confidence. And then I don't like being deposited, like a parcel, or being watched, like a curious animal. I am too fond of my liberty."

"That is the second time you have contradicted yourself," said Bernard. "You said just now that you were not an independent being."

Angela turned toward him quickly, smiling and frowning at once.

"You do watch one, certainly! I see it has already begun." Mrs. Vivian laid her hand upon her daughter's with a little murmur of tender deprecation, and the girl bent over and kissed her. "Mamma will tell you it 's the effect of agitation," she said—"that I am nervous, and don't know what I say. I am supposed to be agitated by Mr. Wright's departure; is n't that it, mamma?"

Mrs. Vivian turned away, with a certain soft severity.

"I don't know, my daughter. I don't understand you."

A charming pink flush had come into Angela's cheek and a noticeable light into her eye. She looked admirably handsome, and Bernard frankly gazed at her. She met his gaze an instant, and then she went on.

"Mr. Longueville does n't understand me either. You must know that I am agitated," she continued. "Every now and then I have moments of talking nonsense. It 's the air of Baden, I think; it 's too exciting. It 's only lately I have been so. When you go away I shall be horribly ashamed."

"If the air of Baden has such an effect upon you," said Bernard, "it is only a proof the more that you need the solicitous attention of your friends."

"That may be; but, as I told you just now, I have no confidence—none whatever, in any one or anything. Therefore, for the present, I shall withdraw from the world—I shall seclude myself. Let us go on being quiet, mamma. Three or four days of it have been so charming. Let the parcel lie till it 's called for. It is much safer it should n't be touched at all. I shall assume that, metaphorically speaking, Mr. Wright, who, as you have intimated, is our earthly providence, has turned the key upon us. I am locked up. I shall not go out, except upon the balcony!" And with this, Angela stepped out of the long window and went and stood beside Miss Evers.

Bernard was extremely amused, but he was also a good deal puzzled, and it came over him that it was not a wonder that poor Wright should not have found this young lady's disposition a perfectly decipherable page. He remained in the room with Mrs. Vivian—he stood there looking at her with his agreeably mystified smile. She had turned away, but on perceiving that her daughter had gone outside she came toward Bernard again, with her habitual little air of eagerness mitigated by discretion. There instantly rose before his mind the vision of that moment when he had stood face to face with this same apologetic mamma, after Angela had turned her back, on the grass-grown terrace at Siena. To make the vision complete, Mrs. Vivian took it into her head to utter the same words.

"I am sure you think she is a strange girl."

Bernard recognized them, and he gave a light laugh.

"You told me that the first time you ever saw me—in that quiet little corner of an Italian town."

Mrs. Vivian gave a little faded, elderly blush.

"Don't speak of that," she murmured, glancing at the open window. "It was a little accident of travel."

"I am dying to speak of it," said Bernard. "It was such a charming accident for me! Tell me this, at least—have you kept my sketch?"

Mrs. Vivian colored more deeply and glanced at the window again.

"No," she just whispered.

Bernard looked out of the window too. Angela was leaning against the railing of the balcony, in profile, just as she had stood while he painted her, against the polished parapet at Siena. The young man's eyes rested on her a moment, then, as he glanced back at her mother:

"Has she kept it?" he asked.

"I don't know," said Mrs. Vivian, with decision.

The decision was excessive—it expressed the poor lady's distress at having her veracity tested. "Dear little daughter of the Puritans—she can't tell a fib!" Bernard exclaimed to himself. And with this flattering conclusion he took leave of her.

CHAPTER XII

It was affirmed at an early stage of this narrative that he was a young man of a contemplative and speculative turn, and he had perhaps never been more true to his character than during an hour or two that evening as he sat by himself on the terrace of the Conversation-house, surrounded by the crowd of its frequenters, but lost in his meditations. The place was full of movement and sound, but he had tilted back his chair against the great green box of an orange-tree, and in this easy attitude, vaguely and agreeably conscious of the music, he directed his gaze to the star-sprinkled vault of the night. There were people coming and going whom he knew, but he said nothing to any one— he preferred to be alone; he found his own company quite absorbing. He felt very happy, very much amused, very curiously preoccupied. The feeling was a singular one. It partook of the nature of intellectual excitement. He had a sense of having received carte blanche for the expenditure of his wits. Bernard liked to feel his intelligence at play; this is, perhaps, the highest luxury of a clever man. It played at present over the whole field of Angela Vivian's oddities of conduct—for, since his visit in the afternoon, Bernard had felt that the spectacle was considerably enlarged. He had come to feel, also, that poor Gordon's predicament was by no means an unnatural one. Longueville had begun to take his friend's dilemma very seriously indeed. The girl was certainly a curious study.

The evening drew to a close and the crowd of Bernard's fellow-loungers dispersed. The lighted windows of the Kursaal still glittered in the bosky darkness, and the lamps along the terrace had not been extinguished; but the great promenade was almost deserted; here and there only a lingering couple—the red tip of a cigar and the vague radiance of a light dress—gave animation to the place. But Bernard sat there still in his tilted chair, beneath his orange-tree; his imagination had wandered very far and he was awaiting its return to the fold. He was on the point of rising, however, when he saw three figures come down the empty vista of the terrace—figures which even at a distance had a familiar air. He immediately left his seat and, taking a dozen steps, recognized Angela Vivian, Blanche Evers and Captain Lovelock. In a moment he met them in the middle of the terrace.

Blanche immediately announced that they had come for a midnight walk.

"And if you think it 's improper," she exclaimed, "it 's not my invention— it 's Miss Vivian's."

"I beg pardon—it 's mine," said Captain Lovelock. "I desire the credit of it. I started the idea; you never would have come without me."

"I think it would have been more proper to come without you than with you," Blanche declared. "You know you 're a dreadful character."

"I 'm much worse when I 'm away from you than when I 'm with you," said Lovelock. "You keep me in order."

The young girl gave a little cry.

"I don't know what you call order! You can't be worse than you have been to-night."

Angela was not listening to this; she turned away a little, looking about at the empty garden.

"This is the third time to-day that you have contradicted yourself," he said. Though he spoke softly he went nearer to her; but she appeared not to hear him—she looked away.

"You ought to have been there, Mr. Longueville," Blanche went on. "We have had a most lovely night; we sat all the evening on Mrs. Vivian's balcony, eating ices. To sit on a balcony, eating ices—that 's my idea of heaven."

"With an angel by your side," said Captain Lovelock.

"You are not my idea of an angel," retorted Blanche.

"I 'm afraid you 'll never learn what the angels are really like," said the Captain. "That 's why Miss Evers got Mrs. Vivian to take rooms over the baker's—so that she could have ices sent up several times a day. Well, I 'm bound to say the baker's ices are not bad."

"Considering that they have been baked! But they affect the mind," Blanche went on. "They would have affected Captain Lovelock's—only he has n't any. They certainly affected Angela's—putting it into her head, at eleven o'clock, to come out to walk."

Angela did nothing whatever to defend herself against this ingenious sally; she simply stood there in graceful abstraction. Bernard was vaguely vexed at her neither looking at him nor speaking to him; her indifference seemed a contravention of that right of criticism which Gordon had bequeathed to him.

"I supposed people went to bed at eleven o'clock," he said.

Angela glanced about her, without meeting his eye.

"They seem to have gone."

Miss Evers strolled on, and her Captain of course kept pace with her; so that Bernard and Miss Vivian were left standing together. He looked at her a moment in silence, but her eye still avoided his own.

"You are remarkably inconsistent," Bernard presently said. "You take a solemn vow of seclusion this afternoon, and no sooner have you taken it than you proceed to break it in this outrageous manner."

She looked at him now—a long time—longer than she had ever done before.

"This is part of the examination, I suppose," she said.

Bernard hesitated an instant.

"What examination?"

"The one you have undertaken—on Mr. Wright's behalf."

"What do you know about that?"

"Ah, you admit it then?" the girl exclaimed, with an eager laugh.

"I don't in the least admit it," said Bernard, conscious only for the moment of the duty of loyalty to his friend and feeling that negation here was simply a point of honor.

"I trust more to my own conviction than to your denial. You have engaged to bring your superior wisdom and your immense experience to bear upon me! That 's the understanding."

"You must think us a pretty pair of wiseacres," said Bernard.

"There it is—you already begin to answer for what I think. When Mr. Wright comes back you will be able to tell him that I am 'outrageous'!" And she turned away and walked on, slowly following her companions.

"What do you care what I tell him?" Bernard asked. "You don't care a straw."

She said nothing for a moment, then, suddenly, she stopped again, dropping her eyes.

"I beg your pardon," she said, very gently; "I care a great deal. It 's as well that you should know that."

Bernard stood looking at her; her eyes were still lowered.

"Do you know what I shall tell him? I shall tell him that about eleven o'clock at night you become peculiarly attractive."

She went on again a few steps; Miss Evers and Captain Lovelock had turned round and were coming toward her.

"It is very true that I am outrageous," she said; "it was extremely silly and in very bad taste to come out at this hour. Mamma was not at all pleased, and I was very unkind to her. I only wanted to take a turn, and now we will go back." On the others coming up she announced this resolution, and though Captain Lovelock and his companion made a great outcry, she carried her point. Bernard offered no opposition. He contented himself with walking back to her mother's lodging with her almost in silence. The little winding streets were still and empty; there was no sound but the chatter and laughter of Blanche and her attendant swain. Angela said nothing.

This incident presented itself at first to Bernard's mind as a sort of declaration of war. The girl had guessed that she was to be made a subject of speculative scrutiny. The idea was not agreeable to her independent spirit, and she placed herself boldly on the defensive. She took her stand upon her right to defeat his purpose by every possible means—to perplex, elude, deceive him—in plain English, to make a fool of him. This was the construction which for several days Bernard put upon her deportment, at the same time that he thought it immensely clever of her to have guessed what had been going on in his mind. She made him feel very much ashamed of his critical attitude, and he did everything he could think of to put her off her guard and persuade her that for the moment he had ceased to be an observer. His position at moments seemed to him an odious one, for he was firmly resolved that between him and the woman to whom his friend had proposed there should be nothing in the way of a vulgar flirtation. Under the circumstances, it savoured both of flirtation and of vulgarity that they should even fall out with each other—a consummation which appeared to be more or less definitely impending. Bernard remarked to himself that his own only reasonable line of conduct would be instantly to leave Baden, but I am almost ashamed to mention the fact which led him to modify this decision. It was simply that he was induced to make the reflection that he had really succeeded in putting Miss Vivian off her guard. How he had done so he would have found it difficult to explain, inasmuch as in one way or another, for a week, he had spent several hours in talk with her. The most effective way of putting her off her guard would have been to leave her alone, to forswear the privilege of conversation with her, to pass the days in other society. This course would have had the drawback of not enabling him to measure the operation of so ingenious a policy, and Bernard liked, of all the things in the world, to know when he was successful. He believed, at all events, that he was successful now, and that the virtue of his conversation itself had persuaded this keen and brilliant girl that he was thinking of anything in the world but herself. He flattered himself that the civil indifference of his manner, the abstract character of the topics he selected, the irrelevancy of his allusions and the laxity of his attention, all contributed to this result.

Such a result was certainly a remarkable one, for it is almost superfluous to intimate that Miss Vivian was, in fact, perpetually in his thoughts. He made it a point of conscience not to think of her, but he was thinking of her most when his conscience was most lively. Bernard had a conscience—a conscience which, though a little irregular in its motions, gave itself in the long run a great deal of exercise; but nothing could have been more natural than that, curious, imaginative, audacious as he was, and delighting, as I have said, in the play of his singularly nimble intelligence, he should have given himself up to a sort of unconscious experimentation. "I will leave her alone—I will be hanged if I attempt to draw her out!" he said to himself; and meanwhile he was roaming afield and plucking personal impressions in great fragrant handfuls. All this, as I say, was natural, given the man and the situation; the only oddity is that he should have fancied himself able to persuade the person most interested that he had renounced his advantage.

He remembered her telling him that she cared very much what he should say of her on Gordon Wright's return, and he felt that this declaration had a particular significance. After this, of her own movement, she never spoke of Gordon, and Bernard made up his mind that she had promised her mother to accept him if he should repeat his proposal, and that as her heart was not in the matter she preferred to drop a veil over the prospect. "She is going to marry him for his money," he said, "because her mother has brought out the advantages of the thing. Mrs. Vivian's persuasive powers have carried the day, and the girl has made herself believe that it does n't matter that she does n't love him. Perhaps it does n't—to her; it 's hard, in such a case, to put one's self in the woman's point of view. But I should think it would matter, some day or other, to poor Gordon. She herself can't help suspecting it may make a difference in his happiness, and she therefore does n't wish to seem any worse to him than is necessary. She wants me to speak well of her; if she intends to deceive him she expects me to back her up. The wish is doubtless natural, but for a proud girl it is rather an odd favor to ask. Oh yes, she 's a proud girl, even though she has been able to arrange it with her conscience to make a mercenary marriage. To expect me to help her is perhaps to treat me as a friend; but she ought to remember—or at least I ought to remember—that Gordon is an older friend than she. Inviting me to help her as against my oldest friend—is n't there a grain of impudence in that?"

It will be gathered that Bernard's meditations were not on the whole favorable to this young lady, and it must be affirmed that he was forcibly struck with an element of cynicism in her conduct. On the evening of her so-called midnight visit to the Kursaal she had suddenly sounded a note of sweet submissiveness which re-appeared again at frequent intervals. She was gentle, accessible, tenderly gracious, expressive, demonstrative, almost flattering. From his own personal point of view Bernard had no complaint to make of this maidenly urbanity, but he kept reminding himself that he was not in question and that everything must be looked at in the light of Gordon's requirements. There was all this time an absurd logical twist in his view of things. In the first place he was not to judge at all; and in the second he was to judge strictly on Gordon's behalf. This latter clause always served as a justification when the former had failed to serve as a deterrent. When Bernard reproached himself for thinking too much of the girl, he drew comfort from the reflection that he was not thinking well. To let it gradually filter into one's mind, through a superficial complexity of more reverent preconceptions, that she was an extremely clever coquette—this, surely, was not to think well! Bernard had luminous glimpses of another situation, in which Angela Vivian's coquetry should meet with a different appreciation; but just now it was not an item to be entered on the credit side of Wright's account. Bernard wiped his pen, mentally speaking, as he made this reflection, and felt like a grizzled old book-keeper, of incorruptible probity. He saw her, as I have said, very often; she continued to break her vow of shutting herself up, and at the end of a fortnight she had reduced it to imperceptible particles. On four different occasions, presenting himself at Mrs. Vivian's lodgings, Bernard found Angela there alone. She made him welcome, receiving him as an American girl, in such circumstances, is free to receive the most gallant of visitors. She smiled and talked and gave herself up to charming gayety, so that there was nothing for Bernard to say but that now at least she was off her guard with a vengeance. Happily he was on his own! He flattered himself that he remained so on occasions that were even more insidiously relaxing—when, in the evening, she strolled away with him to parts of the grounds of the Conversation-house, where the music sank to sweeter softness and the murmur of the tree-tops of the Black Forest, stirred by the warm night-air, became almost audible;

or when, in the long afternoons, they wandered in the woods apart from the others—from Mrs. Vivian and the amiable object of her more avowed solicitude, the object of the sportive adoration of the irrepressible, the ever-present Lovelock. They were constantly having parties in the woods at this time—driving over the hills to points of interest which Bernard had looked out in the guide-book. Bernard, in such matters, was extremely alert and considerate; he developed an unexpected talent for arranging excursions, and he had taken regularly into his service the red-waistcoated proprietor of a big Teutonic landau, which had a courier's seat behind and was always at the service of the ladies. The functionary in the red waistcoat was a capital charioteer; he was constantly proposing new drives, and he introduced our little party to treasures of romantic scenery.

CHAPTER XIII

More than a fortnight had elapsed, but Gordon Wright had not re-appeared, and Bernard suddenly decided that he would leave Baden. He found Mrs. Vivian and her daughter, very opportunely, in the garden of the pleasant, homely Schloss which forms the residence of the Grand Dukes of Baden during their visits to the scene of our narrative, and which, perched upon the hill-side directly above the little town, is surrounded with charming old shrubberies and terraces. To this garden a portion of the public is admitted, and Bernard, who liked the place, had been there more than once. One of the terraces had a high parapet, against which Angela was leaning, looking across the valley. Mrs. Vivian was not at first in sight, but Bernard presently perceived her seated under a tree with Victor Cousin in her hand. As Bernard approached the young girl, Angela, who had not seen him, turned round.

"Don't move," he said. "You were just in the position in which I painted your portrait at Siena."

"Don't speak of that," she answered.

"I have never understood," said Bernard, "why you insist upon ignoring that charming incident."

She resumed for a moment her former position, and stood looking at the opposite hills.

"That 's just how you were—in profile—with your head a little thrown back."

"It was an odious incident!" Angela exclaimed, rapidly changing her attitude.

Bernard was on the point of making a rejoinder, but he thought of Gordon Wright and held his tongue. He presently told her that he intended to leave Baden on the morrow.

They were walking toward her mother. She looked round at him quickly.

"Where are you going?"

"To Paris," he said, quite at hazard; for he had not in the least determined where to go.

"To Paris—in the month of August?" And she gave a little laugh. "What a happy inspiration!"

She gave a little laugh, but she said nothing more, and Bernard gave no further account of his plan. They went and sat down near Mrs. Vivian for ten minutes, and then they got up again and strolled to another part of the garden. They had it all to themselves, and it was filled with things that Bernard liked—inequalities of level, with mossy steps connecting them, rose-trees trained upon old brick walls, horizontal trellises arranged like Italian pergolas, and here and there a towering poplar, looking as if it had survived from some more primitive stage of culture, with its stiff boughs motionless and its leaves forever trembling. They made almost the whole circuit of the garden, and then Angela mentioned very quietly that she had heard that morning from Mr. Wright, and that he would not return for another week.

"You had better stay," she presently added, as if Gordon's continued absence were an added reason.

"I don't know," said Bernard. "It is sometimes difficult to say what one had better do."

I hesitate to bring against him that most inglorious of all charges, an accusation of sentimental fatuity, of the disposition to invent obstacles to enjoyment so that he might have the pleasure of seeing a pretty girl attempt to remove them. But it must be admitted that if Bernard really thought at present that he had better leave Baden, the observation I have just quoted was not so much a sign of this conviction as of the hope that his companion would proceed to gainsay it. The hope was not disappointed, though I must add that no sooner had it been gratified than Bernard began to feel ashamed of it.

"This certainly is not one of those cases," said Angela. "The thing is surely very simple now."

"What makes it so simple?"

She hesitated a moment.

"The fact that I ask you to stay."

"You ask me?" he repeated, softly.

"Ah," she exclaimed, "one does n't say those things twice!"

She turned away, and they went back to her mother, who gave Bernard a wonderful little look of half urgent, half remonstrant inquiry. As they left the garden he walked beside Mrs. Vivian, Angela going in front of them at a distance. The elder lady began immediately to talk to him of Gordon Wright.

"He 's not coming back for another week, you know," she said. "I am sorry he stays away so long."

"Ah yes," Bernard answered, "it seems very long indeed."

And it had, in fact, seemed to him very long.

"I suppose he is always likely to have business," said Mrs. Vivian.

"You may be very sure it is not for his pleasure that he stays away."

"I know he is faithful to old friends," said Mrs. Vivian. "I am sure he has not forgotten us."

"I certainly count upon that," Bernard exclaimed—"remembering him as we do!"

Mrs. Vivian glanced at him gratefully.

"Oh yes, we remember him—we remember him daily, hourly. At least, I can speak for my daughter and myself. He has been so very kind to us." Bernard said nothing, and she went on. "And you have been so very kind to us, too, Mr. Longueville. I want so much to thank you."

"Oh no, don't!" said Bernard, frowning. "I would rather you should n't."

"Of course," Mrs. Vivian added, "I know it 's all on his account; but that makes me wish to thank you all the more. Let me express my gratitude, in advance, for the rest of the time, till he comes back. That 's more responsibility than you bargained for," she said, with a little nervous laugh.

"Yes, it 's more than I bargained for. I am thinking of going away."

Mrs. Vivian almost gave a little jump, and then she paused on the Baden cobble-stones, looking up at him.

"If you must go, Mr. Longueville—don't sacrifice yourself!"

The exclamation fell upon Bernard's ear with a certain softly mocking cadence which was sufficient, however, to make this organ tingle.

"Oh, after all, you know," he said, as they walked on—"after all, you know, I am not like Wright—I have no business."

He walked with the ladies to the door of their lodging. Angela kept always in front. She stood there, however, at the little confectioner's window until the others came up. She let her mother pass in, and then she said to Bernard, looking at him—

"Shall I see you again?"

"Some time, I hope."

"I mean—are you going away?"

Bernard looked for a moment at a little pink sugar cherub—a species of Cupid, with a gilded bow—which figured among the pastry-cook's enticements. Then he said—

"I will come and tell you this evening."

And in the evening he went to tell her; she had mentioned during the walk in the garden of the Schloss that they should not go out. As he approached Mrs. Vivian's door he saw a figure in a light dress standing in the little balcony. He stopped and looked up, and then the person in the light dress, leaning her hands on the railing, with her shoulders a little raised, bent over and looked down at him. It was very dark, but even through the thick dusk he thought he perceived the finest brilliancy of Angela Vivian's smile.

"I shall not go away," he said, lifting his voice a little.

She made no answer; she only stood looking down at him through the warm dusk and smiling. He went into the house, and he remained at Baden-Baden till Gordon came back.

CHAPTER XIV

Gordon asked him no questions for twenty-four hours after his return, then suddenly he began:

"Well, have n't you something to say to me?"

It was at the hotel, in Gordon's apartment, late in the afternoon. A heavy thunder-storm had broken over the place an hour before, and Bernard had been standing at one of his friend's windows, rather idly, with his hands in his pockets, watching the rain-torrents dance upon the empty pavements. At last the deluge abated, the clouds began to break—there was a promise of a fine evening. Gordon Wright, while the storm was at its climax, sat down to write letters, and wrote half a dozen. It was after he had sealed, directed and affixed a postage-stamp to the last of the series that he addressed to his companion the question I have just quoted.

"Do you mean about Miss Vivian?" Bernard asked, without turning round from the window.

"About Miss Vivian, of course." Bernard said nothing and his companion went on. "Have you nothing to tell me about Miss Vivian?"

Bernard presently turned round looking at Gordon and smiling a little.

"She 's a delightful creature!"

"That won't do—you have tried that before," said Gordon. "No," he added in a moment, "that won't do." Bernard turned back to the window, and Gordon continued, as he remained silent. "I shall have a right to consider your saying nothing a proof of an unfavorable judgment. You don't like her!"

Bernard faced quickly about again, and for an instant the two men looked at each other.

"Ah, my dear Gordon," Longueville murmured.

"Do you like her then?" asked Wright, getting up.

"No!" said Longueville.

"That 's just what I wanted to know, and I am much obliged to you for telling me."

"I am not obliged to you for asking me. I was in hopes you would n't."

"You dislike her very much then?" Gordon exclaimed, gravely.

"Won't disliking her, simply, do?" said Bernard.

"It will do very well. But it will do a little better if you will tell me why. Give me a reason or two."

"Well," said Bernard, "I tried to make love to her and she boxed my ears."

"The devil!" cried Gordon.

"I mean morally, you know."

Gordon stared; he seemed a little puzzled.

"You tried to make love to her morally?"

"She boxed my ears morally," said Bernard, laughing out.

"Why did you try to make love to her?"

This inquiry was made in a tone so expressive of an unbiassed truth-seeking habit that Bernard's mirth was not immediately quenched. Nevertheless, he replied with sufficient gravity—

"To test her fidelity to you. Could you have expected anything else? You told me you were afraid she was a latent coquette. You gave me a chance, and I tried to ascertain."

"And you found she was not. Is that what you mean?"

"She 's as firm as a rock. My dear Gordon, Miss Vivian is as firm as the firmest of your geological formations."

Gordon shook his head with a strange positive persistence.

"You are talking nonsense. You are not serious. You are not telling me the truth. I don't believe that you attempted to make love to her. You would n't have played such a game as that. It would n't have been honorable."

Bernard flushed a little; he was irritated.

"Oh come, don't make too much of a point of that! Did n't you tell me before that it was a great opportunity?"

"An opportunity to be wise—not to be foolish!"

"Ah, there is only one sort of opportunity," cried Bernard. "You exaggerate the reach of human wisdom."

"Suppose she had let you make love to her," said Gordon. "That would have been a beautiful result of your experiment."

"I should have seemed to you a rascal, perhaps, but I should have saved you from a latent coquette. You would owe some thanks for that."

"And now you have n't saved me," said Gordon, with a simple air of noting a fact.

"You assume—in spite of what I say—that she is a coquette!"

"I assume something because you evidently conceal something. I want the whole truth."

Bernard turned back to the window with increasing irritation.

"If he wants the whole truth he shall have it," he said to himself.

He stood a moment in thought and then he looked at his companion again.

"I think she would marry you—but I don't think she cares for you."

Gordon turned a little pale, but he clapped his hands together.

"Very good," he exclaimed. "That 's exactly how I want you to speak."

"Her mother has taken a great fancy to your fortune and it has rubbed off on the girl, who has made up her mind that it would be a pleasant thing to have thirty thousand a year, and that her not caring for you is an unimportant detail."

"I see—I see," said Gordon, looking at his friend with an air of admiration for his frank and lucid way of putting things.

Now that he had begun to be frank and lucid, Bernard found a charm in it, and the impulse under which he had spoken urged him almost violently forward.

"The mother and daughter have agreed together to bag you, and Angela, I am sure, has made a vow to be as nice to you after marriage as possible. Mrs. Vivian has insisted upon the importance of that; Mrs. Vivian is a great moralist."

Gordon kept gazing at his friend; he seemed positively fascinated.

"Yes, I have noticed that in Mrs. Vivian," he said.

"Ah, she 's a very nice woman!"

"It 's not true, then," said Gordon, "that you tried to make love to Angela?"

Bernard hesitated a single instant.

"No, it is n't true. I calumniated myself, to save her reputation. You insisted on my giving you a reason for my not liking her—I gave you that one."

"And your real reason—"

"My real reason is that I believe she would do you what I can't help regarding as an injury."

"Of course!" and Gordon, dropping his interested eyes, stared for some moments at the carpet. "But it is n't true, then, that you discovered her to be a coquette?"

"Ah, that 's another matter."

"You did discover it all the same?"

"Since you want the whole truth—I did!"

"How did you discover it?" Gordon asked, clinging to his right of interrogation.

Bernard hesitated.

"You must remember that I saw a great deal of her."

"You mean that she encouraged you?"

"If I had not been a very faithful friend I might have thought so."

Gordon laid his hand appreciatively, gratefully, on Bernard's shoulder.

"And even that did n't make you like her?"

"Confound it, you make me blush!" cried Bernard, blushing a little in fact. "I have said quite enough; excuse me from drawing the portrait of too insensible a man. It was my point of view; I kept thinking of you."

Gordon, with his hand still on his friend's arm, patted it an instant in response to this declaration; then he turned away.

"I am much obliged to you. That 's my notion of friendship. You have spoken out like a man."

"Like a man, yes. Remember that. Not in the least like an oracle."

"I prefer an honest man to all the oracles," said Gordon.

"An honest man has his impressions! I have given you mine—they pretend to be nothing more. I hope they have n't offended you."

"Not in the least."

"Nor distressed, nor depressed, nor in any way discomposed you?"

"For what do you take me? I asked you a favor—a service; I imposed it on you. You have done the thing, and my part is simple gratitude."

"Thank you for nothing," said Bernard, smiling. "You have asked me a great many questions; there is one that in turn I have a right to ask you. What do you propose to do in consequence of what I have told you?"

"I propose to do nothing."

This declaration closed the colloquy, and the young men separated. Bernard saw Gordon no more that evening; he took for granted he had gone to Mrs. Vivian's. The burden of Longueville's confidences was a heavy load to carry there, but Bernard ventured to hope that he would deposit it at the door. He had given Gordon his impressions, and the latter might do with them what he chose—toss them out of the window, or let them grow stale with heedless keeping. So Bernard meditated, as he wandered about alone for the rest of the evening. It was useless to look for Mrs. Vivian's little circle, on the terrace of the Conversation-house, for the storm in the afternoon had made the place so damp that it was almost forsaken of its frequenters. Bernard spent the evening in the gaming-rooms, in the thick of the crowd that pressed about the tables, and by way of a change—he had hitherto been almost nothing of a gambler—he laid down a couple of pieces at roulette. He had played but two or three times, without winning a penny; but now he had the agreeable sensation of drawing in a small handful of gold. He continued to play, and he continued to win. His luck surprised and excited him—so much so that after it had repeated itself half a dozen times he left the place and walked about for half an hour in the outer darkness. He felt amused and exhilarated, but the feeling amounted almost to agitation. He, nevertheless, returned to the tables, where he again found success awaiting him. Again and again he put his money on a happy number, and so steady a run of luck began at last to attract attention. The rumor of it spread through the rooms, and the crowd about the roulette received a large contingent of spectators. Bernard felt that they were looking more or less eagerly for a turn of the tide; but he was in the humor for disappointing them, and he left the place, while his luck was still running high, with ten thousand francs in his pocket. It was very late when he returned to the inn—so late that he forbore to knock at Gordon's door. But though he betook himself to his own quarters, he was far from finding, or even seeking, immediate rest. He knocked about, as he would have said, for half the night—not because he was delighted at having won ten thousand francs, but rather because all of a sudden he found himself disgusted at the manner in which he had spent the evening. It was extremely characteristic of Bernard Longueville that his pleasure should suddenly transform itself into flatness. What he felt was not regret or repentance. He had it not in the least on his conscience that he had given countenance to the reprehensible practice of gaming. It was annoyance that he had passed out of his own control—that he had obeyed a force which he was unable to measure at the time. He had been drunk and he was turning sober. In spite of a great momentary appearance of frankness and a lively relish of any conjunction of agreeable circumstances exerting a pressure to which one could respond, Bernard had really little taste for giving himself up, and he never did so without very soon wishing to take himself back. He had now given himself to something that was not himself, and the fact that he had gained ten thousand francs by it was an insufficient salve to an aching sense of having ceased to be his own master. He had not been playing—he had been played with. He had been the sport of a blind, brutal chance, and he felt humiliated by having been favored by so rudely-operating a divinity. Good luck and bad luck? Bernard felt very scornful of the distinction, save that good luck seemed to him rather the more vulgar. As the night went on his disgust deepened, and at last the weariness it brought with it sent him to sleep. He slept very late, and woke up to a disagreeable consciousness. At first, before collecting his thoughts, he could not imagine what he had on his mind—was it that he had spoken ill of Angela Vivian? It brought him extraordinary relief to remember that he had gone to bed in extreme ill-humor with his exploits at roulette. After he had dressed himself and just as he was leaving his room, a servant brought him a note superscribed in Gordon's hand—a note of which the following proved to be the contents.

"Seven o'clock, A.M.

"My dear Bernard: Circumstances have determined me to leave Baden immediately, and I shall take the train that starts an hour hence. I am told that you came in very late last night, so I won't disturb you for a painful parting at this unnatural hour. I came to this decision last evening, and I put up my things; so I have nothing to do but to take myself off. I shall go to Basel, but after that I don't know where, and in so comfortless an uncertainty I don't ask you to follow me. Perhaps I shall go to America; but in any case I shall see you sooner or later. Meanwhile, my dear Bernard, be as happy as your brilliant talents should properly make you, and believe me yours ever,

"G. W.

"P.S. It is perhaps as well that I should say that I am leaving in consequence of something that happened last evening, but not—by any traceable process—in consequence of the talk we had together. I may also add that I am in very good health and spirits."

Bernard lost no time in learning that his friend had in fact departed by the eight o'clock train—the morning was now well advanced; and then, over his breakfast, he gave himself up to meditative surprise. What had happened during the evening—what had happened after their conversation in Gordon's room? He had gone to Mrs. Vivian's—what had happened there? Bernard found it difficult to believe that he had gone there simply to notify her that, having talked it over with an intimate friend, he gave up her daughter, or to mention to the young lady herself that he had ceased to desire the honor of her hand. Gordon alluded to some definite occurrence, yet it was inconceivable that he should have allowed himself to be determined by Bernard's words—his diffident and irresponsible impression. Bernard resented this idea as an injury to himself, yet it was difficult to imagine what else could have happened. There was Gordon's word for it, however, that there was no "traceable" connection between the circumstances which led to his sudden departure and the information he had succeeded in extracting from his friend. What did he mean by a "traceable" connection? Gordon never used words idly, and he meant to make of this point an intelligible distinction. It was this sense of his usual accuracy of expression that assisted Bernard in fitting a meaning to his late companion's letter. He intended to intimate that he had come back to Baden with his mind made up to relinquish his suit, and that he had questioned Bernard simply from moral curiosity—for the sake of intellectual satisfaction. Nothing was altered by the fact that Bernard had told him a sorry tale; it had not modified his behavior—that effect would have been traceable. It had simply affected his imagination, which was a consequence of the imponderable sort. This view of the case was supported by Gordon's mention of his good spirits. A man always had good spirits when he had acted in harmony with a conviction. Of course, after renouncing the attempt to make himself acceptable to Miss Vivian, the only possible thing for Gordon had been to leave Baden. Bernard, continuing to meditate, at last convinced himself that there had been no explicit rupture, that Gordon's last visit had simply been a visit of farewell, that its character had sufficiently signified his withdrawal, and that he had now gone away because, after giving the girl up, he wished very naturally not to meet her again. This was, on Bernard's part, a sufficiently coherent view of the case; but nevertheless, an hour afterward, as he strolled along the Lichtenthal Alley, he found himself stopping suddenly and exclaiming under his breath—"Have I done her an injury? Have I affected her prospects?" Later in the day he said to himself half a dozen times that he had simply warned Gordon against an incongruous union.

CHAPTER XV

Now that Gordon was gone, at any rate, gone for good, and not to return, he felt a sudden and singular sense of freedom. It was a feeling of unbounded expansion, quite out of proportion, as he said to himself, to any assignable cause. Everything suddenly appeared to have become very optional; but he was quite at a loss what to do with his liberty. It seemed a harmless use to make of it, in the afternoon, to go and pay another visit to the ladies who lived at the confectioner's. Here, however, he met a reception which introduced a fresh element of perplexity into the situation that Gordon had left behind him. The door was opened to him by Mrs. Vivian's maid-servant, a sturdy daughter of the Schwartzwald, who informed him that the ladies—with much regret—were unable to receive any one.

"They are very busy—and they are ill," said the young woman, by way of explanation.

Bernard was disappointed, and he felt like arguing the case.

"Surely," he said, "they are not both ill and busy! When you make excuses, you should make them agree with each other."

The Teutonic soubrette fixed her round blue eyes a minute upon the patch of blue sky revealed to her by her open door.

"I say what I can, lieber Herr. It 's not my fault if I 'm not so clever as a French mamsell. One of the ladies is busy, the other is ill. There you have it."

"Not quite," said Bernard. "You must remember that there are three of them."

"Oh, the little one—the little one weeps."

"Miss Evers weeps!" exclaimed Bernard, to whom the vision of this young lady in tears had never presented itself.

"That happens to young ladies when they are unhappy," said the girl; and with an artless yet significant smile she carried a big red hand to the left side of a broad bosom.

"I am sorry she is unhappy; but which of the other ladies is ill?"

"The mother is very busy."

"And the daughter is ill?"

The young woman looked at him an instant, smiling again, and the light in her little blue eyes indicated confusion, but not perversity.

"No, the mamma is ill," she exclaimed, "and the daughter is very busy. They are preparing to leave Baden."

"To leave Baden? When do they go?"

"I don't quite know, lieber Herr; but very soon."

With this information Bernard turned away. He was rather surprised, but he reflected that Mrs. Vivian had not proposed to spend her life on the banks of the Oos, and that people were leaving Baden every day in the year. In the evening, at the Kursaal, he met Captain Lovelock, who was wandering about with an air of explosive sadness.

"Damn it, they 're going—yes, they 're going," said the Captain, after the two young men had exchanged a few allusions to current events. "Fancy their leaving us in that heartless manner! It 's not the time to run away—it 's the time to keep your rooms, if you 're so lucky as to have any. The races begin next week and there 'll be a tremendous crowd. All the grand-ducal people are coming. Miss Evers wanted awfully to see the Grand Duke, and I promised her an introduction. I can't make out what Mrs. Vivian is up to. I bet you a ten-pound note she 's giving chase. Our friend Wright has come back and gone off again, and Mrs. Vivian means to strike camp and follow. She 'll pot him yet; you see if she does n't!"

"She is running away from you, dangerous man!" said Bernard.

"Do you mean on account of Miss Evers? Well, I admire Miss Evers—I don't mind admitting that; but I ain't dangerous," said Captain Lovelock, with a lustreless eye. "How can a fellow be dangerous when he has n't ten shillings in his pocket? Desperation, do you call it? But Miss Evers has n't money, so far as I have heard. I don't ask you," Lovelock continued—"I don't care a damn whether she has or not. She 's a devilish charming girl, and I don't mind telling you I 'm hit. I stand no chance—I know I stand no chance. Mrs. Vivian 's down on me, and, by Jove, Mrs. Vivian 's right. I 'm not the husband to pick out for a young woman of expensive habits and no expectations. Gordon Wright's the sort of young man that 's wanted, and, hang me, if Mrs. Vivian did n't want him so much for her own daughter, I believe she 'd try and bag him for the little one. Gad, I believe that to keep me off she would like to cut him in two and give half to each of them! I 'm afraid of that little woman. She has got a little voice like a screw-driver. But for all that, if I could get away from this cursed place, I would keep the girl in sight—hang me if I would n't! I 'd cut the races—dash me if I would n't! But I 'm in pawn, if you know what that means. I owe a beastly lot of money at the inn, and that impudent little beggar of a landlord won't let me out of his sight. The luck 's dead against me at those filthy tables; I have n't won a farthing in three weeks. I wrote to my brother the other day, and this morning I got an answer from him—a cursed, canting letter of good advice, remarking that he had already paid my debts seven times. It does n't happen to be seven; it 's only six, or six and a half! Does he expect me to spend the rest of my life at the Hotel de Hollande? Perhaps he would like me to engage as a waiter there and pay it off by serving at the table d'hote. It would be convenient for him the next time he comes abroad with his seven daughters and two governesses. I hate the smell of their beastly table d'hote! You 're sorry I 'm hard up? I 'm sure I 'm much obliged to you. Can you be of any service? My dear fellow, if you are bent on throwing your money about the place I 'm not the man to stop you." Bernard's winnings of the previous night were burning a hole, as the phrase is, in his pocket. Ten thousand francs had never before seemed to him so heavy a load to carry, and to lighten the weight of his good luck by lending fifty pounds to a less fortunate fellow-player was an operation that not only gratified his good-nature but strongly commended itself to his conscience. His conscience, however, made its conditions. "My dear Longueville," Lovelock went on, "I have always gone in for family feeling, early associations, and all that sort of thing. That 's what made me confide my difficulties to Dovedale. But, upon my honor, you remind me of the good Samaritan, or that sort of person; you are fonder of me than my own brother! I 'll take fifty pounds with pleasure, thank you, and you shall have them again—at the earliest opportunity. My earliest convenience—will that do? Damn it, it is a convenience, is n't it? You make your conditions. My dear fellow, I accept them in advance. That I 'm not to follow up Miss Evers—is that what you mean? Have you been commissioned by the family to buy me off? It 's devilish cruel to take advantage of my poverty! Though I 'm poor, I 'm honest. But I am honest, my dear Longueville; that 's the point. I 'll give you my word, and I 'll keep it. I won't go near that girl again—I won't think of her till I 've got rid of your fifty pounds. It 's a dreadful encouragement to extravagance, but that 's your lookout. I 'll stop for their beastly races and the young lady shall be sacred."

Longueville called the next morning at Mrs. Vivian's, and learned that the three ladies had left Baden by the early train, a couple of hours before. This fact produced in his mind a variety of emotions—surprise, annoyance, embarrassment. In spite of his effort to think it natural they should go, he found something precipitate and inexplicable in the manner of their going, and he declared to himself that one of the party, at least, had been unkind and ungracious in not giving him a chance to say good-bye. He took refuge by anticipation, as it were, in this reflection, whenever, for the next three or four days, he foresaw himself stopping short, as he had done before, and asking himself whether he had done an injury to Angela Vivian. This was an idle and unpractical question, inasmuch as the answer was not forthcoming; whereas it was quite simple and conclusive to say, without the note of interrogation, that she was, in spite of many attractive points, an abrupt and capricious young woman. During the three or four days in question, Bernard lingered on at Baden, uncertain what to do or where to go, feeling as if he had received a sudden check—a sort of spiritual snub—which arrested the accumulation of motive. Lovelock, also, whom Bernard saw every day, appeared to think that destiny had given him a slap in the face, for he had not enjoyed the satisfaction of a last interview with Miss Evers.

"I thought she might have written me a note," said the Captain; "but it appears she does n't write. Some girls don't write, you know."

Bernard remarked that it was possible Lovelock would still have news of Miss Blanche; and before he left Baden he learned that she had addressed her forsaken swain a charming little note from Lausanne, where the three ladies had paused in their flight from Baden, and where Mrs. Vivian had decreed that for the present they should remain.

"I 'm devilish glad she writes," said Captain Lovelock; "some girls do write, you know."

Blanche found Lausanne most horrid after Baden, for whose delights she languished. The delights of Baden, however, were not obvious just now to her correspondent, who had taken Bernard's fifty pounds into the Kursaal and left them there. Bernard, on learning his misfortune, lent him another fifty, with which he performed a second series of unsuccessful experiments; and our hero was not at his ease until he had passed over to his luckless friend the whole amount of his own winnings, every penny of which found its way through Captain Lovelock's fingers back into the bank. When this operation was completed, Bernard left Baden, the Captain gloomily accompanying him to the station.

I have said that there had come over Bernard a singular sense of freedom. One of the uses he made of his freedom was to undertake a long journey. He went to the East and remained absent from Europe for upward of two years—a period of his life of which it is not proposed to offer a complete history. The East is a wonderful region, and Bernard, investigating the mysteries of Asia, saw a great many curious and beautiful things. He had moments of keen enjoyment; he laid up a great store of impressions and even a considerable sum of knowledge. But, nevertheless, he was not destined to look back upon this episode with any particular complacency. It was less delightful than it was supposed to be; it was less successful than it might have been. By what unnatural element the cup of pleasure was adulterated, he would have been very much at a loss to say; but it was an incontestable fact that at times he sipped it as a medicine, rather than quaffed it as a nectar. When people congratulated him on his opportunity of seeing the world, and said they envied him the privilege of seeing it so well, he felt even more than the usual degree of irritation produced by an insinuation that fortune thinks so poorly of us as to give us easy terms. Misplaced sympathy is the least available of superfluities, and Bernard at this time found himself thinking that there was a good deal of impertinence in the world. He would, however, readily have confessed that, in so far as he failed to enjoy his Oriental wanderings, the fault was his own; though he would have made mentally the gratifying reflection that never was a fault less deliberate. If, during the period of which I speak, his natural gayety had sunk to a minor key, a partial explanation may be found in the fact that he was deprived of the society of his late companion. It was an odd circumstance that the two young men had not met since Gordon's abrupt departure from Baden. Gordon went to Berlin, and shortly afterward to America, so that they were on opposite sides of the globe. Before he returned to his own country, Bernard made by letter two or three offers to join him in Europe, anywhere that was agreeable to him. Gordon answered that his movements were very uncertain, and that he should be sorry to trouble Bernard to follow him about. He had put him to this inconvenience in making him travel from Venice to Baden, and one such favor at a time was enough to ask, even of the most obliging of men. Bernard was, of course, afraid that what he had told Gordon about Angela Vivian was really the cause of a state of things which, as between two such good friends, wore a perceptible resemblance to alienation. Gordon had given her up; but he bore Bernard a grudge for speaking ill of her, and so long as this disagreeable impression should last, he preferred not to see him. Bernard was frank enough to charge the poor fellow with a lingering rancor, of which he made, indeed, no great crime. But Gordon denied the allegation, and assured him that, to his own perception, there was no decline in their intimacy. He only requested, as a favor and as a tribute to "just susceptibilities," that Bernard would allude no more either to Miss Vivian or to what had happened at Baden. This request was easy to comply with, and Bernard, in writing, strictly conformed to it; but it seemed to him that the act of doing so was in itself a cooling-off. What would be a better proof of what is called a "tension" than an agreement to avoid a natural topic? Bernard moralized a little over Gordon's "just susceptibilities," and felt that the existence of a perverse resentment in so honest a nature was a fact gained to his acquaintance with psychological science. It cannot be said, however, that he suffered this fact to occupy at all times the foreground of his consciousness. Bernard was like some great painters; his foregrounds were very happily arranged. He heard nothing of Mrs. Vivian and her daughter, beyond a rumor that they had gone to Italy; and he learned, on apparently good authority, that Blanche Evers had returned to New York with her mother. He wondered whether Captain Lovelock was still in pawn at the Hotel de Hollande. If he did not allow himself to wonder too curiously whether he had done a harm to Gordon, it may be affirmed that he was haunted by the recurrence of that other question, of which mention has already been made. Had he done a harm to Angela Vivian, and did she know that he had done it? This inquiry by no means made him miserable, and it was far from awaiting him regularly on his pillow. But it visited him at intervals, and sometimes in the strangest places—suddenly, abruptly, in the stillness of an Indian temple, or amid the shrillness of an Oriental crowd. He became familiar with it at last; he called it his Jack-in-the-box. Some invisible touch of circumstance would press the spring, and the little image would pop up, staring him in the face and grinning an interrogation. Bernard always clapped down the lid, for he regarded this phenomenon as strikingly inane. But if it was more frequent than any pang of conscience connected with the remembrance of Gordon himself, this last sentiment was certainly lively enough to make it a great relief to hear at last a rumor that the excellent fellow was about to be married. The rumor reached him at Athens; it was vague and indirect, and it omitted the name of his betrothed. But Bernard made the most of it, and took comfort in the thought that his friend had recovered his spirits and his appetite for matrimony.

CHAPTER XVI

It was not till our hero reached Paris, on his return from the distant East, that the rumor I have just mentioned acquired an appreciable consistency. Here, indeed, it took the shape of authentic information. Among a number of delayed letters which had been awaiting him at his banker's he found a communication from Gordon Wright. During the previous year or two his correspondence with this trusted—and trusting—friend had not been frequent, and Bernard had received little direct news of him. Three or four short letters had overtaken him in his wanderings—letters as cordial, to all appearance, if not as voluminous, as the punctual missives of an earlier time. Bernard made a point of satisfying himself that they were as cordial; he weighed them in the scales of impartial suspicion. It seemed to him on the whole that there was no relaxation of Gordon's epistolary tone. If he wrote less often than he used to do, that was a thing that very commonly happened as men grew older. The closest intimacies, moreover, had phases and seasons, intermissions and revivals, and even if his friend had, in fact, averted his countenance from him, this was simply the accomplishment of a periodical revolution which would bring them in due order face to face again. Bernard made a point, himself, of writing tolerably often and writing always in the friendliest tone. He made it a matter of conscience—he liked to feel that he was treating Gordon generously, and not demanding an eye for an eye. The letter he found in Paris was so short that I may give it entire.

"My dear Bernard (it ran), I must write to you before I write to any one else, though unfortunately you are so far away that you can't be the first to congratulate me. Try and not be the last, however. I am going to be married—as soon as possible. You know the young lady, so you can appreciate the situation. Do you remember little Blanche Evers, whom we used to see three years ago at Baden-Baden? Of course you remember her, for I know you used often to talk with her. You will be rather surprised, perhaps, at my having selected her as the partner of a life-time; but we manage these matters according to our lights. I am very much in love with her, and I hold that an excellent reason. I have been ready any time this year or two to fall in love with some simple, trusting, child-like nature. I find this in perfection in this charming young girl. I find her so natural and fresh. I remember telling you once that I did n't wish to be fascinated—that I wanted to estimate scientifically the woman I should marry. I have altogether got over that, and I don't know how I ever came to talk such nonsense. I am fascinated now, and I assure you I like it! The best of it is that I find it does n't in the least prevent my estimating Blanche. I judge her very fairly—I see just what she is. She 's simple—that 's what I want; she 's tender—that 's what I long for. You will remember how pretty she is; I need n't remind you of that. She was much younger then, and she has greatly developed and improved in these two or three years. But she will always be young and innocent—I don't want her to improve too much. She came back to America with her mother the winter after we met her at Baden, but I never saw her again till three months ago. Then I saw her with new eyes, and I wondered I could have been so blind. But I was n't ready for her till then, and what makes me so happy now is to know that I have come to my present way of feeling by experience. That gives me confidence—you see I am a reasoner still. But I am under the charm, for all my reason. We are to be married in a month—try and come back to the wedding. Blanche sends you a message, which I will give you verbatim. 'Tell him I am not such a silly little chatterbox as I used to be at Baden. I am a great deal wiser; I am almost as clever as Angela Vivian.' She has an idea you thought Miss Vivian very clever—but it is not true that she is equally so. I am very happy; come home and see."

Bernard went home, but he was not able to reach the United States in time for Gordon's wedding, which took place at midsummer. Bernard, arriving late in the autumn, found his friend a married man of some months' standing, and was able to judge, according to his invitation, whether he appeared happy. The first effect of the letter I have just quoted had been an immense surprise; the second had been a series of reflections which were quite the negative of surprise; and these operations of Bernard's mind had finally merged themselves in a simple sentiment of jollity. He was delighted that Gordon should be married; he felt jovial about it; he was almost indifferent to the question of whom he had chosen. Certainly, at first, the choice of

Blanche Evers seemed highly incongruous; it was difficult to imagine a young woman less shaped to minister to Gordon's strenuous needs than the light-hearted and empty-headed little flirt whose inconsequent prattle had remained for Bernard one of the least importunate memories of a charming time. Blanche Evers was a pretty little goose—the prettiest of little geese, perhaps, and doubtless the most amiable; but she was not a companion for a peculiarly serious man, who would like his wife to share his view of human responsibilities. What a singular selection—what a queer infatuation! Bernard had no sooner committed himself to this line of criticism than he stopped short, with the sudden consciousness of error carried almost to the point of naivetae. He exclaimed that Blanche Evers was exactly the sort of girl that men of Gordon Wright's stamp always ended by falling in love with, and that poor Gordon knew very much better what he was about in this case than he had done in trying to solve the deep problem of a comfortable life with Angela Vivian. This was what your strong, solid, sensible fellows always came to; they paid, in this particular, a larger tribute to pure fancy than the people who were supposed habitually to cultivate that muse. Blanche Evers was what the French call an article of fantasy, and Gordon had taken a pleasure in finding her deliciously useless. He cultivated utility in other ways, and it pleased and flattered him to feel that he could afford, morally speaking, to have a kittenish wife. He had within himself a fund of common sense to draw upon, so that to espouse a paragon of wisdom would be but to carry water to the fountain. He could easily make up for the deficiencies of a wife who was a little silly, and if she charmed and amused him, he could treat himself to the luxury of these sensations for themselves. He was not in the least afraid of being ruined by it, and if Blanche's birdlike chatter and turns of the head had made a fool of him, he knew it perfectly well, and simply took his stand upon his rights. Every man has a right to a little flower-bed, and life is not all mere kitchen-gardening. Bernard rapidly extemporized this rough explanation of the surprise his friend had offered him, and he found it all-sufficient for his immediate needs. He wrote Blanche a charming note, to which she replied with a great deal of spirit and grace. Her little letter was very prettily turned, and Bernard, reading it over two or three times, said to himself that, to do her justice, she might very well have polished her intellect a trifle during these two or three years. As she was older, she could hardly help being wiser. It even occurred to Bernard that she might have profited by the sort of experience that is known as the discipline of suffering. What had become of Captain Lovelock and that tender passion which was apparently none the less genuine for having been expressed in the slang of a humorous period? Had they been permanently separated by judicious guardians, and had she been obliged to obliterate his image from her lightly-beating little heart? Bernard had felt sure at Baden that, beneath her contemptuous airs and that impertinent consciousness of the difficulties of conquest by which a pretty American girl attests her allegiance to a civilization in which young women occupy the highest place—he had felt sure that Blanche had a high appreciation of her handsome Englishman, and that if Lovelock should continue to relish her charms, he might count upon the advantages of reciprocity. But it occurred to Bernard that Captain Lovelock had perhaps been faithless; that, at least, the discourtesy of chance and the inhumanity of an elder brother might have kept him an eternal prisoner at the Hotel de Hollande (where, for all Bernard knew to the contrary, he had been obliged to work out his destiny in the arduous character of a polyglot waiter); so that the poor young girl, casting backward glances along the path of Mrs. Vivian's retreat, and failing to detect the onward rush of a rescuing cavalier, had perforce believed herself forsaken, and had been obliged to summon philosophy to her aid. It was very possible that her philosophic studies had taught her the art of reflection; and that, as she would have said herself, she was tremendously toned down. Once, at Baden, when Gordon Wright happened to take upon himself to remark that little Miss Evers was bored by her English gallant, Bernard had ventured to observe, in petto, that Gordon knew nothing about it. But all this was of no consequence now, and Bernard steered further and further away from the liability to detect fallacies in his friend. Gordon had engaged himself to marry, and our critical hero had not a grain of fault to find with this resolution. It was a capital thing; it was just what he wanted; it would do him a world of good. Bernard rejoiced with him sincerely, and regretted extremely that a series of solemn engagements to pay visits in England should prevent his being present at the nuptials.

They were well over, as I have said, when he reached New York. The honeymoon had waned, and the business of married life had begun. Bernard, at the end, had sailed from England rather abruptly. A friend who had a remarkably good cabin on one of the steamers was obliged by a sudden detention to give it up, and on his offering it to Longueville, the latter availed himself gratefully of this opportunity of being a little less discomposed than usual by the Atlantic billows. He therefore embarked at two days' notice, a fortnight earlier than he had intended and than he had written to Gordon to expect him. Gordon, of course, had written that he was to seek no hospitality but that which Blanche was now prepared—they had a charming house—so graciously to dispense; but Bernard, nevertheless, leaving the ship early in the morning, had betaken himself to an hotel. He wished not to anticipate his welcome, and he determined to report himself to Gordon first and to come back with his luggage later in the day. After purifying himself of his sea-stains, he left his hotel and walked up the Fifth Avenue with all a newly-landed voyager's enjoyment of terrestrial locomotion. It was a charming autumn day; there was a golden haze in the air; he supposed it was the Indian summer. The broad sidewalk of the Fifth Avenue was scattered over with dry leaves— crimson and orange and amber. He tossed them with his stick as he passed; they rustled and murmured with the motion, and it reminded him of the way he used to kick them in front of him over these same pavements in his riotous infancy. It was a pleasure, after many wanderings, to find himself in his native land again, and Bernard Longueville, as he went, paid his compliments to his mother-city. The brightness and gayety of the place seemed a greeting to a returning son, and he felt a throb of affection for the freshest, the youngest, the easiest and most good-natured of great capitals. On presenting himself at Gordon's door, Bernard was told that the master of the house was not at home; he went in, however, to see the mistress. She was in her drawing-room, alone; she had on her bonnet, as if she had been going out. She gave him a joyous, demonstrative little welcome; she was evidently very glad to see him. Bernard had thought it possible she had "improved," and she was certainly prettier than ever. He instantly perceived that she was still a chatterbox; it remained to be seen whether the quality of her discourse were finer.

"Well, Mr. Longueville," she exclaimed, "where in the world did you drop from, and how long did it take you to cross the Atlantic? Three days, eh? It could n't have taken you many more, for it was only the other day that Gordon told me you were not to sail till the 20th. You changed your mind, eh? I did n't know you ever changed your mind. Gordon never changes his. That 's not a reason, eh, because you are not a bit like Gordon. Well, I never thought you were, except that you are a man. Now what are you laughing at? What should you like me call you? You are a man, I suppose; you are not a god. That 's what you would like me to call you, I have no doubt. I must keep that for Gordon? I shall certainly keep it a good while. I know a good deal more about gentlemen than I did when I last saw you, and I assure you I don't think they are a bit god-like. I suppose that 's why you always drop down from the sky—you think it 's more divine. I remember that 's the way you arrived at Baden when we were there together; the first thing we knew, you were standing in the midst of us. Do you remember that evening when you presented yourself? You came up and touched Gordon on the shoulder, and he gave a little jump. He will give another little jump when he sees you to-day. He gives a great many little jumps; I keep him skipping about! I remember perfectly the way we were sitting that evening at Baden, and the way you looked at me when you came up. I saw you before Gordon—I see a good many things before Gordon. What did you look at me that way for? I always meant to ask you. I was dying to know."

"For the simplest reason in the world," said Bernard. "Because you were so pretty."

"Ah no, it was n't that! I know all about that look. It was something else—as if you knew something about me. I don't know what you can have known. There was very little to know about me, except that I was intensely silly. Really, I was awfully silly that summer at Baden—you would n't believe how silly I was. But I don't see how you could have known that—before you had spoken to me. It came out in my conversation—it came out awfully. My mother was a good deal disappointed in Mrs. Vivian's influence; she had expected so much from it. But it was not poor Mrs. Vivian's fault, it was some one's else. Have you ever seen the Vivians again? They are always in Europe;

they have gone to live in Paris. That evening when you came up and spoke to Gordon, I never thought that three years afterward I should be married to him, and I don't suppose you did either. Is that what you meant by looking at me? Perhaps you can tell the future. I wish you would tell my future!"

"Oh, I can tell that easily," said Bernard.

"What will happen to me?"

"Nothing particular; it will be a little dull—the perfect happiness of a charming woman married to the best fellow in the world."

"Ah, what a horrid future!" cried Blanche, with a little petulant cry. "I want to be happy, but I certainly don't want to be dull. If you say that again you will make me repent of having married the best fellow in the world. I mean to be happy, but I certainly shall not be dull if I can help it."

"I was wrong to say that," said Bernard, "because, after all, my dear young lady, there must be an excitement in having so kind a husband as you have got. Gordon's devotion is quite capable of taking a new form—of inventing a new kindness—every day in the year."

Blanche looked at him an instant, with less than her usual consciousness of her momentary pose.

"My husband is very kind," she said gently.

She had hardly spoken the words when Gordon came in. He stopped a moment on seeing Bernard, glanced at his wife, blushed, flushed, and with a loud, frank exclamation of pleasure, grasped his friend by both hands. It was so long since he had seen Bernard that he seemed a good deal moved; he stood there smiling, clasping his hands, looking him in the eyes, unable for some moments to speak. Bernard, on his side, was greatly pleased; it was delightful to him to look into Gordon's honest face again and to return his manly grasp. And he looked well—he looked happy; to see that was more delightful yet. During these few instants, while they exchanged a silent pledge of renewed friendship, Bernard's elastic perception embraced several things besides the consciousness of his own pleasure. He saw that Gordon looked well and happy, but that he looked older, too, and more serious, more marked by life. He looked as if something had happened to him—as, in fact, something had. Bernard saw a latent spark in his friend's eye that seemed to question his own for an impression of Blanche—to question it eagerly, and yet to deprecate judgment. He saw, too—with the fact made more vivid by Gordon's standing there beside her in his manly sincerity and throwing it into contrast—that Blanche was the same little posturing coquette of a Blanche whom, at Baden, he would have treated it as a broad joke that Gordon Wright should dream of marrying. He saw, in a word, that it was what it had first struck him as being—an incongruous union. All this was a good deal for Bernard to see in the course of half a minute, especially through the rather opaque medium of a feeling of irreflective joy; and his impressions at this moment have a value only in so far as they were destined to be confirmed by larger opportunity.

"You have come a little sooner than we expected," said Gordon; "but you are all the more welcome."

"It was rather a risk," Blanche observed. "One should be notified, when one wishes to make a good impression."

"Ah, my dear lady," said Bernard, "you made your impression—as far as I am concerned—a long time ago, and I doubt whether it would have gained anything to-day by your having prepared an effect."

They were standing before the fire-place, on the great hearth-rug, and Blanche, while she listened to this speech, was feeling, with uplifted arm, for a curl that had strayed from her chignon.

"She prepares her effects very quickly," said Gordon, laughing gently. "They follow each other very fast!"

Blanche kept her hand behind her head, which was bent slightly forward; her bare arm emerged from her hanging sleeve, and, with her eyes glancing upward from under her lowered brows, she smiled at her two spectators. Her husband laid his hand on Bernard's arm.

"Is n't she pretty?" he cried; and he spoke with a sort of tender delight in being sure at least of this point.

"Tremendously pretty!" said Bernard. "I told her so half an hour before you came in."

"Ah, it was time I should arrive!" Gordon exclaimed.

Blanche was manifestly not in the least discomposed by this frank discussion of her charms, for the air of distinguished esteem adopted by both of her companions diminished the crudity of their remarks. But she gave a little pout of irritated modesty—it was more becoming than anything she had done yet—and declared that if they wished to talk her over, they were very welcome; but she should prefer their waiting till she got out of the room. So she left them, reminding Bernard that he was to send for his luggage and remain, and promising to give immediate orders for the preparation of his apartment. Bernard opened the door for her to pass out; she gave him a charming nod as he stood there, and he turned back to Gordon with the reflection of her smile in his face. Gordon was watching him; Gordon was dying to know what he thought of her. It was a curious mania of Gordon's, this wanting to know what one thought of the women he loved; but Bernard just now felt abundantly able to humor it. He was so pleased at seeing him tightly married.

"She 's a delightful creature," Bernard said, with cordial vagueness, shaking hands with his friend again.

Gordon glanced at him a moment, and then, coloring a little, looked straight out of the window; whereupon Bernard remembered that these were just the terms in which, at Baden, after his companion's absence, he had attempted to qualify Angela Vivian. Gordon was conscious—he was conscious of the oddity of his situation.

"Of course it surprised you," he said, in a moment, still looking out of the window.

"What, my dear fellow?"

"My marriage."

"Well, you know," said Bernard, "everything surprises me. I am of a very conjectural habit of mind. All sorts of ideas come into my head, and yet when the simplest things happen I am always rather startled. I live in a reverie, and I am perpetually waked up by people doing things."

Gordon transferred his eyes from the window to Bernard's face—to his whole person.

"You are waked up? But you fall asleep again!"

"I fall asleep very easily," said Bernard.

Gordon looked at him from head to foot, smiling and shaking his head.

"You are not changed," he said. "You have travelled in unknown lands; you have had, I suppose, all sorts of adventures; but you are the same man I used to know."

"I am sorry for that!"

"You have the same way of representing—of misrepresenting, yourself."

"Well, if I am not changed," said Bernard, "I can ill afford to lose so valuable an art."

"Taking you altogether, I am glad you are the same," Gordon answered, simply; "but you must come into my part of the house."

CHAPTER XVII

Yes, he was conscious—he was very conscious; so Bernard reflected during the two or three first days of his visit to his friend. Gordon knew it must seem strange to so irreverent a critic that a man who had once aspired to the hand of so intelligent a girl—putting other things aside—as Angela Vivian should, as the Ghost in "Hamlet" says, have "declined upon" a young lady who, in force of understanding, was so very much Miss Vivian's inferior; and this knowledge kept him ill at his ease and gave him a certain pitiable awkwardness. Bernard's sense of the anomaly grew rapidly less acute; he made various observations which helped it to seem natural. Blanche was wonderfully pretty; she was very graceful, innocent, amusing. Since Gordon had determined to marry a little goose, he had chosen the animal with extreme discernment. It had quite the plumage of a swan, and it sailed along the stream of life with an extraordinary lightness of motion. He asked himself indeed at times whether Blanche were really so silly as she seemed; he doubted whether any woman could be so silly as Blanche seemed. He had a suspicion at times that, for ends of her own, she was playing a part—the suspicion arising from the fact that, as usually happens in such cases, she over-played it. Her empty chatter, her futility, her childish coquetry and frivolity—such light wares could hardly be the whole substance of any woman's being; there was something beneath them which Blanche was keeping out of sight. She had a scrap of a mind somewhere, and even a little particle of a heart. If one looked long enough one might catch a glimpse of these possessions. But why should she keep them out of sight, and what were the ends that she proposed to serve by this uncomfortable perversity? Bernard wondered whether she were fond of her husband, and he heard it intimated by several good people in New York who had had some observation of the courtship, that she had married him for his money. He was very sorry to find that this was taken for granted, and he determined, on the whole, not to believe it. He was disgusted with the idea of such a want of gratitude; for, if Gordon Wright had loved Miss Evers for herself, the young lady might certainly have discovered the intrinsic value of so disinterested a suitor. Her mother had the credit of having made the match. Gordon was known to be looking for a wife; Mrs. Evers had put her little feather-head of a daughter very much forward, and Gordon was as easily captivated as a child by the sound of a rattle. Blanche had an affection for him now, however; Bernard saw no reason to doubt that, and certainly she would have been a very flimsy creature indeed if she had not been touched by his inexhaustible kindness. She had every conceivable indulgence, and if she married him for his money, at least she had got what she wanted. She led the most agreeable life conceivable, and she ought to be in high good-humor. It was impossible to have a prettier house, a prettier carriage, more jewels and laces for the adornment of a plump little person. It was impossible to go to more parties, to give better dinners, to have fewer privations or annoyances. Bernard was so much struck with all this that, advancing rapidly in the intimacy of his gracious hostess, he ventured to call her attention to her blessings. She answered that she was perfectly aware of them, and there was no pretty speech she was not prepared to make about Gordon.

"I know what you want to say," she went on; "you want to say that he spoils me, and I don't see why you should hesitate. You generally say everything you want, and you need n't be afraid of me. He does n't spoil me, simply because I am so bad I can't be spoiled; but that 's of no consequence. I was spoiled ages ago; every one spoiled me—every one except Mrs. Vivian. I was always fond of having everything I want, and I generally managed to get it. I always had lovely clothes; mamma thought that was a kind of a duty. If it was a duty, I don't suppose it counts as a part of the spoiling. But I was very much indulged, and I know I have everything now. Gordon is a perfect husband; I believe if I were to ask him for a present of his nose, he would cut it off and give it to me. I think I will ask him for a small piece of it some day; it will rather improve him to have an inch or two less. I don't say he 's handsome; but he 's just as good as he can be. Some people say that if you are very fond of a person you always think them handsome; but I don't agree with that at all. I am very fond of Gordon, and yet I am not blinded by affection, as regards his personal appearance. He 's too light for my taste, and too red. And because you think people handsome, it does n't follow that you are fond of them. I used to have a friend who was awfully handsome—the handsomest man I ever saw—and I was perfectly conscious of his defects. But I 'm not conscious of Gordon's, and I don't believe he has got any. He 's so intensely kind; it 's quite pathetic. One would think he had done me an injury in marrying me, and that he wanted to make up for it. If he has done me an injury I have n't discovered it yet, and I don't believe I ever shall. I certainly shall not as long as he lets me order all the clothes I want. I have ordered five dresses this week, and I mean to order two more. When I told Gordon, what do you think he did? He simply kissed me. Well, if that 's not expressive, I don't know what he could have done. He kisses me about seventeen times a day. I suppose it 's very improper for a woman to tell any one how often her husband kisses her; but, as you happen to have seen him do it, I don't suppose you will be scandalized. I know you are not easily scandalized; I am not afraid of you. You are scandalized at my getting so many dresses? Well, I told you I was spoiled—I freely acknowledge it. That 's why I was afraid to tell Gordon—because when I was married I had such a lot of things; I was supposed to have dresses enough to last for a year. But Gordon had n't to pay for them, so there was no harm in my letting him feel that he has a wife. If he thinks I am extravagant, he can easily stop kissing me. You don't think it would be easy to stop? It 's very well, then, for those that have never begun!"

Bernard had a good deal of conversation with Blanche, of which, so far as she was concerned, the foregoing remarks may serve as a specimen. Gordon was away from home during much of the day; he had a chemical laboratory in which he was greatly interested, and which he took Bernard to see; it was fitted up with the latest contrivances for the pursuit of experimental science, and was the resort of needy young students, who enjoyed, at Gordon's expense, the opportunity for pushing their researches. The place did great honor to Gordon's liberality and to his ingenuity; but Blanche, who had also paid it a visit, could never speak of it without a pretty little shudder.

"Nothing would induce me to go there again," she declared, "and I consider myself very fortunate to have escaped from it with my life. It 's filled with all sorts of horrible things, that fizzle up and go off, or that make you turn some dreadful color if you look at them. I expect to hear a great clap some day, and half an hour afterward to see Gordon brought home in several hundred small pieces, put up in a dozen little bottles. I got a horrid little stain in the middle of my dress that one of the young men—the young savants—was so good as to drop there. Did you see the young savants who work under Gordon's orders? I thought they were too forlorn; there is n't one of them you would look at. If you can believe it, there was n't one of them that looked at me; they took no more notice of me than if I had been the charwoman. They might have shown me some attention, at least, as the wife of the proprietor. What is it that Gordon 's called—is n't there some other name? If you say 'proprietor,' it sounds as if he kept an hotel. I certainly don't want to pass for the wife of an hotel-keeper. What does he call himself? He must have some name. I hate telling people he 's a chemist; it sounds just as if he kept a shop. That 's what they call the druggists in England, and I formed the habit while I was there. It makes me feel as if he were some dreadful little man, with big green bottles in the window and 'night-bell' painted outside. He does n't call himself anything? Well, that 's exactly like Gordon! I wonder he consents to have a name at all. When I was telling some one about the young men who work under his orders—the young savants—he said I must not say that—I must not speak of their working 'under his orders.' I don't know what he would like me to say! Under his inspiration!"

During the hours of Gordon's absence, Bernard had frequent colloquies with his friend's wife, whose irresponsible prattle amused him, and in whom he tried to discover some faculty, some quality, which might be a positive guarantee of Gordon's future felicity. But often, of course, Gordon was an auditor as well; I say an auditor, because it seemed to Bernard that he had grown to be less of a talker than of yore. Doubtless, when a man finds himself united to a garrulous wife, he naturally learns to hold his tongue; but sometimes, at the close of one of Blanche's discursive monologues, on glancing at her husband just to see how he took it, and seeing him sit perfectly silent, with a fixed, inexpressive smile, Bernard said to himself that Gordon found the lesson of listening attended with some embarrassments. Gordon, as the years went by, was growing a little inscrutable; but this, too, in certain circumstances, was a usual tendency. The operations of the mind, with deepening experience, became more complex, and people were less apt to emit immature reflections at forty than they had been in their earlier days.

Bernard felt a great kindness in these days for his old friend; he never yet had seemed to him such a good fellow, nor appealed so strongly to the benevolence of his disposition. Sometimes, of old, Gordon used to irritate him; but this danger appeared completely to have passed away. Bernard prolonged his visit; it gave him pleasure to be able to testify in this manner to his good will. Gordon was the kindest of hosts, and if in conversation, when his wife was present, he gave precedence to her superior powers, he had at other times a good deal of pleasant bachelor-talk with his guest. He seemed very happy; he had plenty of occupation and plenty of practical intentions. The season went on, and Bernard enjoyed his life. He enjoyed the keen and brilliant American winter, and he found it very pleasant to be treated as a distinguished stranger in his own land—a situation to which his long and repeated absences had relegated him. The hospitality of New York was profuse; the charm of its daughters extreme; the radiance of its skies superb. Bernard was the restless and professionless mortal that we know, wandering in life from one vague experiment to another, constantly gratified and never satisfied, to whom no imperious finality had as yet presented itself; and, nevertheless, for a time he contrived to limit his horizon to the passing hour, and to make a good many hours pass in the drawing-room of a demonstrative flirt.

For Mrs. Gordon was a flirt; that had become tolerably obvious. Bernard had known of old that Blanche Evers was one, and two or three months' observation of his friend's wife assured him that she did not judge a certain ethereal coquetry to be inconsistent with the conjugal character. Blanche flirted, in fact, more or less with all men, but her opportunity for playing her harmless batteries upon Bernard were of course exceptionally large. The poor fellow was perpetually under fire, and it was inevitable that he should reply with some precision of aim. It seemed to him all child's play, and it is certain that when his back was turned to his pretty hostess he never found himself thinking of her. He had not the least reason to suppose that she thought of him—excessive concentration of mind was the last vice of which he accused her. But before the winter was over, he discovered that Mrs. Gordon Wright was being talked about, and that his own name was, as the newspapers say, mentioned in connection with that of his friend's wife. The discovery greatly disgusted him; Bernard Longueville's chronicler must do him the justice to say that it failed to yield him an even transient thrill of pleasure. He thought it very improbable that this vulgar rumor had reached Gordon's ears; but he nevertheless—very naturally—instantly made up his mind to leave the house. He lost no time in saying to Gordon that he had suddenly determined to go to California, and that he was sure he must be glad to get rid of him. Gordon expressed no surprise and no regret. He simply laid his hand on his shoulder and said, very quietly, looking at him in the eyes—

"Very well; the pleasantest things must come to an end."

It was not till an hour afterwards that Bernard said to himself that his friend's manner of receiving the announcement of his departure had been rather odd. He had neither said a word about his staying longer nor urged him to come back again, and there had been (it now seemed to Bernard) an audible undertone of relief in the single sentence with which he assented to his visitor's withdrawal. Could it be possible that poor Gordon was jealous of him, that he had heard this loathsome gossip, or that his own observation had given him an alarm? He had certainly never betrayed the smallest sense of injury; but it was to be remembered that even if he were uneasy, Gordon was quite capable, with his characteristic habit of weighing everything, his own honor included, in scrupulously adjusted scales, of denying himself the luxury of active suspicion. He would never have let a half suspicion make a difference in his conduct, and he would not have dissimulated; he would simply have resisted belief. His hospitality had been without a flaw, and if he had really been wishing Bernard out of his house, he had behaved with admirable self-control. Bernard, however, followed this train of thought a very short distance. It was odious to him to believe that he could have appeared to Gordon, however guiltlessly, to have invaded even in imagination the mystic line of the marital monopoly; not to say that, moreover, if one came to that, he really cared about as much for poor little Blanche as for the weather-cock on the nearest steeple. He simply hurried his preparations for departure, and he told Blanche that he should have to bid her farewell on the following day. He had found her in the drawing-room, waiting for dinner. She was expecting company to dine, and Gordon had not yet come down.

She was sitting in the vague glow of the fire-light, in a wonderful blue dress, with two little blue feet crossed on the rug and pointed at the hearth. She received Bernard's announcement with small satisfaction, and expended a great deal of familiar ridicule on his project of a journey to California. Then, suddenly getting up and looking at him a moment—

"I know why you are going," she said.

"I am glad to hear my explanations have not been lost."

"Your explanations are all nonsense. You are going for another reason."

"Well," said Bernard, "if you insist upon it, it 's because you are too sharp with me."

"It 's because of me. So much as that is true." Bernard wondered what she was going to say—if she were going to be silly enough to allude to the most impudent of fictions; then, as she stood opening and closing her blue fan and smiling at him in the fire-light, he felt that she was silly enough for anything. "It 's because of all the talk—it 's because of Gordon. You need n't be afraid of Gordon."

"Afraid of him? I don't know what you mean," said Bernard, gravely.

Blanche gave a little laugh.

"You have discovered that people are talking about us—about you and me. I must say I wonder you care. I don't care, and if it 's because of Gordon, you might as well know that he does n't care. If he does n't care, I don't see why I should; and if I don't, I don't see why you should!"

"You pay too much attention to such insipid drivel in even mentioning it."

"Well, if I have the credit of saying what I should n't—to you or to any one else—I don't see why I should n't have the advantage too. Gordon does n't care—he does n't care what I do or say. He does n't care a pin for me!"

She spoke in her usual rattling, rambling voice, and brought out this declaration with a curious absence of resentment.

"You talk about advantage," said Bernard. "I don't see what advantage it is to you to say that."

"I want to—I must—I will! That 's the advantage!" This came out with a sudden sharpness of tone; she spoke more excitedly. "He does n't care a button for me, and he never did! I don't know what he married me for. He cares for something else—he thinks of something else. I don't know what it is—I suppose it 's chemistry!"

These words gave Bernard a certain shock, but he had his intelligence sufficiently in hand to contradict them with energy.

"You labor under a monstrous delusion," he exclaimed. "Your husband thinks you fascinating."

This epithet, pronounced with a fine distinctness, was ringing in the air when the door opened and Gordon came in. He looked for a moment from Bernard to his wife, and then, approaching the latter, he said, softly—

"Do you know that he leaves us to-morrow?"

CHAPTER XVIII

Bernard left then and went to California; but when he arrived there he asked himself why he had come, and was unable to mention any other reason than that he had announced it. He began to feel restless again, and to drift back to that chronic chagrin which had accompanied him through his long journey in the East. He succeeded, however, in keeping these unreasonable feelings at bay for some time, and he strove to occupy himself, to take an interest in Californian problems. Bernard, however, was neither an economist nor a cattle-fancier, and he found that, as the phrase is, there was not a great deal to take hold of. He wandered about, admired the climate and the big peaches, thought a while of going to Japan, and ended by going to Mexico. In this way he passed several months, and justified, in the eyes of other people at least, his long journey across the Continent. At last he made it again, in the opposite sense. He went back to New York, where the summer had already begun, and here he invented a solution for the difficulty presented by life to a culpably unoccupied and ill-regulated man. The solution was not in the least original, and I am almost ashamed to mention so stale and conventional a device. Bernard simply hit upon the plan of returning to Europe. Such as it was, however, he carried it out with an audacity worthy of a better cause, and was sensibly happier since he had made up his mind to it. Gordon Wright and his wife were out of town, but Bernard went into the country, as boldly as you please, to inform them of his little project and take a long leave of them. He had made his arrangements to sail immediately, and, as at such short notice it was impossible to find good quarters on one of the English vessels, he had engaged a berth on a French steamer, which would convey him to Havre. On going down to Gordon's house in the country, he was conscious of a good deal of eagerness to know what had become of that latent irritation of which Blanche had given him a specimen. Apparently it had quite subsided; Blanche was wreathed in smiles; she was living in a bower of roses. Bernard, indeed, had no opportunity for investigating her state of mind, for he found several people in the house, and Blanche, who had an exalted standard of the duties of a hostess, was occupied in making life agreeable to her guests, most of whom were gentlemen. She had in this way that great remedy for dissatisfaction which Bernard lacked—something interesting to do. Bernard felt a good deal of genuine sadness in taking leave of Gordon, to whom he contrived to feel even more kindly than in earlier days. He had quite forgotten that Gordon was jealous of him—which he was not, as Bernard said. Certainly, Gordon showed nothing of it now, and nothing could have been more friendly than their parting. Gordon, also, for a man who was never boisterous, seemed very contented. He was fond of exercising hospitality, and he confessed to Bernard that he was just now in the humor for having his house full of people. Fortune continued to gratify this generous taste; for just as Bernard was coming away another guest made his appearance. The newcomer was none other than the Honourable Augustus Lovelock, who had just arrived in New York, and who, as he added, had long desired to visit the United States. Bernard merely witnessed his arrival, and was struck with the fact that as he presented himself—it seemed quite a surprise—Blanche really stopped chattering.

CHAPTER XIX

I have called it a stale expedient on Bernard Longueville's part to "go to Europe" again, like the most commonplace American; and it is certain that, as our young man stood and looked out of the window of his inn at Havre, an hour after his arrival at that sea-port, his adventure did not strike him as having any great freshness. He had no plans nor intentions; he had not even any very definite desires. He had felt the impulse to come back to Europe, and he had obeyed it; but now that he had arrived, his impulse seemed to have little more to say to him. He perceived it, indeed—mentally—in the attitude of a small street-boy playing upon his nose with that vulgar gesture which is supposed to represent the elation of successful fraud. There was a large blank wall before his window, painted a dirty yellow and much discolored by the weather; a broad patch of summer sunlight rested upon it and brought out the full vulgarity of its complexion. Bernard stared a while at this blank wall, which struck him in some degree as a symbol of his own present moral prospect. Then suddenly he turned away, with the declaration that, whatever truth there might be in symbolism, he, at any rate, had not come to Europe to spend the precious remnant of his youth in a malodorous Norman sea-port. The weather was very hot, and neither the hotel nor the town at large appeared to form an attractive sejour for persons of an irritable nostril. To go to Paris, however, was hardly more attractive than to remain at Havre, for Bernard had a lively vision of the heated bitumen and the glaring frontages of the French capital. But if a Norman town was close and dull, the Norman country was notoriously fresh and entertaining, and the next morning Bernard got into a caleche, with his luggage, and bade its proprietor drive him along the coast. Once he had begun to rumble through this charming landscape, he was in much better humor with his situation; the air was freshened by a breeze from the sea; the blooming country, without walls or fences, lay open to the traveller's eye; the grain-fields and copses were shimmering in the summer wind; the pink-faced cottages peeped through the ripening orchard-boughs, and the gray towers of the old churches were silvered by the morning-light of France.

At the end of some three hours, Bernard arrived at a little watering-place which lay close upon the shore, in the embrace of a pair of white-armed cliffs. It had a quaint and primitive aspect and a natural picturesqueness which commended it to Bernard's taste. There was evidently a great deal of nature about it, and at this moment, nature, embodied in the clear, gay sunshine, in the blue and quiet sea, in the daisied grass of the high-shouldered downs, had an air of inviting the intelligent observer to postpone his difficulties. Blanquais-les-Galets, as Bernard learned the name of this unfashionable resort to be, was twenty miles from a railway, and the place wore an expression of unaffected rusticity. Bernard stopped at an inn for his noonday breakfast, and then, with his appreciation quickened by the homely felicity of this repast, determined to go no further. He engaged a room at the inn, dismissed his vehicle, and gave himself up to the contemplation of French sea-side manners. These were chiefly to be observed upon a pebbly strand which lay along the front of the village and served as the gathering-point of its idler inhabitants. Bathing in the sea was the chief occupation of these good people, including, as it did, prolonged spectatorship of the process and infinite conversation upon its mysteries. The little world of Blanquais appeared to form a large family party, of highly developed amphibious habits, which sat gossiping all day upon the warm pebbles, occasionally dipping into the sea and drying itself in the sun, without any relaxation of personal intimacy. All this was very amusing to Bernard, who in the course of the day took a bath with the rest. The ocean was, after all, very large, and when one took one's plunge one seemed to have it quite to one's self. When he had dressed himself again, Bernard stretched himself on the beach, feeling happier than he had done in a long time, and pulled his hat over his eyes. The feeling of happiness was an odd one; it had come over him suddenly, without visible cause; but, such as it was, our hero made the most of it. As he lay there it seemed to deepen; his immersion and his exercise in the salt water had given him an agreeable languor. This presently became a drowsiness which was not less agreeable, and Bernard felt himself going to sleep. There were sounds in the air above his head—sounds of the crunching and rattling of the loose, smooth stones as his neighbors moved about on them; of high-pitched French voices exchanging colloquial cries; of the plash of the bathers in the distant water, and the short, soft breaking of the waves. But these things came to his ears more vaguely and remotely, and at last they faded away. Bernard enjoyed half an hour of that light and easy slumber which is apt to overtake idle people in recumbent attitudes in the open air on August afternoons. It brought with it an exquisite sense of rest, and the rest was not spoiled by the fact that it was animated by a charming dream. Dreams are vague things, and this one had the defects of its species; but it was somehow concerned with the image of a young lady whom Bernard had formerly known, and who had beautiful eyes, into which—in the dream—he found himself looking. He waked up to find himself looking into the crown of his hat, which had been resting on the bridge of his nose. He removed it, and half raised himself, resting on his elbow and preparing to taste, in another position, of a little more of that exquisite rest of which mention has just been made. The world about him was still amusing and charming; the chatter of his companions, losing itself in the large sea-presence, the plash of the divers and swimmers, the deep blue of the ocean and the silvery white of the cliff, had that striking air of indifference to the fact that his mind had been absent from them which we are apt to find in mundane things on emerging from a nap. The same people were sitting near him on the beach—the same, and yet not quite the same. He found himself noticing a person whom he had not noticed before—a young lady, who was seated in a low portable chair, some dozen yards off, with her eyes bent upon a book. Her head was in shade; her large parasol made, indeed, an awning for her whole person, which in this way, in the quiet attitude of perusal, seemed to abstract itself from the glare and murmur of the beach. The clear shadow of her umbrella—it was lined with blue—was deep upon her face; but it was not deep enough to prevent Bernard from recognizing a profile that he knew. He suddenly sat upright, with an intensely quickened vision. Was he dreaming still, or had he waked? In a moment he felt that he was acutely awake; he heard her, across the interval, turn the page of her book. For a single instant, as she did so, she looked with level brows at the glittering ocean; then, lowering her eyes, she went on with her reading. In this barely perceptible movement he saw Angela Vivian; it was wonderful how well he remembered her. She was evidently reading very seriously; she was much interested in her book. She was alone; Bernard looked about for her mother, but Mrs. Vivian was not in sight. By this time Bernard had become aware that he was agitated; the exquisite rest of a few moments before had passed away. His agitation struck him as unreasonable; in a few minutes he made up his mind that it was absurd. He had done her an injury—yes; but as she sat there losing herself in a French novel—Bernard could see it was a French novel—he could not make out that she was the worse for it. It had not affected her appearance; Miss Vivian was still a handsome girl. Bernard hoped she would not look toward him or recognize him; he wished to look at her at his ease; to think it over; to make up his mind. The idea of meeting Angela Vivian again had often come into his thoughts; I may, indeed, say that it was a tolerably familiar presence there; but the fact, nevertheless, now presented itself with all the violence of an accident for which he was totally unprepared. He had often asked himself what he should say to her, how he should carry himself, and how he should probably find the young lady; but, with whatever ingenuity he might at the moment have answered these questions, his intelligence at present felt decidedly overtaxed. She was a very pretty girl to whom he had done a wrong; this was the final attitude into which, with a good deal of preliminary shifting and wavering, she had settled in his recollection. The wrong was a right, doubtless, from certain points of view; but from the girl's own it could only seem an injury to which its having been inflicted by a clever young man with whom she had been on agreeable terms, necessarily added a touch of baseness.

In every disadvantage that a woman suffers at the hands of a man, there is inevitably, in what concerns the man, an element of cowardice. When I say "inevitably," I mean that this is what the woman sees in it. This is what Bernard believed that Angela Vivian saw in the fact that by giving his friend a bad account of her he had prevented her making an opulent marriage. At first he had said to himself that, whether he had held his tongue or spoken, she had already lost her chance; but with time, somehow, this reflection had lost its weight in the scale. It conveyed little re-assurance to his irritated conscience—it had become imponderable and impertinent. At the moment of which I speak it entirely failed to present itself, even for form's sake; and as he sat looking at this superior creature who came back to him out of an episode of his past, he thought of her simply as an unprotected woman toward whom he had been indelicate. It is not an agreeable thing for a delicate man like Bernard Longueville to have to accommodate himself to such an accident, but this is nevertheless what it seemed needful that he should do. If she bore him a grudge he must think it natural; if she had vowed him a hatred he must allow her the comfort of it. He had done the only thing possible, but that made it no better for her. He had wronged her. The circumstances mattered nothing, and as he could not make it up to her, the only reasonable thing was to keep out of her way. He had stepped into her path now, and the proper thing was to step out of it. If it could give her no pleasure to see him again, it could certainly do him no good to see her. He had seen her by this time pretty well—as far as mere seeing went, and as yet, apparently, he was none the worse for that; but his hope that he should himself escape unperceived had now become acute. It is singular that this hope should not have led him instantly to turn his back and move away; but the explanation of his imprudent delay is simply that he wished to see a little more of Miss Vivian. He was unable to bring himself to the point. Those clever things that he might have said to her quite faded away. The only good taste was to take himself off, and spare her the trouble of inventing civilities that she could not feel. And yet he continued to sit there from moment to moment, arrested, detained, fascinated, by the accident of her not looking round—of her having let him watch her so long. She turned another page, and another, and her reading absorbed her still. He was so near her that he could have touched her dress with the point of his umbrella. At last she raised her eyes and rested them a while on the blue horizon, straight in front of her, but as yet without turning them aside. This, however, augmented the danger of her doing so, and Bernard, with a good deal of an effort, rose to his feet. The effort, doubtless, kept the movement from being either as light or as swift as it might have been, and it vaguely attracted his neighbor's attention. She turned her head and glanced at him, with a glance that evidently expected but to touch him and pass. It touched him, and it was on the point of passing; then it suddenly checked itself; she had recognized him. She looked at him, straight and open-eyed, out of the shadow of her parasol, and Bernard stood there—motionless now—receiving her gaze. How long it lasted need not be narrated. It was probably a matter of a few seconds, but to Bernard it seemed a little eternity. He met her eyes, he looked straight into her face; now that she had seen him he could do nothing else. Bernard's little eternity, however, came to an end; Miss Vivian dropped her eyes upon her book again. She let them rest upon it only a moment; then she closed it and slowly rose from her chair, turning away from Bernard. He still stood looking at her—stupidly, foolishly, helplessly enough, as it seemed to him; no sign of recognition had been exchanged. Angela Vivian hesitated a minute; she now had her back turned to him, and he fancied her light, flexible figure was agitated by her indecision. She looked along the sunny beach which stretched its shallow curve to where the little bay ended and the white wall of the cliffs began. She looked down toward the sea, and up toward the little Casino which was perched on a low embankment, communicating with the beach at two or three points by a short flight of steps. Bernard saw—or supposed he saw—that she was asking herself whither she had best turn to avoid him. He had not blushed when she looked at him—he had rather turned a little pale; but he blushed now, for it really seemed odious to have literally driven the poor girl to bay. Miss Vivian decided to take refuge in the Casino, and she passed along one of the little pathways of planks that were laid here and there across the beach, and directed herself to the nearest flight of steps. Before she had gone two paces a complete change came over Bernard's feeling; his only wish now was to speak to her—to explain—to tell her he would go away. There was another row of steps at a short distance behind him; he rapidly ascended them and reached the little terrace of the Casino. Miss Vivian stood there; she was apparently hesitating again which way to turn. Bernard came straight up to her, with a gallant smile and a greeting. The comparison is a coarse one, but he felt that he was taking the bull by the horns. Angela Vivian stood watching him arrive.

"You did n't recognize me," he said, "and your not recognizing me made me—made me hesitate."

For a moment she said nothing, and then—

"You are more timid than you used to be!" she answered.

He could hardly have said what expression he had expected to find in her face; his apprehension had, perhaps, not painted her obtrusively pale and haughty, aggressively cold and stern; but it had figured something different from the look he encountered. Miss Vivian was simply blushing— that was what Bernard mainly perceived; he saw that her surprise had been extreme—complete. Her blush was re-assuring; it contradicted the idea of impatient resentment, and Bernard took some satisfaction in noting that it was prolonged.

"Yes, I am more timid than I used to be," he said.

In spite of her blush, she continued to look at him very directly; but she had always done that—she always met one's eye; and Bernard now instantly found all the beauty that he had ever found before in her pure, unevasive glance.

"I don't know whether I am more brave," she said; "but I must tell the truth—I instantly recognized you."

"You gave no sign!"

"I supposed I gave a striking one—in getting up and going away."

"Ah!" said Bernard, "as I say, I am more timid than I was, and I did n't venture to interpret that as a sign of recognition."

"It was a sign of surprise."

"Not of pleasure!" said Bernard. He felt this to be a venturesome, and from the point of view of taste perhaps a reprehensible, remark; but he made it because he was now feeling his ground, and it seemed better to make it gravely than with assumed jocosity.

"Great surprises are to me never pleasures," Angela answered; "I am not fond of shocks of any kind. The pleasure is another matter. I have not yet got over my surprise."

"If I had known you were here, I would have written to you beforehand," said Bernard, laughing.

Miss Vivian, beneath her expanded parasol, gave a little shrug of her shoulders.

"Even that would have been a surprise."

"You mean a shock, eh? Did you suppose I was dead?"

Now, at last, she lowered her eyes, and her blush slowly died away.

"I knew nothing about it."

"Of course you could n't know, and we are all mortal. It was natural that you should n't expect—simply on turning your head—to find me lying on the pebbles at Blanquais-les-Galets. You were a great surprise to me, as well; but I differ from you—I like surprises."

"It is rather refreshing to hear that one is a surprise," said the girl.

"Especially when in that capacity one is liked!" Bernard exclaimed.

"I don't say that—because such sensations pass away. I am now beginning to get over mine."

The light mockery of her tone struck him as the echo of an unforgotten air. He looked at her a moment, and then he said—

"You are not changed; I find you quite the same."

"I am sorry for that!" And she turned away.

"What are you doing?" he asked. "Where are you going?"

She looked about her, without answering, up and down the little terrace. The Casino at Blanquais was a much more modest place of reunion than the Conversation-house at Baden-Baden. It was a small, low structure of brightly painted wood, containing but three or four rooms, and furnished all along its front with a narrow covered gallery, which offered a delusive shelter from the rougher moods of the fine, fresh weather. It was somewhat rude and shabby— the subscription for the season was low—but it had a simple picturesqueness. Its little terrace was a very convenient place for a stroll, and the great view of the ocean and of the marble-white crags that formed the broad gate-way of the shallow bay, was a sufficient compensation for the absence of luxuries. There were a few people sitting in the gallery, and a few others scattered upon the terrace; but the pleasure-seekers of Blanquais were, for the most part, immersed in the salt water or disseminated on the grassy downs.

"I am looking for my mother," said Angela Vivian.

"I hope your mother is well."

"Very well, thank you."

"May I help you to look for her?" Bernard asked.

Her eyes paused in their quest, and rested a moment upon her companion.

"She is not here," she said presently. "She has gone home."

"What do you call home?" Bernard demanded.

"The sort of place that we always call home; a bad little house that we have taken for a month."

"Will you let me come and see it?"

"It 's nothing to see."

Bernard hesitated a moment.

"Is that a refusal?"

"I should never think of giving it so fine a name."

"There would be nothing fine in forbidding me your door. Don't think that!" said Bernard, with rather a forced laugh.

It was difficult to know what the girl thought; but she said, in a moment—

"We shall be very happy to see you. I am going home."

"May I walk with you so far?" asked Bernard.

"It is not far; it 's only three minutes." And Angela moved slowly to the gate of the Casino.

CHAPTER XX

Bernard walked beside her, and for some moments nothing was said between them. As the silence continued, he became aware of it, and it vexed him that she should leave certain things unsaid. She had asked him no question—neither whence he had come, nor how long he would stay, nor what had happened to him since they parted. He wished to see whether this was intention or accident. He was already complaining to himself that she expressed no interest in him, and he was perfectly aware that this was a ridiculous feeling. He had come to speak to her in order to tell her that he was going away, and yet, at the end of five minutes, he had asked leave to come and see her. This sudden gyration of mind was grotesque, and Bernard knew it; but, nevertheless, he had an immense expectation that, if he should give her time, she would manifest some curiosity as to his own situation. He tried to give her time; he held his tongue; but she continued to say nothing. They passed along a sort of winding lane, where two or three fishermen's cottages, with old brown nets suspended on the walls and drying in the sun, stood open to the road, on the other side of which was a patch of salt-looking grass, browsed by a donkey that was not fastidious.

"It 's so long since we parted, and we have so much to say to each other!" Bernard exclaimed at last, and he accompanied this declaration with a laugh much more spontaneous than the one he had given a few moments before.

It might have gratified him, however, to observe that his companion appeared to see no ground for joking in the idea that they should have a good deal to say to each other.

"Yes, it 's a long time since we spent those pleasant weeks at Baden," she rejoined. "Have you been there again?"

This was a question, and though it was a very simple one, Bernard was charmed with it.

"I would n't go back for the world!" he said. "And you?"

"Would I go back? Oh yes; I thought it so agreeable."

With this he was less pleased; he had expected the traces of resentment, and he was actually disappointed at not finding them. But here was the little house of which his companion had spoken, and it seemed, indeed, a rather bad one. That is, it was one of those diminutive structures which are known at French watering-places as "chalets," and, with an exiguity of furniture, are let for the season to families that pride themselves upon their powers of contraction. This one was a very humble specimen of its class, though it was doubtless a not inadequate abode for two quiet and frugal women. It had a few inches of garden, and there were flowers in pots in the open windows, where some extremely fresh white curtains were gently fluttering in the breath of the neighboring ocean. The little door stood wide open.

"This is where we live," said Angela; and she stopped and laid her hand upon the little garden-gate.

"It 's very fair," said Bernard. "I think it 's better than the pastry-cook's at Baden."

They stood there, and she looked over the gate at the geraniums. She did not ask him to come in; but, on the other hand, keeping the gate closed, she made no movement to leave him. The Casino was now quite out of sight, and the whole place was perfectly still. Suddenly, turning her eyes upon Bernard with a certain strange inconsequence—

"I have not seen you here before," she observed.

He gave a little laugh.

"I suppose it 's because I only arrived this morning. I think that if I had been here you would have noticed me."

"You arrived this morning?"

"Three or four hours ago. So, if the remark were not in questionable taste, I should say we had not lost time."

"You may say what you please," said Angela, simply. "Where did you come from?"

Interrogation, now it had come, was most satisfactory, and Bernard was glad to believe that there was an element of the unexpected in his answer.

"From California."

"You came straight from California to this place?"

"I arrived at Havre only yesterday."

"And why did you come here?"

"It would be graceful of me to be able to answer—'Because I knew you were here.' But unfortunately I did not know it. It was a mere chance; or rather, I feel like saying it was an inspiration."

Angela looked at the geraniums again.

"It was very singular," she said. "We might have been in so many places besides this one. And you might have come to so many places besides this one."

"It is all the more singular, that one of the last persons I saw in America was your charming friend Blanche, who married Gordon Wright. She did n't tell me you were here."

"She had no reason to know it," said the girl. "She is not my friend—as you are her husband's friend."

"Ah no, I don't suppose that. But she might have heard from you."

"She does n't hear from us. My mother used to write to her for a while after she left Europe, but she has given it up." She paused a moment, and then she added—"Blanche is too silly!"

Bernard noted this, wondering how it bore upon his theory of a spiteful element in his companion. Of course Blanche was silly; but, equally of course, this young lady's perception of it was quickened by Blanche's having married a rich man whom she herself might have married.

"Gordon does n't think so," Bernard said.

Angela looked at him a moment.

"I am very glad to hear it," she rejoined, gently.

"Yes, it is very fortunate."

"Is he well?" the girl asked. "Is he happy?"

"He has all the air of it."

"I am very glad to hear it," she repeated. And then she moved the latch of the gate and passed in. At the same moment her mother appeared in the open door-way. Mrs. Vivian had apparently been summoned by the sound of her daughter's colloquy with an unrecognized voice, and when she saw Bernard she gave a sharp little cry of surprise. Then she stood gazing at him.

Since the dispersion of the little party at Baden-Baden he had not devoted much meditation to this conscientious gentlewoman who had been so tenderly anxious to establish her daughter properly in life; but there had been in his mind a tacit assumption that if Angela deemed that he had played her a trick Mrs. Vivian's view of his conduct was not more charitable. He felt that he must have seemed to her very unkind, and that in so far as a well-regulated conscience permitted the exercise of unpractical passions, she honored him with a superior detestation. The instant he beheld her on her threshold this conviction rose to the surface of his consciousness and made him feel that now, at least, his hour had come.

"It is Mr. Longueville, whom we met at Baden," said Angela to her mother, gravely.

Mrs. Vivian began to smile, and stepped down quickly toward the gate.

"Ah, Mr. Longueville," she murmured, "it 's so long—it 's so pleasant—it 's so strange—"

And suddenly she stopped, still smiling. Her smile had an odd intensity; she was trembling a little, and Bernard, who was prepared for hissing scorn, perceived with a deep, an almost violent, surprise, a touching agitation, an eager friendliness.

"Yes, it 's very long," he said; "it 's very pleasant. I have only just arrived; I met Miss Vivian."

"And you are not coming in?" asked Angela's mother, very graciously.

"Your daughter has not asked me!" said Bernard.

"Ah, my dearest," murmured Mrs. Vivian, looking at the girl.

Her daughter returned her glance, and then the elder lady paused again, and simply began to smile at Bernard, who recognized in her glance that queer little intimation—shy and cautious, yet perfectly discernible—of a desire to have a private understanding with what he felt that she mentally termed his better nature, which he had more than once perceived at Baden-Baden.

"Ah no, she has not asked me," Bernard repeated, laughing gently.

Then Angela turned her eyes upon him, and the expression of those fine organs was strikingly agreeable. It had, moreover, the merit of being easily interpreted; it said very plainly, "Please don't insist, but leave me alone." And it said it not at all sharply—very gently and pleadingly. Bernard found himself understanding it so well that he literally blushed with intelligence.

"Don't you come to the Casino in the evening, as you used to come to the Kursaal?" he asked.

Mrs. Vivian looked again at her daughter, who had passed into the door-way of the cottage; then she said—

"We will go this evening."

"I shall look for you eagerly," Bernard rejoined. "Auf wiedersehen, as we used to say at Baden!"

Mrs. Vivian waved him a response over the gate, her daughter gave him a glance from the threshold, and he took his way back to his inn.

He awaited the evening with great impatience; he fancied he had made a discovery, and he wished to confirm it. The discovery was that his idea that she bore him a grudge, that she was conscious of an injury, that he was associated in her mind with a wrong, had all been a morbid illusion. She had forgiven, she had forgotten, she did n't care, she had possibly never cared! This, at least, was his theory now, and he longed for a little more light upon it. His old sense of her being a complex and intricate girl had, in that quarter of an hour of talk with her, again become lively, so that he was not absolutely sure his apprehensions had been vain. But, with his quick vision of things, he had got the impression, at any rate, that she had no vulgar resentment of any slight he might have put upon her, or any disadvantage he might have caused her. Her feeling about such a matter would be large and original. Bernard desired to see more of that, and in the evening, in fact, it seemed to him that he did so.

The terrace of the Casino was far from offering the brilliant spectacle of the promenade in front of the gaming-rooms at Baden. It had neither the liberal illumination, the distinguished frequenters, nor the superior music which formed the attraction of that celebrated spot; but it had a modest animation of its own, in which the starlight on the open sea took the place of clustered lamps, and the mighty resonance of the waves performed the function of an orchestra. Mrs. Vivian made her appearance with her daughter, and Bernard, as he used to do at Baden, chose a corner to place some chairs for them. The crowd was small, for most of the visitors had compressed themselves into one of the rooms, where a shrill operetta was being performed by a strolling troupe. Mrs. Vivian's visit was a short one; she remained at the Casino less than half an hour. But Bernard had some talk with Angela. He sat beside her—her mother was on the other side, talking with an old French lady whose acquaintance she had made on the beach. Between Bernard and Angela several things were said. When his friends went away Bernard walked home with them. He bade them good-night at the door of their chalet, and then slowly strolled back to the Casino. The terrace was nearly empty; every one had gone to listen to the operetta, the sound of whose contemporary gayety came through the open, hot-looking windows in little thin quavers and catches. The ocean was rumbling just beneath; it made a ruder but richer music. Bernard stood looking at it a moment; then he went down the steps to the beach. The tide was rather low; he walked slowly down to the line of the breaking waves. The sea looked huge and black and simple; everything was vague in the unassisted darkness. Bernard stood there some time; there was nothing but the sound and the sharp, fresh smell. Suddenly he put his hand to his heart; it was beating very fast. An immense conviction had come over him—abruptly, then and there—and for a moment he held his breath. It was like a word spoken in the darkness—he held his breath to listen. He was in love with Angela Vivian, and his love was a throbbing passion! He sat down on the stones where he stood—it filled him with a kind of awe.

CHAPTER XXI

It filled him with a kind of awe, and the feeling was by no means agreeable. It was not a feeling to which even a man of Bernard Longueville's easy power of extracting the savour from a sensation could rapidly habituate himself, and for the rest of that night it was far from making of our hero the happy man that a lover just coming to self-consciousness is supposed to be. It was wrong—it was dishonorable—it was impossible—and yet it was; it was, as nothing in his own personal experience had ever been. He seemed hitherto to have been living by proxy, in a vision, in reflection—to have been an echo, a shadow, a futile attempt; but this at last was life itself, this was a fact, this was reality. For these things one lived; these were the things that people had died for. Love had been a fable before this—doubtless a very pretty one; and passion had been a literary phrase—employed obviously with considerable effect. But now he stood in a personal relation to these familiar ideas, which gave them a very much keener import; they had laid their hand upon him in the darkness, he felt it upon his shoulder, and he knew by its pressure that it was the hand of destiny. What made this sensation a shock was the element that was mixed with it; the fact that it came not simply and singly, but with an attendant shadow in which it immediately merged and lost itself. It was forbidden fruit—he knew it the instant he had touched it. He felt that he had pledged himself not to do just this thing which was gleaming before him so divinely—not to widen the crevice, not to open the door that would flood him with light. Friendship and honor were at stake; they stood at his left hand, as his new-born passion stood already at his right; they claimed him as well, and their grasp had a pressure which might become acutely painful. The soul is a still more tender organism than the body, and it shrinks from the prospect of being subjected to violence. Violence—spiritual violence—was what our luxurious hero feared; and it is not too much to say that as he lingered there by the sea, late into the night, while the gurgitation of the waves grew deeper to his ear, the prospect came to have an element of positive terror. The two faces of his situation stood confronting each other; it was a rigid, brutal opposition, and Bernard held his breath for a while with the wonder of what would come of it. He sat a long time upon the beach; the night grew very cold, but he had no sense of it. Then he went away and passed before the Casino again, and wandered through the village. The Casino was shrouded in darkness and silence, and there was nothing in the streets of the little town but the salt smell of the sea, a vague aroma of fish and the distant sound of the breakers. Little by little, Bernard lost the feeling of having been startled, and began to perceive that he could reason about his trouble. Trouble it was, though this seems an odd name for the consciousness of a bright enchantment; and the first thing that reason, definitely consulted, told him about the matter was that he had been in love with Angela Vivian any time these three years. This sapient faculty supplied him with further information; only two or three of the items of which, however, it is necessary to reproduce. He had been a great fool—an incredible fool—not to have discovered before this what was the matter with him! Bernard's sense of his own shrewdness—always tolerably acute—had never received such a bruise as this present perception that a great many things had been taking place in his clever mind without his clever mind suspecting them. But it little mattered, his reason went on to declare, what he had suspected or what he might now feel about it; his present business was to leave Blanquais-les-Galets at sunrise the next morning and never rest his eyes upon Angela Vivian again. This was his duty; it had the merit of being perfectly plain and definite, easily apprehended, and unattended, as far as he could discover, with the smallest material difficulties. Not only this, reason continued to remark; but the moral difficulties were equally inconsiderable. He had never breathed a word of his passion to Miss Vivian—quite the contrary; he had never committed himself nor given her the smallest reason to suspect his hidden flame; and he was therefore perfectly free to turn his back upon her—he could never incur the reproach of trifling with her affections. Bernard was in that state of mind when it is the greatest of blessings to be saved the distress of choice—to see a straight path before you and to feel that you have only to follow it. Upon the straight path I have indicated, he fixed his eyes very hard; of course he would take his departure at the earliest possible hour on the morrow. There was a streak of morning in the eastern sky by the time he knocked for re-admittance at the door of the inn, which was opened to him by a mysterious old woman in a nightcap and meagre accessories, whose identity he failed to ascertain; and he laid himself down to rest—he was very tired—with his attention fastened, as I say, on the idea—on the very image—of departure.

On waking up the next morning, rather late, he found, however, that it had attached itself to a very different object. His vision was filled with the brightness of the delightful fact itself, which seemed to impregnate the sweet morning air and to flutter in the light, fresh breeze that came through his open window from the sea. He saw a great patch of the sea between a couple of red-tiled roofs; it was bluer than any sea had ever been before. He had not slept long—only three or four hours; but he had quite slept off his dread. The shadow had dropped away and nothing was left but the beauty of his love, which seemed to shine in the freshness of the early day. He felt absurdly happy—as if he had discovered El Dorado; quite apart from consequences—he was not thinking of consequences, which of course were another affair—the feeling was intrinsically the finest one he had ever had, and—as a mere feeling—he had not done with it yet. The consideration of consequences could easily be deferred, and there would, meanwhile, be no injury to any one in his extracting, very quietly, a little subjective joy from the state of his heart. He would let the flower bloom for a day before plucking it up by the roots. Upon this latter course he was perfectly resolved, and in view of such an heroic resolution the subjective interlude appeared no more than his just privilege. The project of leaving Blanquais-les-Galets at nine o'clock in the morning dropped lightly from his mind, making no noise as it fell; but another took its place, which had an air of being still more excellent and which consisted of starting off on a long walk and absenting himself for the day. Bernard grasped his stick and wandered away; he climbed the great shoulder of the further cliff and found himself on the level downs. Here there was apparently no obstacle whatever to his walking as far as his fancy should carry him. The summer was still in a splendid mood, and the hot and quiet day—it was a Sunday—seemed to constitute a deep, silent smile on the face of nature. The sea glistened on one side, and the crops ripened on the other; the larks, losing themselves in the dense sunshine, made it ring here and there in undiscoverable spots; this was the only sound save when Bernard, pausing now and then in his walk, found himself hearing far below him, at the base of the cliff, the drawling murmur of a wave. He walked a great many miles and passed through half a dozen of those rude fishing-hamlets, lodged in some sloping hollow of the cliffs, so many of which, of late years, all along the Norman coast, have adorned themselves with a couple of hotels and a row of bathing-machines. He walked so far that the shadows had begun to lengthen before he bethought himself of stopping; the afternoon had come on and had already begun to wane. The grassy downs still stretched before him, shaded here and there with shallow but windless dells. He looked for the softest place and then flung himself down on the grass; he lay there for a long time, thinking of many things. He had determined to give himself up to a day's happiness; it was happiness of a very harmless kind—the satisfaction of thought, the bliss of mere consciousness; but such as it was it did not elude him nor turn bitter in his heart, and the long summer day closed upon him before his spirit, hovering in perpetual circles round the idea of what might be, had begun to rest its wing. When he rose to his feet again it was too late to return to Blanquais in the same way that he had come; the evening was at hand, the light was already fading, and the walk he had taken was one which even if he had not felt very tired, he would have thought it imprudent to attempt to repeat in the darkness. He made his way to the nearest village, where he was able to hire a rustic carriole, in which primitive conveyance, gaining the high-road, he jogged and jostled through the hours of the evening slowly back to his starting-point. It wanted an hour of midnight by the time he reached his inn, and there was nothing left for him but to go to bed.

He went in the unshaken faith that he should leave Blanquais early on the morrow. But early on the morrow it occurred to him that it would be simply grotesque to go off without taking leave of Mrs. Vivian and her daughter, and offering them some explanation of his intention. He had given them to understand that, so delighted was he to find them there, he would remain at Blanquais at least as long as they. He must have seemed to them wanting in civility, to spend a whole bright Sunday without apparently troubling his head about them, and if the unlucky fact of his being in love with the girl were a reason for doing his duty, it was at least not a reason for being rude. He had not yet come to that—to accepting rudeness as an incident of virtue; it had always been his theory that virtue had the best manners in the world, and he flattered himself at any rate that he could guard his integrity without making himself ridiculous. So, at what he thought a proper hour, in the course of the morning, he retraced his steps along the little lane through which, two days ago, Angela Vivian had shown him the way to her mother's door. At this humble portal he knocked; the windows of the little chalet were open, and the white curtains, behind the flower-pots, were fluttering as he had seen them before. The door was opened by a neat young woman, who informed him very promptly that Madame and Mademoiselle had left Blanquais a couple of hours earlier. They had gone to Paris—yes, very suddenly, taking with them but little luggage, and they had left her— she had the honor of being the femme de chambre of ces dames—to put up their remaining possessions and follow as soon as possible. On Bernard's expressing surprise and saying that he had supposed them to be fixed at the sea-side for the rest of the season, the femme de chambre, who seemed a very intelligent person, begged to remind him that the season was drawing to a close, that Madame had taken the chalet but for five weeks, only ten days of which period were yet to expire, that ces dames, as Monsieur perhaps knew, were great travellers, who had been half over the world and thought nothing of breaking camp at an hour's notice, and that, in fine, Madame might very well have received a telegram summoning her to another part of the country.

"And where have the ladies gone?" asked Bernard.

"For the moment, to Paris."

"And in Paris where have they gone?"

"Dame, chez elles—to their house," said the femme de chambre, who appeared to think that Bernard asked too many questions.

But Bernard persisted.

"Where is their house?"

The waiting-maid looked at him from head to foot.

"If Monsieur wishes to write, many of Madame's letters come to her banker," she said, inscrutably.

"And who is her banker?"

"He lives in the Rue de Provence."

"Very good—I will find him out," said our hero, turning away.

The discriminating reader who has been so good as to interest himself in this little narrative will perhaps at this point exclaim with a pardonable consciousness of shrewdness: "Of course he went the next day to the Rue de Provence!" Of course, yes; only as it happens Bernard did nothing of the kind. He did one of the most singular things he ever did in his life—a thing that puzzled him even at the time, and with regard to which he often afterward wondered whence he had drawn the ability for so remarkable a feat—he simply spent a fortnight at Blanquais-les-Galets. It was a very quiet fortnight; he spoke to no one, he formed no relations, he was company to himself. It may be added that he had never found his own company half so good. He struck himself as a reasonable, delicate fellow, who looked at things in such a way as to make him refrain—refrain successfully, that was the point—from concerning himself practically about Angela Vivian. His saying that he would find out the banker in the Rue de Provence had been for the benefit of the femme de chambre, whom he thought rather impertinent; he had really no intention whatever of entering that classic thoroughfare. He took long walks, rambled on the beach, along the base of the cliffs and among the brown sea-caves, and he thought a good deal of certain incidents which have figured at an earlier stage of this narrative. He had forbidden himself the future, as an object of contemplation, and it was therefore a matter of necessity that his imagination should take refuge among the warm and familiar episodes of the past. He wondered why Mrs. Vivian should have left the place so suddenly, and was of course struck with the analogy between this incident and her abrupt departure from Baden. It annoyed him, it troubled him, but it by no means rekindled the alarm he had felt on first perceiving the injured Angela on the beach. That alarm had been quenched by Angela's manner during the hour that followed and during their short talk in the evening. This evening was to be forever memorable, for it had brought with it the revelation which still, at moments, suddenly made Bernard tremble; but it had also brought him the assurance that Angela cared as little as possible for anything that a chance acquaintance might have said about her. It is all the more singular, therefore, that one evening, after he had been at Blanquais a fortnight, a train of thought should suddenly have been set in motion in his mind. It was kindled by no outward occurrence, but by some wandering spark of fancy or of memory, and the immediate effect of it was to startle our hero very much as he had been startled on the evening I have described. The circumstances were the same; he had wandered down to the beach alone, very late, and he stood looking at the duskily-tumbling sea. Suddenly the same voice that had spoken before murmured another phrase in the darkness, and it rang upon his ear for the rest of the night. It startled him, as I have said, at first; then, the next morning, it led him to take his departure for Paris. During the journey it lingered in his ear; he sat in the corner of the railway-carriage with his eyes closed, abstracted, on purpose to prolong the reverberation. If it were not true it was at least, as the Italians have it, ben trovato, and it was wonderful how well it bore thinking of. It bears telling less well; but I can at least give a hint of it. The theory that Angela hated him had evaporated in her presence, and another of a very different sort had sprung into being. It fitted a great many of the facts, it explained a great many contradictions, anomalies, mysteries, and it accounted for Miss Vivian's insisting upon her mother's leaving Blanquais at a few hours' notice, even better than the theory of her resentment could have done. At any rate, it obliterated Bernard's scruples very effectually, and led him on his arrival in Paris to repair instantly to the Rue de Provence. This street contains more than one banker, but there is one with whom Bernard deemed Mrs. Vivian most likely to have dealings. He found he had reckoned rightly, and he had no difficulty in procuring her address. Having done so, however, he by no means went immediately to see her; he waited a couple of days—perhaps to give those obliterated scruples I have spoken of a chance to revive. They kept very quiet, and it must be confessed that Bernard took no great pains to recall them to life. After he had been in Paris three days, he knocked at Mrs. Vivian's door.

CHAPTER XXII

It was opened by the little waiting-maid whom he had seen at Blanquais, and who looked at him very hard before she answered his inquiry.

"You see I have found Mrs. Vivian's dwelling, though you would n't give me the address," Bernard said to her, smiling.

"Monsieur has put some time to it!" the young woman answered dryly. And she informed him that Madame was at home, though Mademoiselle, for whom he had not asked, was not.

Mrs. Vivian occupied a diminutive apartment at the summit of one of the tall white houses which ornament the neighborhood of the Arc de Triomphe. The early days of September had arrived, but Paris was still a city of absentees. The weather was warm and charming, and a certain savour of early autumn in the air was in accord with the somewhat melancholy aspect of the empty streets and closed shutters of this honorable quarter, where the end of the monumental vistas seemed to be curtained with a hazy emanation from the Seine. It was late in the afternoon when Bernard was ushered into Mrs. Vivian's little high-nestling drawing-room, and a patch of sunset tints, faintly red, rested softly upon the gilded wall. Bernard had seen these ladies only in borrowed and provisional abodes; but here was a place where they were really living and which was stamped with their tastes, their habits, their charm. The little salon was very elegant; it contained a multitude of pretty things, and it appeared to Bernard to be arranged in perfection. The long windows—the ceiling being low, they were really very short—opened upon one of those solid balconies, occupying the width of the apartment, which are often in Paris a compensation for living up five flights of stairs, and this balcony was filled with flowers and cushions. Bernard stepped out upon it to await the coming of Mrs. Vivian, and, as she was not quick to appear, he had time to see that his friends enjoyed a magnificent view. They looked up at the triumphal Arch, which presented itself at a picturesque angle, and near the green tree-tops of the Champs Elysees, beyond which they caught a broad gleam of the Seine and a glimpse, blue in the distance, of the great towers of Notre Dame. The whole vast city lay before them and beneath them, with its ordered brilliancy and its mingled aspect of compression and expansion; and yet the huge Parisian murmur died away before it reached Mrs. Vivian's sky-parlor, which seemed to Bernard the brightest and quietest little habitation he had ever known.

His hostess came rustling in at last; she seemed agitated; she knocked over with the skirt of her dress a little gilded chair which was reflected in the polished parquet as in a sheet of looking-glass. Mrs. Vivian had a fixed smile—she hardly knew what to say.

"I found your address at the banker's," said Bernard. "Your maid, at Blanquais, refused to give it to me."

Mrs. Vivian gave him a little look—there was always more or less of it in her face—which seemed equivalent to an entreaty that her interlocutor should spare her.

"Maids are so strange," she murmured; "especially the French!"

It pleased Bernard for the moment not to spare her, though he felt a sort of delight of kindness for her.

"Your going off from Blanquais so suddenly, without leaving me any explanation, any clue, any message of any sort—made me feel at first as if you did n't wish that I should look you up. It reminded me of the way you left Baden—do you remember?—three years ago."

"Baden was so charming—but one could n't stay forever," said Mrs. Vivian.

"I had a sort of theory one could. Our life was so pleasant that it seemed a shame to break the spell, and if no one had moved I am sure we might be sitting there now."

Mrs. Vivian stared, still with her little fixed smile.

"I think we should have had bad weather."

"Very likely," said Bernard, laughing. "Nature would have grown jealous of our good-humor—of our tranquil happiness. And after all, here we are together again—that is, some of us. But I have only my own audacity to thank for it. I was quite free to believe that you were not at all pleased to see me re-appear—and it is only because I am not easy to discourage—am indeed probably a rather impudent fellow—that I have ventured to come here to-day."

"I am very glad to see you re-appear, Mr. Longueville," Mrs. Vivian declared with the accent of veracity.

"It was your daughter's idea, then, running away from Blanquais?"

Mrs. Vivian lowered her eyes.

"We were obliged to go to Fontainebleau. We have but just come back. I thought of writing to you," she softly added.

"Ah, what pleasure that would have given me!"

"I mean, to tell you where we were, and that we should have been so happy to see you."

"I thank you for the intention. I suppose your daughter would n't let you carry it out."

"Angela is so peculiar," Mrs. Vivian said, simply.

"You told me that the first time I saw you."

"Yes, at Siena," said Mrs. Vivian.

"I am glad to hear you speak frankly of that place!"

"Perhaps it 's better," Mrs. Vivian murmured. She got up and went to the window; then stepping upon the balcony, she looked down a moment into the street. "She will come back in a moment," she said, coming into the room again. "She has gone to see a friend who lives just beside us. We don't mind about Siena now," she added, softly.

Bernard understood her—understood this to be a retraction of the request she had made of him at Baden.

"Dear little woman," he said to himself, "she wants to marry her daughter still—only now she wants to marry her to me!"

He wished to show her that he understood her, and he was on the point of seizing her hand, to do he did n't know what—to hold it, to press it, to kiss it—when he heard the sharp twang of the bell at the door of the little apartment.

Mrs. Vivian fluttered away.

"It 's Angela," she cried, and she stood there waiting and listening, smiling at Bernard, with her handkerchief pressed to her lips.

In a moment the girl came into the drawing-room, but on seeing Bernard she stopped, with her hand on the door-knob. Her mother went to her and kissed her.

"It 's Mr. Longueville, dearest—he has found us out."

"Found us out?" repeated Angela, with a little laugh. "What a singular expression!"

She was blushing as she had blushed when she first saw him at Blanquais. She seemed to Bernard now to have a great and peculiar brightness—something she had never had before.

"I certainly have been looking for you," he said. "I was greatly disappointed when I found you had taken flight from Blanquais."

"Taken flight?" She repeated his words as she had repeated her mother's. "That is also a strange way of speaking!"

"I don't care what I say," said Bernard, "so long as I make you understand that I have wanted very much to see you again, and that I have wondered every day whether I might venture—"

"I don't know why you should n't venture!" she interrupted, giving her little laugh again. "We are not so terrible, are we, mamma?—that is, when once you have climbed our five flights of stairs."

"I came up very fast," said Bernard, "and I find your apartment magnificent."

"Mr. Longueville must come again, must he not, dear?" asked mamma.

"I shall come very often, with your leave," Bernard declared.

"It will be immensely kind," said Angela, looking away.

"I am not sure that you will think it that."

"I don't know what you are trying to prove," said Angela; "first that we ran away from you, and then that we are not nice to our visitors."

"Oh no, not that!" Bernard exclaimed; "for I assure you I shall not care how cold you are with me."

She walked away toward another door, which was masked with a curtain that she lifted.

"I am glad to hear that, for it gives me courage to say that I am very tired, and that I beg you will excuse me."

She glanced at him a moment over her shoulder; then she passed out, dropping the curtain.

Bernard stood there face to face with Mrs. Vivian, whose eyes seemed to plead with him more than ever. In his own there was an excited smile.

"Please don't mind that," she murmured. "I know it 's true that she is tired."

"Mind it, dear lady?" cried the young man. "I delight in it. It 's just what I like."

"Ah, she 's very peculiar!" sighed Mrs. Vivian.

"She is strange—yes. But I think I understand her a little."

"You must come back to-morrow, then."

"I hope to have many to-morrows!" cried Bernard as he took his departure.

CHAPTER XXIII

And he had them in fact. He called the next day at the same hour, and he found the mother and the daughter together in their pretty salon. Angela was very gentle and gracious; he suspected Mrs. Vivian had given her a tender little lecture upon the manner in which she had received him the day before. After he had been there five minutes, Mrs. Vivian took a decanter of water that was standing upon a table and went out on the balcony to irrigate her flowers. Bernard watched her a while from his place in the room; then she moved along the balcony and out of sight. Some ten minutes elapsed without her re-appearing, and then Bernard stepped to the threshold of the window and looked for her. She was not there, and as he came and took his seat near Angela again, he announced, rather formally, that Mrs. Vivian had passed back into one of the other windows.

Angela was silent a moment—then she said—

"Should you like me to call her?"

She was very peculiar—that was very true; yet Bernard held to his declaration of the day before that he now understood her a little.

"No, I don't desire it," he said. "I wish to see you alone; I have something particular to say to you."

She turned her face toward him, and there was something in its expression that showed him that he looked to her more serious than he had ever looked. He sat down again; for some moments he hesitated to go on.

"You frighten me," she said laughing; and in spite of her laugh this was obviously true.

"I assure you my state of mind is anything but formidable. I am afraid of you, on the contrary; I am humble and apologetic."

"I am sorry for that," said Angela. "I particularly dislike receiving apologies, even when I know what they are for. What yours are for, I can't imagine."

"You don't dislike me—you don't hate me?" Bernard suddenly broke out.

"You don't ask me that humbly. Excuse me therefore if I say I have other, and more practical, things to do."

"You despise me," said Bernard.

"That is not humble either, for you seem to insist upon it."

"It would be after all a way of thinking of me, and I have a reason for wishing you to do that."

"I remember very well that you used to have a reason for everything. It was not always a good one."

"This one is excellent," said Bernard, gravely. "I have been in love with you for three years."

She got up slowly, turning away.

"Is that what you wished to say to me?"

She went toward the open window, and he followed her.

"I hope it does n't offend you. I don't say it lightly—it 's not a piece of gallantry. It 's the very truth of my being. I did n't know it till lately—strange as that may seem. I loved you long before I knew it—before I ventured or presumed to know it. I was thinking of you when I seemed to myself to be thinking of other things. It is very strange—there are things in it I don't understand. I travelled over the world, I tried to interest, to divert myself; but at bottom it was a perfect failure. To see you again—that was what I wanted. When I saw you last month at Blanquais I knew it; then everything became clear. It was the answer to the riddle. I wished to read it very clearly—I wished to be sure; therefore I did n't follow you immediately. I questioned my heart—I cross-questioned it. It has borne the examination, and now I am sure. I am very sure. I love you as my life—I beg you to listen to me!"

She had listened—she had listened intently, looking straight out of the window and without moving.

"You have seen very little of me," she said, presently, turning her illuminated eye on him.

"I have seen enough," Bernard added, smiling. "You must remember that at Baden I saw a good deal of you."

"Yes, but that did n't make you like me. I don't understand."

Bernard stood there a moment, frowning, with his eyes lowered.

"I can imagine that. But I think I can explain."

"Don't explain now," said Angela. "You have said enough; explain some other time." And she went out on the balcony.

Bernard, of course, in a moment was beside her, and, disregarding her injunction, he began to explain.

"I thought I disliked you—but I have come to the conclusion it was just the contrary. In reality I was in love with you. I had been so from the first time I saw you—when I made that sketch of you at Siena."

"That in itself needs an explanation. I was not at all nice then—I was very rude, very perverse. I was horrid!"

"Ah, you admit it!" cried Bernard, with a sort of quick elation.

She had been pale, but she suddenly blushed.

"Your own conduct was singular, as I remember it. It was not exactly agreeable."

"Perhaps not; but at least it was meant to be. I did n't know how to please you then, and I am far from supposing that I have learned now. But I entreat you to give me a chance."

She was silent a while; her eyes wandered over the great prospect of Paris.

"Do you know how you can please me now?" she said, at last. "By leaving me alone."

Bernard looked at her a moment, then came straight back into the drawing-room and took his hat.

"You see I avail myself of the first chance. But I shall come back tomorrow."

"I am greatly obliged to you for what you have said. Such a speech as that deserves to be listened to with consideration. You may come back tomorrow," Angela added.

On the morrow, when he came back, she received him alone.

"How did you know, at Baden, that I did n't like you?" he asked, as soon as she would allow him.

She smiled, very gently.

"You assured me yesterday that you did like me."

"I mean that I supposed I did n't. How did you know that?"

"I can only say that I observed."

"You must have observed very closely, for, superficially, I rather had the air of admiring you," said Bernard.

"It was very superficial."

"You don't mean that; for, after all, that is just what my admiration, my interest in you, were not. They were deep, they were latent. They were not superficial—they were subterranean."

"You are contradicting yourself, and I am perfectly consistent," said Angela. "Your sentiments were so well hidden that I supposed I displeased you."

"I remember that at Baden, you used to contradict yourself," Bernard answered.

"You have a terrible memory!"

"Don't call it terrible, for it sees everything now in a charming light—in the light of this understanding that we have at last arrived at, which seems to shine backward—to shine full on those Baden days."

"Have we at last arrived at an understanding?" she asked, with a grave directness which Bernard thought the most beautiful thing he had ever seen.

"It only depends upon you," he declared; and then he broke out again into a protestation of passionate tenderness. "Don't put me off this time," he cried. "You have had time to think about it; you have had time to get over the surprise, the shock. I love you, and I offer you everything that belongs to me in this world." As she looked at him with her dark, clear eyes, weighing this precious vow and yet not committing herself—"Ah, you don't forgive me!" he murmured.

She gazed at him with the same solemn brightness.

"What have I to forgive you?"

This question seemed to him enchanting. He reached forward and took her hands, and if Mrs. Vivian had come in she would have seen him kneeling at her daughter's feet.

But Mrs. Vivian remained in seclusion, and Bernard saw her only the next time he came.

"I am very happy, because I think my daughter is happy," she said.

"And what do you think of me?"

"I think you are very clever. You must promise me to be very good to her."

"I am clever enough to promise that."

"I think you are good enough to keep it," said Mrs. Vivian. She looked as happy as she said, and her happiness gave her a communicative, confidential tendency. "It is very strange how things come about—how the wheel turns round," she went on. "I suppose there is no harm in my telling you that I believe she always cared for you."

"Why did n't you tell me before?" said Bernard, with almost filial reproachfulness.

"How could I? I don't go about the world offering my daughter to people—especially to indifferent people."

"At Baden you did n't think I was indifferent. You were afraid of my not being indifferent enough."

Mrs. Vivian colored.

"Ah, at Baden I was a little too anxious!"

"Too anxious I should n't speak to your daughter!" said Bernard, laughing.

"At Baden," Mrs. Vivian went on, "I had views. But I have n't any now—I have given them up."

"That makes your acceptance of me very flattering!" Bernard exclaimed, laughing still more gaily.

"I have something better," said Mrs. Vivian, laying her finger-tips on his arm. "I have confidence."

Bernard did his best to encourage this gracious sentiment, and it seemed to him that there was something yet to be done to implant it more firmly in Angela's breast.

"I have a confession to make to you," he said to her one day. "I wish you would listen to it."

"Is it something very horrible?" Angela asked.

"Something very horrible indeed. I once did you an injury."

"An injury?" she repeated, in a tone which seemed to reduce the offence to contemptible proportions by simple vagueness of mind about it.

"I don't know what to call it," said Bernard. "A poor service—an ill-turn."

173

Angela gave a shrug, or rather an imitation of a shrug; for she was not a shrugging person.

"I never knew it."

"I misrepresented you to Gordon Wright," Bernard went on.

"Why do you speak to me of him?" she asked rather sadly.

"Does it displease you?"

She hesitated a little.

"Yes, it displeases me. If your confession has anything to do with him, I would rather not hear it."

Bernard returned to the subject another time—he had plenty of opportunities. He spent a portion of every day in the company of these dear women; and these days were the happiest of his life. The autumn weather was warm and soothing, the quartier was still deserted, and the uproar of the great city, which seemed a hundred miles away, reached them through the dense October air with a softened and muffled sound. The evenings, however, were growing cool, and before long they lighted the first fire of the season in Mrs. Vivian's heavily draped little chimney-piece. On this occasion Bernard sat there with Angela, watching the bright crackle of the wood and feeling that the charm of winter nights had begun. These two young persons were alone together in the gathering dusk; it was the hour before dinner, before the lamp had been lighted.

"I insist upon making you my confession," said Bernard. "I shall be very unhappy until you let me do it."

"Unhappy? You are the happiest of men."

"I lie upon roses, if you will; but this memory, this remorse, is a folded rose-leaf. I was completely mistaken about you at Baden; I thought all manner of evil of you—or at least I said it."

"Men are dull creatures," said Angela.

"I think they are. So much so that, as I look back upon that time, there are some things I don't understand even now."

"I don't see why you should look back. People in our position are supposed to look forward."

"You don't like those Baden days yourself," said Bernard. "You don't like to think of them."

"What a wonderful discovery!"

Bernard looked at her a moment in the brightening fire-light.

"What part was it you tried to play there?"

Angela shook her head.

"Men are dull creatures."

"I have already granted that, and I am eating humble pie in asking for an explanation."

"What did you say of me?" Angela asked, after a silence.

"I said you were a coquette. Remember that I am simply historical."

She got up and stood in front of the fire, having her hand on the chimney-piece and looking down at the blaze. For some moments she remained there. Bernard could not see her face.

"I said you were a dangerous woman to marry," he went on deliberately. "I said it because I thought it. I gave Gordon an opinion about you—it was a very unfavorable one. I could n't make you out—I thought you were playing a double part. I believed that you were ready to marry him, and yet I saw—I thought I saw—" and Bernard paused again.

"What did you see?" and Angela turned toward him.

"That you were encouraging me—playing with me."

"And you did n't like that?"

"I liked it immensely—for myself! But did n't like it for Gordon; and I must do myself the justice to say that I thought more of him than of myself."

"You were an excellent friend," said Angela, simply.

"I believe I was. And I am so still," Bernard added.

She shook her head sadly.

"Poor Mr. Wright!"

"He is a dear good fellow," said Bernard.

"Thoroughly good, and dear, doubtless to his wife, the affectionate Blanche."

"You don't like him—you don't like her," said Bernard.

"Those are two very different matters. I am very sorry for Mr. Wright."

"You need n't be that. He is doing very well."

"So you have already informed me. But I am sorry for him, all the same."

"That does n't answer my question," Bernard exclaimed, with a certain irritation. "What part were you playing?"

"What part do you think?"

"Have n't I told you I gave it up, long ago?"

Angela stood with her back to the fire, looking at him; her hands were locked behind her.

"Did it ever strike you that my position at Baden was a charming one?—knowing that I had been handed over to you to be put under the microscope—like an insect with a pin stuck through it!"

"How in the world did you know it? I thought we were particularly careful."

"How can a woman help knowing such a thing? She guesses it—she discovers it by instinct; especially if she be a proud woman."

"Ah," said Bernard, "if pride is a source of information, you must be a prodigy of knowledge!"

"I don't know that you are particularly humble!" the girl retorted. "The meekest and most submissive of her sex would not have consented to have such a bargain as that made about her—such a trick played upon her!"

"My dearest Angela, it was no bargain—no trick!" Bernard interposed.

"It was a clumsy trick—it was a bad bargain!" she declared. "At any rate I hated it—I hated the idea of your pretending to pass judgment upon me; of your having come to Baden for the purpose. It was as if Mr. Wright had been buying a horse and you had undertaken to put me through my paces!"

"I undertook nothing—I declined to undertake."

"You certainly made a study of me—and I was determined you should get your lesson wrong. I determined to embarrass, to mislead, to defeat you. Or rather, I did n't determine; I simply obeyed a natural impulse of self-defence—the impulse to evade the fierce light of criticism. I wished to put you in the wrong."

"You did it all very well. You put me admirably in the wrong."

"The only justification for my doing it at all was my doing it well," said Angela.

"You were justified then! You must have hated me fiercely."

She turned her back to him and stood looking at the fire again.

"Yes, there are some things that I did that can be accounted for only by an intense aversion."

She said this so naturally that in spite of a certain theory that was touched upon a few pages back, Bernard was a good deal bewildered. He rose from the sofa where he had been lounging and went and stood beside her a moment. Then he passed his arm round her waist and murmured an almost timorous—

"Really?"

"I don't know what you are trying to make me say!" she answered.

He looked down at her for a moment as he held her close to him.

"I don't see, after all, why I should wish to make you say it. It would only make my remorse more acute."

She was musing, with her eyes on the fire, and for a moment she made no answer; then, as if her attention were returning—

"Are you still talking about your remorse?" she asked.

"You see I put it very strongly."

"That I was a horrid creature?"

"That you were not a woman to marry."

"Ah, my poor Bernard," said Angela, "I can't attempt to prove to you that you are not inconsistent!"

The month of September drew to a close, and she consented to fix a day for their wedding. The last of October was the moment selected, and the selection was almost all that was wanting to Bernard's happiness. I say "almost," for there was a solitary spot in his consciousness which felt numb and dead—unpervaded by the joy with which the rest of his spirit seemed to thrill and tingle. The removal of this hard grain in the sweet savour of life was needed to complete his felicity. Bernard felt that he had made the necessary excision when, at the end of the month, he wrote to Gordon Wright of his engagement. He had been putting off the performance of this duty from day to day—it seemed so hard to accomplish it gracefully. He did it at the end very briefly; it struck him that this was the best way. Three days after he had sent his letter there arrived one from Gordon himself, informing Bernard that he had suddenly determined to bring Blanche to Europe. She was not well, and they would lose no time. They were to sail within a week after his writing. The letter contained a postscript—"Captain Lovelock comes with us."

CHAPTER XXIV

Bernard prepared for Gordon's arrival in Paris, which, according to his letter, would take place in a few days. He was not intending to stop in England; Blanche desired to proceed immediately to the French capital, to confer with her man-milliner, after which it was probable that they would go to Italy or to the East for the winter. "I have given her a choice of Rome or the Nile," said Gordon, "but she tells me she does n't care a fig where we go."

I say that Bernard prepared to receive his friends, and I mean that he prepared morally—or even intellectually. Materially speaking, he could simply hold himself in readiness to engage an apartment at a hotel and to go to meet them at the station. He expected to hear from Gordon as soon as this interesting trio should reach England, but the first notification he received came from a Parisian hotel. It came to him in the shape of a very short note, in the morning, shortly before lunch, and was to the effect that his friends had alighted in the Rue de la Paix the night before.

"We were tired, and I have slept late," said Gordon; "otherwise you should have heard from me earlier. Come to lunch, if possible. I want extremely to see you."

Bernard, of course, made a point of going to lunch. In as short a time as possible he found himself in Gordon's sitting-room at the Hotel Middlesex. The table was laid for the midday repast, and a gentleman stood with his back to the door, looking out of the window. As Bernard came in, this gentleman turned and exhibited the ambrosial beard, the symmetrical shape, the monocular appendage, of Captain Lovelock.

The Captain screwed his glass into his eye, and greeted Bernard in his usual fashion—that is, as if he had parted with him overnight.

"Oh, good morning! Beastly morning, is n't it? I suppose you are come to luncheon—I have come to luncheon. It ought to be on table, you know—it 's nearly two o'clock. But I dare say you have noticed foreigners are never punctual—it 's only English servants that are punctual. And they don't understand luncheon, you know—they can't make out our eating at this sort of hour. You know they always dine so beastly early. Do you remember the sort of time they used to dine at Baden?—half-past five, half-past six; some unearthly hour of that kind. That 's the sort of time you dine in America. I found they 'd invite a man at half-past six. That 's what I call being in a hurry for your food. You know they always accuse the Americans of making a rush for their victuals. I am bound to say that in New York, and that sort of place, the victuals were very good when you got them. I hope you don't mind my saying anything about America? You know the Americans are so deucedly thin-skinned—they always bristle up if you say anything against their institutions. The English don't care a rap what you say—they 've got a different sort of temper, you know. With the Americans I 'm deuced careful—I never breathe a word about anything. While I was over there I went in for being complimentary. I laid it on thick, and I found they would take all I could give them. I did n't see much of their institutions, after all; I went in for seeing the people. Some of the people were charming—upon my soul, I was surprised at some of the people. I dare say you know some of the people I saw; they were as nice people as you would see anywhere. There were always a lot of people about Mrs. Wright, you know; they told me they were all the best people. You know she is always late for everything. She always comes in after every one is there—looking so devilish pretty, pulling on her gloves. She wears the longest gloves I ever saw in my life. Upon my word, if they don't come, I think I will ring the bell and ask the waiter what 's the matter. Would n't you ring the bell? It 's a great mistake, their trying to carry out their ideas of lunching. That 's Wright's character, you know; he 's always trying to carry out some idea. When I am abroad, I go in for the foreign breakfast myself. You may depend upon it they had better give up trying to do this sort of thing at this hour."

Captain Lovelock was more disposed to conversation than Bernard had known him before. His discourse of old had been languid and fragmentary, and our hero had never heard him pursue a train of ideas through so many involutions. To Bernard's observant eye, indeed, the Captain was an altered man. His manner betrayed a certain restless desire to be agreeable, to anticipate judgment—a disposition to smile, and be civil, and entertain his auditor, a tendency to move about and look out of the window and at the clock. He struck Bernard as a trifle nervous—as less solidly planted on his feet than when he lounged along the Baden gravel-walks by the side of his usual companion—a lady for whom, apparently, his admiration was still considerable. Bernard was curious to see whether he would ring the bell to inquire into the delay attending the service of lunch; but before this sentiment, rather idle under the circumstances, was gratified, Blanche passed into the room from a neighboring apartment. To Bernard's perception Blanche, at least, was always Blanche; she was a person in whom it would not have occurred to him to expect any puzzling variation, and the tone of her little, soft, thin voice instantly rang in his ear like an echo of yesterday's talk. He had already remarked to himself that after however long an interval one might see Blanche, she re-appeared with an air of familiarity. This was in some sense, indeed, a proof of the agreeable impression she made, and she looked exceedingly pretty as she now suddenly stopped on seeing our two gentlemen, and gave a little cry of surprise.

"Ah! I did n't know you were here. They never told me. Have you been waiting a long time? How d' ye do? You must think we are polite." She held out her hand to Bernard, smiling very graciously. At Captain Lovelock she barely glanced. "I hope you are very well," she went on to Longueville; "but I need n't ask that. You 're as blooming as a rose. What in the world has happened to you? You look so brilliant—so fresh. Can you say that to a man—that he looks fresh? Or can you only say that about butter and eggs?"

"It depends upon the man," said Captain Lovelock. "You can't say that a man 's fresh who spends his time in running about after you!"

"Ah, are you here?" cried Blanche with another little cry of surprise. "I did n't notice you—I thought you were the waiter. This is what he calls running about after me," she added, to Bernard; "coming to breakfast without being asked. How queerly they have arranged the table!" she went on, gazing with her little elevated eyebrows at this piece of furniture. "I always thought that in Paris, if they could n't do anything else, they could arrange a table. I don't like that at all—those horrid little dishes on each side! Don't you think those things ought to be off the table, Mr. Longueville? I don't like to see a lot of things I 'm not eating. And I told them to have some flowers—pray, where are the flowers? Do they call those things flowers? They look as if they had come out of the landlady's bonnet! Mr. Longueville, do look at those objects."

"They are not like me—they are not very fresh," laughed Bernard.

"It 's no great matter—we have not got to eat them," growled Captain Lovelock.

"I should think you would expect to—with the luncheon you usually make!" rejoined Blanche. "Since you are here, though I did n't ask you, you might as well make yourself useful. Will you be so good as to ring the bell? If Gordon expects that we are going to wait another quarter of an hour for him he exaggerates the patience of a long-suffering wife. If you are very curious to know what he is about, he is writing letters, by way of a change. He writes about eighty a day; his correspondents must be strong people! It 's a lucky thing for me that I am married to Gordon; if I were not he might write to me—to me, to whom it 's a misery to have to answer even an invitation to dinner! To begin with, I don't know how to spell. If Captain Lovelock ever boasts that he has had letters from me, you may know it 's an invention. He has never had anything but telegrams—three telegrams—that I sent him in America about a pair of slippers that he had left at our house and that I did n't know what to do with. Captain Lovelock's slippers are no trifle to have on one's hands—on one's feet, I suppose I ought to say. For telegrams the spelling does n't matter; the people at the office correct it—or if they don't you can put it off on them. I never see anything nowadays but Gordon's back," she went on, as they took their places at table—"his noble broad back, as he sits writing his letters. That 's my principal view of my husband. I think that now we are in Paris I ought to have a portrait of it by one of the great artists. It would be such a characteristic pose. I have quite forgotten his face and I don't think I should know it."

Gordon's face, however, presented itself just at this moment; he came in quickly, with his countenance flushed with the pleasure of meeting his old friend again. He had the sun-scorched look of a traveller who has just crossed the Atlantic, and he smiled at Bernard with his honest eyes.

"Don't think me a great brute for not being here to receive you," he said, as he clasped his hand. "I was writing an important letter and I put it to myself in this way: 'If I interrupt my letter I shall have to come back and finish it; whereas if I finish it now, I can have all the rest of the day to spend with him.' So I stuck to it to the end, and now we can be inseparable."

"You may be sure Gordon reasoned it out," said Blanche, while her husband offered his hand in silence to Captain Lovelock.

"Gordon's reasoning is as fine as other people's feeling!" declared Bernard, who was conscious of a desire to say something very pleasant to Gordon, and who did not at all approve of Blanche's little ironical tone about her husband.

"And Bernard's compliments are better than either," said Gordon, laughing and taking his seat at table.

"I have been paying him compliments," Blanche went on. "I have been telling him he looks so brilliant, so blooming—as if something had happened to him, as if he had inherited a fortune. He must have been doing something very wicked, and he ought to tell us all about it, to amuse us. I am sure you are a dreadful Parisian, Mr. Longueville. Remember that we are three dull, virtuous people, exceedingly bored with each other's society, and wanting to hear something strange and exciting. If it 's a little improper, that won't spoil it."

"You certainly are looking uncommonly well," said Gordon, still smiling, across the table, at his friend. "I see what Blanche means—"

"My dear Gordon, that 's a great event," his wife interposed.

"It 's a good deal to pretend, certainly," he went on, smiling always, with his red face and his blue eyes. "But this is no great credit to me, because Bernard's superb condition would strike any one. You look as if you were going to marry the Lord Mayor's daughter!"

If Bernard was blooming, his bloom at this juncture must have deepened, and in so doing indeed have contributed an even brighter tint to his expression of salubrious happiness. It was one of the rare occasions of his life when he was at a loss for a verbal expedient.

"It 's a great match," he nevertheless murmured, jestingly. "You must excuse my inflated appearance."

"It has absorbed you so much that you have had no time to write to me," said Gordon. "I expected to hear from you after you arrived."

"I wrote to you a fortnight ago—just before receiving your own letter. You left New York before my letter reached it."

"Ah, it will have crossed us," said Gordon. "But now that we have your society I don't care. Your letters, of course, are delightful, but that is still better."

In spite of this sympathetic statement Bernard cannot be said to have enjoyed his lunch; he was thinking of something else that lay before him and that was not agreeable. He was like a man who has an acrobatic feat to perform—a wide ditch to leap, a high pole to climb—and who has a presentiment of fractures and bruises. Fortunately he was not obliged to talk much, as Mrs. Gordon displayed even more than her usual vivacity, rendering her companions the graceful service of lifting the burden of conversation from their shoulders.

"I suppose you were surprised to see us rushing out here so suddenly," she observed in the course of the repast. "We had said nothing about it when you last saw us, and I believe we are supposed to tell you everything, ain't we? I certainly have told you a great many things, and there are some of them I hope you have n't repeated. I have no doubt you have told them all over Paris, but I don't care what you tell in Paris—Paris is n't so easily shocked. Captain Lovelock does n't repeat what I tell him; I set him up as a model of discretion. I have told him some pretty bad things, and he has liked them so much he has kept them all to himself. I say my bad things to Captain Lovelock, and my good things to other people; he does n't know the difference and he is perfectly content."

"Other people as well often don't know the difference," said Gordon, gravely. "You ought always to tell us which are which."

Blanche gave her husband a little impertinent stare.

"When I am not appreciated," she said, with an attempt at superior dryness, "I am too proud to point it out. I don't know whether you know that I 'm proud," she went on, turning to Gordon and glancing at Captain Lovelock; "it 's a good thing to know. I suppose Gordon will say that I ought to be too proud to point that out; but what are you to do when no one has any imagination? You have a grain or two, Mr. Longueville; but Captain Lovelock has n't a speck. As for Gordon, je n'en parle pas! But even you, Mr. Longueville, would never imagine that I am an interesting invalid—that we are travelling for my delicate health. The doctors have n't given me up, but I have given them up. I know I don't look as if I were out of health; but that 's because I always try to look my best. My appearance proves nothing— absolutely nothing. Do you think my appearance proves anything, Captain Lovelock?"

Captain Lovelock scrutinized Blanche's appearance with a fixed and solemn eye; and then he replied—

"It proves you are very lovely."

Blanche kissed her finger-tips to him in return for this compliment.

"You only need to give Captain Lovelock a chance," she rattled on, "and he is as clever as any one. That 's what I like to do to my friends—I like to make chances for them. Captain Lovelock is like my dear little blue terrier that I left at home. If I hold out a stick he will jump over it. He won't jump without the stick; but as soon as I produce it he knows what he has to do. He looks at it a moment and then he gives his little hop. He knows he will have a lump of sugar, and Captain Lovelock expects one as well. Dear Captain Lovelock, shall I ring for a lump? Would n't it be touching? Garcon, un morceau de sucre pour Monsieur le Capitaine! But what I give Monsieur le Capitaine is moral sugar! I usually administer it in private, and he shall have a good big morsel when you go away."

Gordon got up, turning to Bernard and looking at his watch.

"Let us go away, in that case," he said, smiling, "and leave Captain Lovelock to receive his reward. We will go and take a walk; we will go up the Champs Elysees. Good morning, Monsieur le Capitaine."

185

Neither Blanche nor the Captain offered any opposition to this proposal, and Bernard took leave of his hostess and joined Gordon, who had already passed into the antechamber.

CHAPTER XXV

Gordon took his arm and they gained the street; they strolled in the direction of the Champs Elysees.

"For a little exercise and a good deal of talk, it 's the pleasantest place," said Gordon. "I have a good deal to say; I have a good deal to ask you."

Bernard felt the familiar pressure of his friend's hand, as it rested on his arm, and it seemed to him never to have lain there with so heavy a weight. It held him fast—it held him to account; it seemed a physical symbol of responsibility. Bernard was not re-assured by hearing that Gordon had a great deal to say, and he expected a sudden explosion of bitterness on the subject of Blanche's irremediable triviality. The afternoon was a lovely one—the day was a perfect example of the mellowest mood of autumn. The air was warm and filled with a golden haze, which seemed to hang about the bare Parisian trees, as if with a tender impulse to drape their nakedness. A fine day in Paris brings out a wonderfully bright and appreciative multitude of strollers and loungers, and the liberal spaces of the Champs Elysees were on this occasion filled with those placid votaries of inexpensive entertainment who abound in the French capital. The benches and chairs on the edge of the great avenue exhibited a dense fraternity of gazers, and up and down the broad walk passed the slow-moving and easily pleased pedestrians. Gordon, in spite of his announcement that he had a good deal to say, confined himself at first to superficial allusions, and Bernard after a while had the satisfaction of perceiving that he was not likely, for the moment, to strike the note of conjugal discord. He appeared, indeed, to feel no desire to speak of Blanche in any manner whatever. He fell into the humor of the hour and the scene, looked at the crowd, talked about trifles. He remarked that Paris was a wonderful place after all, and that a little glimpse of the Parisian picture was a capital thing as a change; said he was very glad they had come, and that for his part he was willing to stay three months.

"And what have you been doing with yourself?" he asked. "How have you been occupied, and what are you meaning to do?"

Bernard said nothing for a moment, and Gordon presently glanced at his face to see why he was silent. Bernard, looking askance, met his companion's eyes, and then, resting his own upon them, he stopped short. His heart was beating; it was a question of saying to Gordon outright, "I have been occupied in becoming engaged to Angela Vivian." But he could n't say it, and yet he must say something. He tried to invent something; but he could think of nothing, and still Gordon was looking at him.

"I am so glad to see you!" he exclaimed, for want of something better; and he blushed—he felt foolish, he felt false—as he said it.

"My dear Bernard!" Gordon murmured gratefully, as they walked on. "It 's very good of you to say that; I am very glad we are together again. I want to say something," he added, in a moment; "I hope you won't mind it—" Bernard gave a little laugh at his companion's scruples, and Gordon continued. "To tell the truth, it has sometimes seemed to me that we were not so good friends as we used to be—that something had come between us—I don't know what, I don't know why. I don't know what to call it but a sort of lowering of the temperature. I don't know whether you have felt it, or whether it has been simply a fancy of mine. Whatever it may have been, it 's all over, is n't it? We are too old friends—too good friends—not to stick together. Of course, the rubs of life may occasionally loosen the cohesion; but it is very good to feel that, with a little direct contact, it may easily be re-established. Is n't that so? But we should n't reason about these things; one feels them, and that 's enough."

Gordon spoke in his clear, cheerful voice, and Bernard listened intently. It seemed to him there was an undertone of pain and effort in his companion's speech; it was that of an unhappy man trying to be wise and make the best of things.

"Ah, the rubs of life—the rubs of life!" Bernard repeated vaguely.

"We must n't mind them," said Gordon, with a conscientious laugh. "We must toughen our hides; or, at the worst, we must plaster up our bruises. But why should we choose this particular place and hour for talking of the pains of life?" he went on. "Are we not in the midst of its pleasures? I mean, henceforth, to cultivate its pleasures. What are yours, just now, Bernard? Is n't it supposed that in Paris one must amuse one's self? How have you been amusing yourself?"

"I have been leading a very quiet life," said Bernard.

"I notice that 's what people always say when they have been particularly dissipated. What have you done? Whom have you seen that one knows?"

Bernard was silent a moment.

"I have seen some old friends of yours," he said at last. "I have seen Mrs. Vivian and her daughter."

"Ah!" Gordon made this exclamation, and then stopped short. Bernard looked at him, but Gordon was looking away; his eyes had caught some one in the crowd. Bernard followed the direction they had taken, and then Gordon went on: "Talk of the devil—excuse the adage! Are not those the ladies in question?"

Mrs. Vivian and her daughter were, in fact, seated among a great many other quiet people, in a couple of hired chairs, at the edge of the great avenue. They were turned toward our two friends, and when Bernard distinguished them, in the well-dressed multitude, they were looking straight at Gordon Wright.

"They see you!" said Bernard.

"You say that as if I wished to run away," Gordon answered. "I don't want to run away; on the contrary, I want to speak to them."

"That 's easily done," said Bernard, and they advanced to the two ladies.

Mrs. Vivian and her daughter rose from their chairs as they came; they had evidently rapidly exchanged observations, and had decided that it would facilitate their interview with Gordon Wright to receive him standing. He made his way to them through the crowd, blushing deeply, as he always did when excited; then he stood there bare-headed, shaking hands with each of them, with a fixed smile, and with nothing, apparently, to say. Bernard

189

watched Angela's face; she was giving his companion a beautiful smile. Mrs. Vivian was delicately cordial.

"I was sure it was you," said Gordon at last. "We were just talking of you."

"Did Mr. Longueville deny it was we?" asked Mrs. Vivian, archly; "after we had supposed that we had made an impression on him!"

"I knew you were in Paris—we were in the act of talking of you," Gordon went on. "I am very glad to see you."

Bernard had shaken hands with Angela, looking at her intently; and in her eyes, as his own met them, it seemed to him that there was a gleam of mockery. At whom was she mocking—at Gordon, or at himself? Bernard was uncomfortable enough not to care to be mocked; but he felt even more sorry that Gordon should be.

"We also knew you were coming—Mr. Longueville had told us," said Mrs. Vivian; "and we have been expecting the pleasure of seeing Blanche. Dear little Blanche!"

"Dear little Blanche will immediately come and see you," Gordon replied.

"Immediately, we hope," said Mrs. Vivian. "We shall be so very glad." Bernard perceived that she wished to say something soothing and sympathetic to poor Gordon; having it, as he supposed, on her conscience that, after having once encouraged him to regard himself as indispensable (in the capacity of son-in-law) to her happiness, she should now present to him the spectacle of a felicity which had established itself without his aid. "We were so very much interested in your marriage," she went on. "We thought it so—so delightful."

Gordon fixed his eyes on the ground for a moment.

"I owe it partly to you," he answered. "You had done so much for Blanche. You had so cultivated her mind and polished her manners that her attractions were doubled, and I fell an easy victim to them."

He uttered these words with an exaggerated solemnity, the result of which was to produce, for a moment, an almost embarrassing silence. Bernard was rapidly becoming more and more impatient of his own embarrassment, and now he exclaimed, in a loud and jovial voice—

"Blanche makes victims by the dozen! I was a victim last winter; we are all victims!"

"Dear little Blanche!" Mrs. Vivian murmured again.

Angela had said nothing; she had simply stood there, making no attempt to address herself to Gordon, and yet with no affectation of reserve or of indifference. Now she seemed to feel the impulse to speak to him.

"When Blanche comes to see us, you must be sure to come with her," she said, with a friendly smile.

Gordon looked at her, but he said nothing.

"We were so sorry to hear she is out of health," Angela went on.

Still Gordon was silent, with his eyes fixed on her expressive and charming face.

"It is not serious," he murmured at last.

"She used to be so well—so bright," said Angela, who also appeared to have the desire to say something kind and comfortable.

Gordon made no response to this; he only looked at her.

"I hope you are well, Miss Vivian," he broke out at last.

"Very well, thank you."

"Do you live in Paris?"

"We have pitched our tent here for the present."

"Do you like it?"

"I find it no worse than other places."

Gordon appeared to desire to talk with her; but he could think of nothing to say. Talking with her was a pretext for looking at her; and Bernard, who thought she had never been so handsome as at that particular moment, smiling at her troubled ex-lover, could easily conceive that his friend should desire to prolong this privilege.

"Have you been sitting here long?" Gordon asked, thinking of something at last.

"Half an hour. We came out to walk, and my mother felt tired. It is time we should turn homeward," Angela added.

"Yes, I am tired, my daughter. We must take a voiture, if Mr. Longueville will be so good as to find us one," said Mrs. Vivian.

Bernard, professing great alacrity, looked about him; but he still lingered near his companions. Gordon had thought of something else. "Have you been to Baden again?" Bernard heard him ask. But at this moment Bernard espied at a distance an empty hackney-carriage crawling up the avenue, and he was obliged to go and signal to it. When he came back, followed by the vehicle, the two ladies, accompanied by Gordon, had come to the edge of the pavement. They shook hands with Gordon before getting into the cab, and Mrs. Vivian exclaimed—

"Be sure you give our love to your dear wife!"

Then the two ladies settled themselves and smiled their adieux, and the little victoria rumbled away at an easy pace, while Bernard stood with Gordon, looking after it. They watched it a moment, and then Gordon turned to his companion. He looked at Bernard for some moments intently, with a singular expression.

"It is strange for me to see her!" he said, presently.

"I hope it is not altogether disagreeable," Bernard answered smiling.

"She is delightfully handsome," Gordon went on.

"She is a beautiful woman."

"And the strange thing is that she strikes me now so differently," Gordon continued. "I used to think her so mysterious—so ambiguous. She seems to be now so simple."

"Ah," said Bernard, laughing, "that's an improvement!"

"So simple and so good!" Gordon exclaimed.

Bernard laid his hand on his companion's shoulder, shaking his head slowly.

"You must not think too much about that," he said.

"So simple—so good—so charming!" Gordon repeated.

"Ah, my dear Gordon!" Bernard murmured.

But still Gordon continued.

"So intelligent, so reasonable, so sensible."

"Have you discovered all that in two minutes' talk?"

"Yes, in two minutes' talk. I should n't hesitate about her now!"

"It 's better you should n't say that," said Bernard.

"Why should n't I say it? It seems to me it 's my duty to say it."

"No—your duty lies elsewhere," said Bernard. "There are two reasons. One is that you have married another woman."

"What difference does that make?" cried Gordon.

Bernard made no attempt to answer this inquiry; he simply went on—

"The other is—the other is—"

But here he paused.

"What is the other?" Gordon asked.

"That I am engaged to marry Miss Vivian."

And with this Bernard took his hand off Gordon's shoulder.

Gordon stood staring.

"To marry Miss Vivian?"

Now that Bernard had heard himself say it, audibly, distinctly, loudly, the spell of his apprehension seemed broken, and he went on bravely.

"We are to be married very shortly. It has all come about within a few weeks. It will seem to you very strange—perhaps you won't like it. That 's why I have hesitated to tell you."

Gordon turned pale; it was the first time Bernard had ever seen him do so; evidently he did not like it. He stood staring and frowning.

"Why, I thought—I thought," he began at last—"I thought that you disliked her!"

"I supposed so, too," said Bernard. "But I have got over that."

Gordon turned away, looking up the great avenue into the crowd. Then turning back, he said—

"I am very much surprised."

"And you are not pleased!"

Gordon fixed his eyes on the ground a moment.

"I congratulate you on your engagement," he said at last, looking up with a face that seemed to Bernard hard and unnatural.

"It is very good of you to say that, but of course you can't like it! I was sure you would n't like it. But what could I do? I fell in love with her, and I could n't run away simply to spare you a surprise. My dear Gordon," Bernard added, "you will get used to it."

"Very likely," said Gordon, dryly. "But you must give me time."

"As long as you like!"

Gordon stood for a moment again staring down at the ground.

"Very well, then, I will take my time," he said. "Good-bye!"

And he turned away, as if to walk off alone.

"Where are you going?" asked Bernard, stopping him.

"I don't know—to the hotel, anywhere. To try to get used to what you have told me."

"Don't try too hard; it will come of itself," said Bernard.

"We shall see!"

And Gordon turned away again.

"Do you prefer to go alone?"

"Very much—if you will excuse me!"

"I have asked you to excuse a greater want of ceremony!" said Bernard, smiling.

"I have not done so yet!" Gordon rejoined; and marching off, he mingled with the crowd.

Bernard watched him till he lost sight of him, and then, dropping into the first empty chair that he saw, he sat and reflected that his friend liked it quite as little as he had feared.

CHAPTER XXVI

Bernard sat thinking for a long time; at first with a good deal of mortification—at last with a good deal of bitterness. He felt angry at last; but he was not angry with himself. He was displeased with poor Gordon, and with Gordon's displeasure. He was uncomfortable, and he was vexed at his discomfort. It formed, it seemed to him, no natural part of his situation; he had had no glimpse of it in the book of fate where he registered on a fair blank page his betrothal to a charming girl. That Gordon should be surprised, and even a little shocked and annoyed—this was his right and his privilege; Bernard had been prepared for that, and had determined to make the best of it. But it must not go too far; there were limits to the morsel of humble pie that he was disposed to swallow. Something in Gordon's air and figure, as he went off in a huff, looking vicious and dangerous—yes, that was positively his look—left a sinister impression on Bernard's mind, and, after a while, made him glad to take refuge in being angry. One would like to know what Gordon expected, par exemple! Did he expect Bernard to give up Angela simply to save him a shock; or to back out of his engagement by way of an ideal reparation? No, it was too absurd, and, if Gordon had a wife of his own, why in the name of justice should not Bernard have one?

Being angry was a relief, but it was not exactly a solution, and Bernard, at last, leaving his place, where for an hour or two he had been absolutely unconscious of everything that went on around him, wandered about for some time in deep restlessness and irritation. At one moment he thought of going back to Gordon's hotel, to see him, to explain. But then he became aware that he was too angry for that—to say nothing of Gordon's being too angry also; and, moreover, that there was nothing to explain. He was to marry Angela Vivian; that was a very simple fact—it needed no explanation. Was it so wonderful, so inconceivable, an incident so unlikely to happen? He went, as he always did on Sunday, to dine with Mrs. Vivian, and it seemed to him that he perceived in the two ladies some symptoms of a discomposure which had the same origin as his own. Bernard, on this occasion, at dinner, failed to make himself particularly agreeable; he ate fast—as if he had no idea what he was eating, and talked little; every now and then his eyes rested for some time upon Angela, with a strange, eagerly excited expression, as if he were looking her over and trying to make up his mind about her afresh. This young lady bore his inscrutable scrutiny with a deal of superficial composure; but she was also silent, and she returned his gaze, from time to time, with an air of unusual anxiety. She was thinking, of course, of Gordon, Bernard said to himself; and a woman's first meeting, in after years, with an ex-lover must always make a certain impression upon her. Gordon, however, had never been a lover, and if Bernard noted Angela's gravity it was not because he felt jealous. "She is simply sorry for him," he said to himself; and by the time he had finished his dinner it began to come back to him that he was sorry, too. Mrs. Vivian was probably sorry as well, for she had a slightly confused and preoccupied look—a look from which, even in the midst of his chagrin, Bernard extracted some entertainment. It was Mrs. Vivian's intermittent conscience that had been reminded of one of its lapses; her meeting with Gordon Wright had recalled the least exemplary episode of her life—the time when she whispered mercenary counsel in the ear of a daughter who sat, grave and pale, looking at her with eyes that wondered. Mrs. Vivian blushed a little now, when she met Bernard's eyes; and to remind herself that she was after all a virtuous woman, talked as much as possible about superior and harmless things—the beauty of the autumn weather, the pleasure of seeing French papas walking about on Sunday with their progeny in their hands, the peculiarities of the pulpit-oratory of the country as exemplified in the discourse of a Protestant pasteur whom she had been to hear in the morning.

When they rose from table and went back into her little drawing-room, she left her daughter alone for awhile with Bernard. The two were standing together before the fire; Bernard watched Mrs. Vivian close the door softly behind her. Then, looking for a moment at his companion—

"He is furious!" he announced at last.

"Furious?" said Angela. "Do you mean Mr. Wright?"

"The amiable, reasonable Gordon. He takes it very hard."

"Do you mean about me?" asked Angela.

"It 's not with you he 's furious, of course; it is with me. He won't let me off easily."

Angela looked for a moment at the fire.

"I am very sorry for him," she said, at last.

"It seems to me I am the one to be pitied," said Bernard; "and I don't see what compassion you, of all people in the world, owe him."

Angela again rested her eyes on the fire; then presently, looking up—

"He liked me very much," she remarked.

"All the more shame to him!" cried Bernard.

"What do you mean?" asked the girl, with her beautiful stare.

"If he liked you, why did he give you up?"

"He did n't give me up."

"What do you mean, please?" asked Bernard, staring back at her.

"I sent him away—I refused him," said Angela.

"Yes; but you thought better of it, and your mother had persuaded you that if he should ask you again, you had better accept him. Then it was that he backed out—in consequence of what I said to him on his return from England."

She shook her head slowly, with a strange smile.

"My poor Bernard, you are talking very wildly. He did ask me again."

"That night?" cried Bernard.

"The night he came back from England—the last time I saw him, until to-day."

"After I had denounced you?" our puzzled hero exclaimed, frowning portentously.

"I am sorry to let you know the small effect of your words!"

Bernard folded his hands together—almost devoutly—and stood gazing at her with a long, inarticulate murmur of satisfaction.

"Ah! then, I did n't injure you—I did n't deprive you of a chance?"

"Oh, sir, the intention on your part was the same!" Angela exclaimed.

"Then all my uneasiness, all my remorse, were wasted?" he went on.

But she kept the same tone, and its tender archness only gave a greater sweetness to his sense of relief.

"It was a very small penance for you to pay."

"You dismissed him definitely, and that was why he vanished?" asked Bernard, wondering still.

"He gave me another 'chance,' as you elegantly express it, and I declined to take advantage of it."

"Ah, well, now," cried Bernard, "I am sorry for him!"

"I was very kind—very respectful," said Angela. "I thanked him from the bottom of my heart; I begged his pardon very humbly for the wrong—if wrong it was—that I was doing him. I did n't in the least require of him that he should leave Baden at seven o'clock the next morning. I had no idea that he would do so, and that was the reason that I insisted to my mother that we ourselves should go away. When we went I knew nothing about his having gone, and I supposed he was still there. I did n't wish to meet him again."

Angela gave this information slowly, softly, with pauses between the sentences, as if she were recalling the circumstances with a certain effort; and meanwhile Bernard, with his transfigured face and his eyes fixed upon her lips, was moving excitedly about the room.

"Well, he can't accuse me, then!" he broke out again. "If what I said had no more effect upon him than that, I certainly did him no wrong."

"I think you are rather vexed he did n't believe you," said Angela.

"I confess I don't understand it. He had all the air of it. He certainly had not the air of a man who was going to rush off and give you the last proof of his confidence."

"It was not a proof of confidence," said Angela. "It had nothing to do with me. It was as between himself and you; it was a proof of independence. He did believe you, more or less, and what you said fell in with his own impressions—strange impressions that they were, poor man! At the same time, as I say, he liked me, too; it was out of his liking me that all his trouble came! He caught himself in the act of listening to you too credulously—and that seemed to him unmanly and dishonorable. The sensation brought with it a reaction, and to prove to himself that in such a matter he could be influenced by nobody, he marched away, an hour after he had talked with you, and, in the teeth of his perfect mistrust, confirmed by your account of my irregularities—heaven forgive you both!—again asked me to be his wife. But he hoped I would refuse!"

"Ah," cried Bernard, "the recreant! He deserved—he deserved—"

"That I should accept him?" Angela asked, smiling still.

Bernard was so much affected by this revelation, it seemed to him to make such a difference in his own responsibility and to lift such a weight off his conscience, that he broke out again into the liveliest ejaculations of relief.

"Oh, I don't care for anything, now, and I can do what I please! Gordon may hate me, and I shall be sorry for him; but it 's not my fault, and I owe him no reparation. No, no; I am free!"

"It 's only I who am not, I suppose," said Angela, "and the reparation must come from me! If he is unhappy, I must take the responsibility."

"Ah yes, of course," said Bernard, kissing her.

"But why should he be unhappy?" asked Angela. "If I refused him, it was what he wanted."

"He is hard to please," Bernard rejoined. "He has got a wife of his own."

"If Blanche does n't please him, he is certainly difficult;" and Angela mused a little. "But you told me the other day that they were getting on so well."

"Yes, I believe I told you," Bernard answered, musing a little too.

"You are not attending to what I say."

"No, I am thinking of something else—I am thinking of what it was that made you refuse him that way, at the last, after you had let your mother hope." And Bernard stood there, smiling at her.

"Don't think any more; you will not find out," the girl declared, turning away.

"Ah, it was cruel of you to let me think I was wrong all these years," he went on; "and, at the time, since you meant to refuse him, you might have been more frank with me."

"I thought my fault had been that I was too frank."

"I was densely stupid, and you might have made me understand better."

"Ah," said Angela, "you ask a great deal of a girl!"

"Why have you let me go on so long thinking that my deluded words had had an effect upon Gordon—feeling that I had done you a brutal wrong? It was real to me, the wrong—and I have told you of the pangs and the shame which, for so many months, it has cost me! Why have you never undeceived me until to-day, and then only by accident?"

At this question Angela blushed a little; then she answered, smiling—

"It was my vengeance."

Bernard shook his head.

"That won't do—you don't mean it. You never cared—you were too proud to care; and when I spoke to you about my fault, you did n't even know what I meant. You might have told me, therefore, that my remorse was idle, that what I said to Gordon had not been of the smallest consequence, and that the rupture had come from yourself."

For some time Angela said nothing, then at last she gave him one of the deeply serious looks with which her face was occasionally ornamented.

"If you want really to know, then—can't you see that your remorse seemed to me connected in a certain way with your affection; a sort of guarantee of it? You thought you had injured some one or other, and that seemed to be mixed up with your loving me, and therefore I let it alone."

"Ah," said Bernard, "my remorse is all gone, and yet I think I love you about as much as ever! So you see how wrong you were not to tell me."

"The wrong to you I don't care about. It is very true I might have told you for Mr. Wright's sake. It would perhaps have made him look better. But as you never attacked him for deserting me, it seemed needless for me to defend him."

"I confess," said Bernard, "I am quite at sea about Gordon's look in the matter. Is he looking better now—or is he looking worse? You put it very well just now; I was attending to you, though you said I was not. If he hoped you would refuse him, with whom is his quarrel at present? And why was he so cool to me for months after we parted at Baden? If that was his state of mind, why should he accuse me of inconsistency?"

"There is something in it, after all, that a woman can understand. I don't know whether a man can. He hoped I would refuse him, and yet when I had done so he was vexed. After a while his vexation subsided, and he married poor Blanche; but, on learning to-day that I had accepted you, it flickered up again. I suppose that was natural enough; but it won't be serious."

"What will not be serious, my dear?" asked Mrs. Vivian, who had come back to the drawing-room, and who, apparently, could not hear that the attribute in question was wanting in any direction, without some alarm.

"Shall I tell mamma, Bernard?" said Angela.

"Ah, my dear child, I hope it 's nothing that threatens your mutual happiness," mamma murmured, with gentle earnestness.

"Does it threaten our mutual happiness, Bernard?" the girl went on, smiling.

"Let Mrs. Vivian decide whether we ought to let it make us miserable," said Bernard. "Dear Mrs. Vivian, you are a casuist, and this is a nice case."

"Is it anything about poor Mr. Wright?" the elder lady inquired.

"Why do you say 'poor' Mr. Wright?" asked Bernard.

"Because I am sadly afraid he is not happy with Blanche."

"How did you discover that—without seeing them together?"

"Well, perhaps you will think me very fanciful," said Mrs. Vivian; "but it was by the way he looked at Angela. He has such an expressive face."

"He looked at me very kindly, mamma," Angela observed.

"He regularly stared, my daughter. In any one else I should have said it was rude. But his situation is so peculiar; and one could see that he admired you still." And Mrs. Vivian gave a little soft sigh.

"Ah! she is thinking of the thirty thousand a year," Bernard said to himself.

"I am sure I hope he admires me still," the girl cried, laughing. "There is no great harm in that."

"He was comparing you with Blanche—and he was struck with the contrast."

"It could n't have been in my favor. If it 's a question of being looked at, Blanche bears it better than I."

"Poor little Blanche!" murmured Mrs. Vivian, sweetly.

"Why did you tell me he was so happy with her?" Angela asked, turning to Bernard, abruptly.

Bernard gazed at her a moment, with his eyebrows raised.

"I never saw any one ask such sudden questions!" he exclaimed.

"You can answer me at your leisure," she rejoined, turning away.

"It was because I adored you."

"You would n't say that at your leisure," said the girl.

Mrs. Vivian stood watching them.

"You, who are so happy together, you ought to think kindly of others who are less fortunate."

"That is very true, Mrs. Vivian; and I have never thought of any one so kindly as I have of Gordon for the last year."

Angela turned round again.

"Is Blanche so very bad, then?"

"You will see for yourself!"

"Ah, no," said Mrs. Vivian, "she is not bad; she is only very light. I am so glad she is to be near us again. I think a great deal can be done by association. We must help her, Angela. I think we helped her before."

"It is also very true that she is light, Mrs. Vivian," Bernard observed, "and if you could make her a little heavier, I should be tremendously grateful."

Bernard's prospective mother-in-law looked at him a little.

"I don't know whether you are laughing at me—I always think you are. But I shall not give up Blanche for that. I never give up any one that I have once tried to help. Blanche will come back to me."

Mrs. Vivian had hardly spoken when the sharp little vibration of her door-bell was heard in the hall. Bernard stood for a moment looking at the door of the drawing-room.

"It is poor Gordon come to make a scene!" he announced.

"Is that what you mean—that he opposed your marriage?" asked Mrs. Vivian, with a frightened air.

"I don't know what he proposes to do with Blanche," said Bernard, laughing.

There were voices in the hall. Angela had been listening.

"You say she will come back to you, mamma," she exclaimed. "Here she is arrived!"

CHAPTER XXVII

At the same moment the door was thrown open, and Mrs. Gordon appeared on the threshold with a gentleman behind her. Blanche stood an instant looking into the lighted room and hesitating—flushed a little, smiling, extremely pretty.

"May I come in?" she said, "and may I bring in Captain Lovelock?"

The two ladies, of course, fluttering toward her with every demonstration of hospitality, drew her into the room, while Bernard proceeded to greet the Captain, who advanced with a certain awkward and bashful majesty, almost sweeping with his great stature Mrs. Vivian's humble ceiling. There was a tender exchange of embraces between Blanche and her friends, and the charming visitor, losing no time, began to chatter with her usual volubility. Mrs. Vivian and Angela made her companion graciously welcome; but Blanche begged they would n't mind him—she had only brought him as a watch-dog.

"His place is on the rug," she said. "Captain Lovelock, go and lie down on the rug."

"Upon my soul, there is nothing else but rugs in these French places!" the Captain rejoined, looking round Mrs. Vivian's salon. "Which rug do you mean?"

Mrs. Vivian had remarked to Blanche that it was very kind of her to come first, and Blanche declared that she could not have laid her head on her pillow before she had seen her dear Mrs. Vivian.

"Do you suppose I would wait because I am married?" she inquired, with a keen little smile in her charming eyes. "I am not so much married as that, I can tell you! Do you think I look much as if I were married, with no one to bring me here to-night but Captain Lovelock?"

"I am sure Captain Lovelock is a very gallant escort," said Mrs. Vivian.

"Oh, he was not afraid—that is, he was not afraid of the journey, though it lay all through those dreadful wild Champs Elysees. But when we arrived, he was afraid to come in—to come up here. Captain Lovelock is so modest, you know—in spite of all the success he had in America. He will tell you about the success he had in America; it quite makes up for the defeat of the British army in the Revolution. They were defeated in the Revolution, the British, were n't they? I always told him so, but he insists they were not. 'How do we come to be free, then?' I always ask him; 'I suppose you admit that we are free.' Then he becomes personal and says that I am free enough, certainly. But it 's the general fact I mean; I wish you would tell him about the general fact. I think he would believe you, because he knows you know a great deal about history and all that. I don't mean this evening, but some time when it is convenient. He did n't want to come in—he wanted to stay in the carriage and smoke a cigar; he thought you would n't like it, his coming with me the first time. But I told him he need n't mind that, for I would certainly explain. I would be very careful to let you know that I brought him only as a substitute. A substitute for whom? A substitute for my husband, of course. My dear Mrs. Vivian, of course I ought to bring you some pretty message from Gordon—that he is dying to come and see you, only that he had nineteen letters to write and that he could n't possibly stir from his fireside. I suppose a good wife ought to invent excuses for her husband—ought to throw herself into the breach; is n't that what they call it? But I am afraid I am not a good wife. Do you think I am a good wife, Mr. Longueville? You once stayed three months with us, and you had a chance to see. I don't ask you that seriously, because you never tell the truth. I always do; so I will say I am not a good wife. And then the breach is too big, and I am too little. Oh, I am too little, Mrs. Vivian; I know I am too little. I am the smallest woman living; Gordon can scarcely see me with a microscope, and I believe he has the most powerful one in America. He is going to get another here; that is one of the things he came abroad for; perhaps it will do better. I do tell the truth, don't I, Mrs. Vivian? I have that merit, if I have n't any other. You once told me so at Baden; you said you could say one thing for me, at any rate—that I did n't tell fibs. You were very nice to me at Baden," Blanche went on, with her little intent smile, laying her hand in that of her hostess. "You see, I have never forgotten it. So, to keep up my reputation, I must tell the truth about Gordon. He simply said he would n't come—voila! He gave no reason and he did n't send you any pretty message. He simply declined, and he went out somewhere else. So you see he is n't writing letters. I don't know where he can have gone; perhaps he has gone to the theatre. I know it is n't proper to go to the theatre on Sunday evening; but they say charity begins at home, and as Gordon's does n't begin at home, perhaps it does n't begin anywhere. I told him that if he would n't come with me I would come alone, and he said I might do as I chose—that he was not in a humor for making visits. I wanted to come to you very much; I had been thinking about it all day; and I am so fond of a visit like this in the evening, without being invited. Then I thought perhaps you had a salon—does n't every one in Paris have a salon? I tried to have a salon in New York, only Gordon said it would n't do. He said it was n't in our manners. Is this a salon to-night, Mrs. Vivian? Oh, do say it is; I should like so much to see Captain Lovelock in a salon! By good fortune he happened to have been dining with us; so I told him he must bring me here. I told you I would explain, Captain Lovelock," she added, "and I hope you think I have made it clear."

The Captain had turned very red during this wandering discourse. He sat pulling his beard and shifting the position which, with his stalwart person, he had taken up on a little gilded chair—a piece of furniture which every now and then gave a delicate creak.

"I always understand you well enough till you begin to explain," he rejoined, with a candid, even if embarrassed, laugh. "Then, by Jove, I 'm quite in the woods. You see such a lot more in things than most people. Does n't she, Miss Vivian?"

"Blanche has a fine imagination," said Angela, smiling frankly at the charming visitor.

When Blanche was fairly adrift upon the current of her articulate reflections, it was the habit of her companions—indeed, it was a sort of tacit agreement among them—simply to make a circle and admire. They sat about and looked at her—yawning, perhaps, a little at times, but on the whole very well entertained, and often exchanging a smiling commentary with each other. She looked at them, smiled at them each, in succession. Every one had his turn, and this always helped to give Blanche an audience. Incoherent and aimless as much of her talk was, she never looked prettier than in the attitude of improvisation—or rather, I should say, than in the hundred attitudes which she assumed at such a time. Perpetually moving, she was yet constantly graceful, and while she twisted her body and turned her head, with charming hands that never ceased to gesticulate, and little, conscious, brilliant eyes that looked everywhere at once—eyes that seemed to chatter even faster than her lips—she made you forget the nonsense she poured forth, or think of it only as a part of her personal picturesqueness. The thing was a regular performance; the practice of unlimited chatter had made her perfect. She rested upon her audience and held it together, and the sight of half a dozen pairs of amused and fascinated faces led her from one piece of folly to another. On this occasion, her audience was far from failing her, for they were all greatly interested. Captain Lovelock's interest, as we know, was chronic, and our three other friends were much occupied with a matter with which Blanche was intimately connected. Bernard, as he listened to her, smiling mechanically, was not encouraged. He remembered what Mrs. Vivian had said shortly before she came in, and it was not pleasant to him to think that Gordon had been occupied half the day in contrasting the finest girl in the world with this magnified butterfly. The contrast was sufficiently striking as Angela sat there near her, very still, bending her handsome head a little, with her hands crossed in her lap, and on her lips a kind but inscrutable smile. Mrs. Vivian was on the sofa next to Blanche, one of whose hands, when it was not otherwise occupied, she occasionally took into her own.

"Dear little Blanche!" she softly murmured, at intervals.

These few remarks represent a longer pause than Mrs. Gordon often suffered to occur. She continued to deliver herself upon a hundred topics, and it hardly matters where we take her up.

"I have n't the least idea what we are going to do. I have nothing to say about it whatever. Gordon tells me every day I must decide, and then I ask Captain Lovelock what he thinks; because, you see, he always thinks a great deal. Captain Lovelock says he does n't care a fig—that he will go wherever I go. So you see that does n't carry us very far. I want to settle on some place where Captain Lovelock won't go, but he won't help me at all. I think it will look better for him not to follow us; don't you think it will look better, Mrs. Vivian? Not that I care in the least where we go—or whether Captain Lovelock follows us, either. I don't take any interest in anything, Mrs. Vivian; don't you think that is very sad? Gordon may go anywhere he likes—to St. Petersburg, or to Bombay."

"You might go to a worse place than Bombay," said Captain Lovelock, speaking with the authority of an Anglo-Indian rich in reminiscences.

Blanche gave him a little stare.

"Ah well, that 's knocked on the head! From the way you speak of it, I think you would come after us; and the more I think of that, the more I see it would n't do. But we have got to go to some southern place, because I am very unwell. I have n't the least idea what 's the matter with me, and neither has any one else; but that does n't make any difference. It 's settled that I am out of health. One might as well be out of it as in it, for all the advantage it is. If you are out of health, at any rate you can come abroad. It was Gordon's discovery—he 's always making discoveries. You see it 's because I 'm so silly; he can always put it down to my being an invalid. What I should like to do, Mrs. Vivian, would be to spend the winter with you—just sitting on the sofa beside you and holding your hand. It would be rather tiresome for you; but I really think it would be better for me than anything else. I have never forgotten how kind you were to me before my marriage—that summer at Baden. You were everything to me—you and Captain Lovelock. I am sure I should be happy if I never went out of this lovely room. You have got it so beautifully arranged—I mean to do my own room just like it when I go home. And you have got such lovely clothes. You never used to say anything about it, but you and Angela always had better clothes than I. Are you always so quiet and serious—never talking about chiffons—always reading some wonderful book? I wish you would let me come and stay with you. If you only ask me, Gordon would be too delighted. He would n't have to trouble about me any more. He could go and live over in the Latin Quarter—that 's the desire of his heart—and think of nothing but old bottles. I know it is n't very good manners to beg for an invitation," Blanche went on, smiling with a gentler radiance; "but when it 's a question of one's health. One wants to keep one's self alive—does n't one? One wants to keep one's self going. It would be so good for me, Mrs. Vivian; it would really be very good for me!"

She had turned round more and more to her hostess as she talked; and at last she had given both her hands to Mrs. Vivian, and sat looking at her with a singular mixture of earnestness and jocosity. It was hard to know whether Blanche were expressing a real desire or a momentary caprice, and whether this abrupt little petition were to be taken seriously, or treated merely as a dramatic pose in a series of more or less effective attitudes. Her smile had become almost a grimace, she was flushed, she showed her pretty teeth; but there was a little passionate quiver in her voice.

"My dear child," said Mrs. Vivian, "we should be delighted to have you pay us a visit, and we should be so happy if we could do you any good. But I am afraid you would very soon get tired of us, and I ought to tell you, frankly, that our little home is to be—a broken up. You know there is to be a—a change," the good lady continued, with a hesitation which apparently came from a sense of walking on uncertain ground, while she glanced with a smile at Bernard and Angela.

Blanche sat there with her little excited, yet innocent—too innocent—stare; her eyes followed Mrs. Vivian's. They met Bernard's for an instant, and for some reason, at this moment, Bernard flushed.

He rose quickly and walked away to the window where he stood looking out into the darkness. "The devil—the devil!" he murmured to himself; "she does n't even know we are to be married—Gordon has n't been able to trust himself to tell her!" And this fact seemed pregnant with evidence as to Gordon's state of mind; it did not appear to simplify the situation. After a moment, while Bernard stood there with his back turned—he felt rather awkward and foolish—he heard Blanche begin with her little surprised voice.

"Ah, you are going away? You are going to travel? But that 's charming; we can travel together. You are not going to travel? What then are you going to do? You are going back to America? Ah, but you must n't do that, as soon as I come abroad; that 's not nice or friendly, Mrs. Vivian, to your poor little old Blanche. You are not going back to America? Ah, then, I give it up! What 's the great mystery? Is it something about Angela? There was always a mystery about Angela. I hope you won't mind my saying it, my dear; but I was always afraid of you. My husband—he admires you so much, you know—has often tried to explain you to me; but I have never understood. What are you going to do now? Are you going into a convent? Are you going to be—A-a-h!"

And, suddenly, quickly, interrupting herself, Mrs. Gordon gave a long, wondering cry. Bernard heard her spring to her feet, and the two other ladies rise from their seats. Captain Lovelock got up as well; Bernard heard him knock over his little gilded chair. There was a pause, during which Blanche went through a little mute exhibition of amazement and pleasure. Bernard turned round, to receive half a dozen quick questions.

"What are you hiding away for? What are you blushing for? I never saw you do anything like that before! Why do you look so strange, and what are you making me say? Angela, is it true—is there something like that?" Without waiting for the answer to this last question, Blanche threw herself upon Mrs. Vivian. "My own Mrs. Vivian," she cried, "is she married?"

"My dear Blanche," said Bernard, coming forward, "has not Gordon told you? Angela and I are not married, but we hope to be before long. Gordon only knew it this morning; we ourselves have only known it a short time. There is no mystery about it, and we only want your congratulations."

"Well, I must say you have been very quiet about it!" cried Blanche. "When I was engaged, I wrote you all a letter."

"By Jove, she wrote to me!" observed Captain Lovelock.

Angela went to her and kissed her.

"Your husband does n't seem to have explained me very successfully!"

Mrs. Gordon held Bernard's intended for a moment at arm's length, with both her hands, looking at her with eyes of real excitement and wonder. Then she folded her in a prolonged, an exaggerated, embrace.

"Why did n't he tell me—why did n't he tell me?" she presently began. "He has had all day to tell me, and it was very cruel of him to let me come here without knowing it. Could anything be more absurd—more awkward? You don't think it 's awkward—you don't mind it? Ah well, you are very good! But I like it, Angela—I like it extremely, immensely. I think it 's delightful, and I wonder it never occurred to me. Has it been going on long? Ah, of course, it has been going on! Did n't it begin at Baden, and did n't I see it there? Do you mind my alluding to that? At Baden we were all so mixed up that one could n't tell who was attentive to whom! But Bernard has been very faithful, my dear; I can assure you of that. When he was in America he would n't look at another woman. I know something about that! He stayed three months in my house and he never spoke to me. Now I know why, Mr. Bernard; but you might have told me at the time. The reason was certainly good enough. I always want to know why, you know. Why Gordon never told me, for instance; that 's what I want to know!"

Blanche refused to sit down again; she declared that she was so agitated by this charming news that she could not be quiet, and that she must presently take her departure. Meanwhile she congratulated each of her friends half a dozen times; she kissed Mrs. Vivian again, she almost kissed Bernard; she inquired about details; she longed to hear all about Angela's "things." Of course they would stop for the wedding; but meantime she must be very discreet; she must not intrude too much. Captain Lovelock addressed to Angela a few fragmentary, but well-intentioned sentences, pulling his beard and fixing his eyes on the door-knob—an implement which presently turned in his manly fist, as he opened the door for his companion to withdraw. Blanche went away in a flutter of ejaculations and protestations which left our three friends in Mrs. Vivian's little drawing-room standing looking at each other as the door closed behind her.

"It certainly would have been better taste in him to tell her," said Bernard, frowning, "and not let other people see how little communication there is between them. It has mortified her."

"Poor Mr. Wright had his reasons," Mrs. Vivian suggested, and then she ventured to explain: "He still cares for Angela, and it was painful to him to talk about her marrying some one else."

This had been Bernard's own reflection, and it was no more agreeable as Mrs. Vivian presented it; though Angela herself seemed indifferent to it—seemed, indeed, not to hear it, as if she were thinking of something else.

"We must simply marry as soon as possible; to-morrow, if necessary," said Bernard, with some causticity. "That 's the best thing we can do for every one. When once Angela is married, Gordon will stop thinking of her. He will never permit his imagination to hover about a married woman; I am very sure of that. He does n't approve of that sort of thing, and he has the same law for himself as for other people."

"It does n't matter," said Angela, simply.

"How do you mean, my daughter, it does n't matter?"

"I don't feel obliged to feel so sorry for him now."

"Now? Pray, what has happened? I am more sorry than ever, since I have heard poor Blanche's dreadful tone about him."

The girl was silent a moment; then she shook her head, lightly.

"Her tone—her tone? Dearest mother, don't you see? She is intensely in love with him!"

CHAPTER XXVIII

This observation struck Bernard as extremely ingenious and worthy of his mistress's fine intelligence; he greeted it with enthusiasm, and thought of it for the next twelve hours. The more he thought of it the more felicitous it seemed to him, and he went to Mrs. Vivian's the next day almost for the express purpose of saying to Angela that, decidedly, she was right. He was admitted by his old friend, the little femme de chambre, who had long since bestowed upon him, definitively, her confidence; and as in the ante-chamber he heard the voice of a gentleman raised and talking with some emphasis, come to him from the salon, he paused a moment, looking at her with an interrogative eye.

"Yes," said Mrs. Vivian's attendant, "I must tell Monsieur frankly that another gentleman is there. Moreover, what does it matter? Monsieur would perceive it for himself!"

"Has he been here long?" asked Bernard.

"A quarter of an hour. It probably does n't seem long to the gentleman!"

"Is he alone with Mademoiselle?"

"He asked for Mademoiselle only. I introduced him into the salon, and Mademoiselle, after conversing a little while with Madame, consented to receive him. They have been alone together, as I have told Monsieur, since about three o'clock. Madame is in her own apartment. The position of Monsieur," added this discriminating woman, "certainly justifies him in entering the salon."

Bernard was quite of this opinion, and in a moment more he had crossed the threshold of the little drawing-room and closed the door behind him.

Angela sat there on a sofa, leaning back with her hands clasped in her lap and her eyes fixed upon Gordon Wright, who stood squarely before her, as if he had been making her a resolute speech. Her face wore a look of distress, almost of alarm; she kept her place, but her eyes gave Bernard a mute welcome. Gordon turned and looked at him slowly from head to foot. Bernard remembered, with a good deal of vividness, the last look his friend had given him in the Champs Elysees the day before; and he saw with some satisfaction that this was not exactly a repetition of that expression of cold horror. It was a question, however, whether the horror were changed for the better. Poor Gordon looked intensely sad and grievously wronged. The keen resentment had faded from his face, but an immense reproach was there—a heavy, helpless, appealing reproach. Bernard saw that he had not a scene of violence to dread—and yet, when he perceived what was coming, he would almost have preferred violence. Gordon did not offer him his hand, and before Bernard had had time to say anything, began to speak again, as if he were going on with what he had been saying to Angela.

"You have done me a great wrong—you have done me a cruel wrong! I have been telling it to Miss Vivian; I came on purpose to tell her. I can't really tell her; I can't tell her the details; it 's too painful! But you know what I mean! I could n't stand it any longer. I thought of going away—but I could n't do that. I must come and say what I feel. I can't bear it now."

This outbreak of a passionate sense of injury in a man habitually so undemonstrative, so little disposed to call attention to himself, had in it something at once of the touching and the terrible. Bernard, for an instant, felt almost bewildered; he asked himself whether he had not, after all, been a monster of duplicity. He was guilty of the weakness of taking refuge in what is called, I believe, in legal phrase, a side-issue.

"Don't say all this before Angela!" he exclaimed, with a kind of artificial energy. "You know she is not in the least at fault, and that it can only give her pain. The thing is between ourselves."

Angela was sitting there, looking up at both the men. "I like to hear it," she said.

"You have a singular taste!" Bernard declared.

"I know it 's between ourselves," cried Gordon, "and that Miss Vivian is not at fault. She is only too lovely, too wise, too good! It is you and I that are at fault—horribly at fault! You see I admit it, and you don't. I never dreamed that I should live to say such things as this to you; but I never dreamed you would do what you have done! It 's horrible, most horrible, that such a difference as this should come between two men who believed themselves—or whom I believed, at least—the best friends in the world. For it is a difference—it 's a great gulf, and nothing will ever fill it up. I must say so; I can't help it. You know I don't express myself easily; so, if I break out this way, you may know what I feel. I know it is a pain to Miss Vivian, and I beg her to forgive me. She has so much to forgive that she can forgive that, too. I can't pretend to accept it; I can't sit down and let it pass. And then, it is n't only my feelings; it 's the right; it 's the justice. I must say to her that you have no right to marry her; and beg of her to listen to me and let you go."

"My dear Gordon, are you crazy?" Bernard demanded, with an energy which, this time at least, was sufficiently real.

"Very likely I am crazy. I am crazy with disappointment and the bitterness of what I have lost. Add to that the wretchedness of what I have found!"

"Ah, don't say that, Mr. Wright," Angela begged.

He stood for an instant looking at her, but not heeding her words. "Will you listen to me again? Will you forget the wrong I did you?—my stupidity and folly and unworthiness? Will you blot out the past and let me begin again. I see you as clearly now as the light of that window. Will you give me another chance?"

Angela turned away her eyes and covered her face with her hands. "You do pain me!" she murmured.

"You go too far," said Bernard. "To what position does your extraordinary proposal relegate your wife?"

Gordon turned his pleading eyes on his old friend without a ray of concession; but for a moment he hesitated. "Don't speak to me of my wife. I have no wife."

"Ah, poor girl!" said Angela, springing up from the sofa.

"I am perfectly serious," Gordon went on, addressing himself again to her. "No, after all, I am not crazy; I see only too clearly—I see what should be; when people see that, you call them crazy. Bernard has no right—he must give you up. If you really care for him, you should help him. He is in a very false position; you should n't wish to see him in such a position. I can't explain to you—if it were even for my own sake. But Bernard must have told you; it is not possible that he has not told you?"

"I have told Angela everything, Gordon," said Bernard.

"I don't know what you mean by your having done me a wrong!" the girl exclaimed.

"If he has told you, then—I may say it! In listening to him, in believing him."

"But you did n't believe me," Bernard exclaimed, "since you immediately went and offered yourself to Miss Vivian!"

"I believed you all the same! When did I ever not believe you?"

"The last words I ever heard from Mr. Wright were words of the deepest kindness," said Angela.

She spoke with such a serious, tender grace, that Gordon seemed stirred to his depths again.

"Ah, give me another chance!" he moaned.

The poor girl could not help her tone, and it was in the same tone that she continued—

"If you think so well of me, try and be reasonable."

Gordon looked at her, slowly shaking his head.

"Reasonable—reasonable? Yes, you have a right to say that, for you are full of reason. But so am I. What I ask is within reasonable limits."

"Granting your happiness were lost," said Bernard—"I say that only for the argument—is that a ground for your wishing to deprive me of mine?"

"It is not yours—it is mine, that you have taken! You put me off my guard, and then you took it! Yours is elsewhere, and you are welcome to it!"

"Ah," murmured Bernard, giving him a long look and turning away, "it is well for you that I am willing still to regard you as my best friend!"

Gordon went on, more passionately, to Angela.

"He put me off my guard—I can't call it anything else. I know I gave him a great chance—I encouraged him, urged him, tempted him. But when once he had spoken, he should have stood to it. He should n't have had two opinions—one for me, and one for himself! He put me off my guard. It was because I still resisted him that I went to you again, that last time. But I was still afraid of you, and in my heart I believed him. As I say, I always believed him; it was his great influence upon me. He is the cleverest, the most intelligent, the most brilliant of men. I don't think that a grain less than I ever thought it," he continued, turning again to Bernard. "I think it only the more, and I don't wonder that you find a woman to believe it. But what have you done but deceive me? It was just my belief in your intelligence that reassured me. When Miss Vivian refused me a second time, and I left Baden, it was at first with a sort of relief. But there came back a better feeling—a feeling faint compared to this feeling of to-day, but strong enough to make me uneasy and to fill me with regret. To quench my regret, I kept thinking of what you had said, and it kept me quiet. Your word had such weight with me!"

"How many times more would you have wished to be refused, and how many refusals would have been required to give me my liberty?" asked Bernard.

"That question means nothing, because you never knew that I had again offered myself to Miss Vivian."

"No; you told me very little, considering all that you made me tell you."

"I told you beforehand that I should do exactly as I chose."

"You should have allowed me the same liberty!"

"Liberty!" cried Gordon. "Had n't you liberty to range the whole world over? Could n't he have found a thousand other women?"

"It is not for me to think so," said Angela, smiling a little.

Gordon looked at her a moment.

"Ah, you cared for him from the first!" he cried.

"I had seen him before I ever saw you," said the girl.

Bernard suppressed an exclamation. There seemed to flash through these words a sort of retrospective confession which told him something that she had never directly told him. She blushed as soon as she had spoken, and Bernard found a beauty in this of which the brightness blinded him to the awkward aspect of the fact she had just presented to Gordon. At this fact Gordon stood staring; then at last he apprehended it—largely.

"Ah, then, it had been a plot between you!" he cried out.

Bernard and Angela exchanged a glance of pity.

"We had met for five minutes, and had exchanged a few words before I came to Baden. It was in Italy—at Siena. It was a simple accident that I never told you," Bernard explained.

"I wished that nothing should be said about it," said Angela.

"Ah, you loved him!" Gordon exclaimed.

Angela turned away—she went to the window. Bernard followed her for three seconds with his eyes; then he went on—

"If it were so, I had no reason to suppose it. You have accused me of deceiving you, but I deceived only myself. You say I put you off your guard, but you should rather say you put me on mine. It was, thanks to that, that I fell into the most senseless, the most brutal of delusions. The delusion passed away—it had contained the germ of better things. I saw my error, and I bitterly repented of it; and on the day you were married I felt free."

"Ah, yes, I have no doubt you waited for that!" cried Gordon. "It may interest you to know that my marriage is a miserable failure."

"I am sorry to hear it—but I can't help it."

"You have seen it with your own eyes. You know all about it, and I need n't tell you."

"My dear Mr. Wright," said Angela, pleadingly, turning round, "in Heaven's name, don't say that!"

"Why should n't I say it? I came here on purpose to say it. I came here with an intention—with a plan. You know what Blanche is—you need n't pretend, for kindness to me, that you don't. You know what a precious, what an inestimable wife she must make me—how devoted, how sympathetic she must be, and what a household blessing at every hour of the day. Bernard can tell you all about us—he has seen us in the sanctity of our home." Gordon gave a bitter laugh and went on, with the same strange, serious air of explaining his plan. "She despises me, she hates me, she cares no more for me than for the button on her glove—by which I mean that she does n't care a hundredth part as much. You may say that it serves me right, and that I have got what I deserve. I married her because she was silly. I wanted a silly wife; I had an idea you were too wise. Oh, yes, that 's what I thought of you! Blanche knew why I picked her out, and undertook to supply the article required. Heaven forgive her! She has certainly kept her engagement. But you can imagine how it must have made her like me—knowing why I picked her out! She has disappointed me all the same. I thought she had a heart; but that was a mistake. It does n't matter, though, because everything is over between us."

"What do you mean, everything is over?" Bernard demanded.

"Everything will be over in a few weeks. Then I can speak to Miss Vivian seriously."

"Ah! I am glad to hear this is not serious," said Bernard.

"Miss Vivian, wait a few weeks," Gordon went on. "Give me another chance then. Then it will be perfectly right; I shall be free."

"You speak as if you were going to put an end to your wife!"

"She is rapidly putting an end to herself. She means to leave me."

"Poor, unhappy man, do you know what you are saying?" Angela murmured.

"Perfectly. I came here to say it. She means to leave me, and I mean to offer her every facility. She is dying to take a lover, and she has got an excellent one waiting for her. Bernard knows whom I mean; I don't know whether you do. She was ready to take one three months after our marriage. It is really very good of her to have waited all this time; but I don't think she can go more than a week or two longer. She is recommended a southern climate, and I am pretty sure that in the course of another ten days I may count upon their starting together for the shores of the Mediterranean. The shores of the Mediterranean, you know, are lovely, and I hope they will do her a world of good. As soon as they have left Paris I will let you know; and then you will of course admit that, virtually, I am free."

"I don't understand you."

"I suppose you are aware," said Gordon, "that we have the advantage of being natives of a country in which marriages may be legally dissolved."

Angela stared; then, softly—

"Are you speaking of a divorce?"

"I believe that is what they call it," Gordon answered, gazing back at her with his densely clouded blue eyes. "The lawyers do it for you; and if she goes away with Lovelock, nothing will be more simple than for me to have it arranged."

Angela stared, I say; and Bernard was staring, too. Then the latter, turning away, broke out into a tremendous, irrepressible laugh.

Gordon looked at him a moment; then he said to Angela, with a deeper tremor in his voice—

"He was my dearest friend."

"I never felt more devoted to you than at this moment!" Bernard declared, smiling still.

Gordon had fixed his sombre eyes upon the girl again.

"Do you understand me now?"

Angela looked back at him for some instants.

"Yes," she murmured at last.

"And will you wait, and give me another chance?"

"Yes," she said, in the same tone.

Bernard uttered a quick exclamation, but Angela checked him with a glance, and Gordon looked from one of them to the other.

"Can I trust you?" Gordon asked.

"I will make you happy," said Angela.

Bernard wondered what under the sun she meant; but he thought he might safely add—

"I will abide by her choice."

Gordon actually began to smile.

"It won't be long, I think; two or three weeks."

Angela made no answer to this; she fixed her eyes on the floor.

"I shall see Blanche as often as possible," she presently said.

"By all means! The more you see her the better you will understand me."

"I understand you very well now. But you have shaken me very much, and you must leave me. I shall see you also—often."

Gordon took up his hat and stick; he saw that Bernard did not do the same.

"And Bernard?" he exclaimed.

"I shall ask him to leave Paris," said Angela.

"Will you go?"

"I will do what Angela requests," said Bernard.

"You have heard what she requests; it 's for you to come now."

"Ah, you must at least allow me to take leave!" cried Bernard.

Gordon went to the door, and when he had opened it he stood for a while, holding it and looking at his companions. Then—

"I assure you she won't be long!" he said to Angela, and rapidly passed out.

The others stood silent till they heard the outer door of the apartment close behind him.

"And now please to elucidate!" said Bernard, folding his arms.

Angela gave no answer for some moments; then she turned upon him a smile which appeared incongruous, but which her words presently helped to explain.

"He is intensely in love with his wife!"

CHAPTER XXIX

This statement was very effective, but it might well have seemed at first to do more credit to her satiric powers than to her faculty of observation. This was the light in which it presented itself to Bernard; but, little by little, as she amplified the text, he grew to think well of it, and at last he was quite ready to place it, as a triumph of sagacity, on a level with that other discovery which she had made the evening before and with regard to which his especial errand to-day had been to congratulate her afresh. It brought him, however, less satisfaction than it appeared to bring to his clever companion; for, as he observed plausibly enough, Gordon was quite out of his head, and, this being the case, of what importance was the secret of his heart?

"The secret of his heart and the condition of his head are one and the same thing," said Angela. "He is turned upside down by the wretchedly false position that he has got into with his wife. She has treated him badly, but he has treated her wrongly. They are in love with each other, and yet they both do nothing but hide it. He is not in the least in love with poor me—not to-day any more than he was three years ago. He thinks he is, because he is full of sorrow and bitterness, and because the news of our engagement has given him a shock. But that 's only a pretext—a chance to pour out the grief and pain which have been accumulating in his heart under a sense of his estrangement from Blanche. He is too proud to attribute his feelings to that cause, even to himself; but he wanted to cry out and say he was hurt, to demand justice for a wrong; and the revelation of the state of things between you and me—which of course strikes him as incongruous; we must allow largely for that—came to him as a sudden opportunity. No, no," the girl went on, with a generous ardor in her face, following further the train of her argument, which she appeared to find extremely attractive, "I know what you are going to say and I deny it. I am not fanciful, or sophistical, or irrational, and I know perfectly what I am about. Men are so stupid; it 's only women that have real discernment. Leave me alone, and I shall do something. Blanche is silly, yes, very silly; but she is not so bad as her husband accused her of being, in those dreadful words which he will live to repent of. She is wise enough to care for him, greatly, at bottom, and to feel her little heart filled with rage and shame that he does n't appear to care for her. If he would take her a little more seriously—it 's an immense pity he married her because she was silly!—she would be flattered by it, and she would try and deserve it. No, no, no! she does n't, in reality, care a straw for Captain Lovelock, I assure you, I promise you she does n't. A woman can tell. She is in danger, possibly, and if her present situation, as regards her husband, lasts, she might do something as horrid as he said. But she would do it out of spite—not out of affection for the Captain, who must be got immediately out of the way. She only keeps him to torment her husband and make Gordon come back to her. She would drop him forever to-morrow." Angela paused a moment, reflecting, with a kindled eye. "And she shall!"

Bernard looked incredulous.

"How will that be, Miss Solomon?"

"You shall see when you come back."

"When I come back? Pray, where am I going?"

"You will leave Paris for a fortnight—as I promised our poor friend."

Bernard gave an irate laugh.

"My dear girl, you are ridiculous! Your promising it was almost as childish as his asking it."

"To play with a child you must be childish. Just see the effect of this abominable passion of love, which you have been crying up to me so! By its operation Gordon Wright, the most sensible man of our acquaintance, is reduced to the level of infancy! If you will only go away, I will manage him."

"You certainly manage me! Pray, where shall I go?"

"Wherever you choose. I will write to you every day."

"That will be an inducement," said Bernard. "You know I have never received a letter from you."

"I write the most delightful ones!" Angela exclaimed; and she succeeded in making him promise to start that night for London.

She had just done so when Mrs. Vivian presented herself, and the good lady was not a little astonished at being informed of his intention.

"You surely are not going to give up my daughter to oblige Mr. Wright?" she observed.

"Upon my word, I feel as if I were!" said Bernard.

"I will explain it, dear mamma," said Angela. "It is very interesting. Mr. Wright has made a most fearful scene; the state of things between him and Blanche is dreadful."

Mrs. Vivian opened her clear eyes.

"You really speak as if you liked it!"

"She does like it—she told Gordon so," said Bernard. "I don't know what she is up to! Gordon has taken leave of his wits; he wishes to put away his wife."

"To put her away?"

"To repudiate her, as the historians say!"

"To repudiate little Blanche!" murmured Mrs. Vivian, as if she were struck with the incongruity of the operation.

"I mean to keep them together," said Angela, with a firm decision.

Her mother looked at her with admiration.

"My dear daughter, I will assist you."

The two ladies had such an air of mysterious competence to the task they had undertaken that it seemed to Bernard that nothing was left to him but to retire into temporary exile. He accordingly betook himself to London, where he had social resources which would, perhaps, make exile endurable. He found himself, however, little disposed to avail himself of these resources, and he treated himself to no pleasures but those of memory and expectation. He ached with a sense of his absence from Mrs. Vivian's deeply familiar sky-parlor, which seemed to him for the time the most sacred spot on earth—if on earth it could be called—and he consigned to those generous postal receptacles which ornament with their brilliant hue the London street-corners, an inordinate number of the most voluminous epistles that had ever been dropped into them. He took long walks, alone, and thought all the way of Angela, to whom, it seemed to him, that the character of ministering angel was extremely becoming. She was faithful to her promise of writing to him every day, and she was an angel who wielded—so at least Bernard thought, and he was particular about letters—a very ingenious pen. Of course she had only one topic—the success of her operations with regard to Gordon. "Mamma has undertaken Blanche," she wrote, "and I am devoting myself to Mr. W. It is really very interesting." She told Bernard all about it in detail, and he also found it interesting; doubly so, indeed, for it must be confessed that the charming figure of the mistress of his affections attempting to heal a great social breach with her light and delicate hands, divided his attention pretty equally with the distracted, the distorted, the almost ludicrous, image of his old friend.

Angela wrote that Gordon had come back to see her the day after his first visit, and had seemed greatly troubled on learning that Bernard had taken himself off. "It was because you insisted on it, of course," he said; "it was not from feeling the justice of it himself." "I told him," said Angela, in her letter, "that I had made a point of it, but that we certainly ought to give you a little credit for it. But I could n't insist upon this, for fear of sounding a wrong note and exciting afresh what I suppose he would be pleased to term his jealousy. He asked me where you had gone, and when I told him—'Ah, how he must hate me!' he exclaimed. 'There you are quite wrong,' I answered. 'He feels as kindly to you as—as I do.' He looked as if he by no means believed this; but, indeed, he looks as if he believed nothing at all. He is quite upset and demoralized. He stayed half an hour and paid me his visit—trying hard to 'please' me again! Poor man, he is in a charming state to please the fair sex! But if he does n't please me, he interests me more and more; I make bold to say that to you. You would have said it would be very awkward; but, strangely enough, I found it very easy. I suppose it is because I am so interested. Very likely it was awkward for him, poor fellow, for I can certify that he was not a whit happier at the end of his half-hour, in spite of the privilege he had enjoyed. He said nothing more about you, and we talked of Paris and New York, of Baden and Rome. Imagine the situation! I shall make no resistance whatever to it; I shall simply let him perceive that conversing with me on these topics does not make him feel a bit more comfortable, and that he must look elsewhere for a remedy. I said not a word about Blanche."

She spoke of Blanche, however, the next time. "He came again this afternoon," she said in her second letter, "and he wore exactly the same face as yesterday—namely, a very unhappy one. If I were not entirely too wise to believe his account of himself, I might suppose that he was unhappy because Blanche shows symptoms of not taking flight. She has been with us a great deal—she has no idea what is going on—and I can't honestly say that she chatters any less than usual. But she is greatly interested in certain shops that she is buying out, and especially in her visits to her tailor. Mamma has proposed to her—in view of your absence—to come and stay with us, and she does n't seem afraid of the idea. I told her husband to-day that we had asked her, and that we hoped he had no objection. 'None whatever; but she won't come.' 'On the contrary, she says she will.' 'She will pretend to, up to the last minute; and then she will find a pretext for backing out.' 'Decidedly, you think very ill of her,' I said. 'She hates me,' he answered, looking at me strangely. 'You say that of every one,' I said. 'Yesterday you said it of Bernard.' 'Ah, for him there would be more reason!' he exclaimed. 'I won't attempt to answer for Bernard,' I went on, 'but I will answer for Blanche. Your idea of her hating you is a miserable delusion. She cares for you more than for any one in the world. You only misunderstand each other, and with a little good will on both sides you can easily get out of your tangle.' But he would n't listen to me; he stopped me short. I saw I should excite him if I insisted; so I dropped the subject. But it is not for long; he shall listen to me."

Later she wrote that Blanche had in fact "backed out," and would not come to stay with them, having given as an excuse that she was perpetually trying on dresses, and that at Mrs. Vivian's she should be at an inconvenient distance from the temple of these sacred rites, and the high priest who conducted the worship. "But we see her every day," said Angela, "and mamma is constantly with her. She likes mamma better than me. Mamma listens to her a great deal and talks to her a little—I can't do either when we are alone; I don't know what she says—I mean what mamma says; what Blanche says I know as well as if I heard it. We see nothing of Captain Lovelock, and mamma tells me she has not spoken of him for two days. She thinks this is a better symptom, but I am not so sure. Poor Mr. Wright treats it as a great triumph that Blanche should behave as he foretold. He is welcome to the comfort he can get out of this, for he certainly gets none from anything else. The society of your correspondent is not that balm to his spirit which he appeared to expect, and this in spite of the fact that I have been as gentle and kind with him as I know how to be. He is very silent—he sometimes sits for ten minutes without speaking; I assure you it is n't amusing. Sometimes he looks at me as if he were going to break out with that crazy idea to which he treated me the other day. But he says nothing, and then I see that he is not thinking of me—he is simply thinking of Blanche. The more he thinks of her the better."

"My dear Bernard," she began on another occasion, "I hope you are not dying of ennui, etc. Over here things are going so-so. He asked me yesterday to go with him to the Louvre, and we walked about among the pictures for half an hour. Mamma thinks it a very strange sort of thing for me to be doing, and though she delights, of all things, in a good cause, she is not sure that this cause is good enough to justify the means. I admit that the means are very singular, and, as far as the Louvre is concerned, they were not successful. We sat and looked for a quarter of an hour at the great Venus who has lost her arms, and he said never a word. I think he does n't know what to say. Before we separated he asked me if I heard from you. 'Oh, yes,' I said, 'every day.' 'And does he speak of me?' 'Never!' I answered; and I think he looked disappointed." Bernard had, in fact, in writing to Angela, scarcely mentioned his name. "He had not been here for two days," she continued, at the end of a week; "but last evening, very late—too late for a visitor—he came in. Mamma had left the drawing-room, and I was sitting alone; I immediately saw that we had reached a crisis. I thought at first he was going to tell me that Blanche had carried out his prediction; but I presently saw that this was not where the shoe pinched; and, besides, I knew that mamma was watching her too closely. 'How can I have ever been such a dull-souled idiot?' he broke out, as soon as he had got into the room. 'I like to hear you say that,' I said, 'because it does n't seem to me that you have been at all wise.' 'You are cleverness, kindness, tact, in the most perfect form!' he went on. As a veracious historian I am bound to tell you that he paid me a bushel of compliments, and thanked me in the most flattering terms for my having let him bore me so for a week. 'You have not bored me,' I said; 'you have interested me.' 'Yes,' he cried, 'as a curious case of monomania. It 's a part of your kindness to say that; but I know I have bored you to death; and the end of it all is that you despise me. You can't help despising me; I despise myself. I used to think that I was a man, but I have given that up; I am a poor creature! I used to think I could take things quietly and bear them bravely. But I can't! If it were not for very shame I could sit here and cry to you.' 'Don't mind me,' I said; 'you know it is a part of our agreement that I was not to be critical.' 'Our agreement?' he repeated, vaguely. 'I see you have forgotten it,' I answered; 'but it does n't in the least matter; it is not of that I wish to talk to you. All the more that it has n't done you a particle of good. I have been extremely nice with you for a week; but you are just as unhappy now as you were at the beginning. Indeed, I think you are rather worse.' 'Heaven forgive me, Miss Vivian, I believe I am!' he cried. 'Heaven will easily forgive you; you are on the wrong road. To catch up with your happiness, which has been running away from you, you must take another; you must travel in the same direction as Blanche; you must not separate yourself from your wife.' At the sound of Blanche's name he jumped up and took his usual tone; he knew all about his wife, and needed no information. But I made him sit down again, and I made him listen to me. I made him listen for half an hour, and at the end of the time he was interested. He had all the appearance of it; he sat gazing at me, and at last the tears came into his eyes. I believe I had a moment of eloquence. I don't know what I said, nor how I said it, to what point it would bear examination, nor how, if you had been there, it would seem to you, as a disinterested critic, to hang together; but I know that after a while there were tears in my own eyes. I begged him not to give up Blanche; I assured him that she is not so foolish as she seems; that she is a very delicate little creature to handle, and that, in reality, whatever she does, she is thinking only of him. He had been all goodness and kindness to her, I knew that; but he had not, from the first, been able to conceal from her that he regarded her chiefly as a pretty kitten. She wished to be more than that, and she took refuge in flirting, simply to excite his jealousy and make him feel strongly about her. He has felt strongly, and he was feeling strongly now; he was feeling passionately—that was my whole contention. But he had perhaps never made it plain to those rather near-sighted little mental eyes of hers, and he had let her suppose something that could n't fail to rankle in her mind and torment it. 'You have let her suppose,' I said, 'that you were thinking of me, and the poor girl has been jealous of me. I know it, but from nothing she herself has said. She has said nothing; she has been too proud and too considerate. If you don't think that 's to her honor, I do. She has had a chance every day for a week, but she has treated me without a grain of spite. I have appreciated it, I have understood it, and it has touched me very much. It ought to touch you, Mr. Wright. When she heard I was engaged to Mr. Longueville, it gave her an immense relief. And yet, at the same moment you were protesting, and denouncing, and saying those horrible things about her! I know how she appears—she likes admiration. But the admiration in the world which she would most delight in just now would be yours. She plays with Captain Lovelock as a child does with a wooden harlequin, she pulls a string and he throws up his arms and legs. She has about as much intention of eloping with him as a little girl might have of eloping with a pasteboard Jim Crow. If you were to have a frank explanation with her, Blanche would very soon throw Jim Crow out of the window. I very humbly entreat you to cease thinking of me. I don't know what wrong you have ever done me, or what kindness I have ever done you, that you should feel obliged to trouble your head about me. You see all I am—I tell you now. I am nothing in the least remarkable. As for your thinking ill of me at Baden, I never knew it nor cared about it. If it had been so, you see how I should have got over it. Dear Mr. Wright, we might be such good friends, if you would only believe me. She 's so pretty, so charming, so universally admired. You said just now you had bored me, but it 's nothing—in spite of all the compliments you have paid me—to the way I have bored you. If she could only know it—that I have bored you! Let her see for half an hour that I am out of your mind—the rest will take care of itself. She might so easily have made a quarrel with me. The way she has behaved to me is one of the prettiest things I have ever seen, and you shall see the way I shall always behave to her! Don't think it necessary to say out of politeness that I have not bored you; it is not in the least necessary. You know perfectly well that you are disappointed in the charm of my society. And I have done my best, too. I can honestly affirm that!' For some time he said nothing, and then he remarked that I was very clever, but he did n't see a word of sense in what I said. 'It only proves,' I said, 'that the merit of my conversation is smaller than you had taken it into your head to fancy. But I have done you good, all the same. Don't contradict me; you don't know yet; and it 's too late for us to argue about it. You will tell me to-morrow.'"

CHAPTER XXX

Some three evenings after he received this last report of the progress of affairs in Paris, Bernard, upon whom the burden of exile sat none the more lightly as the days went on, turned out of the Strand into one of the theatres. He had been gloomily pushing his way through the various London densities—the November fog, the nocturnal darkness, the jostling crowd. He was too restless to do anything but walk, and he had been saying to himself, for the thousandth time, that if he had been guilty of a misdemeanor in succumbing to the attractions of the admirable girl who showed to such advantage in letters of twelve pages, his fault was richly expiated by these days of impatience and bereavement. He gave little heed to the play; his thoughts were elsewhere, and, while they rambled, his eyes wandered round the house. Suddenly, on the other side of it, he beheld Captain Lovelock, seated squarely in his orchestra-stall, but, if Bernard was not mistaken, paying as little attention to the stage as he himself had done. The Captain's eyes, it is true, were fixed upon the scene; his head was bent a little, his magnificent beard rippled over the expanse of his shirt-front. But Bernard was not slow to see that his gaze was heavy and opaque, and that, though he was staring at the actresses, their charms were lost upon him. He saw that, like himself, poor Lovelock had matter for reflection in his manly breast, and he concluded that Blanche's ponderous swain was also suffering from a sense of disjunction. Lovelock sat in the same posture all the evening, and that his imagination had not projected itself into the play was proved by the fact that during the entractes he gazed with the same dull fixedness at the curtain. Bernard forebore to interrupt him; we know that he was not at this moment socially inclined, and he judged that the Captain was as little so, inasmuch as causes even more imperious than those which had operated in his own case must have been at the bottom of his sudden appearance in London. On leaving the theatre, however, Bernard found himself detained with the crowd in the vestibule near the door, which, wide open to the street, was a scene of agitation and confusion. It had come on to rain, and the raw dampness mingled itself with the dusky uproar of the Strand. At last, among the press of people, as he was passing out, our hero became aware that he had been brought into contact with Lovelock, who was walking just beside him. At the same moment Lovelock noticed him—looked at him for an instant, and then looked away. But he looked back again the next instant, and the two men then uttered that inarticulate and inexpressive exclamation which passes for a sign of greeting among gentlemen of the Anglo-Saxon race, in their moments of more acute self-consciousness.

"Oh, are you here?" said Bernard. "I thought you were in Paris."

"No; I ain't in Paris," Lovelock answered with some dryness. "Tired of the beastly hole!"

"Oh, I see," said Bernard. "Excuse me while I put up my umbrella."

He put up his umbrella, and from under it, the next moment, he saw the Captain waving two fingers at him out of the front of a hansom. When he returned to his hotel he found on his table a letter superscribed in Gordon Wright's hand. This communication ran as follows:

"I believe you are making a fool of me. In Heaven's name, come back to Paris! G. W."

Bernard hardly knew whether to regard these few words as a further declaration of war, or as an overture to peace; but he lost no time in complying with the summons they conveyed. He started for Paris the next morning, and in the evening, after he had removed the dust of his journey and swallowed a hasty dinner, he rang at Mrs. Vivian's door. This lady and her daughter gave him a welcome which—I will not say satisfied him, but which, at least, did something toward soothing the still unhealed wounds of separation.

"And what is the news of Gordon?" he presently asked.

"We have not seen him in three days," said Angela.

"He is cured, dear Bernard; he must be. Angela has been wonderful," Mrs. Vivian declared.

"You should have seen mamma with Blanche," her daughter said, smiling. "It was most remarkable."

Mrs. Vivian smiled, too, very gently.

"Dear little Blanche! Captain Lovelock has gone to London."

"Yes, he thinks it a beastly hole. Ah, no," Bernard added, "I have got it wrong."

But it little mattered. Late that night, on his return to his own rooms, Bernard sat gazing at his fire. He had not begun to undress; he was thinking of a good many things. He was in the midst of his reflections when there came a rap at his door, which the next moment was flung open. Gordon Wright stood there, looking at him—with a gaze which Bernard returned for a moment before bidding him to come in. Gordon came in and came up to him; then he held out his hand. Bernard took it with great satisfaction; his last feeling had been that he was very weary of this ridiculous quarrel, and it was an extreme relief to find it was over.

"It was very good of you to go to London," said Gordon, looking at him with all the old serious honesty of his eyes.

"I have always tried to do what I could to oblige you," Bernard answered, smiling.

"You must have cursed me over there," Gordon went on.

"I did, a little. As you were cursing me here, it was permissible."

"That 's over now," said Gordon. "I came to welcome you back. It seemed to me I could n't lay my head on my pillow without speaking to you."

"I am glad to get back," Bernard admitted, smiling still. "I can't deny that. And I find you as I believed I should." Then he added, seriously—"I knew Angela would keep us good friends."

For a moment Gordon said nothing. Then, at last—

"Yes, for that purpose it did n't matter which of us should marry her. If it had been I," he added, "she would have made you accept it."

"Ah, I don't know!" Bernard exclaimed.

"I am sure of it," said Gordon earnestly—almost argumentatively. "She 's an extraordinary woman."

"Keeping you good friends with me—that 's a great thing. But it 's nothing to her keeping you good friends with your wife."

Gordon looked at Bernard for an instant; then he fixed his eyes for some time on the fire.

"Yes, that is the greatest of all things. A man should value his wife. He should believe in her. He has taken her, and he should keep her—especially when there is a great deal of good in her. I was a great fool the other day," he went on. "I don't remember what I said. It was very weak."

"It seemed to me feeble," said Bernard. "But it is quite within a man's rights to be a fool once in a while, and you had never abused of the license."

"Well, I have done it for a lifetime—for a lifetime." And Gordon took up his hat. He looked into the crown of it for a moment, and then he fixed his eyes on Bernard's again. "But there is one thing I hope you won't mind my saying. I have come back to my old impression of Miss Vivian."

"Your old impression?"

And Miss Vivian's accepted lover frowned a little.

"I mean that she 's not simple. She 's very strange."

Bernard's frown cleared away in a sudden, almost eager smile.

"Say at once that you dislike her! That will do capitally."

Gordon shook his head, and he, too, almost smiled a little.

"It 's not true. She 's very wonderful. And if I did dislike her, I should struggle with it. It would never do for me to dislike your wife!"

After he had gone, when the night was half over, Bernard, lying awake a while, gave a laugh in the still darkness, as this last sentence came back to him.

On the morrow he saw Blanche, for he went to see Gordon. The latter, at first, was not at home; but he had a quarter of an hour's talk with his wife, whose powers of conversation were apparently not in the smallest degree affected by anything that had occurred.

"I hope you enjoyed your visit to London," she said. "Did you go to buy Angela a set of diamonds in Bond Street? You did n't buy anything—you did n't go into a shop? Then pray what did you go for? Excuse my curiosity—it seems to me it 's rather flattering. I never know anything unless I am told. I have n't any powers of observation. I noticed you went—oh, yes, I observed that very much; and I thought it very strange, under the circumstances. Your most intimate friend arrived in Paris, and you choose the next day to make a little tour! I don't like to see you treat my husband so; he would never have done it to you. And if you did n't stay for Gordon, you might have staid for Angela. I never heard of anything so monstrous as a gentleman rushing away from the object of his affection, for no particular purpose that any one could discover, the day after she has accepted him. It was not the day after? Well, it was too soon, at any rate. Angela could n't in the least tell me what you had gone for; she said it was for a 'change.' That was a charming reason! But she was very much ashamed of you—and so was I; and at last we all sent Captain Lovelock after you to bring you back. You came back without him? Ah, so much the better; I suppose he is still looking for you, and, as he is n't very clever, that will occupy him for some time. We want to occupy him; we don't approve of his being so idle. However, for my own part, I am very glad you were away. I was a great deal at Mrs. Vivian's, and I should n't have felt nearly so much at liberty to go if I had known I should always find you there making love to Mademoiselle. It would n't have seemed to me discreet,—I know what you are going to say—that it 's the first time you ever heard of my wishing to avoid an indiscretion. It 's a taste I have taken up lately,—for the same reason you went to London, for a 'change.'" Here Blanche paused for an appreciable moment; and then she added—"Well, I must say, I have never seen anything so lovely as Mrs. Vivian's influence. I hope mamma won't be disappointed in it this time."

When Bernard next saw the other two ladies, he said to them that he was surprised at the way in which clever women incurred moral responsibilities.

"We like them," said Mrs. Vivian. "We delight in them!"

"Well," said Bernard, "I would n't for the world have it on my conscience to have reconciled poor Gordon to Mrs. Blanche."

"You are not to say a word against Blanche," Angela declared. "She 's a little miracle."

"It will be all right, dear Bernard," Mrs. Vivian added, with soft authority.

"I have taken a great fancy to her," the younger lady went on.

Bernard gave a little laugh.

"Gordon is right in his ultimate opinion. You are very strange!"

"You may abuse me as much as you please; but I will never hear a word against Mrs. Gordon."

And she never would in future; though it is not recorded that Bernard availed himself in any special degree of the license offered him in conjunction with this warning.

Blanche's health within a few days had, according to her own account, taken a marvellous turn for the better; but her husband appeared still to think it proper that they should spend the winter beneath a brilliant sun, and he presently informed his friends that they had at last settled it between them that a voyage up the Nile must be, for a thoroughly united couple, a very agreeable pastime. To perform this expedition advantageously they must repair to Cairo without delay, and for this reason he was sure that Bernard and Angela would easily understand their not making a point of waiting for the wedding. These happy people quite understood it. Their nuptials were to be celebrated with extreme simplicity. If, however, Gordon was not able to be present, he, in conjunction with his wife, bought for Angela, as a bridal gift, a necklace of the most beautiful pearls the Rue de la Paix could furnish; and on his arrival at Cairo, while he waited for his dragoman to give the signal for starting, he found time, in spite of the exactions of that large correspondence which has been more than once mentioned in the course of our narrative, to write Bernard the longest letter he had ever addressed to him. The letter reached Bernard in the middle of his honeymoon.

DAISY MILLER

PART I

At the little town of Vevey, in Switzerland, there is a particularly comfortable hotel. There are, indeed, many hotels, for the entertainment of tourists is the business of the place, which, as many travelers will remember, is seated upon the edge of a remarkably blue lake—a lake that it behooves every tourist to visit. The shore of the lake presents an unbroken array of establishments of this order, of every category, from the "grand hotel" of the newest fashion, with a chalk-white front, a hundred balconies, and a dozen flags flying from its roof, to the little Swiss pension of an elder day, with its name inscribed in German-looking lettering upon a pink or yellow wall and an awkward summerhouse in the angle of the garden. One of the hotels at Vevey, however, is famous, even classical, being distinguished from many of its upstart neighbors by an air both of luxury and of maturity. In this region, in the month of June, American travelers are extremely numerous; it may be said, indeed, that Vevey assumes at this period some of the characteristics of an American watering place. There are sights and sounds which evoke a vision, an echo, of Newport and Saratoga. There is a flitting hither and thither of "stylish" young girls, a rustling of muslin flounces, a rattle of dance music in the morning hours, a sound of high-pitched voices at all times. You receive an impression of these things at the excellent inn of the "Trois Couronnes" and are transported in fancy to the Ocean House or to Congress Hall. But at the "Trois Couronnes," it must be added, there are other features that are much at variance with these suggestions: neat German waiters, who look like secretaries of legation; Russian princesses sitting in the garden; little Polish boys walking about held by the hand, with their governors; a view of the sunny crest of the Dent du Midi and the picturesque towers of the Castle of Chillon.

I hardly know whether it was the analogies or the differences that were uppermost in the mind of a young American, who, two or three years ago, sat in the garden of the "Trois Couronnes," looking about him, rather idly, at some of the graceful objects I have mentioned. It was a beautiful summer morning, and in whatever fashion the young American looked at things, they must have seemed to him charming. He had come from Geneva the day before by the little steamer, to see his aunt, who was staying at the hotel—Geneva having been for a long time his place of residence. But his aunt had a headache—his aunt had almost always a headache—and now she was shut up in her room, smelling camphor, so that he was at liberty to wander about. He was some seven-and-twenty years of age; when his friends spoke of him, they usually said that he was at Geneva "studying." When his enemies spoke of him, they said—but, after all, he had no enemies; he was an extremely amiable fellow, and universally liked. What I should say is, simply, that when certain persons spoke of him they affirmed that the reason of his spending so much time at Geneva was that he was extremely devoted to a lady who lived there—a foreign lady—a person older than himself. Very few Americans—indeed, I think none—had ever seen this lady, about whom there were some singular stories. But Winterbourne had an old attachment for the little metropolis of Calvinism; he had been put to school there as a boy, and he had afterward gone to college there—circumstances which had led to his forming a great many youthful friendships. Many of these he had kept, and they were a source of great satisfaction to him.

After knocking at his aunt's door and learning that she was indisposed, he had taken a walk about the town, and then he had come in to his breakfast. He had now finished his breakfast; but he was drinking a small cup of coffee, which had been served to him on a little table in the garden by one of the waiters who looked like an attache. At last he finished his coffee and lit a cigarette. Presently a small boy came walking along the path—an urchin of nine or ten. The child, who was diminutive for his years, had an aged expression of countenance, a pale complexion, and sharp little features. He was dressed in knickerbockers, with red stockings, which displayed his poor little spindle-shanks; he also wore a brilliant red cravat. He carried in his hand a long alpenstock, the sharp point of which he thrust into everything that he approached—the flowerbeds, the garden benches, the trains of the ladies' dresses. In front of Winterbourne he paused, looking at him with a pair of bright, penetrating little eyes.

"Will you give me a lump of sugar?" he asked in a sharp, hard little voice—a voice immature and yet, somehow, not young.

Winterbourne glanced at the small table near him, on which his coffee service rested, and saw that several morsels of sugar remained. "Yes, you may take one," he answered; "but I don't think sugar is good for little boys."

This little boy stepped forward and carefully selected three of the coveted fragments, two of which he buried in the pocket of his knickerbockers, depositing the other as promptly in another place. He poked his alpenstock, lance-fashion, into Winterbourne's bench and tried to crack the lump of sugar with his teeth.

"Oh, blazes; it's har-r-d!" he exclaimed, pronouncing the adjective in a peculiar manner.

Winterbourne had immediately perceived that he might have the honor of claiming him as a fellow countryman. "Take care you don't hurt your teeth," he said, paternally.

"I haven't got any teeth to hurt. They have all come out. I have only got seven teeth. My mother counted them last night, and one came out right afterward. She said she'd slap me if any more came out. I can't help it. It's this old Europe. It's the climate that makes them come out. In America they didn't come out. It's these hotels."

Winterbourne was much amused. "If you eat three lumps of sugar, your mother will certainly slap you," he said.

"She's got to give me some candy, then," rejoined his young interlocutor. "I can't get any candy here—any American candy. American candy's the best candy."

"And are American little boys the best little boys?" asked Winterbourne.

"I don't know. I'm an American boy," said the child.

"I see you are one of the best!" laughed Winterbourne.

"Are you an American man?" pursued this vivacious infant. And then, on Winterbourne's affirmative reply—"American men are the best," he declared.

His companion thanked him for the compliment, and the child, who had now got astride of his alpenstock, stood looking about him, while he attacked a second lump of sugar. Winterbourne wondered if he himself had been like this in his infancy, for he had been brought to Europe at about this age.

"Here comes my sister!" cried the child in a moment. "She's an American girl."

Winterbourne looked along the path and saw a beautiful young lady advancing. "American girls are the best girls," he said cheerfully to his young companion.

"My sister ain't the best!" the child declared. "She's always blowing at me."

"I imagine that is your fault, not hers," said Winterbourne. The young lady meanwhile had drawn near. She was dressed in white muslin, with a hundred frills and flounces, and knots of pale-colored ribbon. She was bareheaded, but she balanced in her hand a large parasol, with a deep border of embroidery; and she was strikingly, admirably pretty. "How pretty they are!" thought Winterbourne, straightening himself in his seat, as if he were prepared to rise.

The young lady paused in front of his bench, near the parapet of the garden, which overlooked the lake. The little boy had now converted his alpenstock into a vaulting pole, by the aid of which he was springing about in the gravel and kicking it up not a little.

"Randolph," said the young lady, "what ARE you doing?"

"I'm going up the Alps," replied Randolph. "This is the way!" And he gave another little jump, scattering the pebbles about Winterbourne's ears.

"That's the way they come down," said Winterbourne.

"He's an American man!" cried Randolph, in his little hard voice.

The young lady gave no heed to this announcement, but looked straight at her brother. "Well, I guess you had better be quiet," she simply observed.

It seemed to Winterbourne that he had been in a manner presented. He got up and stepped slowly toward the young girl, throwing away his cigarette. "This little boy and I have made acquaintance," he said, with great civility. In Geneva, as he had been perfectly aware, a young man was not at liberty to speak to a young unmarried lady except under certain rarely occurring conditions; but here at Vevey, what conditions could be better than these?—a pretty American girl coming and standing in front of you in a garden. This pretty American girl, however, on hearing Winterbourne's observation, simply glanced at him; she then turned her head and looked over the parapet, at the lake and the opposite mountains. He wondered whether he had gone too far, but he decided that he must advance farther, rather than retreat. While he was thinking of something else to say, the young lady turned to the little boy again.

"I should like to know where you got that pole," she said.

"I bought it," responded Randolph.

"You don't mean to say you're going to take it to Italy?"

"Yes, I am going to take it to Italy," the child declared.

The young girl glanced over the front of her dress and smoothed out a knot or two of ribbon. Then she rested her eyes upon the prospect again. "Well, I guess you had better leave it somewhere," she said after a moment.

"Are you going to Italy?" Winterbourne inquired in a tone of great respect.

The young lady glanced at him again. "Yes, sir," she replied. And she said nothing more.

"Are you—a—going over the Simplon?" Winterbourne pursued, a little embarrassed.

"I don't know," she said. "I suppose it's some mountain. Randolph, what mountain are we going over?"

"Going where?" the child demanded.

"To Italy," Winterbourne explained.

"I don't know," said Randolph. "I don't want to go to Italy. I want to go to America."

"Oh, Italy is a beautiful place!" rejoined the young man.

"Can you get candy there?" Randolph loudly inquired.

"I hope not," said his sister. "I guess you have had enough candy, and mother thinks so too."

"I haven't had any for ever so long—for a hundred weeks!" cried the boy, still jumping about.

The young lady inspected her flounces and smoothed her ribbons again; and Winterbourne presently risked an observation upon the beauty of the view. He was ceasing to be embarrassed, for he had begun to perceive that she was not in the least embarrassed herself. There had not been the slightest alteration in her charming complexion; she was evidently neither offended nor flattered. If she looked another way when he spoke to her, and seemed not particularly to hear him, this was simply her habit, her manner. Yet, as he talked a little more and pointed out some of the objects of interest in the view, with which she appeared quite unacquainted, she gradually gave him more of the benefit of her glance; and then he saw that this glance was perfectly direct and unshrinking. It was not, however, what would have been called an immodest glance, for the young girl's eyes were singularly honest and fresh. They were wonderfully pretty eyes; and, indeed, Winterbourne had not seen for a long time anything prettier than his fair countrywoman's various features—her complexion, her nose, her ears, her teeth. He had a great relish for feminine beauty; he was addicted to observing and analyzing it; and as regards this young lady's face he made several observations. It was not at all insipid, but it was not exactly expressive; and though it was eminently delicate, Winterbourne mentally accused it—very forgivingly—of a want of finish. He thought it very possible that Master Randolph's sister was a coquette; he was sure she had a spirit of her own; but in her bright, sweet, superficial little visage there was no mockery, no irony. Before long it became obvious that she was much disposed toward conversation. She told him that they were going to Rome for the winter—she and her mother and Randolph. She asked him if he was a "real American"; she shouldn't have taken him for one; he seemed more like a German—this was said after a little hesitation—especially when he spoke. Winterbourne, laughing, answered that he had met Germans who spoke like Americans, but that he had not, so far as he remembered, met an American who spoke like a German. Then he asked her if she should not be more comfortable in sitting upon the bench which he had just quitted. She answered that she liked standing up and walking about; but she presently sat down. She told him she was from New York State—"if you know where that is." Winterbourne learned more about her by catching hold of her small, slippery brother and making him stand a few minutes by his side.

"Tell me your name, my boy," he said.

"Randolph C. Miller," said the boy sharply. "And I'll tell you her name;" and he leveled his alpenstock at his sister.

"You had better wait till you are asked!" said this young lady calmly.

"I should like very much to know your name," said Winterbourne.

"Her name is Daisy Miller!" cried the child. "But that isn't her real name; that isn't her name on her cards."

"It's a pity you haven't got one of my cards!" said Miss Miller.

"Her real name is Annie P. Miller," the boy went on.

"Ask him HIS name," said his sister, indicating Winterbourne.

But on this point Randolph seemed perfectly indifferent; he continued to supply information with regard to his own family. "My father's name is Ezra B. Miller," he announced. "My father ain't in Europe; my father's in a better place than Europe."

Winterbourne imagined for a moment that this was the manner in which the child had been taught to intimate that Mr. Miller had been removed to the sphere of celestial reward. But Randolph immediately added, "My father's in Schenectady. He's got a big business. My father's rich, you bet!"

"Well!" ejaculated Miss Miller, lowering her parasol and looking at the embroidered border. Winterbourne presently released the child, who departed, dragging his alpenstock along the path. "He doesn't like Europe," said the young girl. "He wants to go back."

"To Schenectady, you mean?"

"Yes; he wants to go right home. He hasn't got any boys here. There is one boy here, but he always goes round with a teacher; they won't let him play."

"And your brother hasn't any teacher?" Winterbourne inquired.

"Mother thought of getting him one, to travel round with us. There was a lady told her of a very good teacher; an American lady—perhaps you know her—Mrs. Sanders. I think she came from Boston. She told her of this teacher, and we thought of getting him to travel round with us. But Randolph said he didn't want a teacher traveling round with us. He said he wouldn't have lessons when he was in the cars. And we ARE in the cars about half the time. There was an English lady we met in the cars—I think her name was Miss Featherstone; perhaps you know her. She wanted to know why I didn't give Randolph lessons—give him 'instruction,' she called it. I guess he could give me more instruction than I could give him. He's very smart."

"Yes," said Winterbourne; "he seems very smart."

"Mother's going to get a teacher for him as soon as we get to Italy. Can you get good teachers in Italy?"

"Very good, I should think," said Winterbourne.

"Or else she's going to find some school. He ought to learn some more. He's only nine. He's going to college." And in this way Miss Miller continued to converse upon the affairs of her family and upon other topics. She sat there with her extremely pretty hands, ornamented with very brilliant rings, folded in her lap, and with her pretty eyes now resting upon those of Winterbourne, now wandering over the garden, the people who passed by, and the beautiful view. She talked to Winterbourne as if she had known him a long time. He found it very pleasant. It was many years since he had heard a young girl talk so much. It might have been said of this unknown young lady, who had come and sat down beside him upon a bench, that she chattered. She was very quiet; she sat in a charming, tranquil attitude; but her lips and her eyes were constantly moving. She had a soft, slender, agreeable voice, and her tone was decidedly sociable. She gave Winterbourne a history of her movements and intentions and those of her mother and brother, in Europe, and enumerated, in particular, the various hotels at which they had stopped. "That English lady in the cars," she said—"Miss Featherstone—asked me if we didn't all live in hotels in America. I told her I had never been in so many hotels in my life as since I came to Europe. I have never seen so many—it's nothing but hotels." But Miss Miller did not make this remark with a querulous accent; she appeared to be in the best humor with everything. She declared that the hotels were very good, when once you got used to their ways, and that Europe was perfectly sweet. She was not disappointed—not a bit. Perhaps it was because she had heard so much about it before. She had ever so many intimate friends that had been there ever so many times. And then she had had ever so many dresses and things from Paris. Whenever she put on a Paris dress she felt as if she were in Europe.

"It was a kind of a wishing cap," said Winterbourne.

"Yes," said Miss Miller without examining this analogy; "it always made me wish I was here. But I needn't have done that for dresses. I am sure they send all the pretty ones to America; you see the most frightful things here. The only thing I don't like," she proceeded, "is the society. There isn't any society; or, if there is, I don't know where it keeps itself. Do you? I suppose there is some society somewhere, but I haven't seen anything of it. I'm very fond of society, and I have always had a great deal of it. I don't mean only in Schenectady, but in New York. I used to go to New York every winter. In New York I had lots of society. Last winter I had seventeen dinners given me; and three of them were by gentlemen," added Daisy Miller. "I have more friends in New York than in Schenectady—more gentleman friends; and more young lady friends too," she resumed in a moment. She paused again for an instant; she was looking at Winterbourne with all her prettiness in her lively eyes and in her light, slightly monotonous smile. "I have always had," she said, "a great deal of gentlemen's society."

Poor Winterbourne was amused, perplexed, and decidedly charmed. He had never yet heard a young girl express herself in just this fashion; never, at least, save in cases where to say such things seemed a kind of demonstrative evidence of a certain laxity of deportment. And yet was he to accuse Miss Daisy Miller of actual or potential inconduite, as they said at Geneva? He felt that he had lived at Geneva so long that he had lost a good deal; he had become dishabituated to the American tone. Never, indeed, since he had grown old enough to appreciate things, had he encountered a young American girl of so pronounced a type as this. Certainly she was very charming, but how deucedly sociable! Was she simply a pretty girl from New York State? Were they all like that, the pretty girls who had a good deal of gentlemen's society? Or was she also a designing, an audacious, an unscrupulous young person? Winterbourne had lost his instinct in this matter, and his reason could not help him. Miss Daisy Miller looked extremely innocent. Some people had told him that, after all, American girls were exceedingly innocent; and others had told him that, after all, they were not. He was inclined to think Miss Daisy Miller was a flirt—a pretty American flirt. He had never, as yet, had any relations with young ladies of this category. He had known, here in Europe, two or three women—persons older than Miss Daisy Miller, and provided, for respectability's sake, with husbands—who were great coquettes—dangerous, terrible women, with whom one's relations were liable to take a serious turn. But this young girl was not a coquette in that sense; she was very unsophisticated; she was only a pretty American flirt. Winterbourne was almost grateful for having found the formula that applied to Miss Daisy Miller. He leaned back in his seat; he remarked to himself that she had the most charming nose he had ever seen; he wondered what were the regular conditions and limitations of one's intercourse with a pretty American flirt. It presently became apparent that he was on the way to learn.

"Have you been to that old castle?" asked the young girl, pointing with her parasol to the far-gleaming walls of the Chateau de Chillon.

"Yes, formerly, more than once," said Winterbourne. "You too, I suppose, have seen it?"

"No; we haven't been there. I want to go there dreadfully. Of course I mean to go there. I wouldn't go away from here without having seen that old castle."

"It's a very pretty excursion," said Winterbourne, "and very easy to make. You can drive, you know, or you can go by the little steamer."

"You can go in the cars," said Miss Miller.

"Yes; you can go in the cars," Winterbourne assented.

"Our courier says they take you right up to the castle," the young girl continued. "We were going last week, but my mother gave out. She suffers dreadfully from dyspepsia. She said she couldn't go. Randolph wouldn't go either; he says he doesn't think much of old castles. But I guess we'll go this week, if we can get Randolph."

"Your brother is not interested in ancient monuments?" Winterbourne inquired, smiling.

"He says he don't care much about old castles. He's only nine. He wants to stay at the hotel. Mother's afraid to leave him alone, and the courier won't stay with him; so we haven't been to many places. But it will be too bad if we don't go up there." And Miss Miller pointed again at the Chateau de Chillon.

"I should think it might be arranged," said Winterbourne. "Couldn't you get some one to stay for the afternoon with Randolph?"

Miss Miller looked at him a moment, and then, very placidly, "I wish YOU would stay with him!" she said.

Winterbourne hesitated a moment. "I should much rather go to Chillon with you."

"With me?" asked the young girl with the same placidity.

She didn't rise, blushing, as a young girl at Geneva would have done; and yet Winterbourne, conscious that he had been very bold, thought it possible she was offended. "With your mother," he answered very respectfully.

But it seemed that both his audacity and his respect were lost upon Miss Daisy Miller. "I guess my mother won't go, after all," she said. "She don't like to ride round in the afternoon. But did you really mean what you said just now—that you would like to go up there?"

"Most earnestly," Winterbourne declared.

"Then we may arrange it. If mother will stay with Randolph, I guess Eugenio will."

"Eugenio?" the young man inquired.

"Eugenio's our courier. He doesn't like to stay with Randolph; he's the most fastidious man I ever saw. But he's a splendid courier. I guess he'll stay at home with Randolph if mother does, and then we can go to the castle."

Winterbourne reflected for an instant as lucidly as possible—"we" could only mean Miss Daisy Miller and himself. This program seemed almost too agreeable for credence; he felt as if he ought to kiss the young lady's hand. Possibly he would have done so and quite spoiled the project, but at this moment another person, presumably Eugenio, appeared. A tall, handsome man, with superb whiskers, wearing a velvet morning coat and a brilliant watch chain, approached Miss Miller, looking sharply at her companion. "Oh, Eugenio!" said Miss Miller with the friendliest accent.

Eugenio had looked at Winterbourne from head to foot; he now bowed gravely to the young lady. "I have the honor to inform mademoiselle that luncheon is upon the table."

Miss Miller slowly rose. "See here, Eugenio!" she said; "I'm going to that old castle, anyway."

"To the Chateau de Chillon, mademoiselle?" the courier inquired. "Mademoiselle has made arrangements?" he added in a tone which struck Winterbourne as very impertinent.

Eugenio's tone apparently threw, even to Miss Miller's own apprehension, a slightly ironical light upon the young girl's situation. She turned to Winterbourne, blushing a little—a very little. "You won't back out?" she said.

"I shall not be happy till we go!" he protested.

"And you are staying in this hotel?" she went on. "And you are really an American?"

The courier stood looking at Winterbourne offensively. The young man, at least, thought his manner of looking an offense to Miss Miller; it conveyed an imputation that she "picked up" acquaintances. "I shall have the honor of presenting to you a person who will tell you all about me," he said, smiling and referring to his aunt.

"Oh, well, we'll go some day," said Miss Miller. And she gave him a smile and turned away. She put up her parasol and walked back to the inn beside Eugenio. Winterbourne stood looking after her; and as she moved away, drawing her muslin furbelows over the gravel, said to himself that she had the tournure of a princess.

He had, however, engaged to do more than proved feasible, in promising to present his aunt, Mrs. Costello, to Miss Daisy Miller. As soon as the former lady had got better of her headache, he waited upon her in her apartment; and, after the proper inquiries in regard to her health, he asked her if she had observed in the hotel an American family—a mamma, a daughter, and a little boy.

"And a courier?" said Mrs. Costello. "Oh yes, I have observed them. Seen them—heard them—and kept out of their way." Mrs. Costello was a widow with a fortune; a person of much distinction, who frequently intimated that, if she were not so dreadfully liable to sick headaches, she would probably have left a deeper impress upon her time. She had a long, pale face, a high nose, and a great deal of very striking white hair, which she wore in large puffs and rouleaux over the top of her head. She had two sons married in New York and another who was now in Europe. This young man was amusing himself at Hamburg, and, though he was on his travels, was rarely perceived to visit any particular city at the moment selected by his mother for her own appearance there. Her nephew, who had come up to Vevey expressly to see her, was therefore more attentive than those who, as she said, were nearer to her. He had imbibed at Geneva the idea that one must always be attentive to one's aunt. Mrs. Costello had not seen him for many years, and she was greatly pleased with him, manifesting her approbation by initiating him into many of the secrets of that social sway which, as she gave him to understand, she exerted in the American capital. She admitted that she was very exclusive; but, if he were acquainted with New York, he would see that one had to be. And her picture of the minutely hierarchical constitution of the society of that city, which she presented to him in many different lights, was, to Winterbourne's imagination, almost oppressively striking.

He immediately perceived, from her tone, that Miss Daisy Miller's place in the social scale was low. "I am afraid you don't approve of them," he said.

"They are very common," Mrs. Costello declared. "They are the sort of Americans that one does one's duty by not—not accepting."

"Ah, you don't accept them?" said the young man.

"I can't, my dear Frederick. I would if I could, but I can't."

"The young girl is very pretty," said Winterbourne in a moment.

"Of course she's pretty. But she is very common."

"I see what you mean, of course," said Winterbourne after another pause.

"She has that charming look that they all have," his aunt resumed. "I can't think where they pick it up; and she dresses in perfection—no, you don't know how well she dresses. I can't think where they get their taste."

"But, my dear aunt, she is not, after all, a Comanche savage."

"She is a young lady," said Mrs. Costello, "who has an intimacy with her mamma's courier."

"An intimacy with the courier?" the young man demanded.

"Oh, the mother is just as bad! They treat the courier like a familiar friend—like a gentleman. I shouldn't wonder if he dines with them. Very likely they have never seen a man with such good manners, such fine clothes, so like a gentleman. He probably corresponds to the young lady's idea of a count. He sits with them in the garden in the evening. I think he smokes."

Winterbourne listened with interest to these disclosures; they helped him to make up his mind about Miss Daisy. Evidently she was rather wild. "Well," he said, "I am not a courier, and yet she was very charming to me."

"You had better have said at first," said Mrs. Costello with dignity, "that you had made her acquaintance."

"We simply met in the garden, and we talked a bit."

"Tout bonnement! And pray what did you say?"

"I said I should take the liberty of introducing her to my admirable aunt."

"I am much obliged to you."

"It was to guarantee my respectability," said Winterbourne.

"And pray who is to guarantee hers?"

"Ah, you are cruel!" said the young man. "She's a very nice young girl."

"You don't say that as if you believed it," Mrs. Costello observed.

"She is completely uncultivated," Winterbourne went on. "But she is wonderfully pretty, and, in short, she is very nice. To prove that I believe it, I am going to take her to the Chateau de Chillon."

"You two are going off there together? I should say it proved just the contrary. How long had you known her, may I ask, when this interesting project was formed? You haven't been twenty-four hours in the house."

"I have known her half an hour!" said Winterbourne, smiling.

"Dear me!" cried Mrs. Costello. "What a dreadful girl!"

Her nephew was silent for some moments. "You really think, then," he began earnestly, and with a desire for trustworthy information—"you really think that—" But he paused again.

"Think what, sir?" said his aunt.

"That she is the sort of young lady who expects a man, sooner or later, to carry her off?"

"I haven't the least idea what such young ladies expect a man to do. But I really think that you had better not meddle with little American girls that are uncultivated, as you call them. You have lived too long out of the country. You will be sure to make some great mistake. You are too innocent."

"My dear aunt, I am not so innocent," said Winterbourne, smiling and curling his mustache.

"You are guilty too, then!"

Winterbourne continued to curl his mustache meditatively. "You won't let the poor girl know you then?" he asked at last.

"Is it literally true that she is going to the Chateau de Chillon with you?"

"I think that she fully intends it."

"Then, my dear Frederick," said Mrs. Costello, "I must decline the honor of her acquaintance. I am an old woman, but I am not too old, thank Heaven, to be shocked!"

"But don't they all do these things—the young girls in America?" Winterbourne inquired.

Mrs. Costello stared a moment. "I should like to see my granddaughters do them!" she declared grimly.

This seemed to throw some light upon the matter, for Winterbourne remembered to have heard that his pretty cousins in New York were "tremendous flirts." If, therefore, Miss Daisy Miller exceeded the liberal margin allowed to these young ladies, it was probable that anything might be expected of her. Winterbourne was impatient to see her again, and he was vexed with himself that, by instinct, he should not appreciate her justly.

Though he was impatient to see her, he hardly knew what he should say to her about his aunt's refusal to become acquainted with her; but he discovered, promptly enough, that with Miss Daisy Miller there was no great need of walking on tiptoe. He found her that evening in the garden, wandering about in the warm starlight like an indolent sylph, and swinging to and fro the largest fan he had ever beheld. It was ten o'clock. He had dined with his aunt, had been sitting with her since dinner, and had just taken leave of her till the morrow. Miss Daisy Miller seemed very glad to see him; she declared it was the longest evening she had ever passed.

"Have you been all alone?" he asked.

"I have been walking round with mother. But mother gets tired walking round," she answered.

"Has she gone to bed?"

"No; she doesn't like to go to bed," said the young girl. "She doesn't sleep—not three hours. She says she doesn't know how she lives. She's dreadfully nervous. I guess she sleeps more than she thinks. She's gone somewhere after Randolph; she wants to try to get him to go to bed. He doesn't like to go to bed."

"Let us hope she will persuade him," observed Winterbourne.

"She will talk to him all she can; but he doesn't like her to talk to him," said Miss Daisy, opening her fan. "She's going to try to get Eugenio to talk to him. But he isn't afraid of Eugenio. Eugenio's a splendid courier, but he can't make much impression on Randolph! I don't believe he'll go to bed before eleven." It appeared that Randolph's vigil was in fact triumphantly prolonged, for Winterbourne strolled about with the young girl for some time without meeting her mother. "I have been looking round for that lady you want to introduce me to," his companion resumed. "She's your aunt." Then, on Winterbourne's admitting the fact and expressing some curiosity as to how she had learned it, she said she had heard all about Mrs. Costello from the chambermaid. She was very quiet and very comme il faut; she wore white puffs; she spoke to no one, and she never dined at the table d'hote. Every two days she had a headache. "I think that's a lovely description, headache and all!" said Miss Daisy, chattering along in her thin, gay voice. "I want to know her ever so much. I know just what YOUR aunt would be; I know I should like her. She would be very exclusive. I like a lady to be exclusive; I'm dying to be exclusive myself. Well, we ARE exclusive, mother and I. We don't speak to everyone—or they don't speak to us. I suppose it's about the same thing. Anyway, I shall be ever so glad to know your aunt."

Winterbourne was embarrassed. "She would be most happy," he said; "but I am afraid those headaches will interfere."

The young girl looked at him through the dusk. "But I suppose she doesn't have a headache every day," she said sympathetically.

Winterbourne was silent a moment. "She tells me she does," he answered at last, not knowing what to say.

Miss Daisy Miller stopped and stood looking at him. Her prettiness was still visible in the darkness; she was opening and closing her enormous fan. "She doesn't want to know me!" she said suddenly. "Why don't you say so? You needn't be afraid. I'm not afraid!" And she gave a little laugh.

Winterbourne fancied there was a tremor in her voice; he was touched, shocked, mortified by it. "My dear young lady," he protested, "she knows no one. It's her wretched health."

The young girl walked on a few steps, laughing still. "You needn't be afraid," she repeated. "Why should she want to know me?" Then she paused again; she was close to the parapet of the garden, and in front of her was the starlit lake. There was a vague sheen upon its surface, and in the distance were dimly seen mountain forms. Daisy Miller looked out upon the mysterious prospect and then she gave another little laugh. "Gracious! she IS exclusive!" she said. Winterbourne wondered whether she was seriously wounded, and for a moment almost wished that her sense of injury might be such as to make it becoming in him to attempt to reassure and comfort her. He had a pleasant sense that she would be very approachable for consolatory purposes. He felt then, for the instant, quite ready to sacrifice his aunt, conversationally;

to admit that she was a proud, rude woman, and to declare that they needn't mind her. But before he had time to commit himself to this perilous mixture of gallantry and impiety, the young lady, resuming her walk, gave an exclamation in quite another tone. "Well, here's Mother! I guess she hasn't got Randolph to go to bed." The figure of a lady appeared at a distance, very indistinct in the darkness, and advancing with a slow and wavering movement. Suddenly it seemed to pause.

"Are you sure it is your mother? Can you distinguish her in this thick dusk?" Winterbourne asked.

"Well!" cried Miss Daisy Miller with a laugh; "I guess I know my own mother. And when she has got on my shawl, too! She is always wearing my things."

The lady in question, ceasing to advance, hovered vaguely about the spot at which she had checked her steps.

"I am afraid your mother doesn't see you," said Winterbourne. "Or perhaps," he added, thinking, with Miss Miller, the joke permissible— "perhaps she feels guilty about your shawl."

"Oh, it's a fearful old thing!" the young girl replied serenely. "I told her she could wear it. She won't come here because she sees you."

"Ah, then," said Winterbourne, "I had better leave you."

"Oh, no; come on!" urged Miss Daisy Miller.

"I'm afraid your mother doesn't approve of my walking with you."

Miss Miller gave him a serious glance. "It isn't for me; it's for you—that is, it's for HER. Well, I don't know who it's for! But mother doesn't like any of my gentlemen friends. She's right down timid. She always makes a fuss if I introduce a gentleman. But I DO introduce them—almost always. If I didn't introduce my gentlemen friends to Mother," the young girl added in her little soft, flat monotone, "I shouldn't think I was natural."

"To introduce me," said Winterbourne, "you must know my name." And he proceeded to pronounce it.

"Oh, dear, I can't say all that!" said his companion with a laugh. But by this time they had come up to Mrs. Miller, who, as they drew near, walked to the parapet of the garden and leaned upon it, looking intently at the lake and turning her back to them. "Mother!" said the young girl in a tone of decision. Upon this the elder lady turned round. "Mr. Winterbourne," said Miss Daisy Miller, introducing the young man very frankly and prettily. "Common," she was, as Mrs. Costello had pronounced her; yet it was a wonder to Winterbourne that, with her commonness, she had a singularly delicate grace.

Her mother was a small, spare, light person, with a wandering eye, a very exiguous nose, and a large forehead, decorated with a certain amount of thin, much frizzled hair. Like her daughter, Mrs. Miller was dressed with extreme elegance; she had enormous diamonds in her ears. So far as Winterbourne could observe, she gave him no greeting—she certainly was not looking at him. Daisy was near her, pulling her shawl straight. "What are you doing, poking round here?" this young lady inquired, but by no means with that harshness of accent which her choice of words may imply.

"I don't know," said her mother, turning toward the lake again.

"I shouldn't think you'd want that shawl!" Daisy exclaimed.

"Well I do!" her mother answered with a little laugh.

"Did you get Randolph to go to bed?" asked the young girl.

"No; I couldn't induce him," said Mrs. Miller very gently. "He wants to talk to the waiter. He likes to talk to that waiter."

"I was telling Mr. Winterbourne," the young girl went on; and to the young man's ear her tone might have indicated that she had been uttering his name all her life.

"Oh, yes!" said Winterbourne; "I have the pleasure of knowing your son."

Randolph's mamma was silent; she turned her attention to the lake. But at last she spoke. "Well, I don't see how he lives!"

"Anyhow, it isn't so bad as it was at Dover," said Daisy Miller.

"And what occurred at Dover?" Winterbourne asked.

"He wouldn't go to bed at all. I guess he sat up all night in the public parlor. He wasn't in bed at twelve o'clock: I know that."

"It was half-past twelve," declared Mrs. Miller with mild emphasis.

"Does he sleep much during the day?" Winterbourne demanded.

"I guess he doesn't sleep much," Daisy rejoined.

"I wish he would!" said her mother. "It seems as if he couldn't."

"I think he's real tiresome," Daisy pursued.

Then, for some moments, there was silence. "Well, Daisy Miller," said the elder lady, presently, "I shouldn't think you'd want to talk against your own brother!"

"Well, he IS tiresome, Mother," said Daisy, quite without the asperity of a retort.

"He's only nine," urged Mrs. Miller.

"Well, he wouldn't go to that castle," said the young girl. "I'm going there with Mr. Winterbourne."

To this announcement, very placidly made, Daisy's mamma offered no response. Winterbourne took for granted that she deeply disapproved of the projected excursion; but he said to himself that she was a simple, easily managed person, and that a few deferential protestations would take the edge from her displeasure. "Yes," he began; "your daughter has kindly allowed me the honor of being her guide."

Mrs. Miller's wandering eyes attached themselves, with a sort of appealing air, to Daisy, who, however, strolled a few steps farther, gently humming to herself. "I presume you will go in the cars," said her mother.

"Yes, or in the boat," said Winterbourne.

"Well, of course, I don't know," Mrs. Miller rejoined. "I have never been to that castle."

"It is a pity you shouldn't go," said Winterbourne, beginning to feel reassured as to her opposition. And yet he was quite prepared to find that, as a matter of course, she meant to accompany her daughter.

"We've been thinking ever so much about going," she pursued; "but it seems as if we couldn't. Of course Daisy—she wants to go round. But there's a lady here—I don't know her name—she says she shouldn't think we'd want to go to see castles HERE; she should think we'd want to wait till we got to Italy. It seems as if there would be so many there," continued Mrs. Miller with an air of increasing confidence. "Of course we only want to see the principal ones. We visited several in England," she presently added.

"Ah yes! in England there are beautiful castles," said Winterbourne. "But Chillon here, is very well worth seeing."

"Well, if Daisy feels up to it—" said Mrs. Miller, in a tone impregnated with a sense of the magnitude of the enterprise. "It seems as if there was nothing she wouldn't undertake."

"Oh, I think she'll enjoy it!" Winterbourne declared. And he desired more and more to make it a certainty that he was to have the privilege of a tete-a-tete with the young lady, who was still strolling along in front of them, softly vocalizing. "You are not disposed, madam," he inquired, "to undertake it yourself?"

Daisy's mother looked at him an instant askance, and then walked forward in silence. Then—"I guess she had better go alone," she said simply. Winterbourne observed to himself that this was a very different type of maternity from that of the vigilant matrons who massed themselves in the forefront of social intercourse in the dark old city at the other end of the lake. But his meditations were interrupted by hearing his name very distinctly pronounced by Mrs. Miller's unprotected daughter.

"Mr. Winterbourne!" murmured Daisy.

"Mademoiselle!" said the young man.

"Don't you want to take me out in a boat?"

"At present?" he asked.

"Of course!" said Daisy.

"Well, Annie Miller!" exclaimed her mother.

"I beg you, madam, to let her go," said Winterbourne ardently; for he had never yet enjoyed the sensation of guiding through the summer starlight a skiff freighted with a fresh and beautiful young girl.

"I shouldn't think she'd want to," said her mother. "I should think she'd rather go indoors."

"I'm sure Mr. Winterbourne wants to take me," Daisy declared. "He's so awfully devoted!"

"I will row you over to Chillon in the starlight."

"I don't believe it!" said Daisy.

"Well!" ejaculated the elder lady again.

"You haven't spoken to me for half an hour," her daughter went on.

"I have been having some very pleasant conversation with your mother," said Winterbourne.

"Well, I want you to take me out in a boat!" Daisy repeated. They had all stopped, and she had turned round and was looking at Winterbourne. Her face wore a charming smile, her pretty eyes were gleaming, she was swinging her great fan about. No; it's impossible to be prettier than that, thought Winterbourne.

"There are half a dozen boats moored at that landing place," he said, pointing to certain steps which descended from the garden to the lake. "If you will do me the honor to accept my arm, we will go and select one of them."

Daisy stood there smiling; she threw back her head and gave a little, light laugh. "I like a gentleman to be formal!" she declared.

"I assure you it's a formal offer."

"I was bound I would make you say something," Daisy went on.

"You see, it's not very difficult," said Winterbourne. "But I am afraid you are chaffing me."

"I think not, sir," remarked Mrs. Miller very gently.

"Do, then, let me give you a row," he said to the young girl.

"It's quite lovely, the way you say that!" cried Daisy.

"It will be still more lovely to do it."

"Yes, it would be lovely!" said Daisy. But she made no movement to accompany him; she only stood there laughing.

"I should think you had better find out what time it is," interposed her mother.

"It is eleven o'clock, madam," said a voice, with a foreign accent, out of the neighboring darkness; and Winterbourne, turning, perceived the florid personage who was in attendance upon the two ladies. He had apparently just approached.

"Oh, Eugenio," said Daisy, "I am going out in a boat!"

Eugenio bowed. "At eleven o'clock, mademoiselle?"

"I am going with Mr. Winterbourne—this very minute."

"Do tell her she can't," said Mrs. Miller to the courier.

"I think you had better not go out in a boat, mademoiselle," Eugenio declared.

Winterbourne wished to Heaven this pretty girl were not so familiar with her courier; but he said nothing.

"I suppose you don't think it's proper!" Daisy exclaimed. "Eugenio doesn't think anything's proper."

"I am at your service," said Winterbourne.

"Does mademoiselle propose to go alone?" asked Eugenio of Mrs. Miller.

"Oh, no; with this gentleman!" answered Daisy's mamma.

The courier looked for a moment at Winterbourne—the latter thought he was smiling—and then, solemnly, with a bow, "As mademoiselle pleases!" he said.

"Oh, I hoped you would make a fuss!" said Daisy. "I don't care to go now."

"I myself shall make a fuss if you don't go," said Winterbourne.

"That's all I want—a little fuss!" And the young girl began to laugh again.

"Mr. Randolph has gone to bed!" the courier announced frigidly.

"Oh, Daisy; now we can go!" said Mrs. Miller.

Daisy turned away from Winterbourne, looking at him, smiling and fanning herself. "Good night," she said; "I hope you are disappointed, or disgusted, or something!"

He looked at her, taking the hand she offered him. "I am puzzled," he answered.

"Well, I hope it won't keep you awake!" she said very smartly; and, under the escort of the privileged Eugenio, the two ladies passed toward the house.

Winterbourne stood looking after them; he was indeed puzzled. He lingered beside the lake for a quarter of an hour, turning over the mystery of the young girl's sudden familiarities and caprices. But the only very definite conclusion he came to was that he should enjoy deucedly "going off" with her somewhere.

Two days afterward he went off with her to the Castle of Chillon. He waited for her in the large hall of the hotel, where the couriers, the servants, the foreign tourists, were lounging about and staring. It was not the place he should have chosen, but she had appointed it. She came tripping downstairs, buttoning her long gloves, squeezing her folded parasol against her pretty figure, dressed in the perfection of a soberly elegant traveling costume. Winterbourne was a man of imagination and, as our ancestors used to say, sensibility; as he looked at her dress and, on the great staircase, her little rapid, confiding step, he felt as if there were something romantic going forward. He could have believed he was going to elope with her. He passed out with her among all the idle people that were assembled there; they were all looking at her very hard; she had begun to chatter as soon as she joined him. Winterbourne's preference had been that they should be conveyed to Chillon in a carriage; but she expressed a lively wish to go in the little steamer; she declared that she had a passion for steamboats. There was always such a lovely breeze upon the water, and you saw such lots of people. The sail was not long, but Winterbourne's companion found time to say a great many things. To the young man himself their little excursion was so much of an escapade—an adventure—that, even allowing for her habitual sense of freedom, he had some expectation of seeing her regard it in the same way. But it must be confessed that, in this particular, he was disappointed. Daisy Miller was extremely animated, she was in charming spirits; but she was apparently not at all excited; she was not fluttered; she avoided neither his eyes nor those of anyone else; she blushed neither when she looked at him nor when she felt that people were looking at her. People continued to look at her a great deal, and Winterbourne took much satisfaction in his pretty companion's distinguished air. He had been a little afraid that she would talk loud, laugh overmuch, and even, perhaps, desire to move about the boat a good deal. But he quite forgot his fears; he sat smiling, with his eyes upon her face, while, without moving from her place, she delivered herself of a great number of original reflections. It was the most charming garrulity he had ever heard. He had assented to the idea that she was "common"; but was she so, after all, or was he simply getting used to her commonness? Her conversation was chiefly of what metaphysicians term the objective cast, but every now and then it took a subjective turn.

"What on EARTH are you so grave about?" she suddenly demanded, fixing her agreeable eyes upon Winterbourne's.

"Am I grave?" he asked. "I had an idea I was grinning from ear to ear."

"You look as if you were taking me to a funeral. If that's a grin, your ears are very near together."

"Should you like me to dance a hornpipe on the deck?"

"Pray do, and I'll carry round your hat. It will pay the expenses of our journey."

"I never was better pleased in my life," murmured Winterbourne.

She looked at him a moment and then burst into a little laugh. "I like to make you say those things! You're a queer mixture!"

In the castle, after they had landed, the subjective element decidedly prevailed. Daisy tripped about the vaulted chambers, rustled her skirts in the corkscrew staircases, flirted back with a pretty little cry and a shudder from the edge of the oubliettes, and turned a singularly well-shaped ear to everything that Winterbourne told her about the place. But he saw that she cared very little for feudal antiquities and that the dusky traditions of Chillon made but a slight impression upon her. They had the good fortune to have been able to walk about without other companionship than that of the custodian; and Winterbourne arranged with this functionary that they should not be hurried—that they should linger and pause wherever they chose. The custodian interpreted the bargain generously—Winterbourne, on his side, had been generous—and ended by leaving them quite to themselves. Miss Miller's observations were not remarkable for logical consistency; for anything she wanted to say she was sure to find a pretext. She found a great many pretexts in the rugged embrasures of Chillon for asking Winterbourne sudden questions about himself—his family, his previous history, his tastes, his habits, his intentions—and for supplying information upon corresponding points in her own personality. Of her own tastes, habits, and intentions Miss Miller was prepared to give the most definite, and indeed the most favorable account.

"Well, I hope you know enough!" she said to her companion, after he had told her the history of the unhappy Bonivard. "I never saw a man that knew so much!" The history of Bonivard had evidently, as they say, gone into one ear and out of the other. But Daisy went on to say that she wished Winterbourne would travel with them and "go round" with them; they might know something, in that case. "Don't you want to come and teach Randolph?" she asked. Winterbourne said that nothing could possibly please him so much, but that he had unfortunately other occupations. "Other occupations? I don't believe it!" said Miss Daisy. "What do you mean? You are not in business." The young man admitted that he was not in business; but he had engagements which, even within a day or two, would force him to go back to Geneva. "Oh, bother!" she said; "I don't believe it!" and she began to talk about something else. But a few moments later, when he was pointing out to her the pretty design of an antique fireplace, she broke out irrelevantly, "You don't mean to say you are going back to Geneva?"

"It is a melancholy fact that I shall have to return to Geneva tomorrow."

"Well, Mr. Winterbourne," said Daisy, "I think you're horrid!"

"Oh, don't say such dreadful things!" said Winterbourne—"just at the last!"

"The last!" cried the young girl; "I call it the first. I have half a mind to leave you here and go straight back to the hotel alone." And for the next ten minutes she did nothing but call him horrid. Poor Winterbourne was fairly bewildered; no young lady had as yet done him the honor to be so agitated by the announcement of his movements. His companion, after this, ceased to pay any attention to the curiosities of Chillon or the beauties of the lake; she opened fire upon the mysterious charmer in Geneva whom she appeared to have instantly taken it for granted that he was hurrying back to see. How did Miss Daisy Miller know that there was a charmer in Geneva? Winterbourne, who denied the existence of such a person, was quite unable to discover, and he was divided between amazement at the rapidity of her induction and amusement at the frankness of her persiflage. She seemed to him, in all this, an extraordinary mixture of innocence and crudity. "Does she never allow you more than three days at a time?" asked Daisy ironically. "Doesn't she give you a vacation in summer? There's no one so hard worked but they can get leave to go off somewhere at this season. I suppose, if you stay another day, she'll come after you in the boat. Do wait over till Friday, and I will go down to the landing to see her arrive!" Winterbourne began to think he had been wrong to feel disappointed in the temper in which the young lady had embarked. If he had missed the personal accent, the personal accent was now making its appearance. It sounded very distinctly, at last, in her telling him she would stop "teasing" him if he would promise her solemnly to come down to Rome in the winter.

"That's not a difficult promise to make," said Winterbourne. "My aunt has taken an apartment in Rome for the winter and has already asked me to come and see her."

"I don't want you to come for your aunt," said Daisy; "I want you to come for me." And this was the only allusion that the young man was ever to hear her make to his invidious kinswoman. He declared that, at any rate, he would certainly come. After this Daisy stopped teasing. Winterbourne took a carriage, and they drove back to Vevey in the dusk; the young girl was very quiet.

In the evening Winterbourne mentioned to Mrs. Costello that he had spent the afternoon at Chillon with Miss Daisy Miller.

"The Americans—of the courier?" asked this lady.

"Ah, happily," said Winterbourne, "the courier stayed at home."

"She went with you all alone?"

"All alone."

Mrs. Costello sniffed a little at her smelling bottle. "And that," she exclaimed, "is the young person whom you wanted me to know!"

PART II

Winterbourne, who had returned to Geneva the day after his excursion to Chillon, went to Rome toward the end of January. His aunt had been established there for several weeks, and he had received a couple of letters from her. "Those people you were so devoted to last summer at Vevey have turned up here, courier and all," she wrote. "They seem to have made several acquaintances, but the courier continues to be the most intime. The young lady, however, is also very intimate with some third-rate Italians, with whom she rackets about in a way that makes much talk. Bring me that pretty novel of Cherbuliez's—Paule Mere—and don't come later than the 23rd."

In the natural course of events, Winterbourne, on arriving in Rome, would presently have ascertained Mrs. Miller's address at the American banker's and have gone to pay his compliments to Miss Daisy. "After what happened at Vevey, I think I may certainly call upon them," he said to Mrs. Costello.

"If, after what happens—at Vevey and everywhere—you desire to keep up the acquaintance, you are very welcome. Of course a man may know everyone. Men are welcome to the privilege!"

"Pray what is it that happens—here, for instance?" Winterbourne demanded.

"The girl goes about alone with her foreigners. As to what happens further, you must apply elsewhere for information. She has picked up half a dozen of the regular Roman fortune hunters, and she takes them about to people's houses. When she comes to a party she brings with her a gentleman with a good deal of manner and a wonderful mustache."

"And where is the mother?"

"I haven't the least idea. They are very dreadful people."

Winterbourne meditated a moment. "They are very ignorant—very innocent only. Depend upon it they are not bad."

"They are hopelessly vulgar," said Mrs. Costello. "Whether or no being hopelessly vulgar is being 'bad' is a question for the metaphysicians. They are bad enough to dislike, at any rate; and for this short life that is quite enough."

The news that Daisy Miller was surrounded by half a dozen wonderful mustaches checked Winterbourne's impulse to go straightway to see her. He had, perhaps, not definitely flattered himself that he had made an ineffaceable impression upon her heart, but he was annoyed at hearing of a state of affairs so little in harmony with an image that had lately flitted in and out of his own meditations; the image of a very pretty girl looking out of an old Roman window and asking herself urgently when Mr. Winterbourne would arrive. If, however, he determined to wait a little before reminding Miss Miller of his claims to her consideration, he went very soon to call upon two or three other friends. One of these friends was an American lady who had spent several winters at Geneva, where she had placed her children at school. She was a very accomplished woman, and she lived in the Via Gregoriana. Winterbourne found her in a little crimson drawing room on a third floor; the room was filled with southern sunshine. He had not been there ten minutes when the servant came in, announcing "Madame Mila!" This announcement was presently followed by the entrance of little Randolph Miller, who stopped in the middle of the room and stood staring at Winterbourne. An instant later his pretty sister crossed the threshold; and then, after a considerable interval, Mrs. Miller slowly advanced.

"I know you!" said Randolph.

"I'm sure you know a great many things," exclaimed Winterbourne, taking him by the hand. "How is your education coming on?"

Daisy was exchanging greetings very prettily with her hostess, but when she heard Winterbourne's voice she quickly turned her head. "Well, I declare!" she said.

"I told you I should come, you know," Winterbourne rejoined, smiling.

"Well, I didn't believe it," said Miss Daisy.

"I am much obliged to you," laughed the young man.

"You might have come to see me!" said Daisy.

"I arrived only yesterday."

"I don't believe that!" the young girl declared.

Winterbourne turned with a protesting smile to her mother, but this lady evaded his glance, and, seating herself, fixed her eyes upon her son. "We've got a bigger place than this," said Randolph. "It's all gold on the walls."

Mrs. Miller turned uneasily in her chair. "I told you if I were to bring you, you would say something!" she murmured.

"I told YOU!" Randolph exclaimed. "I tell YOU, sir!" he added jocosely, giving Winterbourne a thump on the knee. "It IS bigger, too!"

Daisy had entered upon a lively conversation with her hostess; Winterbourne judged it becoming to address a few words to her mother. "I hope you have been well since we parted at Vevey," he said.

Mrs. Miller now certainly looked at him—at his chin. "Not very well, sir," she answered.

"She's got the dyspepsia," said Randolph. "I've got it too. Father's got it. I've got it most!"

This announcement, instead of embarrassing Mrs. Miller, seemed to relieve her. "I suffer from the liver," she said. "I think it's this climate; it's less bracing than Schenectady, especially in the winter season. I don't know whether you know we reside at Schenectady. I was saying to Daisy that I certainly hadn't found any one like Dr. Davis, and I didn't believe I should. Oh, at Schenectady he stands first; they think everything of him. He has so much to do, and yet there was nothing he wouldn't do for me. He said he never saw anything like my dyspepsia, but he was bound to cure it. I'm sure there was nothing he wouldn't try. He was just going to try something new when we came off. Mr. Miller wanted Daisy to see Europe for herself. But I wrote to Mr. Miller that it seems as if I couldn't get on without Dr. Davis. At Schenectady he stands at the very top; and there's a great deal of sickness there, too. It affects my sleep."

Winterbourne had a good deal of pathological gossip with Dr. Davis's patient, during which Daisy chattered unremittingly to her own companion. The young man asked Mrs. Miller how she was pleased with Rome. "Well, I must say I am disappointed," she answered. "We had heard so much about it; I suppose we had heard too much. But we couldn't help that. We had been led to expect something different."

"Ah, wait a little, and you will become very fond of it," said Winterbourne.

"I hate it worse and worse every day!" cried Randolph.

"You are like the infant Hannibal," said Winterbourne.

"No, I ain't!" Randolph declared at a venture.

"You are not much like an infant," said his mother. "But we have seen places," she resumed, "that I should put a long way before Rome." And in reply to Winterbourne's interrogation, "There's Zurich," she concluded, "I think Zurich is lovely; and we hadn't heard half so much about it."

"The best place we've seen is the City of Richmond!" said Randolph.

"He means the ship," his mother explained. "We crossed in that ship. Randolph had a good time on the City of Richmond."

"It's the best place I've seen," the child repeated. "Only it was turned the wrong way."

"Well, we've got to turn the right way some time," said Mrs. Miller with a little laugh. Winterbourne expressed the hope that her daughter at least found some gratification in Rome, and she declared that Daisy was quite carried away. "It's on account of the society—the society's splendid. She goes round everywhere; she has made a great number of acquaintances. Of course she goes round more than I do. I must say they have been very sociable; they have taken her right in. And then she knows a great many gentlemen. Oh, she thinks there's nothing like Rome. Of course, it's a great deal pleasanter for a young lady if she knows plenty of gentlemen."

By this time Daisy had turned her attention again to Winterbourne. "I've been telling Mrs. Walker how mean you were!" the young girl announced.

"And what is the evidence you have offered?" asked Winterbourne, rather annoyed at Miss Miller's want of appreciation of the zeal of an admirer who on his way down to Rome had stopped neither at Bologna nor at Florence, simply because of a certain sentimental impatience. He remembered that a cynical compatriot had once told him that American women—the pretty ones, and this gave a largeness to the axiom—were at once the most exacting in the world and the least endowed with a sense of indebtedness.

"Why, you were awfully mean at Vevey," said Daisy. "You wouldn't do anything. You wouldn't stay there when I asked you."

"My dearest young lady," cried Winterbourne, with eloquence, "have I come all the way to Rome to encounter your reproaches?"

"Just hear him say that!" said Daisy to her hostess, giving a twist to a bow on this lady's dress. "Did you ever hear anything so quaint?"

"So quaint, my dear?" murmured Mrs. Walker in the tone of a partisan of Winterbourne.

"Well, I don't know," said Daisy, fingering Mrs. Walker's ribbons. "Mrs. Walker, I want to tell you something."

"Mother-r," interposed Randolph, with his rough ends to his words, "I tell you you've got to go. Eugenio'll raise—something!"

"I'm not afraid of Eugenio," said Daisy with a toss of her head. "Look here, Mrs. Walker," she went on, "you know I'm coming to your party."

"I am delighted to hear it."

"I've got a lovely dress!"

"I am very sure of that."

"But I want to ask a favor—permission to bring a friend."

"I shall be happy to see any of your friends," said Mrs. Walker, turning with a smile to Mrs. Miller.

"Oh, they are not my friends," answered Daisy's mamma, smiling shyly in her own fashion. "I never spoke to them."

"It's an intimate friend of mine—Mr. Giovanelli," said Daisy without a tremor in her clear little voice or a shadow on her brilliant little face.

Mrs. Walker was silent a moment; she gave a rapid glance at Winterbourne. "I shall be glad to see Mr. Giovanelli," she then said.

"He's an Italian," Daisy pursued with the prettiest serenity. "He's a great friend of mine; he's the handsomest man in the world—except Mr. Winterbourne! He knows plenty of Italians, but he wants to know some Americans. He thinks ever so much of Americans. He's tremendously clever. He's perfectly lovely!"

It was settled that this brilliant personage should be brought to Mrs. Walker's party, and then Mrs. Miller prepared to take her leave. "I guess we'll go back to the hotel," she said.

"You may go back to the hotel, Mother, but I'm going to take a walk," said Daisy.

"She's going to walk with Mr. Giovanelli," Randolph proclaimed.

"I am going to the Pincio," said Daisy, smiling.

"Alone, my dear—at this hour?" Mrs. Walker asked. The afternoon was drawing to a close—it was the hour for the throng of carriages and of contemplative pedestrians. "I don't think it's safe, my dear," said Mrs. Walker.

"Neither do I," subjoined Mrs. Miller. "You'll get the fever, as sure as you live. Remember what Dr. Davis told you!"

"Give her some medicine before she goes," said Randolph.

The company had risen to its feet; Daisy, still showing her pretty teeth, bent over and kissed her hostess. "Mrs. Walker, you are too perfect," she said. "I'm not going alone; I am going to meet a friend."

"Your friend won't keep you from getting the fever," Mrs. Miller observed.

"Is it Mr. Giovanelli?" asked the hostess.

Winterbourne was watching the young girl; at this question his attention quickened. She stood there, smiling and smoothing her bonnet ribbons; she glanced at Winterbourne. Then, while she glanced and smiled, she answered, without a shade of hesitation, "Mr. Giovanelli—the beautiful Giovanelli."

"My dear young friend," said Mrs. Walker, taking her hand pleadingly, "don't walk off to the Pincio at this hour to meet a beautiful Italian."

"Well, he speaks English," said Mrs. Miller.

"Gracious me!" Daisy exclaimed, "I don't to do anything improper. There's an easy way to settle it." She continued to glance at Winterbourne. "The Pincio is only a hundred yards distant; and if Mr. Winterbourne were as polite as he pretends, he would offer to walk with me!"

Winterbourne's politeness hastened to affirm itself, and the young girl gave him gracious leave to accompany her. They passed downstairs before her mother, and at the door Winterbourne perceived Mrs. Miller's carriage drawn up, with the ornamental courier whose acquaintance he had made at Vevey seated within. "Goodbye, Eugenio!" cried Daisy; "I'm going to take a walk." The distance from the Via Gregoriana to the beautiful garden at the other end of the Pincian Hill is, in fact, rapidly traversed. As the day was splendid, however, and the concourse of vehicles, walkers, and loungers numerous, the young Americans found their progress much delayed. This fact was highly agreeable to Winterbourne, in spite of his consciousness of his singular situation. The slow-moving, idly gazing Roman crowd bestowed much attention upon the extremely pretty young foreign lady who was passing through it upon his arm; and he wondered what on earth had been in Daisy's mind when she proposed to expose herself, unattended, to its appreciation.

His own mission, to her sense, apparently, was to consign her to the hands of Mr. Giovanelli; but Winterbourne, at once annoyed and gratified, resolved that he would do no such thing.

"Why haven't you been to see me?" asked Daisy. "You can't get out of that."

"I have had the honor of telling you that I have only just stepped out of the train."

"You must have stayed in the train a good while after it stopped!" cried the young girl with her little laugh. "I suppose you were asleep. You have had time to go to see Mrs. Walker."

"I knew Mrs. Walker—" Winterbourne began to explain.

"I know where you knew her. You knew her at Geneva. She told me so. Well, you knew me at Vevey. That's just as good. So you ought to have come." She asked him no other question than this; she began to prattle about her own affairs. "We've got splendid rooms at the hotel; Eugenio says they're the best rooms in Rome. We are going to stay all winter, if we don't die of the fever; and I guess we'll stay then. It's a great deal nicer than I thought; I thought it would be fearfully quiet; I was sure it would be awfully poky. I was sure we should be going round all the time with one of those dreadful old men that explain about the pictures and things. But we only had about a week of that, and now I'm enjoying myself. I know ever so many people, and they are all so charming. The society's extremely select. There are all kinds—English, and Germans, and Italians. I think I like the English best. I like their style of conversation. But there are some lovely Americans. I never saw anything so hospitable. There's something or other every day. There's not much dancing; but I must say I never thought dancing was everything. I was always fond of conversation. I guess I shall have plenty at Mrs. Walker's, her rooms are so small." When they had passed the gate of the Pincian Gardens, Miss Miller began to wonder where Mr. Giovanelli might be. "We had better go straight to that place in front," she said, "where you look at the view."

"I certainly shall not help you to find him," Winterbourne declared.

"Then I shall find him without you," cried Miss Daisy.

"You certainly won't leave me!" cried Winterbourne.

She burst into her little laugh. "Are you afraid you'll get lost—or run over? But there's Giovanelli, leaning against that tree. He's staring at the women in the carriages: did you ever see anything so cool?"

Winterbourne perceived at some distance a little man standing with folded arms nursing his cane. He had a handsome face, an artfully poised hat, a glass in one eye, and a nosegay in his buttonhole. Winterbourne looked at him a moment and then said, "Do you mean to speak to that man?"

"Do I mean to speak to him? Why, you don't suppose I mean to communicate by signs?"

"Pray understand, then," said Winterbourne, "that I intend to remain with you."

Daisy stopped and looked at him, without a sign of troubled consciousness in her face, with nothing but the presence of her charming eyes and her happy dimples. "Well, she's a cool one!" thought the young man.

"I don't like the way you say that," said Daisy. "It's too imperious."

"I beg your pardon if I say it wrong. The main point is to give you an idea of my meaning."

The young girl looked at him more gravely, but with eyes that were prettier than ever. "I have never allowed a gentleman to dictate to me, or to interfere with anything I do."

"I think you have made a mistake," said Winterbourne. "You should sometimes listen to a gentleman—the right one."

Daisy began to laugh again. "I do nothing but listen to gentlemen!" she exclaimed. "Tell me if Mr. Giovanelli is the right one?"

The gentleman with the nosegay in his bosom had now perceived our two friends, and was approaching the young girl with obsequious rapidity. He bowed to Winterbourne as well as to the latter's companion; he had a brilliant smile, an intelligent eye; Winterbourne thought him not a bad-looking fellow. But he nevertheless said to Daisy, "No, he's not the right one."

Daisy evidently had a natural talent for performing introductions; she mentioned the name of each of her companions to the other. She strolled alone with one of them on each side of her; Mr. Giovanelli, who spoke English very cleverly—Winterbourne afterward learned that he had practiced the idiom upon a great many American heiresses—addressed her a great deal of very polite nonsense; he was extremely urbane, and the young American, who said nothing, reflected upon that profundity of Italian cleverness which enables people to appear more gracious in proportion as they are more acutely disappointed. Giovanelli, of course, had counted upon something more intimate; he had not bargained for a party of three. But he kept his temper in a manner which suggested far-stretching intentions. Winterbourne flattered himself that he had taken his measure. "He is not a gentleman," said the young American; "he is only a clever imitation of one. He is a music master, or a penny-a-liner, or a third-rate artist. D__n his good looks!" Mr. Giovanelli had certainly a very pretty face; but Winterbourne felt a superior indignation at his own lovely fellow countrywoman's not knowing the difference between a spurious gentleman and a real one. Giovanelli chattered and jested and made himself wonderfully agreeable. It was true that, if he was an imitation, the imitation was brilliant. "Nevertheless," Winterbourne said to himself, "a nice girl ought to know!" And then he came back to the question whether this was, in fact, a nice girl. Would a nice girl, even allowing for her being a little American flirt, make a rendezvous with a presumably low-lived foreigner? The rendezvous in this case, indeed, had been in broad daylight and in the most crowded corner of Rome, but was it not impossible to regard the choice of these circumstances as a proof of extreme cynicism? Singular though it may seem, Winterbourne was vexed that the young girl, in joining her amoroso, should not appear more impatient of his own company, and he was vexed because of his inclination. It was impossible to regard her as a perfectly well-conducted young lady; she was wanting in a certain indispensable delicacy. It would therefore simplify matters greatly to be able to treat her as the object of one of those sentiments which are called by romancers "lawless passions." That she should seem to wish to get rid of him would help him to think more lightly of her, and to be able to think more lightly of her would make her much less perplexing. But Daisy, on this occasion, continued to present herself as an inscrutable combination of audacity and innocence.

She had been walking some quarter of an hour, attended by her two cavaliers, and responding in a tone of very childish gaiety, as it seemed to Winterbourne, to the pretty speeches of Mr. Giovanelli, when a carriage that had detached itself from the revolving train drew up beside the path. At the same moment Winterbourne perceived that his friend Mrs. Walker—the lady whose house he had lately left—was seated in the vehicle and was beckoning to him. Leaving Miss Miller's side, he hastened to obey her summons. Mrs. Walker was flushed; she wore an excited air. "It is really too dreadful," she said. "That girl must not do this sort of thing. She must not walk here with you two men. Fifty people have noticed her."

Winterbourne raised his eyebrows. "I think it's a pity to make too much fuss about it."

"It's a pity to let the girl ruin herself!"

"She is very innocent," said Winterbourne.

"She's very crazy!" cried Mrs. Walker. "Did you ever see anything so imbecile as her mother? After you had all left me just now, I could not sit still for thinking of it. It seemed too pitiful, not even to attempt to save her. I ordered the carriage and put on my bonnet, and came here as quickly as possible. Thank Heaven I have found you!"

"What do you propose to do with us?" asked Winterbourne, smiling.

"To ask her to get in, to drive her about here for half an hour, so that the world may see she is not running absolutely wild, and then to take her safely home."

"I don't think it's a very happy thought," said Winterbourne; "but you can try."

Mrs. Walker tried. The young man went in pursuit of Miss Miller, who had simply nodded and smiled at his interlocutor in the carriage and had gone her way with her companion. Daisy, on learning that Mrs. Walker wished to speak to her, retraced her steps with a perfect good grace and with Mr. Giovanelli at her side. She declared that she was delighted to have a chance to present this gentleman to Mrs. Walker. She immediately achieved the introduction, and declared that she had never in her life seen anything so lovely as Mrs. Walker's carriage rug.

"I am glad you admire it," said this lady, smiling sweetly. "Will you get in and let me put it over you?"

"Oh, no, thank you," said Daisy. "I shall admire it much more as I see you driving round with it."

"Do get in and drive with me!" said Mrs. Walker.

"That would be charming, but it's so enchanting just as I am!" and Daisy gave a brilliant glance at the gentlemen on either side of her.

"It may be enchanting, dear child, but it is not the custom here," urged Mrs. Walker, leaning forward in her victoria, with her hands devoutly clasped.

"Well, it ought to be, then!" said Daisy. "If I didn't walk I should expire."

"You should walk with your mother, dear," cried the lady from Geneva, losing patience.

"With my mother dear!" exclaimed the young girl. Winterbourne saw that she scented interference. "My mother never walked ten steps in her life. And then, you know," she added with a laugh, "I am more than five years old."

"You are old enough to be more reasonable. You are old enough, dear Miss Miller, to be talked about."

Daisy looked at Mrs. Walker, smiling intensely. "Talked about? What do you mean?"

"Come into my carriage, and I will tell you."

Daisy turned her quickened glance again from one of the gentlemen beside her to the other. Mr. Giovanelli was bowing to and fro, rubbing down his gloves and laughing very agreeably; Winterbourne thought it a most unpleasant scene. "I don't think I want to know what you mean," said Daisy presently. "I don't think I should like it."

Winterbourne wished that Mrs. Walker would tuck in her carriage rug and drive away, but this lady did not enjoy being defied, as she afterward told him. "Should you prefer being thought a very reckless girl?" she demanded.

"Gracious!" exclaimed Daisy. She looked again at Mr. Giovanelli, then she turned to Winterbourne. There was a little pink flush in her cheek; she was tremendously pretty. "Does Mr. Winterbourne think," she asked slowly, smiling, throwing back her head, and glancing at him from head to foot, "that, to save my reputation, I ought to get into the carriage?"

Winterbourne colored; for an instant he hesitated greatly. It seemed so strange to hear her speak that way of her "reputation." But he himself, in fact, must speak in accordance with gallantry. The finest gallantry, here, was simply to tell her the truth; and the truth, for Winterbourne, as the few indications I have been able to give have made him known to the reader, was that Daisy Miller should take Mrs. Walker's advice. He looked at her exquisite prettiness, and then he said, very gently, "I think you should get into the carriage."

Daisy gave a violent laugh. "I never heard anything so stiff! If this is improper, Mrs. Walker," she pursued, "then I am all improper, and you must give me up. Goodbye; I hope you'll have a lovely ride!" and, with Mr. Giovanelli, who made a triumphantly obsequious salute, she turned away.

Mrs. Walker sat looking after her, and there were tears in Mrs. Walker's eyes. "Get in here, sir," she said to Winterbourne, indicating the place beside her. The young man answered that he felt bound to accompany Miss Miller, whereupon Mrs. Walker declared that if he refused her this favor she would never speak to him again. She was evidently in earnest. Winterbourne overtook Daisy and her companion, and, offering the young girl his hand, told her that Mrs. Walker had made an imperious claim upon his society. He expected that in answer she would say something rather free, something to commit herself still further to that "recklessness" from which Mrs. Walker had so charitably endeavored to dissuade her. But she only shook his hand, hardly looking at him, while Mr. Giovanelli bade him farewell with a too emphatic flourish of the hat.

Winterbourne was not in the best possible humor as he took his seat in Mrs. Walker's victoria. "That was not clever of you," he said candidly, while the vehicle mingled again with the throng of carriages.

"In such a case," his companion answered, "I don't wish to be clever; I wish to be EARNEST!"

"Well, your earnestness has only offended her and put her off."

"It has happened very well," said Mrs. Walker. "If she is so perfectly determined to compromise herself, the sooner one knows it the better; one can act accordingly."

"I suspect she meant no harm," Winterbourne rejoined.

"So I thought a month ago. But she has been going too far."

"What has she been doing?"

"Everything that is not done here. Flirting with any man she could pick up; sitting in corners with mysterious Italians; dancing all the evening with the same partners; receiving visits at eleven o'clock at night. Her mother goes away when visitors come."

"But her brother," said Winterbourne, laughing, "sits up till midnight."

"He must be edified by what he sees. I'm told that at their hotel everyone is talking about her, and that a smile goes round among all the servants when a gentleman comes and asks for Miss Miller."

"The servants be hanged!" said Winterbourne angrily. "The poor girl's only fault," he presently added, "is that she is very uncultivated."

"She is naturally indelicate," Mrs. Walker declared.

"Take that example this morning. How long had you known her at Vevey?"

"A couple of days."

"Fancy, then, her making it a personal matter that you should have left the place!"

Winterbourne was silent for some moments; then he said, "I suspect, Mrs. Walker, that you and I have lived too long at Geneva!" And he added a request that she should inform him with what particular design she had made him enter her carriage.

"I wished to beg you to cease your relations with Miss Miller—not to flirt with her—to give her no further opportunity to expose herself—to let her alone, in short."

"I'm afraid I can't do that," said Winterbourne. "I like her extremely."

"All the more reason that you shouldn't help her to make a scandal."

"There shall be nothing scandalous in my attentions to her."

"There certainly will be in the way she takes them. But I have said what I had on my conscience," Mrs. Walker pursued. "If you wish to rejoin the young lady I will put you down. Here, by the way, you have a chance."

The carriage was traversing that part of the Pincian Garden that overhangs the wall of Rome and overlooks the beautiful Villa Borghese. It is bordered by a large parapet, near which there are several seats. One of the seats at a distance was occupied by a gentleman and a lady, toward whom Mrs. Walker gave a toss of her head. At the same moment these persons rose and walked toward the parapet. Winterbourne had asked the coachman to stop; he now descended from the carriage. His companion looked at him a moment in silence; then, while he raised his hat, she drove majestically away. Winterbourne stood there; he had turned his eyes toward Daisy and her cavalier. They evidently saw no one; they were too deeply occupied with each other. When they reached the low garden wall, they stood a moment looking off at the great flat-topped pine clusters of the Villa Borghese; then Giovanelli seated himself, familiarly, upon the broad ledge of the wall. The western sun in the opposite sky sent out a brilliant shaft through a couple of cloud bars, whereupon Daisy's companion took her parasol out of her hands and opened it. She came a little nearer, and he held the parasol over her; then, still holding it, he let it rest upon her shoulder, so that both of their heads were hidden from Winterbourne. This young man lingered a moment, then he began to walk. But he walked—not toward the couple with the parasol; toward the residence of his aunt, Mrs. Costello.

He flattered himself on the following day that there was no smiling among the servants when he, at least, asked for Mrs. Miller at her hotel. This lady and her daughter, however, were not at home; and on the next day after, repeating his visit, Winterbourne again had the misfortune not to find them. Mrs. Walker's party took place on the evening of the third day, and, in spite of the frigidity of his last interview with the hostess, Winterbourne was among the guests. Mrs. Walker was one of those American ladies who, while residing abroad, make a point, in their own phrase, of studying European society, and she had on this occasion collected several specimens of her diversely born fellow mortals to serve, as it were, as textbooks. When Winterbourne arrived, Daisy Miller was not there, but in a few moments he saw her mother come in alone, very shyly and ruefully. Mrs. Miller's hair above her exposed-looking temples was more frizzled than ever. As she approached Mrs. Walker, Winterbourne also drew near.

"You see, I've come all alone," said poor Mrs. Miller. "I'm so frightened; I don't know what to do. It's the first time I've ever been to a party alone, especially in this country. I wanted to bring Randolph or Eugenio, or someone, but Daisy just pushed me off by myself. I ain't used to going round alone."

"And does not your daughter intend to favor us with her society?" demanded Mrs. Walker impressively.

"Well, Daisy's all dressed," said Mrs. Miller with that accent of the dispassionate, if not of the philosophic, historian with which she always recorded the current incidents of her daughter's career. "She got dressed on purpose before dinner. But she's got a friend of hers there; that gentleman—the Italian—that she wanted to bring. They've got going at the piano; it seems as if they couldn't leave off. Mr. Giovanelli sings splendidly. But I guess they'll come before very long," concluded Mrs. Miller hopefully.

"I'm sorry she should come in that way," said Mrs. Walker.

"Well, I told her that there was no use in her getting dressed before dinner if she was going to wait three hours," responded Daisy's mamma. "I didn't see the use of her putting on such a dress as that to sit round with Mr. Giovanelli."

"This is most horrible!" said Mrs. Walker, turning away and addressing herself to Winterbourne. "Elle s'affiche. It's her revenge for my having ventured to remonstrate with her. When she comes, I shall not speak to her."

Daisy came after eleven o'clock; but she was not, on such an occasion, a young lady to wait to be spoken to. She rustled forward in radiant loveliness, smiling and chattering, carrying a large bouquet, and attended by Mr. Giovanelli. Everyone stopped talking and turned and looked at her. She came straight to Mrs. Walker. "I'm afraid you thought I never was coming, so I sent mother off to tell you. I wanted to make Mr. Giovanelli practice some things before he came; you know he sings beautifully, and I want you to ask him to sing. This is Mr. Giovanelli; you know I introduced him to you; he's got the most lovely voice, and he knows the most charming set of songs. I made him go over them this evening on purpose; we had the greatest time at the hotel." Of all this Daisy delivered herself with the sweetest, brightest audibleness, looking now at her hostess and now round the room, while she gave a series of little pats, round her shoulders, to the edges of her dress. "Is there anyone I know?" she asked.

"I think every one knows you!" said Mrs. Walker pregnantly, and she gave a very cursory greeting to Mr. Giovanelli. This gentleman bore himself gallantly. He smiled and bowed and showed his white teeth; he curled his mustaches and rolled his eyes and performed all the proper functions of a handsome Italian at an evening party. He sang very prettily half a dozen songs, though Mrs. Walker afterward declared that she had been quite unable to find out who asked him. It was apparently not Daisy who had given him his orders. Daisy sat at a distance from the piano, and though she had publicly, as it were, professed a high admiration for his singing, talked, not inaudibly, while it was going on.

"It's a pity these rooms are so small; we can't dance," she said to Winterbourne, as if she had seen him five minutes before.

"I am not sorry we can't dance," Winterbourne answered; "I don't dance."

"Of course you don't dance; you're too stiff," said Miss Daisy. "I hope you enjoyed your drive with Mrs. Walker!"

"No. I didn't enjoy it; I preferred walking with you."

"We paired off: that was much better," said Daisy. "But did you ever hear anything so cool as Mrs. Walker's wanting me to get into her carriage and drop poor Mr. Giovanelli, and under the pretext that it was proper? People have different ideas! It would have been most unkind; he had been talking about that walk for ten days."

"He should not have talked about it at all," said Winterbourne; "he would never have proposed to a young lady of this country to walk about the streets with him."

"About the streets?" cried Daisy with her pretty stare. "Where, then, would he have proposed to her to walk? The Pincio is not the streets, either; and I, thank goodness, am not a young lady of this country. The young ladies of this country have a dreadfully poky time of it, so far as I can learn; I don't see why I should change my habits for THEM."

"I am afraid your habits are those of a flirt," said Winterbourne gravely.

"Of course they are," she cried, giving him her little smiling stare again. "I'm a fearful, frightful flirt! Did you ever hear of a nice girl that was not? But I suppose you will tell me now that I am not a nice girl."

"You're a very nice girl; but I wish you would flirt with me, and me only," said Winterbourne.

"Ah! thank you—thank you very much; you are the last man I should think of flirting with. As I have had the pleasure of informing you, you are too stiff."

"You say that too often," said Winterbourne.

Daisy gave a delighted laugh. "If I could have the sweet hope of making you angry, I should say it again."

"Don't do that; when I am angry I'm stiffer than ever. But if you won't flirt with me, do cease, at least, to flirt with your friend at the piano; they don't understand that sort of thing here."

"I thought they understood nothing else!" exclaimed Daisy.

"Not in young unmarried women."

"It seems to me much more proper in young unmarried women than in old married ones," Daisy declared.

"Well," said Winterbourne, "when you deal with natives you must go by the custom of the place. Flirting is a purely American custom; it doesn't exist here. So when you show yourself in public with Mr. Giovanelli, and without your mother—"

"Gracious! poor Mother!" interposed Daisy.

"Though you may be flirting, Mr. Giovanelli is not; he means something else."

"He isn't preaching, at any rate," said Daisy with vivacity. "And if you want very much to know, we are neither of us flirting; we are too good friends for that: we are very intimate friends."

"Ah!" rejoined Winterbourne, "if you are in love with each other, it is another affair."

She had allowed him up to this point to talk so frankly that he had no expectation of shocking her by this ejaculation; but she immediately got up, blushing visibly, and leaving him to exclaim mentally that little American flirts were the queerest creatures in the world. "Mr. Giovanelli, at least," she said, giving her interlocutor a single glance, "never says such very disagreeable things to me."

Winterbourne was bewildered; he stood, staring. Mr. Giovanelli had finished singing. He left the piano and came over to Daisy. "Won't you come into the other room and have some tea?" he asked, bending before her with his ornamental smile.

Daisy turned to Winterbourne, beginning to smile again. He was still more perplexed, for this inconsequent smile made nothing clear, though it seemed to prove, indeed, that she had a sweetness and softness that reverted instinctively to the pardon of offenses. "It has never occurred to Mr. Winterbourne to offer me any tea," she said with her little tormenting manner.

"I have offered you advice," Winterbourne rejoined.

"I prefer weak tea!" cried Daisy, and she went off with the brilliant Giovanelli. She sat with him in the adjoining room, in the embrasure of the window, for the rest of the evening. There was an interesting performance at the piano, but neither of these young people gave heed to it. When Daisy came to take leave of Mrs. Walker, this lady conscientiously repaired the weakness of which she had been guilty at the moment of the young girl's arrival. She turned her back straight upon Miss Miller and left her to depart with what grace she might. Winterbourne was standing near the door; he saw it all. Daisy turned very pale and looked at her mother, but Mrs. Miller was humbly unconscious of any violation of the usual social forms. She appeared, indeed, to have felt an incongruous impulse to draw attention to her own striking observance of them. "Good night, Mrs. Walker," she said; "we've had a beautiful evening. You see, if I let Daisy come to parties without me, I don't want her to go away without me." Daisy turned away, looking with a pale, grave face at the circle near the door; Winterbourne saw that, for the first moment, she was too much shocked and puzzled even for indignation. He on his side was greatly touched.

"That was very cruel," he said to Mrs. Walker.

"She never enters my drawing room again!" replied his hostess.

Since Winterbourne was not to meet her in Mrs. Walker's drawing room, he went as often as possible to Mrs. Miller's hotel. The ladies were rarely at home, but when he found them, the devoted Giovanelli was always present. Very often the brilliant little Roman was in the drawing room with Daisy alone, Mrs. Miller being apparently constantly of the opinion that discretion is the better part of surveillance. Winterbourne noted, at first with surprise, that Daisy on these occasions was never embarrassed or annoyed by his own entrance; but he very presently began to feel that she had no more surprises for him; the unexpected in her behavior was the only thing to expect. She showed no displeasure at her tete-a-tete with Giovanelli being interrupted; she could chatter as freshly and freely with two gentlemen as with one; there was always, in her conversation, the same odd mixture of audacity and puerility. Winterbourne remarked to himself that if she was seriously interested in Giovanelli, it was very singular that she should not take more trouble to preserve the sanctity of their interviews; and he liked her the more for her innocent-looking indifference and her apparently inexhaustible good humor. He could hardly have said why, but she seemed to him a girl who would never be jealous. At the risk of exciting a somewhat derisive smile on the reader's part, I may affirm that with regard to the women who had hitherto interested him, it very often seemed to Winterbourne among the possibilities that, given certain contingencies, he should be afraid—literally afraid—of these ladies; he had a pleasant sense that he should never be afraid of Daisy Miller. It must be added that this sentiment was not altogether flattering to Daisy; it was part of his conviction, or rather of his apprehension, that she would prove a very light young person.

But she was evidently very much interested in Giovanelli. She looked at him whenever he spoke; she was perpetually telling him to do this and to do that; she was constantly "chaffing" and abusing him. She appeared completely to have forgotten that Winterbourne had said anything to displease her at Mrs. Walker's little party. One Sunday afternoon, having gone to St. Peter's with his aunt, Winterbourne perceived Daisy strolling about the great church in company with the inevitable Giovanelli. Presently he pointed out the young girl and her cavalier to Mrs. Costello. This lady looked at them a moment through her eyeglass, and then she said:

"That's what makes you so pensive in these days, eh?"

"I had not the least idea I was pensive," said the young man.

"You are very much preoccupied; you are thinking of something."

"And what is it," he asked, "that you accuse me of thinking of?"

"Of that young lady's—Miss Baker's, Miss Chandler's—what's her name?—Miss Miller's intrigue with that little barber's block."

"Do you call it an intrigue," Winterbourne asked—"an affair that goes on with such peculiar publicity?"

"That's their folly," said Mrs. Costello; "it's not their merit."

"No," rejoined Winterbourne, with something of that pensiveness to which his aunt had alluded. "I don't believe that there is anything to be called an intrigue."

"I have heard a dozen people speak of it; they say she is quite carried away by him."

"They are certainly very intimate," said Winterbourne.

Mrs. Costello inspected the young couple again with her optical instrument. "He is very handsome. One easily sees how it is. She thinks him the most elegant man in the world, the finest gentleman. She has never seen anything like him; he is better, even, than the courier. It was the courier probably who introduced him; and if he succeeds in marrying the young lady, the courier will come in for a magnificent commission."

"I don't believe she thinks of marrying him," said Winterbourne, "and I don't believe he hopes to marry her."

"You may be very sure she thinks of nothing. She goes on from day to day, from hour to hour, as they did in the Golden Age. I can imagine nothing more vulgar. And at the same time," added Mrs. Costello, "depend upon it that she may tell you any moment that she is 'engaged.'"

"I think that is more than Giovanelli expects," said Winterbourne.

"Who is Giovanelli?"

"The little Italian. I have asked questions about him and learned something. He is apparently a perfectly respectable little man. I believe he is, in a small way, a cavaliere avvocato. But he doesn't move in what are called the first circles. I think it is really not absolutely impossible that the courier introduced him. He is evidently immensely charmed with Miss Miller. If she thinks him the finest gentleman in the world, he, on his side, has never found himself in personal contact with such splendor, such opulence, such expensiveness as this young lady's. And then she must seem to him wonderfully pretty and interesting. I rather doubt that he dreams of marrying her. That must appear to him too impossible a piece of luck. He has nothing but his handsome face to offer, and there is a substantial Mr. Miller in that mysterious land of dollars. Giovanelli knows that he hasn't a title to offer. If he were only a count or a marchese! He must wonder at his luck, at the way they have taken him up."

"He accounts for it by his handsome face and thinks Miss Miller a young lady qui se passe ses fantaisies!" said Mrs. Costello.

"It is very true," Winterbourne pursued, "that Daisy and her mamma have not yet risen to that stage of—what shall I call it?—of culture at which the idea of catching a count or a marchese begins. I believe that they are intellectually incapable of that conception."

"Ah! but the avvocato can't believe it," said Mrs. Costello.

Of the observation excited by Daisy's "intrigue," Winterbourne gathered that day at St. Peter's sufficient evidence. A dozen of the American colonists in Rome came to talk with Mrs. Costello, who sat on a little portable stool at the base of one of the great pilasters. The vesper service was going forward in splendid chants and organ tones in the adjacent choir, and meanwhile, between Mrs. Costello and her friends, there was a great deal said about poor little Miss Miller's going really "too far." Winterbourne was not pleased with what he heard, but when, coming out upon the great steps of the church, he saw Daisy, who had emerged before him, get into an open cab with her accomplice and roll away through the cynical streets of Rome, he could not deny to himself that she was going very far indeed. He felt very sorry for her—not exactly that he believed that she had completely lost her head, but because it was painful to hear so much that was pretty, and undefended, and natural assigned to a vulgar place among the categories of disorder. He made an attempt after this to give a hint to Mrs. Miller. He met one day in the Corso a friend, a tourist like himself, who had just come out of the Doria Palace, where he had been walking through the beautiful gallery. His friend talked for a moment about the superb portrait of Innocent X by Velasquez which hangs in one of the cabinets of the palace, and then said, "And in the same cabinet, by the way, I had the pleasure of contemplating a picture of a different kind—that pretty American girl whom you pointed out to me last week." In answer to Winterbourne's inquiries, his friend narrated that the pretty American girl—prettier than ever—was seated with a companion in the secluded nook in which the great papal portrait was enshrined.

"Who was her companion?" asked Winterbourne.

"A little Italian with a bouquet in his buttonhole. The girl is delightfully pretty, but I thought I understood from you the other day that she was a young lady du meilleur monde."

"So she is!" answered Winterbourne; and having assured himself that his informant had seen Daisy and her companion but five minutes before, he jumped into a cab and went to call on Mrs. Miller. She was at home; but she apologized to him for receiving him in Daisy's absence.

"She's gone out somewhere with Mr. Giovanelli," said Mrs. Miller. "She's always going round with Mr. Giovanelli."

"I have noticed that they are very intimate," Winterbourne observed.

"Oh, it seems as if they couldn't live without each other!" said Mrs. Miller. "Well, he's a real gentleman, anyhow. I keep telling Daisy she's engaged!"

"And what does Daisy say?"

"Oh, she says she isn't engaged. But she might as well be!" this impartial parent resumed; "she goes on as if she was. But I've made Mr. Giovanelli promise to tell me, if SHE doesn't. I should want to write to Mr. Miller about it—shouldn't you?"

Winterbourne replied that he certainly should; and the state of mind of Daisy's mamma struck him as so unprecedented in the annals of parental vigilance that he gave up as utterly irrelevant the attempt to place her upon her guard.

After this Daisy was never at home, and Winterbourne ceased to meet her at the houses of their common acquaintances, because, as he perceived, these shrewd people had quite made up their minds that she was going too far. They ceased to invite her; and they intimated that they desired to express to observant Europeans the great truth that, though Miss Daisy Miller was a young American lady, her behavior was not representative—was regarded by her compatriots as abnormal. Winterbourne wondered how she felt about all the cold shoulders that were turned toward her, and sometimes it annoyed him to suspect that she did not feel at all. He said to himself that she was too light and childish, too uncultivated and unreasoning, too provincial, to have reflected upon her ostracism, or even to have perceived it. Then at other moments he believed that she carried about in her elegant and irresponsible little organism a defiant, passionate, perfectly observant consciousness of the impression she produced. He asked himself whether Daisy's defiance came from the consciousness of innocence, or from her being, essentially, a young person of the reckless class. It must be admitted that holding one's self to a belief in Daisy's "innocence" came to seem to Winterbourne more and more a matter of fine-spun gallantry. As I have already had occasion to relate, he was angry at finding himself reduced to chopping logic about this young lady; he was vexed at his want of instinctive certitude as to how far her eccentricities were generic, national, and how far they were personal. From either view of them he had somehow missed her, and now it was too late. She was "carried away" by Mr. Giovanelli.

A few days after his brief interview with her mother, he encountered her in that beautiful abode of flowering desolation known as the Palace of the Caesars. The early Roman spring had filled the air with bloom and perfume, and the rugged surface of the Palatine was muffled with tender verdure. Daisy was strolling along the top of one of those great mounds of ruin that are embanked with mossy marble and paved with monumental inscriptions. It seemed to him that Rome had never been so lovely as just then. He stood, looking off at the enchanting harmony of line and color that remotely encircles the city, inhaling the softly humid odors, and feeling the freshness of the year and the antiquity of the place reaffirm themselves in mysterious interfusion. It seemed to him also that Daisy had never looked so pretty, but this had been an observation of his whenever he met her. Giovanelli was at her side, and Giovanelli, too, wore an aspect of even unwonted brilliancy.

"Well," said Daisy, "I should think you would be lonesome!"

"Lonesome?" asked Winterbourne.

"You are always going round by yourself. Can't you get anyone to walk with you?"

"I am not so fortunate," said Winterbourne, "as your companion."

Giovanelli, from the first, had treated Winterbourne with distinguished politeness. He listened with a deferential air to his remarks; he laughed punctiliously at his pleasantries; he seemed disposed to testify to his belief that Winterbourne was a superior young man. He carried himself in no degree like a jealous wooer; he had obviously a great deal of tact; he had no objection to your expecting a little humility of him. It even seemed to Winterbourne at times that Giovanelli would find a certain mental relief in being able to have a private understanding with him—to say to him, as an intelligent man, that, bless you, HE knew how extraordinary was this young lady, and didn't flatter himself with delusive—or at least TOO delusive—hopes of matrimony and dollars. On this occasion he strolled away from his companion to pluck a sprig of almond blossom, which he carefully arranged in his buttonhole.

"I know why you say that," said Daisy, watching Giovanelli. "Because you think I go round too much with HIM." And she nodded at her attendant.

"Every one thinks so—if you care to know," said Winterbourne.

"Of course I care to know!" Daisy exclaimed seriously. "But I don't believe it. They are only pretending to be shocked. They don't really care a straw what I do. Besides, I don't go round so much."

"I think you will find they do care. They will show it disagreeably."

Daisy looked at him a moment. "How disagreeably?"

"Haven't you noticed anything?" Winterbourne asked.

"I have noticed you. But I noticed you were as stiff as an umbrella the first time I saw you."

"You will find I am not so stiff as several others," said Winterbourne, smiling.

"How shall I find it?"

"By going to see the others."

"What will they do to me?"

"They will give you the cold shoulder. Do you know what that means?"

Daisy was looking at him intently; she began to color. "Do you mean as Mrs. Walker did the other night?"

"Exactly!" said Winterbourne.

She looked away at Giovanelli, who was decorating himself with his almond blossom. Then looking back at Winterbourne, "I shouldn't think you would let people be so unkind!" she said.

"How can I help it?" he asked.

"I should think you would say something."

"I do say something;" and he paused a moment. "I say that your mother tells me that she believes you are engaged."

"Well, she does," said Daisy very simply.

Winterbourne began to laugh. "And does Randolph believe it?" he asked.

"I guess Randolph doesn't believe anything," said Daisy. Randolph's skepticism excited Winterbourne to further hilarity, and he observed that Giovanelli was coming back to them. Daisy, observing it too, addressed herself again to her countryman. "Since you have mentioned it," she said, "I AM engaged." * * * Winterbourne looked at her; he had stopped laughing. "You don't believe!" she added.

He was silent a moment; and then, "Yes, I believe it," he said.

"Oh, no, you don't!" she answered. "Well, then—I am not!"

The young girl and her cicerone were on their way to the gate of the enclosure, so that Winterbourne, who had but lately entered, presently took leave of them. A week afterward he went to dine at a beautiful villa on the Caelian Hill, and, on arriving, dismissed his hired vehicle. The evening was charming, and he promised himself the satisfaction of walking home beneath the Arch of Constantine and past the vaguely lighted monuments of the Forum. There was a waning moon in the sky, and her radiance was not brilliant, but she was veiled in a thin cloud curtain which seemed to diffuse and equalize it. When, on his return from the villa (it was eleven o'clock), Winterbourne approached the dusky circle of the Colosseum, it recurred to him, as a lover of the picturesque, that the interior, in the pale moonshine, would be well worth a glance. He turned aside and walked to one of the empty arches, near which, as he observed, an open carriage—one of the little Roman streetcabs—was stationed. Then he passed in, among the cavernous shadows of the great structure, and emerged upon the clear and silent arena. The place had never seemed to him more impressive. One-half of the gigantic circus was in deep shade, the other was sleeping in the luminous dusk. As he stood there he began to murmur Byron's famous lines, out of "Manfred," but before he had finished his quotation he remembered that if nocturnal meditations in the Colosseum are recommended by the poets, they are deprecated by the doctors. The historic atmosphere was there, certainly; but the historic atmosphere, scientifically considered, was no better than a villainous miasma. Winterbourne walked to the middle of the arena, to take a more general glance, intending thereafter to make a hasty retreat. The great cross in the center was covered with shadow; it was only as he drew near it that he made it out distinctly. Then he saw that two persons were stationed upon the low steps which formed its base. One of these was a woman, seated; her companion was standing in front of her.

Presently the sound of the woman's voice came to him distinctly in the warm night air. "Well, he looks at us as one of the old lions or tigers may have looked at the Christian martyrs!" These were the words he heard, in the familiar accent of Miss Daisy Miller.

"Let us hope he is not very hungry," responded the ingenious Giovanelli. "He will have to take me first; you will serve for dessert!"

Winterbourne stopped, with a sort of horror, and, it must be added, with a sort of relief. It was as if a sudden illumination had been flashed upon the ambiguity of Daisy's behavior, and the riddle had become easy to read. She was a young lady whom a gentleman need no longer be at pains to respect. He stood there, looking at her—looking at her companion and not reflecting that though he saw them vaguely, he himself must have been more brightly visible. He felt angry with himself that he had bothered so much about the right way of regarding Miss Daisy Miller. Then, as he was going to advance again, he checked himself, not from the fear that he was doing her injustice, but from a sense of the danger of appearing unbecomingly exhilarated by this sudden revulsion from cautious criticism. He turned away toward the entrance of the place, but, as he did so, he heard Daisy speak again.

"Why, it was Mr. Winterbourne! He saw me, and he cuts me!"

What a clever little reprobate she was, and how smartly she played at injured innocence! But he wouldn't cut her. Winterbourne came forward again and went toward the great cross. Daisy had got up; Giovanelli lifted his hat. Winterbourne had now begun to think simply of the craziness, from a sanitary point of view, of a delicate young girl lounging away the evening in this nest of malaria. What if she WERE a clever little reprobate? that was no reason for her dying of the perniciosa. "How long have you been here?" he asked almost brutally.

Daisy, lovely in the flattering moonlight, looked at him a moment. Then—"All the evening," she answered, gently. * * * "I never saw anything so pretty."

"I am afraid," said Winterbourne, "that you will not think Roman fever very pretty. This is the way people catch it. I wonder," he added, turning to Giovanelli, "that you, a native Roman, should countenance such a terrible indiscretion."

"Ah," said the handsome native, "for myself I am not afraid."

"Neither am I—for you! I am speaking for this young lady."

Giovanelli lifted his well-shaped eyebrows and showed his brilliant teeth. But he took Winterbourne's rebuke with docility. "I told the signorina it was a grave indiscretion, but when was the signorina ever prudent?"

"I never was sick, and I don't mean to be!" the signorina declared. "I don't look like much, but I'm healthy! I was bound to see the Colosseum by moonlight; I shouldn't have wanted to go home without that; and we have had the most beautiful time, haven't we, Mr. Giovanelli? If there has been any danger, Eugenio can give me some pills. He has got some splendid pills."

"I should advise you," said Winterbourne, "to drive home as fast as possible and take one!"

"What you say is very wise," Giovanelli rejoined. "I will go and make sure the carriage is at hand." And he went forward rapidly.

Daisy followed with Winterbourne. He kept looking at her; she seemed not in the least embarrassed. Winterbourne said nothing; Daisy chattered about the beauty of the place. "Well, I HAVE seen the Colosseum by moonlight!" she exclaimed. "That's one good thing." Then, noticing Winterbourne's silence, she asked him why he didn't speak. He made no answer; he only began to laugh. They passed under one of the dark archways; Giovanelli was in front with the carriage. Here Daisy stopped a moment, looking at the young American. "DID you believe I was engaged, the other day?" she asked.

"It doesn't matter what I believed the other day," said Winterbourne, still laughing.

"Well, what do you believe now?"

"I believe that it makes very little difference whether you are engaged or not!"

He felt the young girl's pretty eyes fixed upon him through the thick gloom of the archway; she was apparently going to answer. But Giovanelli hurried her forward. "Quick! quick!" he said; "if we get in by midnight we are quite safe."

Daisy took her seat in the carriage, and the fortunate Italian placed himself beside her. "Don't forget Eugenio's pills!" said Winterbourne as he lifted his hat.

"I don't care," said Daisy in a little strange tone, "whether I have Roman fever or not!" Upon this the cab driver cracked his whip, and they rolled away over the desultory patches of the antique pavement.

Winterbourne, to do him justice, as it were, mentioned to no one that he had encountered Miss Miller, at midnight, in the Colosseum with a gentleman; but nevertheless, a couple of days later, the fact of her having been there under these circumstances was known to every member of the little American circle, and commented accordingly. Winterbourne reflected that they had of course known it at the hotel, and that, after Daisy's return, there had been an exchange of remarks between the porter and the cab driver. But the young man was conscious, at the same moment, that it had ceased to be a matter of serious regret to him that the little American flirt should be "talked about" by low-minded menials. These people, a day or two later, had serious information to give: the little American flirt was alarmingly ill. Winterbourne, when the rumor came to him, immediately went to the hotel for more news. He found that two or three charitable friends had preceded him, and that they were being entertained in Mrs. Miller's salon by Randolph.

"It's going round at night," said Randolph—"that's what made her sick. She's always going round at night. I shouldn't think she'd want to, it's so plaguy dark. You can't see anything here at night, except when there's a moon. In America there's always a moon!" Mrs. Miller was invisible; she was now, at least, giving her daughter the advantage of her society. It was evident that Daisy was dangerously ill.

Winterbourne went often to ask for news of her, and once he saw Mrs. Miller, who, though deeply alarmed, was, rather to his surprise, perfectly composed, and, as it appeared, a most efficient and judicious nurse. She talked a good deal about Dr. Davis, but Winterbourne paid her the compliment of saying to himself that she was not, after all, such a monstrous goose. "Daisy spoke of you the other day," she said to him. "Half the time she doesn't know what she's saying, but that time I think she did. She gave me a message she told me to tell you. She told me to tell you that she never was engaged to that handsome Italian. I am sure I am very glad; Mr. Giovanelli hasn't been near us since she was taken ill. I thought he was so much of a gentleman; but I don't call that very polite! A lady told me that he was afraid I was angry with him for taking Daisy round at night. Well, so I am, but I suppose he knows I'm a lady. I would scorn to scold him. Anyway, she says she's not engaged. I don't know why she wanted you to know, but she said to me three times, 'Mind you tell Mr. Winterbourne.' And then she told me to ask if you remembered the time you went to that castle in Switzerland. But I said I wouldn't give any such messages as that. Only, if she is not engaged, I'm sure I'm glad to know it."

But, as Winterbourne had said, it mattered very little. A week after this, the poor girl died; it had been a terrible case of the fever. Daisy's grave was in the little Protestant cemetery, in an angle of the wall of imperial Rome, beneath the cypresses and the thick spring flowers. Winterbourne stood there beside it, with a number of other mourners, a number larger than the scandal excited by the young lady's career would have led you to expect. Near him stood Giovanelli, who came nearer still before Winterbourne turned away. Giovanelli was very pale: on this occasion he had no flower in his buttonhole; he seemed to wish to say something. At last he said, "She was the most beautiful young lady I ever saw, and the most amiable;" and then he added in a moment, "and she was the most innocent."

Winterbourne looked at him and presently repeated his words, "And the most innocent?"

"The most innocent!"

Winterbourne felt sore and angry. "Why the devil," he asked, "did you take her to that fatal place?"

Mr. Giovanelli's urbanity was apparently imperturbable. He looked on the ground a moment, and then he said, "For myself I had no fear; and she wanted to go."

"That was no reason!" Winterbourne declared.

The subtle Roman again dropped his eyes. "If she had lived, I should have got nothing. She would never have married me, I am sure."

"She would never have married you?"

"For a moment I hoped so. But no. I am sure."

Winterbourne listened to him: he stood staring at the raw protuberance among the April daisies. When he turned away again, Mr. Giovanelli, with his light, slow step, had retired.

Winterbourne almost immediately left Rome; but the following summer he again met his aunt, Mrs. Costello at Vevey. Mrs. Costello was fond of Vevey. In the interval Winterbourne had often thought of Daisy Miller and her mystifying manners. One day he spoke of her to his aunt—said it was on his conscience that he had done her injustice.

"I am sure I don't know," said Mrs. Costello. "How did your injustice affect her?"

"She sent me a message before her death which I didn't understand at the time; but I have understood it since. She would have appreciated one's esteem."

"Is that a modest way," asked Mrs. Costello, "of saying that she would have reciprocated one's affection?"

Winterbourne offered no answer to this question; but he presently said, "You were right in that remark that you made last summer. I was booked to make a mistake. I have lived too long in foreign parts."

Nevertheless, he went back to live at Geneva, whence there continue to come the most contradictory accounts of his motives of sojourn: a report that he is "studying" hard—an intimation that he is much interested in a very clever foreign lady.

EMBARRASSMENTS

THE FIGURE IN THE CARPET

I

I had done a few things and earned a few pence—I had perhaps even had time to begin to think I was finer than was perceived by the patronising; but when I take the little measure of my course (a fidgety habit, for it's none of the longest yet) I count my real start from the evening George Corvick, breathless and worried, came in to ask me a service. He had done more things than I, and earned more pence, though there were chances for cleverness I thought he sometimes missed. I could only however that evening declare to him that he never missed one for kindness. There was almost rapture in hearing it proposed to me to prepare for *The Middle_*, the organ of our lucubrations, so called from the position in the week of its day of appearance, an article for which he had made himself responsible and of which, tied up with a stout string, he laid on my table the subject. I pounced upon my opportunity—that is on the first volume of it—and paid scant attention to my friend's explanation of his appeal. What explanation could be more to the point than my obvious fitness for the task? I had written on Hugh Vereker, but never a word in *The Middle*, where my dealings were mainly with the ladies and the minor poets. This was his new novel, an advance copy, and whatever much or little it should do for his reputation I was clear on the spot as to what it should do for mine. Moreover, if I always read him as soon as I could get hold of him, I had a particular reason for wishing to read him now: I had accepted an invitation to Bridges for the following Sunday, and it had been mentioned in Lady Jane's note that Mr. Vereker was to be there. I was young enough to have an emotion about meeting a man of his renown, and innocent enough to believe the occasion would demand the display of an acquaintance with his "last."

Corvick, who had promised a review of it, had not even had time to read it; he had gone to pieces in consequence of news requiring—as on precipitate reflection he judged—that he should catch the night-mail to Paris. He had had a telegram from Gwendolen Erme in answer to his letter offering to fly to her aid. I knew already about Gwendolen Erme; I had never seen her, but I had my ideas, which were mainly to the effect that Corvick would marry her if her mother would only die. That lady seemed now in a fair way to oblige him; after some dreadful mistake about some climate or some waters, she had suddenly collapsed on the return from abroad. Her daughter, unsupported and alarmed, desiring to make a rush for home but hesitating at the risk, had accepted our friend's assistance, and it was my secret belief that at the sight of him Mrs. Erme would pull round. His own belief was scarcely to be called secret; it discernibly at any rate differed from mine. He had showed me Gwendolen's photograph with the remark that she wasn't pretty but was awfully interesting; she had published at the age of nineteen a novel in three volumes, "Deep Down," about which, in *The Middle*, he had been really splendid. He appreciated my present eagerness and undertook that the periodical in question should do no less; then at the last, with his hand on the door, he said to me: "Of course you'll be all right, you know." Seeing I was a trifle vague he added: "I mean you won't be silly."

"Silly—about Vereker! Why, what do I ever find him but awfully clever?"

"Well, what's that but silly? What on earth does 'awfully clever' mean? For God's sake try to get *at* him. Don't let him suffer by our arrangement. Speak of him, you know, if you can, as should have spoken of him."

I wondered an instant. "You mean as far and away the biggest of the lot—that sort of thing?"

Corvick almost groaned. "Oh, you know, I don't put them back to back that way; it's the infancy of art! But he gives me a pleasure so rare; the sense of "—he mused a little—"something or other."

I wondered again. "The sense, pray, of what?"

"My dear man, that's just what I want *you* to say!"

Even before Corvick had banged the door I had begun, book in hand, to prepare myself to say it. I sat up with Vereker half the night; Corvick couldn't have done more than that. He was awfully clever—I stuck to that, but he wasn't a bit the biggest of the lot. I didn't allude to the lot, however; I flattered myself that I emerged on this occasion from the infancy of art. "It's all right," they declared vividly at the office; and when the number appeared I felt there was a basis on which I could meet the great man; It gave me confidence for a day or two, and then that confidence dropped. I had fancied him reading it with relish, but if Corvick was not satisfied how could Vereker himself be? I reflected indeed that the heat of the admirer was sometimes grosser even than the appetite of the scribe. Corvick at all events wrote me from Paris a little ill-humouredly. Mrs. Erme was pulling round, and I hadn't at all said what Vereker gave him the sense of.

II

The effect of my visit to Bridges was to turn me out for more profundity. Hugh Vereker, as I saw him there, was of a contact so void of angles that I blushed for the poverty of imagination involved in my small precautions. If he was in spirits it was not because he had read my review; in fact on the Sunday morning I felt sure he hadn't read it, though *The Middle* had been out three days and bloomed, I assured myself, in the stiff garden of periodicals which gave one of the ormolu tables the air of a stand at a station. The impression he made on me personally was such that I wished him to read it, and I corrected to this end with a surreptitious hand what might be wanting in the careless conspicuity of the sheet. I am afraid I even watched the result of my manouvre, but up to luncheon I watched in vain.

When afterwards, in the course of our gregarious walk, I found myself for half an hour, not perhaps without another manoeuvre, at the great man's side, the result of his affability was a still livelier desire that he should not remain in ignorance of the peculiar justice I had done him. It was not that he seemed to thirst for justice; on the contrary I had not yet caught in his talk the faintest grunt of a grudge—a note for which my young experience had already given me an ear. Of late he had had more recognition, and it was pleasant, as we used to say in *The Middle*, to see that it drew him out. He wasn't of course popular, but I judged one of the sources of his good humour to be precisely that his success was independent of that. He had none the less become in a manner the fashion; the critics at least had put on a spurt and caught up with him. We had found out at last how clever he was, and he had had to make the best of the loss of his mystery. I was strongly tempted, as I walked beside him, to let him know how much of that unveiling was my act; and there was a moment when I probably should have done so had not one of the ladies of our party, snatching a place at his other elbow, just then appealed to him in a spirit comparatively selfish. It was very discouraging: I almost felt the liberty had been taken with myself.

I had had on my tongue's end, for my own part, a phrase or two about the right word at the right time; but later on I was glad not to have spoken, for when on our return we clustered at tea I perceived Lady Jane, who had not been out with us, brandishing *The Middle* with her longest arm. She had taken it up at her leisure; she was delighted with what she had found, and I saw that, as a mistake in a man may often be a felicity in a woman, she would practically do for me what I hadn't been able to do for myself. "Some sweet little truths that needed to be spoken," I heard her declare, thrusting the paper at rather a bewildered couple by the fireplace. She grabbed it away from them again on the reappearance of Hugh Vereker, who after our walk had been upstairs to change something. "I know you don't in general look at this kind of thing, but it's an occasion really for doing so. You *haven't* seen it? Then you must. The man has actually got *at* you, at what *I* always feel, you know." Lady Jane threw into her eyes a look evidently intended to give an idea of what she always felt; but she added that she couldn't have expressed it. The man in the paper expressed it in a striking manner. "Just see there, and there, where I've dashed it, how he brings it out." She had literally marked for him the brightest patches of my prose, and if I was a little amused Vereker himself may well have been. He showed how much he was when before us all Lady Jane wanted to read something aloud. I liked at any rate the way he defeated her purpose by jerking the paper affectionately out of her clutch. He would take it upstairs with him, would look at it on going to dress. He did this half an hour later—I saw it in his hand when he repaired to his room. That was the moment at which, thinking to give her pleasure, I mentioned to Lady Jane that I was the author of the review. I did give her pleasure, I judged, but perhaps not quite so much as I had expected. If the author was "only me" the thing didn't seem quite so remarkable. Hadn't I had the effect rather of diminishing the lustre of the article than of adding to my own? Her ladyship was subject to the most extraordinary drops. It didn't matter; the only effect I cared about was the one it would have on Vereker up there by his bedroom fire.

At dinner I watched for the signs of this impression, tried to fancy there was some happier light in his eyes; but to my disappointment Lady Jane gave me no chance to make sure. I had hoped she would call triumphantly down the table, publicly demand if she hadn't been right. The party was large—there were people from outside as well, but I had never seen a table long enough to deprive Lady Jane of a triumph. I was just reflecting in truth that this interminable board would deprive *me* of one, when the guest next me, dear woman—she was Miss Poyle, the vicar's sister, a robust, unmodulated person—had the happy inspiration and the unusual courage to address herself across it to Vereker, who was opposite, but not directly, so that when he replied they were both leaning forward. She inquired, artless body, what he thought of Lady Jane's "panegyric," which she had read—not connecting it however with her right-hand neighbour; and while I strained my ear for his reply I heard him, to my stupefaction, call back gaily, with his mouth full of bread: "Oh, it's all right—it's the usual twaddle!"

I had caught Vereker's glance as he spoke, but Miss Poyle's surprise was a fortunate cover for my own. "You mean he doesn't do you justice?" said the excellent woman.

Vereker laughed out, and I was happy to be able to do the same. "It's a charming article," he tossed us.

Miss Poyle thrust her chin half across the cloth.

"Oh you're so deep!" she drove home.

"As deep as the ocean! All I pretend is, the author doesn't see—"

A dish was at this point passed over his shoulder, and we had to wait while he helped himself.

"Doesn't see what?" my neighbour continued.

"Doesn't see anything."

"Dear me—how very stupid!"

"Not a bit," Vereker laughed again. "Nobody does."

The lady on his further side appealed to him, and Miss Poyle sank back to me. "Nobody sees anything!" she cheerfully announced; to which I replied that I had often thought so too, but had somehow taken the thought for a proof on my own part of a tremendous eye. I didn't tell her the article was mine; and I observed that Lady Jane, occupied at the end of the table, had not caught Vereker's words.

I rather avoided him after dinner, for I confess he struck me as cruelly conceited, and the revelation was a pain. "The usual twaddle"—my acute little study! That one's admiration should have had a reserve or two could gall him to that point? I had thought him placid, and he was placid enough; such a surface was the hard, polished glass that encased the bauble of his vanity. I was really ruffled, the only comfort was that if nobody saw anything George Corvick was quite as much out of it as I. This comfort however was not sufficient, after the ladies had dispersed, to carry me in the proper manner—I mean in a spotted jacket and humming an air—into the smoking-room. I took my way in some dejection to bed; but in the passage I encountered Mr. Vereker, who had been up once more to change, coming out of his room. *He* was humming an air and had on a spotted jacket, and as soon as he saw me his gaiety gave a start.

"My dear young man," he exclaimed, "I'm so glad to lay hands on you! I'm afraid I most unwittingly wounded you by those words of mine at dinner to Miss Poyle. I learned but half an hour ago from Lady Jane that you wrote the little notice in *The Middle*."

I protested that no bones were broken; but he moved with me to my own door, his hand on my shoulder, kindly feeling for a fracture; and on hearing that I had come up to bed he asked leave to cross my threshold and just tell me in three words what his qualification of my remarks had represented. It was plain he really feared I was hurt, and the sense of his solicitude suddenly made all the difference to me. My cheap review fluttered off into space, and the best things I had said in it became flat enough beside the brilliancy of his being there. I can see him there still, on my rug, in the firelight and his spotted jacket, his fine, clear face all bright with the desire to be tender to my youth. I don't know what he had at first meant to say, but I think the sight of my relief touched him, excited him, brought up words to his lips from far within. It was so these words presently conveyed to me something that, as I afterwards knew, he had never uttered to any one. I have always done justice to the generous impulse that made him speak; it was simply compunction for a snub unconsciously administered to a man of letters in a position inferior to his own, a man of letters moreover in the very act of praising him. To make the thing right he talked to me exactly as an equal and on the ground of what we both loved best. The hour, the place, the unexpectedness deepened the impression: he couldn't have done anything more exquisitely successful

III.

"I don't quite know how to explain it to you," he said, "but it was the very fact that your notice of my book had a spice of intelligence, it was just your exceptional sharpness that produced the feeling—a very old story with me, I beg you to believe—under the momentary influence of which I used in speaking to that good lady the words you so naturally resent. I don't read the things in the newspapers unless they're thrust upon me as that one was—it's always one's best friend that does it! But I used to read them sometimes—ten years ago. I daresay they were in general rather stupider then; at any rate it always seemed to me that they missed my little point with a perfection exactly as admirable when they patted me on the back as when they kicked me in the shins. Whenever since I've happened to have a glimpse of them they were still blazing away—still missing it, I mean, deliciously. *You* miss it, my dear fellow, with inimitable assurance; the fact of your being awfully clever and your article's being awfully nice doesn't make a hair's breadth of difference. It's quite with you rising young men," Vereker laughed, "that I feel most what a failure I am!"

I listened with intense interest; it grew intenser as he talked. "*You* a failure—heavens! What then may your 'little point' happen to be?"

"Have I got to *tell* you, after all these years and labours?" There was something in the friendly reproach of this—jocosely exaggerated—that made me, as an ardent young seeker for truth, blush to the roots of my hair. I'm as much in the dark as ever, though I've grown used in a sense to my obtuseness; at that moment, however, Vereker's happy accent made me appear to myself, and probably to him, a rare donkey. I was on the point of exclaiming, "Ah, yes, don't tell me: for my honour, for that of the craft, don't!" when he went on in a manner that showed he had read my thought and had his own idea of the probability of our some day redeeming ourselves. "By my little point I mean—what shall I call it?—the particular thing I've written my books most *for*. Isn't there for every writer a particular thing of that sort, the thing that most makes him apply himself, the thing without the effort to achieve which he wouldn't write at all, the very passion of his passion, the part of the business in which, for him, the flame of art burns most intensely? Well, it's *that!*"

I considered a moment. I was fascinated—easily, you'll say; but I wasn't going after all to be put off my guard. "Your description's certainly beautiful, but it doesn't make what you describe very distinct."

"I promise you it would be distinct if it should dawn on you at all." I saw that the charm of our topic overflowed for my companion into an emotion as lively as my own. "At any rate," he went on, "I can speak for myself: there's an idea in my work without which I wouldn't have given a straw for the whole job. It's the finest, fullest intention of the lot, and the application of it has been, I think, a triumph of patience, of ingenuity. I ought to leave that to somebody else to say; but that nobody does say it is precisely what we're talking about. It stretches, this little trick of mine, from book to book, and everything else, comparatively, plays over the surface of it. The order, the form, the texture of my books will perhaps some day constitute for the initiated a complete representation of it. So it's naturally the thing for the critic to look for. It strikes me," my visitor added, smiling, "even as the thing for the critic to find."

This seemed a responsibility indeed. "You call it a little trick?"

"That's only my little modesty. It's really an exquisite scheme."

"And you hold that you've carried the scheme out?"

"The way I've carried it out is the thing in life I think a bit well of myself for."

I was silent a moment. "Don't you think you ought—just a trifle—to assist the critic?"

"Assist him? What else have I done with every stroke of my pen? I've shouted my intention in his great blank face!" At this, laughing out again, Vereker laid his hand on my shoulder to show that the allusion was not to my personal appearance.

"But you talk about the initiated. There must therefore, you see, be initiation."

"What else in heaven's name is criticism supposed to be?" I'm afraid I coloured at this too; but I took refuge in repeating that his account of his silver lining was poor in something or other that a plain man knows things by. "That's only because you've never had a glimpse of it," he replied. "If you had had one the element in question would soon have become practically all you'd see. To me it's exactly as palpable as the marble of this chimney. Besides, the critic just *isn't* a plain man: if he were, pray, what would he be doing in his neighbour's garden? You're anything but a plain man yourself, and the very *raison d'être* of you all is that you're little demons of subtlety. If my great affair's a secret, that's only because it's a secret in spite of itself—the amazing event has made it one. I not only never took the smallest precaution to do so, but never dreamed of any such accident. If I had I shouldn't in advance have had the heart to go on. As it was I only became aware little by little, and meanwhile I had done my work."

"And now you quite like it?" I risked.

"My work?"

"Your secret. It's the same thing."

"Your guessing that," Vereker replied, "is a proof that you're as clever as I say!" I was encouraged by this to remark that he would clearly be pained to part with it, and he confessed that it was indeed with him now the great amusement of life. "I live almost to see if it will ever be detected." He looked at me for a jesting challenge; something at the back of his eyes seemed to peep out. "But I needn't worry—it won't!"

"You fire me as I've never been fired," I returned; "you make me determined to do or die." Then I asked: "Is it a kind of esoteric message?"

His countenance fell at this—he put out his hand as if to bid me good-night. "Ah, my dear fellow, it can't be described in cheap journalese!"

I knew of course he would be awfully fastidious, but our talk had made me feel how much his nerves were exposed. I was unsatisfied—I kept hold of his hand. "I won't make use of the expression then," I said, "in the article in which I shall eventually announce my discovery, though I daresay I shall have hard work to do without it. But meanwhile, just to hasten that difficult birth, can't you give a fellow a clue?" I felt much more at my ease.

"My whole lucid effort gives him a clue—every page and line and letter. The thing's as concrete there as a bird in a cage, a bait on a hook, a piece of cheese in a mouse-trap. It's stuck into every volume as your foot is stuck into your shoe. It governs every line, it chooses every word, it dots every i, it places every comma."

I scratched my head. "Is it something in the style or something in the thought? An element of form or an element of feeling?"

He indulgently shook my hand again, and I felt my questions to be crude and my distinctions pitiful. "Good-night, my dear boy—don't bother about it. After all, you do like a fellow."

"And a little intelligence might spoil it?" I still detained him.

He hesitated. "Well, you've got a heart in your body. Is that an element of form or an element of feeling? What I contend that nobody has ever mentioned in my work is the organ of life."

"I see—it's some idea about life, some sort of philosophy. Unless it be," I added with the eagerness of a thought perhaps still happier, "some kind of game you're up to with your style, something you're after in the language. Perhaps it's a preference for the letter P!" I ventured profanely to break out. "Papa, potatoes, prunes—that sort of thing?" He was suitably indulgent: he only said I hadn't got the right letter. But his amusement was over; I could see he was bored. There was nevertheless something else I had absolutely to learn. "Should you be able, pen in hand, to state it clearly yourself—to name it, phrase it, formulate it?"

"Oh," he almost passionately sighed, "if I were only, pen in hand, one of *you* chaps!"

"That would be a great chance for you of course. But why should you despise us chaps for not doing what you can't do yourself?"

"Can't do?" He opened his eyes. "Haven't I done it in twenty volumes? I do it in my way," he continued. "You don't do it in yours."

"Ours is so devilish difficult," I weakly observed.

"So is mine. We each choose our own. There's no compulsion. You won't come down and smoke?"

"No. I want to think this thing out."

"You'll tell me then in the morning that you've laid me bare?"

"I'll see what I can do; I'll sleep on it. But just one word more," I added. We had left the room—I walked again with him a few steps along the passage.

"This extraordinary 'general intention,' as you call it—for that's the most vivid description I can induce you to make of it—is then generally a sort of buried treasure?"

His face lighted. "Yes, call it that, though it's perhaps not for me to do so."

"Nonsense!" I laughed. "You know you're hugely proud of it."

"Well, I didn't propose to tell you so; but it *is* the joy of my soul!"

"You mean it's a beauty so rare, so great?"

He hesitated a moment. "The loveliest thing in the world!" We had stopped, and on these words he left me; but at the end of the corridor, while I looked after him rather yearningly, he turned and caught sight of my puzzled face. It made him earnestly, indeed I thought quite anxiously, shake his head and wave his finger. "Give it up—give it up!"

This wasn't a challenge—it was fatherly advice. If I had had one of his books at hand I would have repeated my recent act of faith—I would have spent half the night with him. At three o'clock in the morning, not sleeping, remembering moreover how indispensable he was to Lady Jane, I stole down to the library with a candle. There wasn't, so far as I could discover, a line of his writing in the house.

IV

Returning to town I feverishly collected them all; I picked out each in its order and held it up to the light. This gave me a maddening month, in the course of which several things took place. One of these, the last, I may as well immediately mention, was that I acted on Vereker's advice: I renounced my ridiculous attempt. I could really make nothing of the business; it proved a dead loss. After all, before, as he had himself observed, I liked him; and what now occurred was simply that my new intelligence and vain preoccupation damaged my liking. I not only failed to find his general intention—I found myself missing the subordinate intentions I had formerly found. His books didn't even remain the charming things they had been for me; the exasperation of my search put me out of conceit of them. Instead of being a pleasure the more they became a resource the less; for from the moment I was unable to follow up the author's hint I of course felt it a point of honour not to make use professionally of my knowledge of them. I *had* no knowledge—nobody had any. It was humiliating, but I could bear it—they only annoyed me now. At last they even bored me, and I accounted for my confusion—perversely, I confess—by the idea that Vereker had made a fool of me. The buried treasure was a bad joke, the general intention a monstrous *pose*.

The great incident of the time however was that I told George Corvick all about the matter and that my information had an immense effect upon him. He had at last come back, but so, unfortunately, had Mrs. Erme, and there was as yet, I could see, no question of his nuptials. He was immensely stirred up by the anecdote I had brought from Bridges; it fell in so completely with the sense he had had from the first that there was more in Vereker than met the eye. When I remarked that the eye seemed what the printed page had been expressly invented to meet he immediately accused me of being spiteful because I had been foiled. Our commerce had always that pleasant latitude. The thing Vereker had mentioned to me was exactly the thing he, Corvick, had wanted me to speak of in my review. On my suggesting at last that with the assistance I had now given him he would doubtless be prepared to speak of it himself he admitted freely that before doing this there was more he must understand. What he would have said, had he reviewed the new book, was that there was evidently in the writer's inmost art something to *be* understood. I hadn't so much as hinted at that: no wonder the writer hadn't been flattered! I asked Corvick what he really considered he meant by his own supersubtlety, and, unmistakably kindled, he replied: "It isn't for the vulgar—it isn't for the vulgar!" He had hold of the tail of something; he would pull hard, pull it right out. He pumped me dry on Vereker's strange confidence and, pronouncing me the luckiest of mortals, mentioned half a dozen questions he wished to goodness I had had the gumption to put. Yet on the other hand he didn't want to be told too much—it would spoil the fun of seeing what would come. The failure of my fun was at the moment of our meeting not complete, but I saw it ahead, and Corvick saw that I saw it. I, on my side, saw likewise that one of the first things he would do would be to rush off with my story to Gwendolen.

On the very day after my talk with him I was surprised by the receipt of a note from Hugh Vereker, to whom our encounter at Bridges had been recalled, as he mentioned, by his falling, in a magazine, on some article to which my signature was appended. "I read it with great pleasure," he wrote, "and remembered under its influence our lively conversation by your bedroom fire. The consequence of this has been that I begin to measure the temerity of my having saddled you with a knowledge that you may find something of a burden. Now that the fit's over I can't imagine how I came to be moved so much beyond my wont. I had never before related, no matter in what expansion, the history of my little secret, and I shall never speak of the business again. I was accidentally so much more explicit with you than it had ever entered into my game to be, that I find this game—I mean the pleasure of playing it—suffers considerably. In short, if you can understand it, I've spoiled a part of my fun. I really don't want to give anybody what I believe you clever young men call the tip. That's of course a selfish solicitude, and I name it to you for what it may be worth to you. If you're disposed to humour me, don't repeat my revelation. Think me demented—it's your right; but don't tell anybody why."

The sequel to this communication was that as early on the morrow as I dared I drove straight to Mr. Vereker's door. He occupied in those years one of the honest old houses in Kensington-square. He received me immediately, and as soon as I came in I saw I had not lost my power to minister to his mirth. He laughed out at the sight of my face, which doubtless expressed my perturbation. I had been indiscreet—my compunction was great. "I *have* told somebody," I panted, "and I'm sure that, person will by this time have told somebody else! It's a woman, into the bargain."

"The person you've told?"

"No, the other person. I'm quite sure he must have told her."

"For all the good it will do her—or do *me!* A woman will never find out."

"No, but she'll talk all over the place: she'll do just what you don't want."

Vereker thought a moment, but he was not so disconcerted as I had feared: he felt that if the harm was done it only served him right. "It doesn't matter—don't worry."

"I'll do my best, I promise you, that your talk with me shall go no further."

"Very good; do what you can."

"In the meantime," I pursued, "George Corvick's possession of the tip may, on his part, really lead to something."

"That will be a brave day."

I told him about Corvick's cleverness, his admiration, the intensity of his interest in my anecdote; and without making too much of the divergence of our respective estimates mentioned that my friend was already of opinion that he saw much further into a certain affair than most people. He was quite as fired as I had been at Bridges. He was moreover in love with the young lady: perhaps the two together would puzzle something out.

Vereker seemed struck with this. "Do you mean they're to be married?"

"I daresay that's what it will come to."

"That may help them," he conceded, "but we must give them time!"

I spoke of my own renewed assault and confessed my difficulties; whereupon he repeated his former advice: "Give it up, give it up!" He evidently didn't think me intellectually equipped for the adventure. I stayed half an hour, and he was most good-natured, but I couldn't help pronouncing him a man of shifting moods. He had been free with me in a mood, he had repented in a mood, and now in a mood he had turned indifferent. This general levity helped me to believe that, so far as the subject of the tip went, there wasn't much in it. I contrived however to make him answer a few more questions about it, though he did so with visible impatience. For himself, beyond doubt, the thing we were all so blank about was vividly there. It was something, I guessed, in the primal plan, something like a complex figure in a Persian carpet. He highly approved of this image when I used it, and he used another himself. "It's the very string," he said, "that my pearls are strung on!" The reason of his note to me had been that he really didn't want to give us a grain of succour—our destiny was a thing too perfect in its way to touch. He had formed the habit of depending upon it, and if the spell was to break it must break by some force of its own. He comes back to me from that last occasion—for I was never to speak to him again—as a man with some safe secret for enjoyment. I wondered as I walked away where he had got *his* tip.

V

When I spoke to George Corvick of the caution I had received he made me feel that any doubt of his delicacy would be almost an insult. He had instantly told Gwendolen, but Gwendolen's ardent response was in itself a pledge of discretion. The question would now absorb them, and they would enjoy their fun too much to wish to share it with the crowd. They appeared to have caught instinctively Vereker's peculiar notion of fun. Their intellectual pride, however, was not such as to make them indifferent to any further light I might throw on the affair they had in hand. They were indeed of the "artistic temperament," and I was freshly struck with my colleague's power to excite himself over a question of art. He called it letters, he called it life—it was all one thing. In what he said I now seemed to understand that he spoke equally for Gwendolen, to whom, as soon as Mrs. Erme was sufficiently better to allow her a little leisure, he made a point of introducing me. I remember our calling together one Sunday in August at a huddled house in Chelsea, and my renewed envy of Corvick's possession of a friend who had some light to mingle with his own. He could say things to her that I could never say to him. She had indeed no sense of humour and, with her pretty way of holding her head on one side, was one of those persons whom you want, as the phrase is, to shake, but who have learnt Hungarian by themselves. She conversed perhaps in Hungarian with Corvick; she had remarkably little English for his friend. Corvick afterwards told me that I had chilled her by my apparent indisposition to oblige her with the detail of what Vereker had said to me. I admitted that I felt I had given thought enough to this exposure: hadn't I even made up my mind that it was hollow, wouldn't stand the test? The importance they attached to it was irritating—it rather envenomed my dissent.

That statement looks unamiable, and what probably happened was that I felt humiliated at seeing other persons derive a daily joy from an experiment which had brought me only chagrin. I was out in the cold while, by the evening fire, under the lamp, they followed the chase for which I myself had sounded the horn. They did as I had done, only more deliberately and sociably—they went over their author from the beginning. There was no hurry, Corvick said—the future was before them and the fascination could only grow; they would take him page by page, as they would take one of the classics, inhale him in slow draughts and let him sink deep in. I doubt whether they would have got so wound up if they had not been in love: poor Vereker's secret gave them endless occasion to put their young heads together. None the less it represented the kind of problem for which Corvick had a special aptitude, drew out the particular pointed patience of which, had he lived, he would have given more striking and, it is to be hoped, more fruitful examples. He at least was, in Vereker's words, a little demon of subtlety. We had begun by disputing, but I soon saw that without my stirring a finger his infatuation would have its bad hours. He would bound off on false scents as I had done—he would clap his hands over new lights and see them blown out by the wind of the turned page. He was like nothing, I told him, but the maniacs who embrace some bedlamitical theory of the cryptic character of Shakespeare. To this he replied that if we had had Shakespeare's own word for his being cryptic he would immediately have accepted it. The case there was altogether different—we had nothing but the word of Mr. Snooks. I rejoined that I was stupefied to see him attach such importance even to the word of Mr. Vereker. He inquired thereupon whether I treated Mr. Vereker's word as a lie. I wasn't perhaps prepared, in my unhappy rebound, to go as far as that, but I insisted that till the contrary was proved I should view it as too fond an imagination. I didn't, I confess, say—I didn't at that time quite know—all I felt. Deep down, as Miss Erme would have said, I was uneasy, I was expectant. At the core of my personal confusion—for my curiosity lived in its ashes—was the sharpness of a sense that Corvick would at last probably come out somewhere. He made, in defence of his credulity, a great point of the fact that from of old, in his study of this genius, he had caught whiffs and hints of he didn't know what, faint wandering notes of a hidden music. That was just the rarity, that was the charm: it fitted so perfectly into what I reported.

If I returned on several occasions to the little house in Chelsea I daresay it was as much for news of Vereker as for news of Miss Erme's mamma. The hours spent there by Corvick were present to my fancy as those of a chessplayer bent with a silent scowl, all the lamplit winter, over his board and his moves. As my imagination filled it out the picture held me fast. On the other side of the table was a ghostlier form, the faint figure of an antagonist good-humouredly but a little wearily secure—an antagonist who leaned back in his chair with his hands in his pockets and a smile on his fine clear face. Close to Corvick, behind him, was a girl who had begun to strike me as pale and wasted and even, on more familiar view, as rather handsome, and who rested on his shoulder and hung upon his moves. He would take up a chessman and hold it poised a while over one of the little squares, and then he would put it back in its place with a long sigh of disappointment. The young lady, at this, would slightly but uneasily shift her position and look across, very hard, very long, very strangely, at their dim participant. I had asked them at an early stage of the business if it mightn't contribute to their success to have some closer communication with him. The special circumstances would surely be held to have given me a right to introduce them. Corvick immediately replied that he had no wish to approach the altar before he had prepared the sacrifice. He quite agreed with our friend both as to the sport and as to the honour—he would bring down the animal with his own rifle. When I asked him if Miss Erme were as keen a shot he said after an hesitation: "No; I'm ashamed to say she wants to set a trap. She'd give anything to see him; she says she requires another tip. She's really quite morbid about it. But she must play fair—she *shan't* see him!" he emphatically added. I had a suspicion that they had even quarrelled a little on the subject—a suspicion not corrected by the way he more than once exclaimed to me: "She's quite incredibly literary, you know—quite fantastically!" I remember his saying of her that she felt in italics and thought in capitals. "Oh, when I've run him to earth," he also said, "then, you know, I shall knock at his door. Rather—I beg you to believe. I'll have it from his own lips: 'Right you are, my boy; you've done it this time!' He shall crown me victor—with the critical laurel."

Meanwhile he really avoided the chances London life might have given him of meeting the distinguished novelist; a danger however that disappeared with Vereker's leaving England for an indefinite absence, as the newspapers announced—going to the south for motives connected with the health of his wife, which had long kept her in retirement. A year—more than a year—had elapsed since the incident at Bridges, but I had not encountered him again. I think at bottom I was rather ashamed—I hated to remind him that though I had irremediably missed his point a reputation for acuteness was rapidly overtaking me. This scruple led me a dance; kept me out of Lady Jane's house, made me even decline, when in spite of my bad manners she was a second time so good as to make me a sign, an invitation to her beautiful seat. I once saw her with Vereker at a concert and was sure I was seen by them, but I slipped out without being caught. I felt, as on that occasion I splashed along in the rain, that I couldn't have done anything else; and yet I remember saying to myself that it was hard, was even cruel. Not only had I lost the books, but I had lost the man himself: they and their author had been alike spoiled for me. I knew too which was the loss I most regretted. I had liked the man still better than I had liked the books.

VI

Six months after Vereker had left England George Corvick, who made his living by his pen, contracted for a piece of work which imposed on him an absence of some length and a journey of some difficulty, and his undertaking of which was much of a surprise to me. His brother-in-law had become editor of a great provincial paper, and the great provincial paper, in a fine flight of fancy, had conceived the idea of sending a "special commissioner" to India. Special commissioners had begun, in the "metropolitan press," to be the fashion, and the journal in question felt that it had passed too long for a mere country cousin. Corvick had no hand, I knew, for the big brush of the correspondent, but that was his brother-in-law's affair, and the fact that a particular task was not in his line was apt to be with himself exactly a reason for accepting it. He was prepared to out-Herod the metropolitan press; he took solemn precautions against priggishness, he exquisitely outraged taste. Nobody ever knew it—the taste was all his own. In addition to his expenses he was to be conveniently paid, and I found myself able to help him, for the usual fat book, to a plausible arrangement with the usual fat publisher. I naturally inferred that his obvious desire to make a little money was not unconnected with the prospect of a union with Gwendolen Erme. I was aware that her mother's opposition was largely addressed to his want of means and of lucrative abilities, but it so happened that, on my saying the last time I saw him something that bore on the question of his separation from our young lady, he exclaimed with an emphasis that startled me: "Ah, I'm not a bit engaged to her, you know!"

"Not overtly," I answered, "because her mother doesn't like you. But I've always taken for granted a private understanding."

"Well, there *was* one. But there isn't now." That was all he said, except something about Mrs. Erme's having got on her feet again in the most extraordinary way—a remark from which I gathered he wished me to think he meant that private understandings were of little use when the doctor didn't share them. What I took the liberty of really thinking was that the girl might in some way have estranged him. Well, if he had taken the turn of jealousy for instance it could scarcely be jealousy of me. In that case (besides the absurdity of it) he wouldn't have gone away to leave us together. For some time before his departure we had indulged in no allusion to the buried treasure, and from his silence, of which mine was the consequence, I had drawn a sharp conclusion. His courage had dropped, his ardour had gone the way of mine—this inference at least he left me to enjoy. More than that he couldn't do; he couldn't face the triumph with which I might have greeted an explicit admission. He needn't have been afraid, poor dear, for I had by this time lost all need to triumph. In fact I considered that I showed magnanimity in not reproaching him with his collapse, for the sense of his having thrown up the game made me feel more than ever how much I at last depended on him. If Corvick had broken down I should never know; no one would be of any use if *he* wasn't. It wasn't a bit true that I had ceased to care for knowledge; little by little my curiosity had not only begun to ache again, but had become the familiar torment of my consciousness. There are doubtless people to whom torments of such an order appear hardly more natural than the contortions of disease; but I don't know after all why I should in this connection so much as mention them. For the few persons, at any rate, abnormal or not, with whom my anecdote is concerned, literature was a game of skill, and skill meant courage, and courage meant honour, and honour meant passion, meant life. The stake on the table was of a different substance, and our roulette was the revolving mind, but we sat round the green board as intently as the grim gamblers at Monte Carlo. Gwendolen Erme, for that matter, with her white face and her fixed eyes, was of the very type of the lean ladies one had met in the temples of chance. I recognised in Corvick's absence that she made this analogy vivid. It was extravagant, I admit, the way she lived for the art of the pen. Her passion visibly preyed upon her, and in her presence I felt almost tepid. I got hold of "Deep Down" again: it was a desert in which she had lost herself, but in which too she had dug a wonderful hole in the sand—a cavity out of which Corvick had still more remarkably pulled her.

Early in March I had a telegram from her, in consequence of which I repaired immediately to Chelsea, where the first thing she said to me was: "He has got it, he has got it!"

She was moved, as I could see, to such depths that she must mean the great thing. "Vereker's idea?"

"His general intention. George has cabled from Bombay."

She had the missive open there; it was emphatic, but it was brief. "Eureka. Immense." That was all—he had saved the money of the signature. I shared her emotion, but I was disappointed. "He doesn't say what it is."

"How could he—in a telegram? He'll write it."

"But how does he know?"

"Know it's the real thing? Oh, I'm sure when you see it you do know. *Vera incessu patuit dea!*"

"It's you, Miss Erme, who are a dear for bringing me such news!"—I went all lengths in my high spirits. "But fancy finding our goddess in the temple of Vishnu! How strange of George to have been able to go into the thing again in the midst of such different and such powerful solicitations!"

"He hasn't gone into it, I know; it's the thing itself, let severely alone for six months, that has simply sprung out at him like a tigress out of the jungle. He didn't take a book with him—on purpose; indeed he wouldn't have needed to—he knows every page, as I do, by heart. They all worked in him together, and some day somewhere, when he wasn't thinking, they fell, in all their superb intricacy, into the one right combination. The figure in the carpet came out. That's the way he knew it would come and the real reason—you didn't in the least understand, but I suppose I may tell you now—why he went and why I consented to his going. We knew the change would do it, the difference of thought, of scene, would give the needed touch, the magic shake. We had perfectly, we had admirably calculated. The elements were all in his mind, and in the *secousse* of a new and intense experience they just struck light." She positively struck light herself—she was literally, facially luminous. I stammered something about unconscious cerebration, and she continued: "He'll come right home—this will bring him."

"To see Vereker, you mean?"

"To see Vereker—and to see *me*. Think what he'll have to tell me!"

I hesitated. "About India?"

"About fiddlesticks! About Vereker—about the figure in the carpet."

"But, as you say, we shall surely have that in a letter."

She thought like one inspired, and I remembered how Corvick had told me long before that her face was interesting. "Perhaps it won't go in a letter if it's 'immense.'"

"Perhaps not if it's immense bosh. If he has got something that won't go in a letter he hasn't got *the* thing. Vereker's own statement to me was exactly that the 'figure' *would* go in a letter."

"Well, I cabled to George an hour ago—two words," said Gwendolen.

"Is it indiscreet of me to inquire what they were?"

She hung fire, but at last she brought them out. "'Angel, write.'"

"Good!" I exclaimed. "I'll make it sure—I'll send him the same."

VII

My words however were not absolutely the same—I put something instead of "angel"; and in the sequel my epithet seemed the more apt, for when eventually we heard from Corvick it was merely, it was thoroughly to be tantalised. He was magnificent in his triumph, he described his discovery as stupendous; but his ecstasy only obscured it—there were to be no particulars till he should have submitted his conception to the supreme authority. He had thrown up his commission, he had thrown up his book, he had thrown up everything but the instant need to hurry to Rapallo, on the Genoese shore, where Vereker was making a stay. I wrote him a letter which was to await him at Aden—I besought him to relieve my suspense. That he found my letter was indicated by a telegram which, reaching me after weary days and without my having received an answer to my laconic dispatch at Bombay, was evidently intended as a reply to both communications. Those few words were in familiar French, the French of the day, which Corvick often made use of to show he wasn't a prig. It had for some persons the opposite effect, but his message may fairly be paraphrased. "Have patience; I want to see, as it breaks on you, the face you'll make!" "*Tellement envie de voir ta tête!*"—that was what I had to sit down with. I can certainly not be said to have sat down, for I seem to remember myself at this time as rushing constantly between the little house in Chelsea and my own. Our impatience, Gwendolen's and mine, was equal, but I kept hoping her light would be greater. We all spent during this episode, for people of our means, a great deal of money in telegrams, and I counted on the receipt of news from Rapallo immediately after the junction of the discoverer with the discovered. The interval seemed an age, but late one day I heard a hansom rattle up to my door with a crash engendered by a hint of liberality. I lived with my heart in my mouth and I bounded to the window—a movement which gave me a view of a young lady erect on the footboard of the vehicle and eagerly looking up at my house. At sight of me she flourished a paper with a movement that brought me straight down, the movement with which, in melodramas, handkerchiefs and reprieves are flourished at the foot of the scaffold.

"Just seen Vereker—not a note wrong. Pressed me to bosom—keeps me a month." So much I read on her paper while the cabby dropped a grin from his perch. In my excitement I paid him profusely and in hers she suffered it; then as he drove away we started to walk about and talk. We had talked, heaven knows, enough before, but this was a wondrous lift. We pictured the whole scene at Rapallo, where he would have written, mentioning my name, for permission to call; that is *I* pictured it, having more material than my companion, whom I felt hang on my lips as we stopped on purpose before shop-windows we didn't look into. About one thing we were clear: if he was staying on for fuller communication we should at least have a letter from him that would help us through the dregs of delay. We understood his staying on, and yet each of us saw, I think, that the other hated it. The letter we were clear about arrived; it was for Gwendolen, and I called upon her in time to save her the trouble of bringing it to me. She didn't read it out, as was natural enough; but she repeated to me what it chiefly embodied. This consisted of the remarkable statement that he would tell her when they were married exactly what she wanted to know.

"Only when we're married—not before," she explained. "It's tantamount to saying—isn't it?—that I must marry him straight off!" She smiled at me while I flushed with disappointment, a vision of fresh delay that made me at first unconscious of my surprise. It seemed more than a hint that on me as well he would impose some tiresome condition. Suddenly, while she reported several more things from his letter, I remembered what he had told me before going away. He found Mr. Vereker deliriously interesting and his own possession of the secret a kind of intoxication. The buried treasure was all gold and gems. Now that it was there it seemed to grow and grow before him; it was in all time, in all tongues, one of the most wonderful flowers of art. Nothing, above all, when once one was face to face with it, had been more consummately done. When once it came out it came out, was there with a splendour that made you ashamed; and there had not been, save in the bottomless vulgarity of the age, with every one tasteless and tainted, every sense stopped, the smallest reason why it should have been overlooked. It was immense, but it was simple—it was simple, but it was immense, and the final knowledge of it was an experience quite apart. He intimated that the charm of such an experience, the desire to drain it, in its freshness, to the last drop, was what kept him there close to the source. Gwendolen, frankly radiant as she tossed me these fragments, showed the elation of a prospect more assured than my own. That brought me back to the question of her marriage, prompted me to ask her if what she meant by what she had just surprised me with was that she was under an engagement.

"Of course I am!" she answered. "Didn't you know it?" She appeared astonished; but I was still more so, for Corvick had told me the exact contrary. I didn't mention this, however; I only reminded her that I had not been to that degree in her confidence, or even in Corvick's, and that moreover I was not in ignorance of her mother's interdict. At bottom I was troubled by the disparity of the two assertions; but after a moment I felt that Corvick's was the one I least doubted. This simply reduced me to asking myself if the girl had on the spot improvised an engagement—vamped up an old one or dashed off a new—in order to arrive at the satisfaction she desired. I reflected that she had resources of which I was destitute; but she made her case slightly more intelligible by rejoining presently: "What the state of things has been is that we felt of course bound to do nothing in mamma's lifetime."

"But now you think you'll just dispense with your mother's consent?"

"Ah, it may not come to that!" I wondered what it might come to, and she went on: "Poor dear, she may swallow the dose. In fact, you know," she added with a laugh, "she really *must!*"—a proposition of which, on behalf of every one concerned, I fully acknowledged the force.

VIII

Nothing more annoying had ever happened to me than to become aware before Corvick's arrival in England that I should not be there to put him through. I found myself abruptly called to Germany by the alarming illness of my younger brother, who, against my advice, had gone to Munich to study, at the feet indeed of a great master, the art of portraiture in oils. The near relative who made him an allowance had threatened to withdraw it if he should, under specious pretexts, turn for superior truth to Paris—Paris being somehow, for a Cheltenham aunt, the school of evil, the abyss. I deplored this prejudice at the time, and the deep injury of it was now visible—first in the fact that it had not saved the poor boy, who was clever, frail and foolish, from congestion of the lungs, and second in the greater remoteness from London to which the event condemned me. I am afraid that what was uppermost in my mind during several anxious weeks was the sense that if we had only been in Paris I might have run over to see Corvick. This was actually out of the question from every point of view: my brother, whose recovery gave us both plenty to do, was ill for three months, during which I never left him and at the end of which we had to face the absolute prohibition of a return to England. The consideration of climate imposed itself, and he was in no state to meet it alone. I took him to Meran and there spent the summer with him, trying to show him by example how to get back to work and nursing a rage of another sort that I tried not to show him.

The whole business proved the first of a series of phenomena so strangely combined that, taken together (which was how I had to take them) they form as good an illustration as I can recall of the manner in which, for the good of his soul doubtless, fate sometimes deals with a man's avidity. These incidents certainly had larger bearings than the comparatively meagre consequence we are here concerned with—though I feel that consequence also to be a thing to speak of with some respect. It's mainly in such a light, I confess, at any rate, that at this hour the ugly fruit of my exile is present to me. Even at first indeed the spirit in which my avidity, as I have called it, made me regard this term owed no element of ease to the fact that before coming back from Rapallo George Corvick addressed me in a way I didn't like. His letter had none of the sedative action that I must to-day profess myself sure he had wished to give it, and the march of occurrences was not so ordered as to make up for what it lacked. He had begun on the spot, for one of the quarterlies, a great last word on Vereker's writings, and this exhaustive study, the only one that would have counted, have existed, was to turn on the new light, to utter—oh, so quietly!—the unimagined truth. It was in other words to trace the figure in the carpet through every convolution, to reproduce it in every tint. The result, said Corvick, was to be the greatest literary portrait ever painted, and what he asked of me was just to be so good as not to trouble him with questions till he should hang up his masterpiece before me. He did me the honour to declare that, putting aside the great sitter himself, all aloft in his indifference, I was individually the connoisseur he was most working for. I was therefore to be a good boy and not try to peep under the curtain before the show-was ready: I should enjoy it all the more if I sat very still.

I did my best to sit very still, but I couldn't help giving a jump on seeing in *The Times* after I had been a week or two in Munich and before, as I knew, Corvick had reached London, the announcement of the sudden death of poor Mrs. Erme. I instantly wrote to Gwendolen for particulars, and she replied that her mother had succumbed to long-threatened failure of the heart. She didn't say, but I took the liberty of reading into her words, that from the point of view of her marriage and also of her eagerness, which was quite a match for mine, this was a solution more prompt than could have been expected and more radical than waiting for the old lady to swallow the dose. I candidly admit indeed that at the time—for I heard from her repeatedly—I read some singular things into Gwendolen's words and some still more extraordinary ones into her silences. Pen in hand, this way, I live the time over, and it brings back the oddest sense of my having been for months and in spite of myself a kind of coerced spectator. All my life had taken refuge in my eyes, which the procession of events appeared to have committed itself to keep astare. There were days when I thought of writing to Hugh Vereker and simply throwing myself on his charity. But I felt more deeply that I hadn't fallen quite so low, besides which, quite properly, he would send me about my business. Mrs.

Erme's death brought Corvick straight home, and within the month he was united "very quietly"—as quietly I suppose as he meant in his article to bring out his *trouvaille*—to the young lady he had loved and quitted. I use this last term, I may parenthetically say, because I subsequently grew sure that at the time he went to India, at the time of his great news from Bombay, there was no engagement whatever. There was none at the moment she affirmed the opposite. On the other hand he certainly became engaged the day he returned. The happy pair went down to Torquay for their honeymoon, and there, in a reckless hour, it occurred to poor Corvick to take his young bride a drive. He had no command of that business: this had been brought home to me of old in a little tour we had once made together in a dogcart. In a dogcart he perched his companion for a rattle over Devonshire hills, on one of the likeliest of which he brought his horse, who, it was true, had bolted, down with such violence that the occupants of the cart were hurled forward and that he fell horribly on his head. He was killed on the spot; Gwendolen escaped unhurt.

I pass rapidly over the question of this unmitigated tragedy, of what the loss of my best friend meant for me, and I complete my little history of my patience and my pain by the frank statement of my having, in a postscript to my very first letter to her after the receipt of the hideous news, asked Mrs. Corvick whether her husband had not at least finished the great article on Vereker. Her answer was as prompt as my inquiry: the article, which had been barely begun, was a mere heartbreaking scrap. She explained that Corvick had just settled down to it when he was interrupted by her mother's death; then, on his return, he had been kept from work by the engrossments into which that calamity plunged them. The opening pages were all that existed; they were striking, they were promising, but they didn't unveil the idol. That great intellectual feat was obviously to have formed his climax. She said nothing more, nothing to enlighten me as to the state of her own knowledge—the knowledge for the acquisition of which I had conceived her doing prodigious things. This was above all what I wanted to know: had *she* seen the idol unveiled? Had there been a private ceremony for a palpitating audience of one? For what else but that ceremony had the previous ceremony been enacted? I didn't like as yet to press her, though when I thought of what had passed between us on the subject in Corvick's absence her reticence surprised me. It was therefore not till much later, from Meran, that I risked another appeal, risked it in some trepidation, for she continued to tell me nothing. "Did you hear in those few days of your blighted bliss," I wrote, "what we desired so to hear?" I said "we" as a little hint; and she showed me she could take a little hint. "I heard everything," she replied, "and I mean to keep it to myself!"

IX

It was impossible not to be moved with the strongest sympathy for her, and on my return to England I showed her every kindness in my power. Her mother's death had made her means sufficient, and she had gone to live in a more convenient quarter. But her loss had been great and her visitation cruel; it never would have occurred to me moreover to suppose she could come to regard the enjoyment of a technical tip, of a piece of literary experience, as a counterpoise to her grief. Strange to say, none the less, I couldn't help fancying after I had seen her a few times that I caught a glimpse of some such oddity. I hasten to add that there had been other things I couldn't help fancying; and as I never felt I was really clear about these, so, as to the point I here touch on, I give her memory the benefit of every doubt. Stricken and solitary, highly accomplished and now, in her deep mourning, her maturer grace, and her uncomplaining sorrow incontestably handsome, she presented herself as leading a life of singular dignity and beauty. I had at first found a way to believe that I should soon get the better of the reserve formulated the week after the catastrophe in her reply to an appeal as to which I was not unconscious that it might strike her as mistimed. Certainly that reserve was something of a shock to me—certainly it puzzled me the more I thought of it, though I tried to explain it, with moments of success, by the supposition of exalted sentiments, of superstitious scruples, of a refinement of loyalty. Certainly it added at the same time hugely to the price of Vereker's secret, precious as that mystery already appeared. I may as well confess abjectly that Mrs. Corvick's unexpected attitude was the final tap on the nail that was to fix, as they say, my luckless idea, convert it into the obsession of which I am for ever conscious. But this only helped me the more to be artful, to be adroit, to allow time to elapse before renewing my suit. There were plenty of speculations for the interval, and one of them was deeply absorbing. Corvick had kept his information from his young friend till after the removal of the last barriers to their intimacy; then he had let the cat out of the bag. Was it Gwendolen's idea, taking a hint from him, to liberate this animal only on the basis of the renewal of such a relation? Was the figure in the carpet traceable or describable only for husbands and wives—for lovers supremely united? It came back to me in a mystifying manner that in Kensington-square, when I told him that Corvick would have told the girl he loved, some word had dropped from Vereker that gave colour to this possibility. There might be little in it, but there was enough to make me wonder if I should have to marry Mrs. Corvick to get what I wanted. Was I prepared to offer her this price for the blessing of her knowledge? Ah! that way madness lay—so I said to myself at least in bewildered hours. I could see meanwhile the torch she refused to pass on flame away in her chamber of memory—pour through her eyes a light that made a glow in her lonely house. At the end of six months I was fully sure of what this warm presence made up to her for. We had talked again and again of the man who had brought us together, of his talent, his character, his personal charm, his certain career, his dreadful doom, and even of his clear purpose in that great study which was to have been a supreme literary portrait, a kind of critical Vandyke or Velasquez. She had conveyed to me in abundance that she was tongue-tied by her perversity, by her piety, that she would never break the silence it had not been given to the "right person," as she said, to break. The hour however finally arrived. One evening when I had been sitting with her longer than usual I laid my hand firmly on her arm.

"Now, at last, what *is* it?"

She had been expecting me; she was ready. She gave a long, slow, soundless headshake, merciful only in being inarticulate. This mercy didn't prevent its hurling at me the largest, finest, coldest "Never!" I had yet, in the course of a life that had known denials, had to take full in the face. I took it and was aware that with the hard blow the tears had come into my eyes. So for a while we sat and looked at each other; after which I slowly rose. I was wondering if some day she would accept me; but this was not what I brought out. I said as I smoothed down my hat: "I know what to think then; it's nothing!"

A remote, disdainful pity for me shone out of her dim smile; then she exclaimed in a voice that I hear at this moment: "It's my *life!*" As I stood at the door she added: "You've insulted him!"

"Do you mean Vereker?"

"I mean—the Dead!"

I recognised when I reached the street the justice of her charge. Yes, it was her life—I recognised that too; but her life none the less made room with the lapse of time for another interest. A year and a half after Corvick's death she published in a single volume her second novel, "Overmastered," which I pounced on in the hope of finding in it some tell-tale echo or some peeping face. All I found was a much better book than her younger performance, showing I thought the better company she had kept. As a tissue tolerably intricate it was a carpet with a figure of its own; but the figure was not the figure I was looking for. On sending a review of it to *The Middle* I was surprised to learn from the office that a notice was already in type. When the paper came out I had no hesitation in attributing this article, which I thought rather vulgarly overdone, to Drayton Deane, who in the old days had been something of a friend of Corvick's, yet had only within a few weeks made the acquaintance of his widow. I had had an early copy of the book, but Deane had evidently had an earlier. He lacked all the same the light hand with which Corvick had gilded the gingerbread—he laid on the tinsel in splotches.

X

Six months later appeared "The Right of Way," the last chance, though we didn't know it, that we were to have to redeem ourselves. Written wholly during Vereker's absence, the book had been heralded, in a hundred paragraphs, by the usual ineptitudes. I carried it, as early a copy as any, I this time flattered myself, straightway to Mrs. Corvick. This was the only use I had for it; I left the inevitable tribute of *The Middle* to some more ingenious mind and some less irritated temper. "But I already have it," Gwendolen said. "Drayton Deane was so good as to bring it to me yesterday, and I've just finished it."

"Yesterday? How did he get it so soon?"

"He gets everything soon. He's to review it in *The Middle*."

"He—Drayton Deane—review Vereker?" I couldn't believe my ears.

"Why not? One fine ignorance is as good as another."

I winced, but I presently said: "You ought to review him yourself!"

"I don't 'review,'" she laughed. "I'm reviewed!"

Just then the door was thrown open. "Ah yes, here's your reviewer!" Drayton Deane was there with his long legs and his tall forehead: he had come to see what she thought of "The Right of Way," and to bring news which was singularly relevant. The evening papers were just out with a telegram on the author of that work, who, in Rome, had been ill for some days with an attack of malarial fever. It had at first not been thought grave, but had taken in consequence of complications a turn that might give rise to anxiety. Anxiety had indeed at the latest hour begun to be felt.

I was struck in the presence of these tidings with the fundamental detachment that Mrs. Corvick's public regret quite failed to conceal: it gave me the measure of her consummate independence. That independence rested on her knowledge, the knowledge which nothing now could destroy and which nothing could make different. The figure in the carpet might take on another twist or two, but the sentence had virtually been written. The writer might go down to his grave: she was the person in the world to whom—as if she had been his favoured heir—his continued existence was least of a need. This reminded me how I had observed at a particular moment—after Corvick's death—the drop of her desire to see him face to face. She had got what she wanted without that. I had been sure that if she hadn't got it she wouldn't have been restrained from the endeavour to sound him personally by those superior reflections, more conceivable on a man's part than on a woman's, which in my case had served as a deterrent. It wasn't however, I hasten to add, that my case, in spite of this invidious comparison, wasn't ambiguous enough. At the thought that Vereker was perhaps at that moment dying there rolled over me a wave of anguish—a poignant sense of how inconsistently I still depended on him. A delicacy that it was my one compensation to suffer to rule me had left the Alps and the Apennines between us, but the vision of the waning opportunity made me feel as if I might in my despair at last have gone to him. Of course I would really have done nothing of the sort. I remained five minutes, while my companions talked of the new book, and when Drayton Deane appealed to me for my opinion of it I replied, getting up, that I detested Hugh Vereker—simply couldn't read him. I went away with the moral certainty that as the door closed behind me Deane would remark that I was awfully superficial. His hostess wouldn't contradict him.

I continue to trace with a briefer touch our intensely odd concatenation. Three weeks after this came Vereker's death, and before the year was out the death of his wife. That poor lady I had never seen, but I had had a futile theory that, should she survive him long enough to be decorously accessible, I might approach her with the feeble flicker of my petition. Did she know and if she knew would she speak? It was much to be presumed that for more reasons than one she would have nothing to say; but when she passed out of all reach I felt that renouncement was indeed my appointed lot. I was shut up in my obsession for ever—my gaolers had gone off with the key. I find myself quite as vague as a captive in a dungeon about the time that further elapsed before Mrs. Corvick became the wife of Drayton Deane. I had foreseen, through my bars, this end of the business, though there was no indecent haste and our friendship had rather fallen off. They were both so "awfully intellectual" that it struck people as a suitable match, but I knew better than any one the wealth of understanding the bride would contribute to the partnership. Never, for a marriage in literary circles—so the newspapers described the alliance—had a bride been so handsomely dowered. I began with due promptness to look for the fruit of their union—that fruit, I mean, of which the premonitory symptoms would be peculiarly visible in the husband. Taking for granted the splendour of the lady's nuptial gift, I expected to see him make a show commensurate with his increase of means. I knew what his means had been—his article on "The Right of Way" had distinctly given one the figure. As he was now exactly in the position in which still more exactly I was not I watched from month to month, in the likely periodicals, for the heavy message poor Corvick had been unable to deliver and the responsibility of which would have fallen on his successor. The widow and wife would have broken by the rekindled hearth the silence that only a widow and wife might break, and Deane would be as aflame with the knowledge as Corvick in his own hour, as Gwendolen in hers had been. Well, he was aflame doubtless, but the fire was apparently not to become a public blaze. I scanned the periodicals in vain: Drayton Deane filled them with exuberant pages, but he withheld the page I most feverishly sought. He wrote on a thousand subjects, but never on the subject of Vereker. His special line was to tell truths that other people either "funked," as he said, or overlooked, but he never told the only truth that seemed to me in these days to signify. I met the couple in those literary circles referred to in the papers: I have sufficiently intimated that it was only in such circles we were all constructed to revolve. Gwendolen was more than ever committed to them by the publication of her third novel, and I myself definitely classed by holding the opinion that this work was inferior to its immediate predecessor. Was it worse because she had been keeping worse company? If her secret was, as she had told me, her life—a fact discernible in her increasing bloom, an air of conscious privilege that, cleverly corrected by pretty charities, gave distinction to her appearance—it had yet not a direct influence on her work. That only made—everything only made—one yearn the more for it, rounded it off with a mystery finer and subtler.

XI

It was therefore from her husband I could never remove my eyes: I hovered about him in a manner that might have made him uneasy. I went even so far as to engage him in conversation. *Didn't* he know, hadn't he come into it as a matter of course?—that question hummed in my brain. Of course he knew; otherwise he wouldn't return my stare so queerly. His wife had told him what I wanted, and he was amiably amused at my impotence. He didn't laugh—he was not a laugher: his system was to present to my irritation, so that I should crudely expose myself, a conversational blank as vast as his big bare brow. It always happened that I turned away with a settled conviction from these unpeopled expanses, which seemed to complete each other geographically and to symbolise together Drayton Deane's want of voice, want of form. He simply hadn't the art to use what he knew; he literally was incompetent to take up the duty where Corvick had left it. I went still further—it was the only glimpse of happiness I had. I made up my mind that the duty didn't appeal to him. He wasn't interested, he didn't care. Yes, it quite comforted me to believe him too stupid to have joy of the thing I lacked. He was as stupid after as before, and that deepened for me the golden glory in which the mystery was wrapped. I had of course however to recollect that his wife might have imposed her conditions and exactions. I had above all to recollect that with Vereker's death the major incentive dropped. He was still there to be honoured by what might be done—he was no longer there to give it his sanction. Who, alas, but he had the authority?

Two children were born to the pair, but the second cost the mother her life. After this calamity I seemed to see another ghost of a chance. I jumped at it in thought, but I waited a certain time for manners, and at last my opportunity arrived in a remunerative way. His wife had been dead a year when I met Drayton Deane in the smoking-room of a small club of which we both were members, but where for months—perhaps because I rarely entered it—I had not seen him. The room was empty and the occasion propitious. I deliberately offered him, to have done with the matter for ever, that advantage for which I felt he had long been looking.

"As an older acquaintance of your late wife's than even you were," I began, "you must let me say to you something I have on my mind. I shall be glad to make any terms with you that you see fit to name for the information she had from George Corvick—the information, you know, that he, poor fellow, in one of the happiest hours of his life, had straight from Hugh Vereker."

He looked at me like a dim phrenological bust. "The information——?"

"Vereker's secret, my dear man—the general intention of his books: the string the pearls were strung on, the buried treasure, the figure in the carpet."

He began to flush—the numbers on his bumps to come out. "Vereker's books had a general intention?"

I stared in my turn. "You don't mean to say you don't know it?" I thought for a moment he was playing with me. "Mrs. Deane knew it; she had it, as I say, straight from Corvick, who had, after infinite search and to Vereker's own delight, found the very mouth of the cave. Where *is* the mouth? He told after their marriage—and told alone—the person who, when the circumstances were reproduced, must have told you. Have I been wrong in taking for granted that she admitted you, as one of the highest privileges of the relation in which you stood to her, to the knowledge of which she was after Corvick's death the sole depositary? All *I* know is that that knowledge is infinitely precious, and what I want you to understand is that if you will in your turn admit *me* to it you will do me a kindness for which I shall be everlastingly grateful."

He had turned at last very red; I daresay he had begun by thinking I had lost my wits. Little by little he followed me; on my own side I stared with a livelier surprise. "I don't know what you're talking about," he said.

He wasn't acting—it was the absurd truth. "She *didn't* tell you——"

"Nothing about Hugh Vereker."

I was stupefied; the room went round. It had been too good even for that! "Upon your honour?"

"Upon my honour. What the devil's the matter with you?" he demanded.

"I'm astounded—I'm disappointed. I wanted to get it out of you."

"It isn't *in* me!" he awkwardly laughed. "And even if it were——"

"If it were you'd let me have it—oh yes, in common humanity. But I believe you. I see—I see!" I went on, conscious, with the full turn of the wheel, of my great delusion, my false view of the poor man's attitude. What I saw, though I couldn't say it, was that his wife hadn't thought him worth enlightening. This struck me as strange for a woman who had thought him worth marrying. At last I explained it by the reflection that she couldn't possibly have married him for his understanding. She had married him for something else. He was to some extent enlightened now, but he was even more astonished, more disconcerted: he took a moment to compare my story with his quickened memories. The result of his meditation was his presently saying with a good deal of rather feeble form:

"This is the first I hear of what you allude to. I think you must be mistaken as to Mrs. Drayton Deane's having had any unmentioned, and still less any unmentionable, knowledge about Hugh Vereker. She would certainly have wished it—if it bore on his literary character—to be used."

"It *was* used. She used it herself. She told me with her own lips that she 'lived' on it."

I had no sooner spoken than I repented of my words; he grew so pale that I felt as if I had struck him. "Ah, 'lived'—!" he murmured, turning short away from me.

My compunction was real; I laid my hand on his shoulder. "I beg you to forgive me—I've made a mistake. You *don't* know what I thought you knew. You could, if I had been right, have rendered me a service; and I had my reasons for assuming that you would be in a position to meet me."

"Your reasons?" he asked. "What were your reasons?"

I looked at him well; I hesitated; I considered. "Come and sit down with me here, and I'll tell you." I drew him to a sofa, I lighted another cigarette and, beginning with the anecdote of Vereker's one descent from the clouds, I gave him an account of the extraordinary chain of accidents that had in spite of it kept me till that hour in the dark. I told him in a word just what I've written out here. He listened with deepening attention, and I became aware, to my surprise, by his ejaculations, by his questions, that he would have been after all not unworthy to have been trusted by his wife. So abrupt an experience of her want of trust had an agitating effect on him, but I saw that immediate shock throb away little by little and then gather again into waves of wonder and curiosity—waves that promised, I could perfectly judge, to break in the end with the fury of my own highest tides. I may say that to-day as victims of unappeased desire there isn't a pin to choose between us. The poor man's state is almost my consolation; there are indeed moments when I feel it to be almost my revenge.

GLASSES

I

Yes indeed, I say to myself, pen in hand, I can keep hold of the thread and let it lead me back to the first impression. The little story is all there, I can touch it from point to point; for the thread, as I call it, is a row of coloured beads on a string. None of the beads are missing—at least I think they're not: that's exactly what I shall amuse myself with finding out.

I had been all summer working hard in town and then had gone down to Folkestone for a blow. Art was long, I felt, and my holiday short; my mother was settled at Folkestone, and I paid her a visit when I could. I remember how on this occasion, after weeks, in my stuffy studio, with my nose on my palette, I sniffed up the clean salt air and cooled my eyes with the purple sea. The place was full of lodgings, and the lodgings were at that season full of people, people who had nothing to do but to stare at one another on the great flat down. There were thousands of little chairs and almost as many little Jews; and there was music in an open rotunda, over which the little Jews wagged their big noses. We all strolled to and fro and took pennyworths of rest; the long, level cliff-top, edged in places with its iron rail, might have been the deck of a huge crowded ship. There were old folks in Bath chairs, and there was one dear chair, creeping to its last full stop, by the side of which I always walked. There was in fine weather the coast of France to look at, and there were the usual things to say about it; there was also in every state of the atmosphere our friend Mrs. Meldrum, a subject of remark not less inveterate. The widow of an officer in the Engineers, she had settled, like many members of the martial miscellany, well within sight of the hereditary enemy, who however had left her leisure to form in spite of the difference of their years a close alliance with my mother. She was the heartiest, the keenest, the ugliest of women, the least apologetic, the least morbid in her misfortune. She carried it high aloft, with loud sounds and free gestures, made it flutter in the breeze as if it had been the flag of her country. It consisted mainly of a big red face, indescribably out of drawing, from which she glared at you through gold-rimmed aids to vision, optic circles of such diameter and so frequently displaced that some one had vividly spoken of her as flattening her nose against the glass of her spectacles. She was extraordinarily near-sighted, and whatever they did to other objects they magnified immensely the kind eyes behind them. Blessed conveniences they were, in their hideous, honest strength—they showed the good lady everything in the world but her own queerness. This element was enhanced by wild braveries of dress, reckless charges of colour and stubborn resistances of cut, wonderous encounters in which the art of the toilet seemed to lay down its life. She had the tread of a grenadier and the voice of an angel.

In the course of a walk with her the day after my arrival I found myself grabbing her arm with sudden and undue familiarity. I had been struck by the beauty of a face that approached us and I was still more affected when I saw the face, at the sight of my companion, open like a window thrown wide. A smile fluttered out of it as brightly as a drapery dropped from a sill—a drapery shaken there in the sun by a young lady flanked with two young men, a wonderful young lady who, as we drew nearer, rushed up to Mrs. Meldrum with arms flourished for an embrace. My immediate impression of her had been that she was dressed in mourning, but during the few moments she stood talking with our friend I made more discoveries. The figure from the neck down was meagre, the stature insignificant, but the desire to please towered high, as well as the air of infallibly knowing how and of never, never missing it. This was a little person whom I would have made a high bid for a good chance to paint. The head, the features, the colour, the whole facial oval and radiance had a wonderful purity; the deep grey eyes—the most agreeable, I thought, that I had ever seen—brushed with a kind of winglike grace every object they encountered. Their possessor was just back from Boulogne, where she had spent a week with dear Mrs. Floyd-Taylor: this accounted for the effusiveness of her reunion with dear Mrs. Meldrum. Her black garments were of the freshest and daintiest; she suggested a pink-and-white wreath at a showy funeral. She confounded us for three minutes with her presence; she was a beauty of the great conscious, public, responsible order. The young men, her companions, gazed at her and grinned: I could see there were very few moments of the day at which young men, these or others, would not be so occupied. The people who approached took leave of their manners; every one seemed to linger and gape. When she brought her face close to Mrs. Meldrum's—and she appeared to be always bringing it close to somebody's—it was a marvel that objects so dissimilar should express the same general identity, the unmistakable character of the English gentlewoman. Mrs. Meldrum sustained the comparison with her usual courage, but I wondered why she didn't introduce me: I should have had no objection to the bringing of such a face close to mine. However, when the young lady moved on with her escort she herself bequeathed me a sense that some such *rapprochement* might still occur. Was this by reason of the general frequency of encounters at Folkestone, or by reason of a subtle acknowledgment that she contrived to make of the rights, on the part of others, that such beauty as hers created? I was in a position to answer that question after Mrs. Meldrum had answered a few of mine.

II

Flora Saunt, the only daughter of an old soldier, had lost both her parents, her mother within a few months. Mrs. Meldrum had known them, disapproved of them, considerably avoided them: she had watched the girl, off and on, from her early childhood. Flora, just twenty, was extraordinarily alone in the world—so alone that she had no natural chaperon, no one to stay with but a mercenary stranger, Mrs. Hammond Synge, the sister-in-law of one of the young men I had just seen. She had lots of friends, but none of them nice: she kept picking up impossible people. The Floyd-Taylors, with whom she had been at Boulogne, were simply horrid. The Hammond Synges were perhaps not so vulgar, but they had no conscience in their dealings with her.

"She knows what I think of them," said Mrs. Meldrum, "and indeed she knows what I think of most things."

"She shares that privilege with most of your friends!" I replied laughing.

"No doubt; but possibly to some of my friends it makes a little difference. That girl doesn't care a button. She knows best of all what I think of Flora Saunt."

"And what may your opinion be?"

"Why, that she's not worth talking about—an idiot too abysmal."

"Doesn't she care for that?"

"Just enough, as you saw, to hug me till I cry out. She's too pleased with herself for anything else to matter."

"Surely, my dear friend," I rejoined, "she has a good deal to be pleased with!"

"So every one tells her, and so you would have told her if I had given you a chance. However, that doesn't signify either, for her vanity is beyond all making or mending. She believes in herself, and she's welcome, after all, poor dear, having only herself to look to. I've seldom met a young woman more completely at liberty to be silly. She has a clear course—she'll make a showy finish."

"Well," I replied, "as she probably will reduce many persons to the same degraded state, her partaking of it won't stand out so much."

"If you mean that the world's full of twaddlers I quite agree with you!" cried Mrs. Meldrum, trumpeting her laugh half across the Channel.

I had after this to consider a little what she would call my mother's son, but I didn't let it prevent me from insisting on her making me acquainted with Flora Saunt; indeed I took the bull by the horns, urging that she had drawn the portrait of a nature which common charity now demanded that she should put into relation with a character really fine. Such a frail creature was just an object of pity. This contention on my part had at first of course been jocular; but strange to say it was quite the ground I found myself taking with regard to our young lady after I had begun to know her. I couldn't have said what I felt about her except that she was undefended; from the first of my sitting with her there after dinner, under the stars—that was a week at Folkestone of balmy nights and muffled tides and crowded chairs—I became aware both that protection was wholly absent from her life and that she was wholly indifferent to its absence.

The odd thing was that she was not appealing: she was abjectly, divinely conceited, absurdly, fantastically happy. Her beauty was as yet all the world to her, a world she had plenty to do to live in. Mrs. Meldrum told me more about her, and there was nothing that, as the centre of a group of giggling, nudging spectators, she was not ready to tell about herself. She held her little court in the crowd, upon the grass, playing her light over Jews and Gentiles, completely at ease in all promiscuities. It was an effect of these things that from the very first, with every one listening, I could mention that my main business with her would be just to have a go at her head and to arrange in that view for an early sitting. It would have been as impossible, I think, to be impertinent to her as it would have been to throw a stone at a plate-glass window; so any talk that went forward on the basis of her loveliness was the most natural thing in the world and immediately became the most general and sociable. It was when I saw all this that I judged how, though it was the last thing she asked for, what one would ever most have at her service was a curious compassion. That sentiment was coloured by the vision of the dire exposure of a being whom vanity had put so off her guard. Hers was the only vanity I have ever known that made its possessor superlatively soft. Mrs. Meldrum's further information contributed moreover to these indulgences—her account of the girl's neglected childhood and queer continental relegations, with straying, squabbling, Monte-Carlo-haunting parents; the more invidious picture, above all, of her pecuniary arrangement, still in force, with the Hammond Synges, who really, though they never took her out—practically she went out alone—had their hands half the time in her pocket. She had to pay for everything, down to her share of the wine-bills and the horses' fodder, down to Bertie Hammond Synge's fare in the "Underground" when he went to the City for her. She had been left with just money enough to turn her head; and it hadn't even been put in trust, nothing prudent or proper had been done with it. She could spend her capital, and at the rate she was going, expensive, extravagant and with a swarm of parasites to help, it certainly wouldn't last very long.

"Couldn't *you* perhaps take her, independent, unencumbered as you are?" I asked of Mrs. Meldrum. "You're probably, with one exception, the sanest person she knows, and you at least wouldn't scandalously fleece her."

"How do you know what I wouldn't do?" my humorous friend demanded. "Of course I've thought how I can help her—it has kept me awake at night. But I can't help her at all; she'll take nothing from me. You know what she does—she hugs me and runs away. She has an instinct about me, she feels that I've one about her. And then she dislikes me for another reason that I'm not quite clear about, but that I'm well aware of and that I shall find out some day. So far as her settling with me goes it would be impossible moreover here: she wants naturally enough a much wider field. She must live in London—her game is there. So she takes the line of adoring me, of saying she can never forget that I was devoted to her mother—which I wouldn't for the world have been—and of giving me a wide berth. I think she positively dislikes to look at me. It's all right; there's no obligation; though people in general can't take their eyes off me."

"I see that at this moment," I replied. "But what does it matter where or how, for the present, she lives? She'll marry infallibly, marry early, and everything then will change."

"Whom will she marry?" my companion gloomily asked.

"Any one she likes. She's so abnormally pretty she can do anything. She'll fascinate some nabob or some prince."

"She'll fascinate him first and bore him afterwards. Moreover she's not so pretty as you make her out; she has a scrappy little figure."

"No doubt; but one doesn't in the least notice it."

"Not now," said Mrs. Meldrum, "but one will when she's older."

"When she's older she'll be a princess, so it won't matter."

"She has other drawbacks," my companion went on. "Those wonderful eyes are good for nothing but to roll about like sugar-balls—which they greatly resemble—in a child's mouth. She can't use them."

"Use them? Why, she does nothing else."

"To make fools of young men, but not to read or write, not to do any sort of work. She never opens a book, and her maid writes her notes. You'll say that those who live in glass houses shouldn't throw stones. Of course I know that if I didn't wear my goggles I shouldn't be good for much."

"Do you mean that Miss Saunt ought to sport such things?" I exclaimed with more horror than I meant to show.

"I don't prescribe for her; I don't know that they're what she requires."

"What's the matter with her eyes?" I asked after a moment.

"I don't exactly know; but I heard from her mother years ago that even as a child they had had for a while to put her into spectacles and that, though she hated them and had been in a fury of disgust, she would always have to be extremely careful. I'm sure I hope she is!"

I echoed the hope, but I remember well the impression this made upon me—my immediate pang of resentment, a disgust almost equal to Flora's own. I felt as if a great rare sapphire had split in my hand.

III

This conversation occurred the night before I went back to town. I settled on the morrow to take a late train, so that I had still my morning to spend at Folkestone, where during the greater part of it I was out with my mother. Every one in the place was as usual out with some one else, and even had I been free to go and take leave of her I should have been sure that Flora Saunt would not be at home. Just where she was I presently discovered: she was at the far end of the cliff, the point at which it overhangs the pretty view of Sandgate and Hythe. Her back however was turned to this attraction; it rested with the aid of her elbows, thrust slightly behind her so that her scanty little shoulders were raised toward her ears, on the high rail that inclosed the down. Two gentlemen stood before her whose faces we couldn't see but who even as observed from the rear were visibly absorbed in the charming figure-piece submitted to them. I was freshly struck with the fact that this meagre and defective little person, with the cock of her hat and the flutter of her crape, with her eternal idleness, her eternal happiness, her absence of moods and mysteries and the pretty presentation of her feet, which especially now in the supported slope of her posture occupied with their imperceptibility so much of the foreground—I was reminded anew, I say, how our young lady dazzled by some art that the enumeration of her merits didn't explain and that the mention of her lapses didn't affect. Where she was amiss nothing counted, and where she was right everything did. I say she was wanting in mystery, but that after all was her secret. This happened to be my first chance of introducing her to my mother, who had not much left in life but the quiet look from under the hood of her chair at the things which, when she should have quitted those she loved, she could still trust to make the world good for them. I wondered an instant how much she might be moved to trust Flora Saunt, and then while the chair stood still and she waited I went over and asked the girl to come and speak to her. In this way I saw that if one of Flora's attendants was the inevitable young Hammond Synge, master of ceremonies of her regular court, always offering the use of a telescope and accepting that of a cigar, the other was a personage I had not yet encountered, a small pale youth in showy knickerbockers, whose eyebrows and nose and the glued points of whose little moustache were extraordinarily uplifted and sustained. I remember taking him at first for a foreigner and for something of a pretender: I scarcely know why, unless because of the motive I felt in the stare he fixed on me when I asked Miss Saunt to come away. He struck me a little as a young man practising the social art of "impertinence"; but it didn't matter, for Flora came away with alacrity, bringing all her prettiness and pleasure and gliding over the grass in that rustle of delicate mourning which made the endless variety of her garments, as a painter could take heed, strike one always as the same obscure elegance. She seated herself on the floor of my mother's chair, a little too much on her right instep as I afterwards gathered, caressing her stiff hand, smiling up into her cold face, commending and approving her without a reserve and without a doubt. She told her immediately, as if it were something for her to hold on by, that she was soon to sit to me for a "likeness," and these words gave me a chance to inquire if it would be the fate of the picture, should I finish it, to be presented to the young man in the knickerbockers. Her lips, at this, parted in a stare; her eyes darkened to the purple of one of the shadow-patches on the sea. She showed for the passing instant the face of some splendid tragic mask, and I remembered for the inconsequence of it what Mrs. Meldrum had said about her sight. I had derived from this lady a worrying impulse to catechise her, but that didn't seem exactly kind; so I substituted another question, inquired who the pretty young man in knickerbockers might happen to be.

"Oh, a gentleman I met at Boulogne. He has come over to see me." After a moment she added: "He's Lord Iffield."

I had never heard of Lord Iffield, but her mention of his having been at Boulogne helped me to give him a niche. Mrs. Meldrum had incidentally thrown a certain light on the manners of Mrs. Floyd-Taylor, Flora's recent hostess in that charming town, a lady who, it appeared, had a special vocation for helping rich young men to find a use for their leisure. She had always one or other in hand and she had apparently on this occasion pointed her lesson at the rare creature on the opposite coast. I had a vague idea that Boulogne was not a resort of the aristocracy; at the same time there might very well have been a strong attraction there even for one of the darlings of fortune. I could perfectly understand in any case that such a darling should be drawn to Folkestone by Flora Saunt. But it was not in truth of these things I was thinking; what was uppermost in my mind was a matter which, though it had no sort of keeping, insisted just then on coming out.

"Is it true, Miss Saunt," I suddenly demanded, "that you're so unfortunate as to have had some warning about your beautiful eyes?"

I was startled by the effect of my words; the girl threw back her head, changing colour from brow to chin. "True? Who in the world says so?" I repented of my question in a flash; the way she met it made it seem cruel, and I saw that my mother looked at me in some surprise. I took care, in answer to Flora's challenge, not to incriminate Mrs. Meldrum. I answered that the rumour had reached me only in the vaguest form and that if I had been moved to put it to the test my very real interest in her must be held responsible. Her blush died away, but a pair of still prettier tears glistened in its track. "If you ever hear such a thing said again you can say it's a horrid lie!" I had brought on a commotion deeper than any I was prepared for; but it was explained in some degree by the next words she uttered: "I'm happy to say there's nothing the matter with any part of my body; not the least little thing!" She spoke with her habitual complacency, with triumphant assurance; she smiled again, and I could see that she was already sorry she had shown herself too disconcerted. She turned it off with a laugh. "I've good eyes, good teeth, a good digestion and a good temper. I'm sound of wind and limb!" Nothing could have been more characteristic than her blush and her tears, nothing less acceptable to her than to be thought not perfect in every particular. She couldn't submit to the imputation of a flaw. I expressed my delight in what she told me, assuring her I should always do battle for her; and as if to rejoin her companions she got up from her place on my mother's toes. The young men presented their backs to us; they were leaning on the rail of the cliff. Our incident had produced a certain awkwardness, and while I was thinking of what next to say she exclaimed irrelevantly: "Don't you know? He'll be Lord Considine." At that moment the youth marked for this high destiny turned round, and she went on, to my mother: "I'll introduce him to you—he's awfully nice." She beckoned and invited him with her parasol; the movement struck me as taking everything for granted. I had heard of Lord Considine and if I had not been able to place Lord Iffield it was because I didn't know the name of his eldest son. The young man took no notice of Miss Saunt's appeal; he only stared a moment and then on her repeating it quietly turned his back. She was an odd creature: she didn't blush at this; she only said to my mother apologetically, but with the frankest, sweetest amusement: "You don't mind, do you? He's a monster of shyness!" It was as if she were sorry for every one—for Lord Iffield, the victim of a complaint so painful, and for my mother, the object of a trifling incivility. "I'm sure I don't want him!" said my mother; but Flora added some remark about the rebuke she would give him for slighting us. She would clearly never explain anything by any failure of her own power. There rolled over me while she took leave of us and floated back to her friends a wave of tenderness superstitious and silly. I seemed somehow to see her go forth to her fate; and yet what should fill out this orb of a high destiny if not such beauty and such joy? I had a dim idea that Lord Considine was a great proprietor, and though there mingled with it a faint impression that I shouldn't like his son the result of the two images was a whimsical prayer that the girl mightn't miss her possible fortune.

IV

One day in the course of the following June there was ushered into my studio a gentleman whom I had not yet seen but with whom I had been very briefly in correspondence. A letter from him had expressed to me some days before his regret on learning that my "splendid portrait" of Titras Flora Louisa Saunt, whose full name figured by her own wish in the catalogue of the exhibition of the Academy, had found a purchaser before the close of the private view. He took the liberty of inquiring whether I might have at his service some other memorial of the same lovely head, some preliminary sketch, some study for the picture. I had replied that I had indeed painted Miss Saunt more than once and that if he were interested in my work I should be happy to show him what I had done. Mr. Geoffrey Dawling, the person thus introduced to me, stumbled into my room with awkward movements and equivocal sounds—a long, lean, confused, confusing young man, with a bad complexion and large, protrusive teeth. He bore in its most indelible pressure the postmark, as it were, of Oxford, and as soon as he opened his mouth I perceived, in addition to a remarkable revelation of gums, that the text of the queer communication matched the registered envelope. He was full of refinements and angles, of dreary and distinguished knowledge. Of his unconscious drollery his dress freely partook; it seemed, from the gold ring into which his red necktie was passed to the square toe-caps of his boots, to conform with a high sense of modernness to the fashion before the last. There were moments when his overdone urbanity, all suggestive stammers and interrogative quavers, made him scarcely intelligible; but I felt him to be a gentleman and I liked the honesty of his errand and the expression of his good green eyes.

As a worshipper at the shrine of beauty however he needed explaining, especially when I found he had no acquaintance with my brilliant model; had on the mere evidence of my picture taken, as he said, a tremendous fancy to her face. I ought doubtless to have been humiliated by the simplicity of his judgment of it, a judgment for which the rendering was lost in the subject, quite leaving out the element of art. He was like the innocent reader for whom the story is "really true" and the author a negligible quantity. He had come to me only because he wanted to purchase, and I remember being so amused at his attitude, which I had never seen equally marked in a person of education, that I asked him why, for the sort of enjoyment he desired, it wouldn't be more to the point to deal directly with the lady. He stared and blushed at this: it was plain the idea frightened him. He was an extraordinary case—personally so modest that I could see it had never occurred to him. He had fallen in love with a painted sign and seemed content just to dream of what it stood for. He was the young prince in the legend or the comedy who loses his heart to the miniature of the outland princess. Until I knew him better this puzzled me much—the link was so missing between his sensibility and his type. He was of course bewildered by my sketches, which implied in the beholder some sense of intention and quality; but for one of them, a comparative failure, he ended by conceiving a preference so arbitrary and so lively that, taking no second look at the others, he expressed the wish to possess it and fell into the extremity of confusion over the question of the price. I simplified that problem, and he went off without having asked me a direct question about Miss Saunt, yet with his acquisition under his arm. His delicacy was such that he evidently considered his rights to be limited; he had acquired none at all in regard to the original of the picture. There were others—for I was curious about him—that I wanted him to feel I conceded: I should have been glad of his carrying away a sense of ground acquired for coming back. To insure this I had probably only to invite him, and I perfectly recall the impulse that made me forbear. It operated suddenly from within while he hung about the door and in spite of the diffident appeal that blinked in his gentle grin. If he was smitten with Flora's ghost what mightn't be the direct force of the luminary that could cast such a shadow? This source of radiance, flooding my poor place, might very well happen to be present the next time he should turn up. The idea was sharp within me that there were complications it was no mission of mine to bring about. If they were to occur they might occur by a logic of their own.

Let me say at once that they did occur and that I perhaps after all had something to do with it. If Mr. Dawling had departed without a fresh appointment he was to reappear six months later under protection no less adequate than that of our young lady herself. I had seen her repeatedly for months: she had grown to regard my studio as the tabernacle of her face. This prodigy was frankly there the sole object of interest; in other places there were occasionally other objects. The freedom of her manners continued to be stupefying; there was nothing so extraordinary save the absence in connection with it of any catastrophe. She was kept innocent by her egotism, but she was helped also, though she had now put off her mourning, by the attitude of the lone orphan who had to be a law unto herself. It was as a lone orphan that she came and went, as a lone orphan that she was the centre of a crush. The neglect of the Hammond Synges gave relief to this character, and she paid them handsomely to be, as every one said, shocking. Lord Iffield had gone to India to shoot tigers, but he returned in time for the private view: it was he who had snapped up, as Flora called it, the gem of the exhibition.

My hope for the girl's future had slipped ignominiously off his back, but after his purchase of the portrait I tried to cultivate a new faith. The girl's own faith was wonderful. It couldn't however be contagious: too great was the limit of her sense of what painters call values. Her colours were laid on like blankets on a cold night. How indeed could a person speak the truth who was always posturing and bragging? She was after all vulgar enough, and by the time I had mastered her profile and could almost with my eyes shut do it in a single line I was decidedly tired of her perfection. There grew to be something silly in its eternal smoothness. One moved with her moreover among phenomena mismated and unrelated; nothing in her talk ever matched with anything out of it. Lord Iffield was dying of love for her, but his family was leading him a life. His mother, horrid woman, had told some one that she would rather he should be swallowed by a tiger than marry a girl not absolutely one of themselves. He had given his young friend unmistakable signs, but he was lying low, gaining time: it was in his father's power to be, both in personal and in pecuniary ways, excessively nasty to him. His father wouldn't last for ever—quite the contrary; and he knew how thoroughly, in spite of her youth, her beauty and the swarm of her admirers, some of them positively threatening in their passion, he could trust her to hold out. There were richer, cleverer men, there were greater personages too, but she liked her "little viscount" just as he was, and liked to think that, bullied and persecuted, he had her there so luxuriously to rest upon. She came back to me with tale upon tale, and it all might be or mightn't. I never met my pretty model in the world—she moved, it appeared, in exalted circles—and could only admire, in her wealth of illustration, the grandeur of her life and the freedom of her hand.

I had on the first opportunity spoken to her of Geoffrey Dawling, and she had listened to my story so far as she had the art of such patience, asking me indeed more questions about him than I could answer; then she had capped my anecdote with others much more striking, revelations of effects produced in the most extraordinary quarters: on people who had followed her into railway-carriages; guards and porters even who had literally stuck there; others who had spoken to her in shops and hung about her house-door; cabmen, upon her honour, in London, who, to gaze their fill at her, had found excuses to thrust their petrifaction through the very glasses of four-wheelers. She lost herself in these reminiscences, the moral of which was that poor Mr. Dawling was only one of a million. When therefore the next autumn she flourished into my studio with her odd companion at her heels her first care was to make clear to me that if he was now in servitude it wasn't because she had run after him. Dawling hilariously explained that when one wished very much to get anything one usually ended by doing so—a proposition which led me wholly to dissent and our young lady to asseverate that she hadn't in the least wished to get Mr. Dawling. She mightn't have wished to get him, but she wished to show him, and I seemed to read that if she could treat him as a trophy her affairs were rather at the ebb. True there always hung from her belt a promiscuous fringe of scalps. Much at any rate would have come and gone since our separation in July. She had spent four months abroad, where, on Swiss and Italian lakes, in German cities, in Paris, many accidents might have happened.

V

I had been again with my mother, but except Mrs. Meldrum and the gleam of France had not found at Folkestone my old resources and pastimes. Mrs. Meldrum, much edified by my report of the performances, as she called them, in my studio, had told me that to her knowledge Flora would soon be on the straw: she had cut from her capital such fine fat slices that there was almost nothing more left to swallow. Perched on her breezy cliff the good lady dazzled me as usual by her universal light: she knew so much more about everything and everybody than I could ever squeeze out of my colour-tubes. She knew that Flora was acting on system and absolutely declined to be interfered with: her precious reasoning was that her money would last as long as she should need it, that a magnificent marriage would crown her charms before she should be really pinched. She had a sum put by for a liberal outfit; meanwhile the proper use of the rest was to decorate her for the approaches to the altar, keep her afloat in the society in which she would most naturally meet her match. Lord Iffield had been seen with her at Lucerne, at Cadenabbia; but it was Mrs. Meldrum's conviction that nothing was to be expected of him but the most futile flirtation. The girl had a certain hold of him, but with a great deal of swagger he hadn't the spirit of a sheep: he was in fear of his father and would never commit himself in Lord Considine's lifetime. The most Flora might achieve would be that he wouldn't marry some one else. Geoffrey Dawling, to Mrs. Meldrum's knowledge (I had told her of the young man's visit) had attached himself on the way back from Italy to the Hammond Synge group. My informant was in a position to be definite about this dangler; she knew about his people: she had heard of him before. Hadn't he been, at Oxford, a friend of one of her nephews? Hadn't he spent the Christmas holidays precisely three years before at her brother-in-law's in Yorkshire, taking that occasion to get himself refused with derision by wilful

Betty, the second daughter of the house? Her sister, who liked the floundering youth, had written to her to complain of Betty, and that the young man should now turn up as an appendage of Flora's was one of those oft-cited proofs that the world is small and that there are not enough people to go round. His father had been something or other in the Treasury; his grandfather, on the mother's side, had been something or other in the Church. He had come into the paternal estate, two or three thousand a year in Hampshire; but he had let the place advantageously and was generous to four ugly sisters who lived at Bournemouth and adored him. The family was hideous all round, but the salt of the earth. He was supposed to be unspeakably clever; he was fond of London, fond of books, of intellectual society and of the idea of a political career. That such a man should be at the same time fond of Flora Saunt attested, as the phrase in the first volume of Gibbon has it, the variety of his inclinations. I was soon to learn that he was fonder of her than of all the other things together. Betty, one of five and with views above her station, was at any rate felt at home to have dished herself by her perversity. Of course no one had looked at her since and no one would ever look at her again. It would be eminently desirable that Flora should learn the lesson of Betty's fate.

I was not struck, I confess, with all this in my mind, by any symptoms on our young lady's part of that sort of meditation. The only moral she saw in anything was that of her incomparable countenance, which Mr. Dawling, smitten even like the railway porters and the cabmen by the doom-dealing gods, had followed from London to Venice and from Venice back to London again. I afterwards learned that her version of this episode was profusely inexact: his personal acquaintance with her had been determined by an accident remarkable enough, I admit, in connection with what had gone before—a coincidence at all events superficially striking. At Munich, returning from a tour in the Tyrol with two of his sisters, he had found himself at the *table d'hôte* of his inn opposite to the full presentment of that face of which the mere clumsy copy had made him dream and desire. He had been tossed by it to a height so vertiginous as to involve a retreat from the table; but the next day he had dropped with a resounding thud at the very feet of his apparition. On the following, with an equal incoherence, a sacrifice even of his bewildered sisters, whom he left behind, he made an heroic effort to escape by flight from a fate of which he already felt the cold breath. That fate, in London, very little later, drove him straight before it—drove him one Sunday afternoon, in the rain, to the door of the Hammond Synges. He marched in other words close up to the cannon that was to blow him to pieces. But three weeks, when he reappeared to me, had elapsed since then, yet (to vary my metaphor) the burden he was to carry for the rest of his days was firmly lashed to his back. I don't mean by this that Flora had been persuaded to contract her scope; I mean that he had been treated to the unconditional snub which, as the event was to show, couldn't have been bettered as a means of securing him. She hadn't calculated, but she had said "Never!" and that word had made a bed big enough for his long-legged patience. He became from this moment to my mind the interesting figure in the piece.

Now that he had acted without my aid I was free to show him this, and having on his own side something to show me he repeatedly knocked at my door. What he brought with him on these occasions was a simplicity so huge that, as I turn my ear to the past, I seem even now to hear it bumping up and down my stairs. That was really what I saw of him in the light of his behaviour. He had fallen in love as he might have broken his leg, and the fracture was of a sort that would make him permanently lame. It was the whole man who limped and lurched, with nothing of him left in the same position as before. The tremendous cleverness, the literary society, the political ambition, the Bournemouth sisters all seemed to flop with his every movement a little nearer to the floor. I hadn't had an Oxford training and I had never encountered the great man at whose feet poor Dawling had most submissively sat and who had addressed him his most destructive sniffs; but I remember asking myself if such privileges had been an indispensable preparation to the career on which my friend appeared now to have embarked. I remember too making up my mind about the cleverness, which had its uses and I suppose in impenetrable shades even its critics, but from which the friction of mere personal intercourse was not the sort of process to extract a revealing spark. He accepted without a question both his fever and his chill, and the only thing he showed any subtlety about was this convenience of my friendship. He doubtless told me his simple story, but the matter comes back to me in a kind of sense of *my* being rather the mouthpiece, of my having had to thresh it out for him. He took it from me without a groan, and I gave it to him, as we used to say, pretty hot; he took it again and again, spending his odd half-hours with me as if for the very purpose of learning how idiotically he was in love. He told me I made him see things: to begin with, hadn't I first made him see Flora Saunt? I wanted him to give her up and luminously informed him why; on which he never protested nor contradicted, never was even so alembicated as to declare just for the sake of the drama that he wouldn't. He simply and undramatically didn't, and when at the end of three months I asked him what was the use of talking with such a fellow his nearest approach to a justification was to say that what made him want to help her was just the deficiencies I dwelt on. I could only reply without pointing the moral: "Oh, if you're as sorry for her as that!" I too was nearly as sorry for her as that, but it only led me to be sorrier still for other victims of this compassion. With Dawling as with me the compassion was at first in excess of any visible motive; so that when eventually the motive was supplied each could to a certain extent compliment the other on the fineness of his foresight.

After he had begun to haunt my studio Miss Saunt quite gave it up, and I finally learned that she accused me of conspiring with him to put pressure on her to marry him. She didn't know I would take it that way; else she wouldn't have brought him to see me. It was in her view a part of the conspiracy; that to show him a kindness I asked him at last to sit to me. I daresay moreover she was disgusted to hear that I had ended by attempting almost as many sketches of his beauty as I had attempted of hers. What was the value of tributes to beauty by a hand that luxuriated in ugliness? My relation to poor Dawling's want of modelling was simple enough. I was really digging in that sandy desert for the buried treasure of his soul.

VI

It befell at this period, just before Christmas, that on my having gone under pressure of the season into a great shop to buy a toy or two, my eye, fleeing from superfluity, lighted at a distance on the bright concretion of Flora Saunt, an exhibitability that held its own even against the most plausible pinkness of the most developed dolls. A huge quarter of the place, the biggest bazaar "on earth," was peopled with these and other effigies and fantasies, as well as with purchasers and vendors, haggard alike in the blaze of the gas with hesitations. I was just about to appeal to Flora to avert that stage of my errand when I saw that she was accompanied by a gentleman whose identity, 'though more than a year had elapsed, came back to me from the Folkestone cliff.' It had been associated in that scene with showy knickerbockers; at present it overflowed more splendidly into a fur-trimmed overcoat. Lord Iffield's presence made me waver an instant before crossing over; and during that instant Flora, blank and undistinguishing, as if she too were after all weary of alternatives, looked straight across at me. I was on the point of raising my hat to her when I observed that her face gave no sign. I was exactly in the line of her vision, but she either didn't see me or didn't recognise me, or else had a reason to pretend she didn't. Was her reason that I had displeased her and that she wished to punish me? I had always thought it one of her merits that she wasn't vindictive. She at any rate simply looked away; and at this moment one of the shop-girls, who had apparently gone off in search of it, bustled up to her with a small mechanical toy. It so happened that I followed closely what then took place, afterwards recognising that I had been led to do so, led even through the crowd to press nearer for the purpose, by an impression of which in the act I was not fully conscious.

Flora, with the toy in her hand, looked round at her companion; then seeing his attention had been solicited in another quarter she moved away with the shop-girl, who had evidently offered to conduct her into the presence of more objects of the same sort. When she reached the indicated spot I was in a position still to observe her. She had asked some question about the working of the toy, and the girl, taking it herself, began to explain the little secret. Flora bent her head over it, but she clearly didn't understand. I saw her, in a manner that quickened my curiosity, give a glance back at the place from which she had come. Lord Iffield was talking with another young person: she satisfied herself of this by the aid of a question addressed to her own attendant. She then drew closer to the table near which she stood and, turning her back to me, bent her head lower over the collection of toys and more particularly over the small object the girl had attempted to explain.

She took it back and, after a moment, with her face well averted, made an odd motion of her arms and a significant little duck of her head. These slight signs, singular as it may appear, produced in my bosom an agitation so great that I failed to notice Lord Iffield's whereabouts. He had rejoined her; he was close upon her before I knew it or before she knew it herself. I felt at that instant the strangest of all impulses: if it could have operated more rapidly it would have caused me to dash between them in some such manner as to give Flora a warning. In fact as it was I think I could have done this in time had I not been checked by a curiosity stronger still than my impulse. There were three seconds during which I saw the young man and yet let him come on. Didn't I make the quick calculation that if he didn't catch what Flora was doing I too might perhaps not catch it? She at any rate herself took the alarm. On perceiving her companion's nearness she made, still averted, another duck of her head and a shuffle of her hands so precipitate that a little tin steamboat she had been holding escaped from them and rattled down to the floor with a sharpness that I hear at this hour. Lord Iffield had already seized her arm; with a violent jerk he brought her round toward him. Then it was that there met my eyes a quite distressing sight: this exquisite creature, blushing, glaring, exposed, with a pair of big black-rimmed eyeglasses, defacing her by their position, crookedly astride of her beautiful nose. She made a grab at them with her free hand while I turned confusedly away.

VII

I don't remember how soon it was I spoke to Geoffrey Dawling; his sittings were irregular, but it was certainly the very next time he gave me one.

"Has any rumour ever reached you of Miss Saunt's having anything the matter with her eyes?" He stared with a candour that was a sufficient answer to my question, backing it up with a shocked and mystified "Never!" Then I asked him if he had observed in her any symptom, however disguised, of embarrassed sight: on which, after a moment's thought, he exclaimed "Disguised?" as if my use of that word had vaguely awakened a train. "She's not a bit myopic," he said; "she doesn't blink or contract her lids." I fully recognised this and I mentioned that she altogether denied the impeachment; owing it to him moreover to explain the ground of my inquiry, I gave him a sketch of the incident that had taken place before me at the shop. He knew all about Lord Iffield: that nobleman had figured freely in our conversation as his preferred, his injurious rival. Poor Daw-ling's contention was that if there had been a definite engagement between his lordship and the young lady, the sort of thing that was announced in *The Morning Post*, renunciation and retirement would be comparatively easy to him; but that having waited in vain for any such assurance he was entitled to act as if the door were not really closed or were at any rate not cruelly locked. He was naturally much struck with my anecdote and still more with my interpretation of it.

"There *is* something, there *is* something—possibly something very grave, certainly something that requires she should make use of artificial aids. She won't admit it publicly, because with her idolatry of her beauty, the feeling she is all made up of, she sees in such aids nothing but the humiliation and the disfigurement. She has used them in secret, but that is evidently not enough, for the affection she suffers from, apparently some definite ailment, has lately grown much worse. She looked straight at me in the shop, which was violently lighted, without seeing it was I. At the same distance, at Folkestone, where as you know I first met her, where I heard this mystery hinted at and where she indignantly denied the thing, she appeared easily enough to recognise people. At present she couldn't really make out anything the shop-girl showed her. She has successfully concealed from the man I saw her with that she resorts in private to a pince-nez and that she does so not only under the strictest orders from an oculist, but because literally the poor thing can't accomplish without such help half the business of life. Iffield however has suspected something, and his suspicions, whether expressed or kept to himself, have put him on the watch. I happened to have a glimpse of the movement at which he pounced on her and caught her in the act."

I had thought it all out; my idea explained many things, and Dawling turned pale as he listened to me.

"Was he rough with her?" he anxiously asked.

"How can I tell what passed between them? I fled from the place."

My companion stared at me a moment. "Do you mean to say her eyesight's going?"

"Heaven forbid! In that case how could she take life as she does?"

"How *does* she take life? That's the question!" He sat there bewilderedly brooding; the tears had come into his eyes; they reminded me of those I had seen in Flora's the day I risked my inquiry. The question he had asked was one that to my own satisfaction I was ready to answer, but I hesitated to let him hear as yet all that my reflections had suggested. I was indeed privately astonished at their ingenuity. For the present I only rejoined that it struck me she was playing a particular game; at which he went on as if he hadn't heard me, suddenly haunted with a fear, lost in the dark possibility I had opened up: "Do you mean there's a danger of anything very bad?" "My dear fellow, you must ask her oculist." "Who in the world *is* her oculist?" "I haven't a conception. But we mustn't get too excited. My impression would be that she has only to observe a few ordinary rules, to exercise a little common sense."

Dawling jumped at this. "I see—to stick to the pince-nez."

"To follow to the letter her oculist's prescription, whatever it is and at whatever cost to her prettiness. It's not a thing to be trifled with."

"Upon my honour it *shan't* be trifled with!" he roundly declared; and he adjusted himself to his position again as if we had quite settled the business. After a considerable interval, while I botched away, he suddenly said: "Did they make a great difference?"

"A great difference?"

"Those things she had put on."

"Oh, the glasses—in her beauty? She looked queer of course, but it was partly because one was unaccustomed. There are women who look charming in nippers. What, at any rate, if she does look queer? She must be mad not to accept that alternative."

"She *is* mad," said Geoffrey Dawling.

"Mad to refuse you, I grant. Besides," I went on, "the pince-nez, which was a large and peculiar one, was all awry: she had half pulled it off, but it continued to stick, and she was crimson, she was angry."

"It must have been horrible!" my companion murmured.

"It *was* horrible. But it's still more horrible to defy all warnings; it's still more horrible to be landed in—" Without saying in what I disgustedly shrugged my shoulders.

After a glance at me Dawling jerked round. "Then you do believe that she may be?"

I hesitated. "The thing would be to make *her* believe it. She only needs a good scare."

"But if that fellow is shocked at the precautions she does take?"

"Oh, who knows?" I rejoined with small sincerity. "I don't suppose Iffield is absolutely a brute."

"I would take her with leather blinders, like a shying mare!" cried Geoffrey Dawling.

I had an impression that Iffield wouldn't, but I didn't communicate it, for I wanted to pacify my friend, whom I had discomposed too much for the purposes of my sitting. I recollect that I did some good work that morning, but it also comes back to me that before we separated he had practically revealed to me that my anecdote, connecting itself in his mind with a series of observations at the time unconscious and unregistered, had covered with light the subject of our colloquy. He had had a formless perception of some secret that drove Miss Saunt to subterfuges, and the more he thought of it the more he guessed this secret to be the practice of making believe she saw when she didn't and of cleverly keeping people from finding out how little she saw. When one patched things together it was astonishing what ground they covered. Just as he was going away he asked me from what source, at Folkestone, the horrid tale had proceeded. When I had given him, as I saw no reason not to do, the name of Mrs. Meldrum, he exclaimed: "Oh, I know all about her; she's a friend of some friends of mine!" At this I remembered wilful Betty and said to myself that I knew some one who would probably prove more wilful still.

VIII

A few days later I again heard Dawling on my stairs, and even before he passed my threshold I knew he had something to tell me.

"I've been down to Folkestone—it was necessary I should see her!" I forget whether he had come straight from the station; he was at any rate out of breath with his news, which it took me however a minute to interpret.

"You mean that you've been with Mrs. Meldrum?"

"Yes; to ask her what she knows and how she comes to know it. It worked upon me awfully—I mean what you told me." He made a visible effort to seem quieter than he was, and it showed me sufficiently that he had not been reassured. I laid, to comfort him and smiling at a venture, a friendly hand on his arm, and he dropped into my eyes, fixing them an instant, a strange, distended look which might have expressed the cold clearness of all that was to come. "I *know*—now!" he said with an emphasis he rarely used.

"What then did Mrs. Meldrum tell you?"

"Only one thing that signified, for she has no real knowledge. But that one thing was everything."

"What is it then?"

"Why, that she can't bear the sight of her." His pronouns required some arranging, but after I had successfully dealt with them I replied that I knew perfectly Miss Saunt had a trick of turning her back on the good lady of Folkestone. But what did that prove? "Have you never guessed? I guessed as soon as she spoke!" Dawling towered over me in dismal triumph. It was the first time in our acquaintance that, intellectually speaking, this had occurred;

but even so remarkable an incident still left me sufficiently at sea to cause him to continue: "Why, the effect of those spectacles!"

I seemed to catch the tail of his idea. "Mrs. Meldrum's?"

"They're so awfully ugly and they increase so the dear woman's ugliness." This remark began to flash a light, and when he quickly added "She sees herself, she sees her own fate!" my response was so immediate that I had almost taken the words out of his mouth. While I tried to fix this sudden image of Flora's face glazed in and cross-barred even as Mrs. Meldrum's was glazed and barred, he went on to assert that only the horror of that image, looming out at herself, could be the reason of her avoiding such a monitress. The fact he had encountered made everything hideously vivid and more vivid than anything else that just such another pair of goggles was what would have been prescribed to Flora.

"I see—I see," I presently rejoined. "What would become of Lord Iffield if she were suddenly to come out in them? What indeed would become of every one, what would become of *everything?*" This was an inquiry that Dawling was evidently unprepared to meet, and I completed it by saying at last: "My dear fellow, for that matter, what would become of *you?*"

Once more he turned on me his good green eyes. "Oh, I shouldn't mind!"

The tone of his words somehow made his ugly face beautiful, and I felt that there dated from this moment in my heart a confirmed affection for him. None the less, at the same time, perversely and rudely, I became aware of a certain drollery in our discussion of such alternatives. It made me laugh out and say to him while I laughed: "You'd take her even with those things of Mrs. Meldrum's?"

He remained mournfully grave; I could see that he was surprised at my rude mirth. But he summoned back a vision of the lady at Folkestone and conscientiously replied: "Even with those things of Mrs. Meldrum's." I begged him not to think my laughter in bad taste: it was only a practical recognition of the fact that we had built a monstrous castle in the air. Didn't he see on what flimsy ground the structure rested? The evidence was preposterously small. He believed the worst, but we were utterly ignorant.

"I shall find out the truth," he promptly replied.

"How can you? If you question her you'll simply drive her to perjure herself. Wherein after all does it concern you to know the truth? It's the girl's own affair."

"Then why did you tell me your story?"

I was a trifle embarrassed. "To warn you off," I returned smiling. He took no more notice of these words than presently to remark that Lord Iffield had no serious intentions. "Very possibly," I said. "But you mustn't speak as if Lord Iffield and you were her only alternatives."

Dawling thought a moment. "Wouldn't the people she has consulted give some information? She must have been to people. How else can she have been condemned?"

"Condemned to what? Condemned to perpetual nippers? Of course she has consulted some of the big specialists, but she has done it, you may be sure, in the most clandestine manner; and even if it were supposable that they would tell you anything—which I altogether doubt—you would have great difficulty in finding out which men they are. Therefore leave it alone; never show her what you suspect."

I even, before he quitted me, asked him to promise me this. "All right, I promise," he said gloomily enough. He was a lover who could tacitly grant the proposition that there was no limit to the deceit his loved one was ready to practise: it made so remarkably little difference. I could see that from this moment he would be filled with a passionate pity ever so little qualified by a sense of the girl's fatuity and folly. She was always accessible to him—that I knew; for if she had told him he was an idiot to dream she could dream of him, she would have resented the imputation of having failed to make it clear that she would always be glad to regard him as a friend. What were most of her friends—what were all of them—but repudiated idiots? I was perfectly aware that in her conversations and confidences I myself for instance had a niche in the gallery. As regards poor Dawling I knew how often he still called on the Hammond Synges. It was not there but under the wing of the Floyd-Taylors that her intimacy with Lord Iffield most flourished. At all events when a week after the visit I have just summarised Flora's name was one morning brought up to me I jumped at the conclusion that Dawling had been with her and even I fear briefly entertained the thought that he had broken his word.

IX

She left me, after she had been introduced, in no suspense about her present motive; she was on the contrary in a visible fever to enlighten me; but I promptly learned that for the alarm with which she pitiably panted our young man was not accountable. She had but one thought in the world, and that thought was for Lord Iffield. I had the strangest, saddest scene with her, and if it did me no other good it at least made me at last completely understand why insidiously, from the first, she had struck me as a creature of tragedy. In showing me the whole of her folly it lifted the curtain of her misery. I don't know how much she meant to tell me when she came—I think she had had plans of elaborate misrepresentation; at any rate she found it at the end of ten minutes the simplest way to break down and sob, to be wretched and true. When she had once begun to let herself go the movement took her off her feet: the relief of it was like the cessation of a cramp. She shared in a word her long secret; she shifted her sharp pain. She brought, I confess, tears to my own eyes, tears of helpless tenderness for her helpless poverty. Her visit however was not quite so memorable in itself as in some of its consequences, the most immediate of which was that I went that afternoon to see Geoffrey Dawling, who had in those days rooms in Welbeck Street, where I presented myself at an hour late enough to warrant the supposition that he might have come in. He had not come in, but he was expected, and I was invited to enter and wait for him: a lady, I was informed, was already in his sitting-room. I hesitated, a little at a loss: it had wildly coursed through my brain that the lady was perhaps Flora Saunt. But when I asked if she were young and remarkably pretty I received so significant a "No, sir!" that I risked an advance and after a minute in this manner found myself, to my astonishment, face to face with Mrs. Meldrum. "Oh, you dear thing," she exclaimed, "I'm delighted to see you: you spare me another compromising *démarche!* But for this I should have called on you also. Know the worst at once: if you see me here it's at least deliberate—it's planned, plotted, shameless. I came up on purpose to see him; upon my word, I'm in love with him. Why, if you valued my peace of mind, did you let him, the other day at Folkestone, dawn upon my delighted eyes? I took there in half an hour the most extraordinary fancy to him. With a perfect sense of everything that can be urged against him, I find him none the less the very pearl of men. However, I haven't come up to declare my passion—I've come to bring him news that will interest him much more. Above all I've come to urge upon him to be careful."

"About Flora Saunt?"

"About what he says and does: he must be as still as a mouse! She's at last really engaged."

"But it's a tremendous secret?" I was moved to merriment.

"Precisely: she telegraphed me this noon, and spent another shilling to tell me that not a creature in the world is yet to know it."

"She had better have spent it to tell you that she had just passed an hour with the creature you see before you."

"She has just passed an hour with every one in the place!" Mrs. Meldrum cried. "They've vital reasons, she wired, for it's not coming out for a month. Then it will be formally announced, but meanwhile her happiness is delirious. I daresay Mr. Dawling already knows, and he may, as it's nearly seven o'clock, have jumped off London Bridge; but an effect of the talk I had with him the other day was to make me, on receipt of my telegram, feel it to be my duty to warn him in person against taking action, as it were, on the horrid certitude which I could see he carried away with him. I had added somehow to that certitude. He told me what you had told him you had seen in your shop."

Mrs. Meldrum, I perceived, had come to Welbeck Street on an errand identical with my own—a circumstance indicating her rare sagacity, inasmuch as her ground for undertaking it was a very different thing from what Flora's wonderful visit had made of mine. I remarked to her that what I had seen in the shop was sufficiently striking, but that I had seen a great deal more that morning in my studio. "In short," I said, "I've seen everything."

She was mystified. "Everything?"

"The poor creature is under the darkest of clouds. Oh, she came to triumph, but she remained to talk something approaching to sense! She put herself completely in my hands—she does me the honour to intimate that of all her friends I'm the most disinterested. After she had announced to me that Lord Iffield was bound hands and feet and that for the present I was absolutely the only person in the secret, she arrived at her real business. She had had a suspicion of me ever since the day, at Folkestone, I asked her for the truth about her eyes. The truth is what you and I both guessed. She has no end of a danger hanging over her."

"But from what cause? I, who by God's mercy have kept mine, know everything that can be known about eyes," said Mrs. Meldrum.

"She might have kept hers if she had profited by God's mercy, if she had done in time, done years ago, what was imperatively ordered her; if she hadn't in fine been cursed with the loveliness that was to make her behaviour a thing of fable. She may keep them still if she'll sacrifice—and after all so little—that purely superficial charm. She must do as you've done; she must wear, dear lady, what you wear!"

What my companion wore glittered for the moment like a melon-frame in August. "Heaven forgive her—now I understand!" She turned pale.

But I wasn't afraid of the effect on her good nature of her thus seeing, through her great goggles, why it had always been that Flora held her at such a distance. "I can't tell you," I said, "from what special affection, what state of the eye, her danger proceeds: that's the one thing she succeeded this morning in keeping from me. She knows it herself perfectly; she has had the best advice in Europe. 'It's a thing that's awful, simply awful'—that was the only account she would give me. Year before last, while she was at Boulogne, she went for three days with Mrs. Floyd-Taylor to Paris. She there surreptitiously consulted the greatest man—even Mrs. Floyd-Taylor doesn't know. Last autumn, in Germany, she did the same. 'First put on certain special spectacles with a straight bar in the middle: then we'll talk'—that's practically what they say. What *she* says is that she'll put on anything in nature when she's married, but that she must get married first. She has always meant to do everything as soon as she's married. Then and then only she'll be safe. How will any one ever look at her if she makes herself a fright? How could she ever have got engaged if she had made herself a fright from the first? It's no use to insist that with her beauty she can never *be* a fright. She said to me this morning, poor girl, the most characteristic, the most harrowing things. 'My face is all I have—and *such* a face! I knew from the first I could do anything with it. But I needed it all—I need it still, every exquisite inch of it. It isn't as if I had a figure or anything else. Oh, if God had only given me a figure too, I don't say! Yes, with a figure, a really good one, like Fanny Floyd-Taylor's, who's hideous, I'd have risked plain glasses. *Que voulez-vous?* No one is perfect.' She says she still has money left, but I don't believe a word of it. She has been speculating on her impunity, on the idea that her danger would hold off: she has literally been running a race with it. Her theory has been, as you from the first so clearly saw, that she'd get in ahead. She swears to me that though the 'bar' is too cruel she wears when she's alone what she has been ordered to wear. But when the deuce is she alone? It's herself of course that she has swindled worst: she has put herself off, so insanely that even her vanity but half accounts for it, with little inadequate concessions, little false measures and preposterous evasions and childish hopes. Her great terror is now that Iffield, who already has suspicions, who has found out her pince-nez but whom she has beguiled with some unblushing hocus-pocus, may discover the dreadful facts; and the essence of what she wanted this morning was in that interest to square me, to get me to deny indignantly and authoritatively (for isn't she my 'favourite sitter'?) that she has anything whatever the matter with any part of her. She sobbed, she 'went on,' she entreated; after we got talking her extraordinary nerve left her and she showed me what she has been through—showed me also all her terror of the harm I could do her. 'Wait till I'm married! wait till I'm married!' She took hold of me, she almost sank on her knees. It seems to me highly immoral, one's participation in her fraud; but there's no doubt that she *must* be married: I don't know what I don't see behind it! Therefore," I wound up, "Dawling must keep his hands off."

Mrs. Meldrum had held her breath; she exhaled a long moan. "Well, that's exactly what I came here to tell him."

"Then here he is." Our unconscious host had just opened the door. Immensely startled at finding us he turned a frightened look from one to the other, as if to guess what disaster we were there to announce or avert.

Mrs. Meldrum, on the spot, was all gaiety. "I've come to return your sweet visit. Ah," she laughed, "I mean to keep up the acquaintance!"

"Do—do," he murmured mechanically and absently, continuing to look at us. Then abruptly he broke out: "He's going to marry her."

I was surprised. "You already know?"

He had had in his hand an evening newspaper; he tossed it down on the table. "It's in that."

"Published—already?" I was still more surprised.

"Oh, Flora can't keep a secret!" Mrs. Meldrum humorously declared. She went up to poor Dawling and laid a motherly hand upon him. "It's all right—it's just as it ought to be: don't think about her ever any more." Then as he met this adjuration with a dismal stare in which the thought of her was as abnormally vivid as the colour of the pupil, the excellent woman put up her funny face and tenderly kissed him on the cheek.

X

I have spoken of these reminiscences as of a row of coloured beads, and I confess that as I continue to straighten out my chaplet I am rather proud of the comparison. The beads are all there, as I said—they slip along the string in their small, smooth roundness. Geoffrey Daw-ling accepted like a gentleman the event his evening paper had proclaimed; in view of which I snatched a moment to murmur him a hint to offer Mrs. Meldrum his hand. He returned me a heavy head-shake, and I judged that marriage would henceforth strike him very much as the traffic of the street may strike some poor incurable at the window of an hospital. Circumstances arising at this time promptly led to my making an absence from England, and circumstances already existing offered him a solid basis for similar action. He had after all the usual resource of a Briton—he could take to his boats.

He started on a journey round the globe, and I was left with nothing but my inference as to what might have happened. Later observation however only confirmed my belief that if at any time during the couple of months that followed Flora Saunt's brilliant engagement he had made up, as they say, to the good lady of Folkestone, that good lady would not have pushed him over the cliff. Strange as she was to behold I knew of cases in which she had been obliged to administer that shove. I went to New York to paint a couple of portraits; but I found, once on the spot, that I had counted without Chicago, where I was invited to blot out this harsh discrimination by the production of no less than ten. I spent a year in America and should probably have spent a second had I not been summoned back to England by alarming news from my mother. Her strength had failed, and as soon as I reached London I hurried down to Folkestone, arriving just at the moment to offer a welcome to some slight symptom of a rally. She had been much worse, but she was now a little better; and though I found nothing but satisfaction in having come to her I saw after a few hours that my London studio, where arrears of work had already met me, would be my place to await whatever might next occur. Before returning to town however I had every reason to sally forth in search of Mrs. Meldrum, from whom, in so many months, I had not had a line, and my view of whom, with the adjacent objects, as I had left them, had been intercepted by a luxuriant foreground.

Before I had gained her house I met her, as I supposed, coming toward me across the down, greeting me from afar with the familiar twinkle of her great vitreous badge; and as it was late in the autumn and the esplanade was a blank I was free to acknowledge this signal by cutting a caper on the grass.

My enthusiasm dropped indeed the next moment, for it had taken me but a few seconds to perceive that the person thus assaulted had by no means the figure of my military friend. I felt a shock much greater than any I should have thought possible as on this person's drawing near I identified her as poor little Flora Saunt. At what moment Flora had recognised me belonged to an order of mysteries over which, it quickly came home to me, one would never linger again: I could intensely reflect that once we were face to face it chiefly mattered that I should succeed in looking still more intensely unastonished. All I saw at first was the big gold bar crossing each of her lenses, over which something convex and grotesque, like the eyes of a large insect, something that now represented her whole personality, seemed, as out of the orifice of a prison, to strain forward and press. The face had shrunk away: it looked smaller, appeared even to look plain; it was at all events, so far as the effect on a spectator was concerned, wholly sacrificed to this huge apparatus of sight. There was no smile in it, and she made no motion to take my offered hand.

"I had no idea you were down here!" I exclaimed; and I wondered whether she didn't know me at all or knew me only by my voice.

"You thought I was Mrs. Meldrum," she very quietly remarked.

It was the quietness itself that made me feel the necessity of an answer almost violently gay. "Oh yes," I laughed, "you have a tremendous deal in common with Mrs. Meldrum! I've just returned to England after a long absence and I'm on my way to see her. Won't you come with me?" It struck me that her old reason for keeping clear of our friend was well disposed of now.

"I've just left her; I'm staying with her." She stood solemnly fixing me with her goggles. "Would you like to paint me *now?*" she asked. She seemed to speak, with intense gravity, from behind a mask or a cage.

There was nothing to do but to treat the question with the same exuberance. "It would be a fascinating little artistic problem!" That something was wrong it was not difficult to perceive; but a good deal more than met the eye might be presumed to be wrong if Flora was under Mrs. Meldrum's roof. I had not for a year had much time to think of her, but my imagination had had sufficient warrant for lodging her in more gilded halls. One of the last things I had heard before leaving England was that in commemoration of the new relationship she had gone to stay with Lady Considine. This had made me take everything else for granted, and the noisy American world had deafened my ears to possible contradictions. Her spectacles were at present a direct contradiction; they seemed a negation not only of new relationships but of every old one as well. I remember nevertheless that when after a moment she walked beside me on the grass I found myself nervously hoping she wouldn't as yet at any rate tell me anything very dreadful; so that to stave off this danger I harried her with questions about Mrs. Meldrum and, without waiting for replies, became profuse on the subject of my own doings. My companion was completely silent, and I felt both as if she were watching my nervousness with a sort of sinister irony and as if I were talking to some different, strange person. Flora plain and obscure and soundless was no Flora at all. At Mrs. Meldrum's door she turned off with the observation that as there was certainly a great deal I should have to say to our friend she had better not go in with me. I looked at her again—I had been keeping my eyes away from her— but only to meet her magnified stare. I greatly desired in truth to see Mrs. Meldrum alone, but there was something so pitiful in the girl's predicament that I hesitated to fall in with this idea of dropping her. Yet one couldn't express a compassion without seeming to take too much wretchedness for granted. I reflected that I must really figure to her as a fool, which was an entertainment I had never expected to give her. It rolled over me there for the first time—it has come back to me since—that there is, strangely, in very deep misfortune a dignity finer even than in the most inveterate habit of being all right. I couldn't have to her the manner of treating it as a mere detail that I was face to face with a part of what, at our last meeting, we had had such a scene about; but while I was trying to think of some manner that I *could* have she said quite colourlessly, yet somehow as if she might never see me again: "Goodbye. I'm going to take my walk."

"All alone?"

She looked round the great bleak cliff-top. "With whom should I go? Besides, I like to be alone—for the present."

This gave me the glimmer of a vision that she regarded her disfigurement as temporary, and the confidence came to me that she would never, for her happiness, cease to be a creature of illusions. It enabled me to exclaim, smiling brightly and feeling indeed idiotic: "Oh, I shall see you again! But I hope you'll have a very pleasant walk."

"All my walks are very pleasant, thank you—they do me such a lot of good." She was as quiet as a mouse, and her words seemed to me stupendous in their wisdom. "I take several a day," she continued. She might have been an ancient woman responding with humility at the church door to the patronage of the parson. "The more I take the better I feel. I'm ordered by the doctors to keep all the while in the air and go in for plenty of exercise. It keeps up my general health, you know, and if that goes on improving as it has lately done everything will soon be all right. All that was the matter with me before—and always; it was too reckless!—was that I neglected my general health. It acts directly on the state of the particular organ. So I'm going three miles."

I grinned at her from the doorstep while Mrs. Meldrum's maid stood there to admit me. "Oh, I'm so glad," I said, looking at her as she paced away with the pretty flutter she had kept and remembering the day when, while she rejoined Lord Iffield, I had indulged in the same observation. Her air of assurance was on this occasion not less than it had been on that; but I recalled that she had then struck me as marching off to her doom. Was she really now marching away from it?

XI

As soon as I saw Mrs. Meldrum I broke out to her. "Is there anything in it? *Is* her general health—?"

Mrs. Meldrum interrupted me with her great amused blare. "You've already seen her and she has told you her wondrous tale? What's 'in it' is what has been in everything she has ever done—the most comical, tragical belief in herself. She thinks she's doing a 'cure.'"

"And what does her husband think?"

"Her husband? What husband?"

"Hasn't she then married Lord Iffield?"

"*Vous-en-êtes là?*" cried my hostess. "He behaved like a regular beast."

"How should I know? You never wrote to me."

Mrs. Meldrum hesitated, covering me with what poor Flora called the particular organ. "No, I didn't write to you; and I abstained on purpose. If I didn't I thought you mightn't, over there, hear what had happened. If you should hear I was afraid you would stir up Mr. Dawling."

"Stir him up?"

"Urge him to fly to the rescue; write out to him that there was another chance for him."

"I wouldn't have done it," I said.

"Well," Mrs. Meldrum replied, "it was not my business to give you an opportunity."

"In short you were afraid of it."

Again she hesitated and though it may have been only my fancy I thought she considerably reddened. At all events she laughed out. Then "I was afraid of it!" she very honestly answered.

"But doesn't he know? Has he given no sign?"

"Every sign in life—he came straight back to her. He did everything to get her to listen to him; but she hasn't the smallest idea of it."

"Has he seen her as she is now?" I presently and just a trifle awkwardly inquired.

"Indeed he has, and borne it like a hero. He told me all about it."

"How much you've all been through!" I ventured to ejaculate. "Then what has become of him?"

"He's at home in Hampshire. He has got back his old place and I believe by this time his old sisters. It's not half a bad little place."

"Yet its attractions say nothing to Flora?"

"Oh, Flora's by no means on her back!" my interlocutress laughed.

"She's not on her back because she's on yours. Have you got her for the rest of your life?"

Once more my hostess genially glared at me. "Did she tell you how much the Hammond Synges have kindly left her to live on? Not quite eighty pounds a year."

"That's a good deal, but it won't pay the oculist. What was it that at last induced her to submit to him?"

"Her general collapse after that brute of an Iffield's rupture. She cried her eyes out—she passed through a horror of black darkness. Then came a gleam of light, and the light appears to have broadened. She went into goggles as repentant Magdalens go into the Catholic Church."

"Yet you don't think she'll be saved?"

"*She* thinks she will—that's all I can tell you. There's no doubt that when once she brought herself to accept her real remedy, as she calls it, she began to enjoy a relief that she had never known. That feeling, very new and in spite of what she pays for it most refreshing, has given her something to hold on by, begotten in her foolish little mind a belief that, as she says, she's on the mend and that in the course of time, if she leads a tremendously healthy life, she'll be able to take off her muzzle and become as dangerous again as ever. It keeps her going."

"And what keeps *you?* You're good until the parties begin again."

"Oh, she doesn't object to me now!" smiled Mrs. Meldrum. "I'm going to take her abroad; we shall be a pretty pair." I was struck with this energy and after a moment I inquired the reason of it. "It's to divert her mind," my friend replied, reddening again, I thought, a little. "We shall go next week: I've only waited, to start, to see how your mother would be." I expressed to her hereupon my sense of her extraordinary merit and also that of the inconceivability of Flora's fancying herself still in a situation not to jump at the chance of marrying a man like Dawling. "She says he's too ugly; she says he's too dreary; she says in fact he's 'nobody,'" Mrs. Meldrum pursued. "She says above all that he's not 'her own sort.' She doesn't deny that he's good, but she insists on the fact that he's grotesque. He's quite the last person she would ever dream of." I was almost disposed on hearing this to protest that if the girl had so little proper feeling her noble suitor had perhaps served her right; but after a while my curiosity as to just how her noble suitor *had* served her got the better of that emotion, and I asked a question or two which led my companion again to apply to him the invidious epithet I have already quoted. What had happened was simply that Flora had at the eleventh hour broken down in the attempt to put him off with an uncandid account of her infirmity and that his lordship's interest in her had not been proof against the discovery of the way she had practised on him. Her dissimulation, he was obliged to perceive, had been infernally deep. The future in short assumed a new complexion for him when looked at through the grim glasses of a bride who, as he had said to some one, couldn't really, when you came to find out, see her hand before her face. He had conducted himself like any other jockeyed customer—he had returned the animal as unsound. He had backed out in his own way, giving the business, by some sharp shuffle, such a turn as to make the rupture ostensibly Flora's, but he had none the less remorselessly and basely backed out. He had cared for her lovely face, cared for it in the amused and haunted way it had been her poor little delusive gift to make men care; and her lovely face, damn it, with the monstrous gear she had begun to rig upon it, was just what had let him in. He had in the judgment of his family done everything that could be expected of him; he had made—Mrs. Meldrum had herself seen the letter—a "handsome" offer of pecuniary compensation. Oh, if Flora, with her incredible buoyancy, was in a manner on her feet again now, it was not that she had not for weeks and weeks been prone in the dust. Strange were the humiliations, the prostrations it was given

Henry James

to some natures to survive. That Flora had survived was perhaps after all a sort of sign that she was reserved for some final mercy. "But she has been in the abysses at any rate," said Mrs. Meldrum, "and I really don't think I can tell you what pulled her through."

"I think I can tell *you*," I said. "What in the world but Mrs. Meldrum?"

At the end of an hour Flora had not come in, and I was obliged to announce that I should have but time to reach the station, where, in charge of my mother's servant, I was to find my luggage. Mrs. Meldrum put before me the question of waiting till a later train, so as not to lose our young lady; but I confess I gave this alternative a consideration less profound than I pretended. Somehow I didn't care if I did lose our young lady. Now that I knew the worst that had befallen her it struck me still less as possible to meet her on the ground of condolence; and with the melancholy aspect she wore to me what other ground was left? I lost her, but I caught my train. In truth she was so changed that one hated to see it; and now that she was in charitable hands one didn't feel compelled to make great efforts. I had studied her face for a particular beauty; I had lived with that beauty and reproduced it; but I knew what belonged to my trade well enough to be sure it was gone for ever.

XII

I was soon called back to Folkestone; but Mrs. Meldrum and her young friend had already left England, finding to that end every convenience on the spot and not having had to come up to town. My thoughts however were so painfully engaged there that I should in any case have had little attention for them: the event occurred that was to bring my series of visits to a close. When this high tide had ebbed I returned to America and to my interrupted work, which had opened out on such a scale that, with a deep plunge into a great chance, I was three good years in rising again to the surface. There are nymphs and naiads moreover in the American depths: they may have had something to do with the duration of my dive. I mention them to account for a grave misdemeanour—the fact that after the first year I rudely neglected

385

Mrs. Meldrum. She had written to me from Florence after my mother's death and had mentioned in a postscript that in our young lady's calculations the lowest numbers were now Italian counts. This was a good omen, and if in subsequent letters there was no news of a sequel I was content to accept small things and to believe that grave tidings, should there be any, would come to me in due course. The gravity of what might happen to a featherweight became indeed with time and distance less appreciable, and I was not without an impression that Mrs. Meldrum, whose sense of proportion was not the least of her merits, had no idea of boring the world with the ups and downs of her pensioner. The poor girl grew dusky and dim, a small fitful memory, a regret tempered by the comfortable consciousness of how kind Mrs. Meldrum would always be to her. I was professionally more preoccupied than I had ever been, and I had swarms of pretty faces in my eyes and a chorus of high voices in my ears. Geoffrey Dawling had on his return to England written me two or three letters: his last information had been that he was going into the figures of rural illiteracy. I was delighted to receive it and had no doubt that if he should go into figures they would, as they are said to be able to prove anything, prove at least that my advice was sound and that he had wasted time enough. This quickened on my part another hope, a hope suggested by some roundabout rumour—I forget how it reached me—that he was engaged to a girl down in Hampshire. He turned out not to be, but I felt sure that if only he went into figures deep enough he would become, among the girls down in Hampshire or elsewhere, one of those numerous prizes of battle whose defences are practically not on the scale of their provocations. I nursed in short the thought that it was probably open to him to become one of the types as to which, as the years go on, frivolous and superficial spectators lose themselves in the wonder that they ever succeeded in winning even the least winsome mates. He never alluded to Flora Saunt; and there was in his silence about her, quite as in Mrs. Meldrum's, an element of instinctive tact, a brief implication that if you didn't happen to have been in love with her she was not an inevitable topic.

Within a week after my return to London I went to the opera, of which I had always been much of a devotee. I arrived too late for the first act of "Lohengrin," but the second was just beginning, and I gave myself up to it with no more than a glance at the house. When it was over I treated myself, with my glass, from my place in the stalls, to a general survey of the boxes, making doubtless on their contents the reflections, pointed by comparison, that are most familiar to the wanderer restored to London. There was a certain proportion of pretty women, but I suddenly became aware that one of these was far prettier than the others. This lady, alone in one of the smaller receptacles of the grand tier and already the aim of fifty tentative glasses, which she sustained with admirable serenity—this single exquisite figure, placed in the quarter furthest removed from my stall, was a person, I immediately felt, to cause one's curiosity to linger. Dressed in white, with diamonds in her hair and pearls on her neck, she had a pale radiance of beauty which even at that distance made her a distinguished presence and, with the air that easily attaches to lonely loveliness in public places, an agreeable mystery. A mystery however she remained to me only for a minute after I had levelled my glass at her: I feel to this moment the startled thrill, the shock almost of joy with which I suddenly encountered in her vague brightness a rich revival of Flora Saunt. I say a revival because, to put it crudely, I had on that last occasion left poor Flora for dead. At present perfectly alive again, she was altered only, as it were, by resurrection. A little older, a little quieter, a little finer and a good deal fairer, she was simply transfigured by recovery. Sustained by the reflection that even recovery wouldn't enable her to distinguish me in the crowd, I was free to look at her well. Then it was it came home to me that my vision of her in her great goggles had been cruelly final. As her beauty was all there was of her, that machinery had extinguished her, and so far as I had thought of her in the interval I had thought of her as buried in the tomb her stern specialist had built. With the sense that she had escaped from it came a lively wish to return to her; and if I didn't straightway leave my place and rush round the theatre and up to her box it was because I was fixed to the spot some moments longer by the simple inability to cease looking at her.

She had been from the first of my seeing her practically motionless, leaning back in her chair with a kind of thoughtful grace and with her eyes vaguely directed, as it seemed to me, to one of the boxes on my side of the house and consequently over my head and out of my sight. The only movement she made for some time was to finger with an ungloved hand

and as if with the habit of fondness the row of pearls on her neck, which my glass showed me to be large and splendid. Her diamonds and pearls, in her solitude, mystified me, making me, as she had had no such brave jewels in the days of the Hammond Synges, wonder what undreamt-of improvement had taken place in her fortunes. The ghost of a question hovered there a moment: could anything so prodigious have happened as that on her tested and proved amendment Lord Iffield had taken her back? This could not have occurred without my hearing of it; and moreover if she had become a person of such fashion where was the little court one would naturally see at her elbow? Her isolation was puzzling, though it could easily suggest that she was but momentarily alone. If she had come with Mrs. Meldrum that lady would have taken advantage of the interval to pay a visit to some other box—doubtless the box at which Flora had just been looking. Mrs. Meldrum didn't account for the jewels, but the refreshment of Flora's beauty accounted for anything. She presently moved her eyes over the house, and I felt them brush me again like the wings of a dove. I don't know what quick pleasure flickered into the hope that she would at last see me. She did see me: she suddenly bent forward to take up the little double-barrelled ivory glass that rested on the edge of the box and, to all appearance, fix me with it. I smiled from my place straight up at the searching lenses, and after an instant she dropped them and smiled as straight back at me. Oh, her smile: it was her old smile, her young smile, her peculiar smile made perfect! I instantly left my stall and hurried off for a nearer view of it; quite flushed, I remember, as I went, with the annoyance of having happened to think of the idiotic way I had tried to paint her. Poor Iffield with his sample of that error, and still poorer Dawling in particular with his! I hadn't touched her, I was professionally humiliated, and as the attendant in the lobby opened her box for me I felt that the very first thing I should have to say to her would be that she must absolutely sit to me again.

XIII

She gave me the smile once more as over her shoulder, from her chair, she turned her face to me. "Here you are again!" she exclaimed with her disgloved hand put up a little backward for me to take. I dropped into a chair just behind her and, having taken it and noted that one of the curtains of the box would make the demonstration sufficiently private, bent my lips over it and impressed them on its finger-tips. It was given me however, to my astonishment, to feel next that all the privacy in the world couldn't have sufficed to mitigate the start with which she greeted this free application of my moustache: the blood had jumped to her face, she quickly recovered her hand and jerked at me, twisting herself round, a vacant, challenging stare. During the next few instants several extraordinary things happened, the first of which was that now I was close to them the eyes of loveliness I had come up to look into didn't show at all the conscious light I had just been pleased to see them flash across the house: they showed on the contrary, to my confusion, a strange, sweet blankness, an expression I failed to give a meaning to until, without delay, I felt on my arm, directed to it as if instantly to efface the effect of her start, the grasp of the hand she had impulsively snatched from me. It was the irrepressible question in this grasp that stopped on my lips all sound of salutation. She had mistaken my entrance for that of another person, a pair of lips without a moustache. She was feeling me to see who I was! With the perception of this and of her not seeing me I sat gaping at her and at the wild word that didn't come, the right word to express or to disguise my stupefaction. What was the right word to commemorate one's sudden discovery, at the very moment too at which one had been most encouraged to count on better things, that one's dear old friend had gone blind? Before the answer to this question dropped upon me—and the moving moments, though few, seemed many—I heard, with the sound of voices, the click of the attendant's key on the other side of the door. Poor Flora heard also, and with the hearing, still with her hand on my arm, she brightened again as I had a minute since seen her brighten across the house: she had the sense of the return of the person she had taken me for—the person with the right pair of lips, as to whom I was for that matter much more in the dark than she. I gasped, but my word had come: if she had lost her sight it was in this very loss that she had found again her beauty. I managed to speak while we were still alone, before her companion had appeared. "You're lovelier at this day than you have ever been in your life!" At the sound of my voice and that of the opening of the door her excitement broke into audible joy. She sprang up, recognising me, always holding me, and gleefully cried to a gentleman who was arrested in the doorway by the sight of me: "He has come back, he has come back, and you should have heard what he says of me!" The gentleman was Geoffrey Dawling, and I thought it best to let him hear on the spot. "How beautiful she is, my dear man—but how extraordinarily beautiful! More beautiful at this hour than ever, ever before!"

It gave them almost equal pleasure and made Dawling blush up to his eyes; while this in turn produced, in spite of deepened astonishment, a blessed snap of the strain that I had been under for some moments. I wanted to embrace them both, and while the opening bars of another scene rose from the orchestra I almost did embrace Dawling, whose first emotion on beholding me had visibly and ever so oddly been a consciousness of guilt. I had caught him somehow in the act, though that was as yet all I knew; but by the time we had sunk noiselessly into our chairs again (for the music was supreme, Wagner passed first) my demonstration ought pretty well to have given him the limit of the criticism he had to fear. I myself indeed, while the opera blazed, was only too afraid he might divine in our silent closeness the very moral of my optimism, which was simply the comfort I had gathered from seeing that if our companion's beauty lived again her vanity partook of its life. I had hit on the right note—that was what eased me off: it drew all pain for the next half-hour from the sense of the deep darkness in which the stricken woman sat there. If the music, in that darkness, happily soared and swelled for her, it beat its wings in unison with those of a gratified passion. A great deal came and went between us without profaning the occasion, so that I could feel at the end of twenty minutes as if I knew almost everything he might in kindness have to tell me; knew even why Flora, while I stared at her from the stalls, had misled me by the use of ivory and crystal and by appearing to recognise me and smile. She leaned back in her chair in luxurious ease: I had from the first become aware that the way she fingered her pearls was a sharp image of the wedded state. Nothing of old had seemed wanting to her assurance; but I hadn't then dreamed of the art with which she would wear that assurance as a married woman. She had taken him when everything had failed; he had taken her when she herself had done so. His embarrassed eyes confessed it all, confessed the deep peace he found in it. They only didn't tell me why he had not written to me, nor clear up as yet a minor obscurity. Flora after a while again lifted the glass from the ledge of the box and elegantly swept the house with it. Then, by the mere instinct of her grace, a motion but half conscious, she inclined her head into the void with the sketch of a salute, producing, I could see, a perfect imitation of a response to some homage. Dawling and I looked at each other again: the tears came into his eyes. She was playing at perfection still, and her misfortune only simplified the process.

I recognised that this was as near as I should ever come, certainly as I should come that night, to pressing on her misfortune. Neither of us would name it more than we were doing then, and Flora would never name it at all. Little by little I perceived that what had occurred was, strange as it might appear, the best thing for her happiness. The question was now only of her beauty and her being seen and marvelled at: with Dawling to do for her everything in life her activity was limited to that. Such an activity was all within her scope: it asked nothing of her that she couldn't splendidly give. As from time to time in our delicate communion she turned her face to me with the parody of a look I lost none of the signs of its strange new glory. The expression of the eyes was a bit of pastel put in by a master's thumb; the whole head, stamped with a sort of showy suffering, had gained a fineness from what she had passed through. Yes, Flora was settled for life—nothing could hurt her further. I foresaw the particular praise she would mostly incur—she would be incomparably "interesting." She would charm with her pathos more even than she had charmed with her pleasure. For herself above all she was fixed for ever, rescued from all change and ransomed from all doubt. Her old certainties, her old vanities were justified and sanctified, and in the darkness that had closed upon her one object remained clear. That object, as unfading as a mosaic mask, was fortunately the loveliest she could possibly look upon. The greatest blessing of all was of course that Dawling thought so. Her future was ruled with the straightest line, and so for that matter was his. There were two facts to which before I left my friends I gave time to sink into my spirit. One of them was that he had changed by some process as effective as Flora's change; had been simplified somehow into service as she had been simplified into success. He was such a picture of inspired intervention as I had never yet encountered: he would exist henceforth for the sole purpose of rendering unnecessary, or rather impossible, any reference even on her own part to his wife's infirmity. Oh yes, how little desire he would ever give *me* to refer to it! He principally after a while made me feel—and this was my second lesson—that, good-natured as he was, my being there to see it all oppressed him; so that by the time the act ended I recognised that I too had filled out my hour. Dawling remembered things; I think he caught in my very face the irony of old judgments: they made him thresh about in his chair. I said to Flora as I took leave of her that I would come to see her; but I may mention that I never went. I'll go to-morrow if I hear she wants me; but what in the world can she ever want? As I quitted them I laid my hand on Dawling's arm and drew him for a moment into the lobby.

"Why did you never write to me of your marriage?"

He smiled uncomfortably, showing his long yellow teeth and something more. "I don't know—the whole thing gave me such a tremendous lot to do."

This was the first dishonest speech I had heard him make: he really hadn't written to me because he had an idea I would think him a still bigger fool than before. I didn't insist, but I tried there, in the lobby, so far as a pressure of his hand could serve me, to give him a notion of what I thought him. "I can't at any rate make out," I said, "why I didn't hear from Mrs. Meldrum."

"She didn't write to you?"

"Never a word. What has become of her?"

"I think she's at Folkestone," Dawling returned; "but I'm sorry to say that practically she has ceased to see us."

"You haven't quarrelled with her?"

"How *could* we? Think of all we owe her. At the time of our marriage, and for months before, she did everything for us: I don't know how we should have managed without her. But since then she has never been near us and has given us rather markedly little encouragement to try and keep up our relations with her."

I was struck with this though of course I admit I am struck with all sorts of things. "Well," I said after a moment, "even if I could imagine a reason for that attitude it wouldn't explain why she shouldn't have taken account of *my* natural interest."

"Just so." Dawling's face was a windowless wall. He could contribute nothing to the mystery, and, quitting him, I carried it away. It was not till I went down to see Mrs. Meldrum that it was really dispelled. She didn't want to hear of them or to talk of them, not a bit, and it was just in the same spirit that she hadn't wanted to write of them. She had done everything in the world for them, but now, thank heaven, the hard business was over. After I had taken this in, which I was quick to do, we quite avoided the subject. She simply couldn't bear it.

THE NEXT TIME

Mrs. Highmore's errand this morning was odd enough to deserve commemoration: she came to ask me to write a notice of her great forthcoming work. Her great works have come forth so frequently without my assistance that I was sufficiently entitled on this occasion to open my eyes; but what really made me stare was the ground on which her request reposed, and what leads me to record the incident is the train of memory lighted by that explanation. Poor Ray Limbert, while we talked, seemed to sit there between us: she reminded me that my acquaintance with him had begun, eighteen years ago, with her having come in precisely as she came in this morning to bespeak my charity for him. If she didn't know then how little my charity was worth she is at least enlightened about it to-day, and this is just the circumstance that makes the drollery of her visit. As I hold up the torch to the dusky years—by which I mean as I cipher up with a pen that stumbles and stops the figured column of my reminiscences—I see that Limbert's public hour, or at least my small apprehension of it, is rounded by those two occasions. It was *finis*, with a little moralising flourish, that Mrs. Highmore seemed to trace to-day at the bottom of the page. "One of the most voluminous writers of the time," she has often repeated this sign; but never, I daresay, in spite of her professional command of appropriate emotion, with an equal sense of that mystery and that sadness of things which to people of imagination generally hover over the close of human histories. This romance at any rate is bracketed by her early and her late appeal; and when its melancholy protrusions had caught the declining light again from my half-hour's talk with her I took a private vow to recover while that light still lingers something of the delicate flush, to pick out with a brief patience the perplexing lesson.

It was wonderful to observe how for herself Mrs. Highmore had already done so: she wouldn't have hesitated to announce to me what was the matter with Ralph Limbert, or at all events to give me a glimpse of the high admonition she had read in his career. There could have been no better proof of the vividness of this parable, which we were really in our pleasant sympathy quite at one about, than that Mrs. Highmore, of all hardened sinners, should have been converted. This indeed was not news to me: she impressed upon me that for the last ten years she had wanted to do something artistic, something as to which she was prepared not to care a rap whether or no it should sell. She brought home to me further that it had been mainly seeing what her brother-in-law did and how he did it that had wedded her to this perversity. As *he* didn't sell, dear soul, and as several persons, of whom I was one, thought highly of that, the fancy had taken her—taken her even quite early in her prolific course—of reaching, if only once, the same heroic eminence. She yearned to be, like Limbert, but of course only once, an exquisite failure. There was something a failure was, a failure in the market, that a success somehow wasn't. A success was as prosaic as a good dinner: there was nothing more to be said about it than that you had had it. Who but vulgar people, in such a case, made gloating remarks about the courses? It was often by such vulgar people that a success was attested. It made if you came to look at it nothing but money; that is it made so much that any other result showed small in comparison. A failure now could make—oh, with the aid of immense talent of course, for there were failures and failures—such a reputation! She did me the honour—she had often done it—to intimate that what she meant by reputation was seeing *me* toss a flower. If it took a failure to catch a failure I was by my own admission well qualified to place the laurel. It was because she had made so much money and Mr. Highmore had taken such care of it that she could treat herself to an hour of pure glory. She perfectly remembered that as often as I had heard her heave that sigh I had been prompt with my declaration that a book sold might easily be as glorious as a book unsold. Of course she knew this, but she knew also that it was the age of trash triumphant and that she had never heard me speak of anything that had "done well" exactly as she had sometimes heard me speak of something that hadn't—with just two or three words of respect which, when I used them, seemed to convey more than they commonly stood for, seemed to hush up the discussion a little, as if for the very beauty of the secret.

I may declare in regard to these allusions that, whatever I then thought of myself as a holder of the scales I had never scrupled to laugh out at the humour of Mrs. Highmore's pursuit of quality at any price. It had never rescued her even for a day from the hard doom of popularity, and though I never gave her my word for it there was no reason at all why it should. The public *would* have her, as her husband used roguishly to remark; not indeed that, making her bargains, standing up to her publishers and even, in his higher flights, to her reviewers, he ever had a glimpse of her attempted conspiracy against her genius, or rather as I may say against mine. It was not that when she tried to be what she called subtle (for wasn't Limbert subtle, and wasn't I?) her fond consumers, bless them, didn't suspect the trick nor show what they thought of it: they straightway rose on the contrary to the morsel she had hoped to hold too high, and, making but a big, cheerful bite of it, wagged their great collective tail artlessly for more. It was not given to her not to please, nor granted even to her best refinements to affright. I have always respected the mystery of those humiliations, but I was fully aware this morning that they were practically the reason why she had come to me. Therefore when she said with the flush of a bold joke in her kind, coarse face "What I feel is, you know, that *you* could settle me if you only would." I knew quite well what she meant. She meant that of old it had always appeared to be the fine blade, as some one had hyperbolically called it, of my particular opinion that snapped the silken thread by which Limbert's chance in the market was wont to hang. She meant that my favour was compromising, that my praise indeed was fatal. I had made myself a little specialty of seeing nothing in certain celebrities, of seeing overmuch in an occasional nobody, and of judging from a point of view that, say what I would for it (and I had a monstrous deal to say) remained perverse and obscure. Mine was in short the love that killed, for my subtlety, unlike Mrs. Highmore's, produced no tremor of the public tail. She had not forgotten how, toward the end, when his case was worst, Limbert would absolutely come to me with a funny, shy pathos in his eyes and say: "My dear fellow, I think I've done it this time, if you'll only keep quiet." If my keeping quiet in those days was to help him to appear to have hit the usual taste, for the want of which he was starving, so now my breaking out was to help Mrs. Highmore to appear to have hit the unusual.

The moral of all this was that I had frightened the public too much for our late friend, but that as she was not starving this was exactly what her grosser reputation required. And then, she good-naturedly and delicately intimated, there would always be, if further reasons were wanting, the price of my clever little article. I think she gave that hint with a flattering impression— spoiled child of the booksellers as she is—that the price of my clever little articles is high. Whatever it is, at any rate, she had evidently reflected that poor Limbert's anxiety for his own profit used to involve my sacrificing mine. Any inconvenience that my obliging her might entail would not in fine be pecuniary. Her appeal, her motive, her fantastic thirst for quality and her ingenious theory of my influence struck me all as excellent comedy, and when I consented contingently to oblige her she left me the sheets of her new novel. I could plead no inconvenience and have been looking them over; but I am frankly appalled at what she expects of me. What is she thinking of, poor dear, and what has put it into her head that "quality" has descended upon her? Why does she suppose that she has been "artistic"? She hasn't been anything whatever, I surmise, that she has not inveterately been. What does she imagine she has left out? What does she conceive she has put in? She has neither left out nor put in anything. I shall have to write her an embarrassed note. The book doesn't exist, and there's nothing in life to say about it. How can there be anything but the same old faithful rush for it?

I

This rush had already begun when, early in the seventies, in the interest of her prospective brother-in-law, she approached me on the singular ground of the unencouraged sentiment I had entertained for her sister. Pretty pink Maud had cast me out, but I appear to have passed in the flurried little circle for a magnanimous youth. Pretty pink Maud, so lovely then, before her troubles, that dusky Jane was gratefully conscious of all she made up for, Maud Stannace, very literary too, very languishing and extremely bullied by her mother, had yielded, invidiously as it might have struck me, to Ray Limbert's suit, which Mrs. Stannace was not the woman to stomach. Mrs.

Stannace was seldom the woman to do anything: she had been shocked at the way her children, with the grubby taint of their father's blood (he had published pale Remains or flat Conversations of *his* father) breathed the alien air of authorship. If not the daughter, nor even the niece, she was, if I am not mistaken, the second cousin of a hundred earls and a great stickler for relationship, so that she had other views for her brilliant child, especially after her quiet one (such had been her original discreet forecast of the producer of eighty volumes) became the second wife of an ex-army-surgeon, already the father of four children. Mrs. Stannace had too manifestly dreamed it would be given to pretty pink Maud to detach some one of the hundred, who wouldn't be missed, from the cluster. It was because she cared only for cousins that I unlearnt the way to her house, which she had once reminded me was one of the few paths of gentility I could hope to tread. Ralph Limbert, who belonged to nobody and had done nothing—nothing even at Cambridge—had only the uncanny spell he had cast upon her younger daughter to recommend him; but if her younger daughter had a spark of filial feeling she wouldn't commit the indecency of deserting for his sake a deeply dependent and intensely aggravated mother.

These things I learned from Jane Highmore, who, as if her books had been babies (they remained her only ones) had waited till after marriage to show what she could do and now bade fair to surround her satisfied spouse (he took for some mysterious reason, a part of the credit) with a little family, in sets of triplets, which properly handled would be the support of his declining years. The young couple, neither of whom had a penny, were now virtually engaged: the thing was subject to Ralph's putting his hand on some regular employment. People more enamoured couldn't be conceived, and Mrs. Highmore, honest woman, who had moreover a professional sense for a love-story, was eager to take them under her wing. What was wanted was a decent opening for Limbert, which it had occurred to her I might assist her to find, though indeed I had not yet found any such matter for myself. But it was well known that I was too particular, whereas poor Ralph, with the easy manners of genius, was ready to accept almost anything to which a salary, even a small one, was attached. If he could only for instance get a place on a newspaper the rest of his maintenance would come freely enough. It was true that his two novels, one of which she had brought to leave with me, had passed unperceived and that to her, Mrs. Highmore personally, they didn't irresistibly appeal; but she could all the same assure me that I should have only to spend ten minutes with him (and our encounter must speedily take place) to receive an impression of latent power.

Our encounter took place soon after I had read the volumes Mrs. Highmore had left with me, in which I recognised an intention of a sort that I had then pretty well given up the hope of meeting. I daresay that without knowing it I had been looking out rather hungrily for an altar of sacrifice: however that may be I submitted when I came across Ralph Limbert to one of the rarest emotions of my literary life, the sense of an activity in which I could critically rest. The rest was deep and salutary, and it has not been disturbed to this hour. It has been a long, large surrender, the luxury of dropped discriminations. He couldn't trouble me, whatever he did, for I practically enjoyed him as much when he was worse as when he was better. It was a case, I suppose, of natural prearrangement, in which, I hasten to add, I keep excellent company. We are a numerous band, partakers of the same repose, who sit together in the shade of the tree, by the plash of the fountain, with the glare of the desert around us and no great vice that I know of but the habit perhaps of estimating people a little too much by what they think of a certain style. If it had been laid upon these few pages, none the less, to be the history of an enthusiasm, I should not have undertaken them: they are concerned with Ralph Limbert in relations to which I was a stranger or in which I participated only by sympathy. I used to talk about his work, but I seldom talk now: the brotherhood of the faith have become, like the Trappists, a silent order. If to the day of his death, after mortal disenchantments, the impression he first produced always evoked the word "ingenuous," those to whom his face was familiar can easily imagine what it must have been when it still had the light of youth. I had never seen a man of genius look so passive, a man of experience so off his guard. At the period I made his acquaintance this freshness was all un-brushed. His foot had begun to stumble, but he was full of big intentions and of sweet Maud Stannace. Black-haired and pale, deceptively languid, he had the eyes of a clever child and the voice of a bronze bell. He saw more even than I had done in the girl he was engaged to;

as time went on I became conscious that we had both, properly enough, seen rather more than there was. Our odd situation, that of the three of us, became perfectly possible from the moment I observed that he had more patience with her than I should have had. I was happy at not having to supply this quantity, and she, on her side, found pleasure in being able to be impertinent to me without incurring the reproach of a bad wife.

Limbert's novels appeared to have brought him no money: they had only brought him, so far as I could then make out, tributes that took up his time. These indeed brought him from several quarters some other things, and on my part at the end of three months *The Blackport Beacon*. I don't to-day remember how I obtained for him the London correspondence of the great northern organ, unless it was through somebody's having obtained it for myself. I seem to recall that I got rid of it in Limbert's interest, persuaded the editor that he was much the better man. The better man was naturally the man who had pledged himself to support a charming wife. We were neither of us good, as the event proved, but he had a finer sort of badness. *The Blackport Beacon* had two London correspondents—one a supposed haunter of political circles, the other a votary of questions sketchily classified as literary. They were both expected to be lively, and what was held out to each was that it was honourably open to him to be livelier than the other. I recollect the political correspondent of that period and how the problem offered to Ray Limbert was to try to be livelier than Pat Moyle. He had not yet seemed to me so candid as when he undertook this exploit, which brought matters to a head with Mrs. Stannace, inasmuch as her opposition to the marriage now logically fell to the ground. It's all tears and laughter as I look back upon that admirable time, in which nothing was so romantic as our intense vision of the real. No fool's paradise ever rustled such a cradle-song. It was anything but Bohemia—it was the very temple of Mrs. Grundy. We knew we were too critical, and that made us sublimely indulgent; we believed we did our duty or wanted to, and that made us free to dream. But we dreamed over the multiplication-table; we were nothing if not practical. Oh, the long smokes and sudden ideas, the knowing hints and banished scruples! The great thing was for Limbert to bring out his next book, which was just what his delightful engagement with the *Beacon* would give him leisure and liberty to do. The kind of work, all human and elastic and suggestive, was capital experience: in picking up things for his bi-weekly letter he would pick up life as well, he would pick up literature. The new publications, the new pictures, the new people—there would be nothing too novel for us and nobody too sacred. We introduced everything and everybody into Mrs. Stannace's drawing-room, of which I again became a familiar.

Mrs. Stannace, it was true, thought herself in strange company; she didn't particularly mind the new books, though some of them seemed queer enough, but to the new people she had decided objections. It was notorious however that poor Lady Robeck secretly wrote for one of the papers, and the thing had certainly, in its glance at the doings of the great world, a side that might be made attractive. But we were going to make every side attractive, and we had everything to say about the sort of thing a paper like the *Beacon* would want. To give it what it would want and to give it nothing else was not doubtless an inspiring, but it was a perfectly respectable task, especially for a man with an appealing bride and a contentious mother-in-law. I thought Lambert's first letters as charming as the type allowed, though I won't deny that in spite of my sense of the importance of concessions I was just a trifle disconcerted at the way he had caught the tone. The tone was of course to be caught, but need it have been caught so in the act? The creature was even cleverer, as Maud Stannace said, than she had ventured to hope. Verily it was a good thing to have a dose of the wisdom of the serpent. If it had to be journalism—well, it *was* journalism. If he had to be "chatty "—well, he *was* chatty. Now and then he made a hit that—it was stupid of me—brought the blood to my face. I hated him to be so personal; but still, if it would make his fortune—! It wouldn't of course directly, but the book would, practically and in the sense to which our pure ideas of fortune were confined; and these things were all for the book. The daily balm meanwhile was in what one knew of the book—there were exquisite things to know; in the quiet monthly cheques from Blackport and in the deeper rose of Maud's little preparations, which were as dainty, on their tiny scale, as if she had been a humming-bird building a nest. When at the end of three months her betrothed had fairly settled down to his correspondence—in which Mrs. Highmore was the only person, so far as we could discover, disappointed, even she moreover being in this particular tortuous and possibly jealous; when the situation had assumed such a comfortable shape it was quite time to prepare. I published at that moment my first volume, mere faded ink to-day, a little collection of literary impressions, odds and ends of criticism contributed to a journal less remunerative but also less chatty than the *Beacon*, small ironies and ecstasies, great phrases and mistakes; and the very week it came out poor Limbert devoted half of one of his letters to it, with the happy sense this time of gratifying both himself and me as well as the Blackport breakfast-tables. I remember his saying it wasn't literature, the stuff, superficial stuff, he had to write about me; but what did that matter if it came back, as we knew, to the making for literature in the roundabout way? I sold the thing, I remember, for ten pounds, and with the money I bought in Vigo Street a quaint piece of old silver for Maud Stannace, which I carried to her with my own hand as a wedding-gift. In her mother's small drawing-room, a faded bower of photography fenced in and bedimmed by folding screens out of which sallow persons of fashion with dashing signatures looked at you from retouched eyes and little windows of plush, I was left to wait long enough to feel in the air of the house a hushed vibration of disaster. When our young lady came in she was very pale and her eyes too had been retouched.

"Something horrid has happened," I immediately said; and having really all along but half believed in her mother's meagre permission I risked with an unguarded groan the introduction of Mrs. Stannace's name.

"Yes, she has made a dreadful scene; she insists on our putting it off again. We're very unhappy: poor Ray has been turned off." Her tears began to flow again.

I had such a good conscience that I stared. "Turned off what?"

"Why, his paper of course. The *Beacon* has given him what he calls the sack. They don't like his letters: they're not the style of thing they want."

My blankness could only deepen. "Then what style of thing *do* they want?"

"Something more chatty."

"More?" I cried, aghast.

"More gossipy, more personal. They want 'journalism.' They want tremendous trash."

"Why, that's just what his letters have *been!*" I broke out.

This was strong, and I caught myself up, but the girl offered me the pardon of a beautiful wan smile. "So Ray himself declares. He says he has stooped so low."

"Very well—he must stoop lower. He *must* keep the place."

"He can't!" poor Maud wailed. "He says he has tried all he knows, has been abject, has gone on all fours, and that if they don't like that—"

"He accepts his dismissal?" I interposed in dismay.

She gave a tragic shrug. "What other course is open to him? He wrote to them that such work as he has done is the very worst he can do for the money."

"Therefore," I inquired with a flash of hope, "they'll offer him more for worse?"

"No indeed," she answered, "they haven't even offered him to go on at a reduction. He isn't funny enough."

I reflected a moment. "But surely such a thing as his notice of my book—!"

"It was your wretched book that was the last straw! He should have treated it superficially."

"Well, if he didn't—!" I began. Then I checked myself. "*Je vous porte malheur.*"

She didn't deny this; she only went, on: "What on earth is he to do?"

"He's to do better than the monkeys! He's to write!"

"But what on earth are we to marry on?"

I considered once more. "You're to marry on *The Major Key*."

II

The Major Key was the new novel, and the great thing accordingly was to finish it; a consummation for which three months of the *Beacon* had in some degree prepared the way. The action of that journal was indeed a shock, but I didn't know then the worst, didn't know that in addition to being a shock it was also a symptom. It was the first hint of the difficulty to which poor Limbert was eventually to succumb. His state was the happier of a truth for his not immediately seeing all that it meant. Difficulty was the law of life, but one could thank heaven it was exceptionally present in that horrid quarter. There was the difficulty that inspired, the difficulty of *The Major Key* to wit, which it was after all base to sacrifice to the turning of somersaults for pennies. These convictions Ray Limbert beguiled his fresh wait by blandly entertaining: not indeed, I think, that the failure of his attempt to be chatty didn't leave him slightly humiliated. If it was bad enough to have grinned through a horse-collar it was very bad indeed to have grinned in vain. Well, he would try no more grinning or at least no more horse-collars. The only success worth one's powder was success in the line of one's idiosyncrasy. Consistency was in itself distinction, and what was talent but the art of being completely whatever it was that one happened to be? One's things were characteristic or they were nothing. I look back rather fondly on our having exchanged in those days these admirable remarks and many others; on our having been very happy too, in spite of postponements and obscurities, in spite also of such occasional hauntings as could spring from our lurid glimpse of the fact that even twaddle cunningly calculated was far above people's heads. It was easy to wave away spectres by the reflection that all one had to do was not to write for people; it was certainly not for people that Limbert wrote while he hammered at *The Major Key*. The taint of literature was fatal only in a certain kind of air, which was precisely the kind against which we had now closed our window. Mrs. Stannace rose from her crumpled cushions as soon as she had obtained an adjournment, and Maud looked pale and proud, quite victorious and superior, at her having obtained nothing more. Maud behaved well, I thought, to her mother, and well indeed for a girl who had mainly been taught to be flowerlike to every one. What she gave Ray Limbert her fine, abundant needs made him then and ever pay for; but the gift was liberal, almost wonderful—an assertion I make even while remembering to how many clever women, early and late, his work has been dear. It was not only that the woman he was to marry was in love with him, but that (this was the strangeness) she had really seen almost better than any one what he could do. The greatest strangeness was that she didn't want him to do something different. This boundless belief was indeed the main way of her devotion; and as an act of faith it naturally asked for miracles. She was a rare wife for a poet if she was not perhaps the best who could have been picked out for a poor man.

Well, we were to have the miracles at all events and we were in a perfect state of mind to receive them. There were more of us every day, and we thought highly even of our friend's odd jobs and pot-boilers. The *Beacon* had had no successor, but he found some quiet comers and stray chances. Perpetually poking the fire and looking out of the window, he was certainly not a monster of facility, but he was, thanks perhaps to a certain method in that madness, a monster of certainty. It wasn't every one however who knew him for this: many editors printed him but once. He was getting a small reputation as a man it was well to have the first time; he created obscure apprehensions as to what might happen the second. He was good for making an impression, but no one seemed exactly to know what the impression was good for when made. The reason was simply that they had not seen yet *The Major Key* that fiery-hearted rose as to which we watched in private the formation of petal after petal and flame after flame. Nothing mattered but this, for it had already elicited a splendid bid, much talked about in Mrs. Highmore's drawing-room, where at this point my reminiscences grow particularly thick. *Her* roses bloomed all the year and her sociability increased with her row of prizes. We had an idea that we "met every one" there—so we naturally thought when we met each other. Between our hostess and Ray Limbert flourished the happiest relation, the only cloud on which was that her husband eyed him rather askance. When he was called clever this personage wanted to know what he had to "show;" and it was certain that he showed nothing that could compare with Jane Highmore. Mr. Highmore took his stand on accomplished work and, turning up his coat-tails, warmed his rear with a good conscience at the neat bookcase in which the generations of triplets were chronologically arranged. The harmony between his companions rested on the fact that, as I have already hinted, each would have liked so much to be the other. Limbert couldn't but have a feeling about a woman who in addition to being the best creature and her sister's backer would have made, could she have condescended, such a success with the *Beacon*. On the other hand Mrs. Highmore used freely to say: "Do you know, he'll do exactly the thing that *I* want to do? I shall never do it myself, but he'll do it instead. Yes, he'll do *my* thing, and I shall hate him for it—the wretch." Hating him was her pleasant humour, for the wretch was personally to her taste.

She prevailed on her own publisher to promise to take *The Major Key* and to engage to pay a considerable sum down, as the phrase is, on the presumption of its attracting attention. This was good news for the evening's end at Mrs. Highmore's when there were only four or five left and cigarettes ran low; but there was better news to come, and I have never forgotten how, as it was I who had the good fortune to bring it, I kept it back on one of those occasions, for the sake of my effect, till only the right people remained. The right people were now more and more numerous, but this was a revelation addressed only to a choice residuum—a residuum including of course Limbert himself, with whom I haggled for another cigarette before I announced that as a consequence of an interview I had had with him that afternoon, and of a subtle argument I had brought to bear, Mrs. Highmore's pearl of publishers had agreed to put forth the new book as a serial. He was to "run" it in his magazine and he was to pay ever so much more for the privilege. I produced a fine gasp which presently found a more articulate relief, but poor Limbert's voice failed him once for all (he knew he was to walk away with me) and it was some one else who asked me in what my subtle argument had resided. I forget what florid description I then gave of it: to-day I have no reason not to confess that it had resided in the simple plea that the book was exquisite. I had said: "Come, my dear friend, be original; just risk it for that!" My dear friend seemed to rise to the chance, and I followed up my advantage, permitting him honestly no illusion as to the quality of the work. He clutched interrogatively at two or three attenuations, but I dashed them aside, leaving him face to face with the formidable truth. It was just a pure gem: was he the man not to flinch? His danger appeared to have acted upon him as the anaconda acts upon the rabbit; fascinated and paralysed, he had been engulfed in the long pink throat. When a week before, at my request, Limbert had let me possess for a day the complete manuscript, beautifully copied out by Maud Stannace, I had flushed with indignation at its having to be said of the author of such pages that he hadn't the common means to marry. I had taken the field in a great glow to repair this scandal, and it was therefore quite directly my fault if three months later, when *The Major Key* began to run, Mrs. Stannace was driven to the wall. She had made a condition of a fixed income; and at last a fixed income was achieved.

She had to recognise it, and after much prostration among the photographs she recognised it to the extent of accepting some of the convenience of it in the form of a project for a common household, to the expenses of which each party should proportionately contribute. Jane Highmore made a great point of her not being left alone, but Mrs. Stannace herself determined the proportion, which on Limbert's side at least and in spite of many other fluctuations was never altered. His income had been "fixed" with a vengeance: having painfully stooped to the comprehension of it Mrs. Stannace rested on this effort to the end and asked no further question on the subject. *The Major Key* in other words ran ever so long, and before it was half out Limbert and Maud had been married and the common household set up. These first months were probably the happiest in the family annals, with wedding-bells and budding laurels, the quiet, assured course of the book and the friendly, familiar note, round the corner, of Mrs. Highmore's big guns. They gave Ralph time to block in another picture as well as to let me know after a while that he had the happy prospect of becoming a father. We had at times some dispute as to whether *The Major Key* was making an impression, but our contention could only be futile so long as we were not agreed as to what an impression consisted of. Several persons wrote to the author and several others asked to be introduced to him:

wasn't that an impression? One of the lively "weeklies," snapping at the deadly "monthlies," said the whole thing was "grossly inartistic"—wasn't that? It was somewhere else proclaimed "a wonderfully subtle character-study"—wasn't that too? The strongest effect doubtless was produced on the publisher when, in its lemon-coloured volumes, like a little dish of three custards, the book was at last served cold: he never got his money back and so far as I know has never got it back to this day. *The Major Key* was rather a great performance than a great success. It converted readers into friends and friends into lovers; it placed the author, as the phrase is—placed him all too definitely; but it shrank to obscurity in the account of sales eventually rendered. It was in short an exquisite thing, but it was scarcely a thing to have published and certainly not a thing to have married on. I heard all about the matter, for my intervention had much exposed me. Mrs. Highmore said the second volume had given her ideas, and the ideas are probably to be found in some of her works, to the circulation of which they have even perhaps contributed. This was not absolutely yet the very thing she wanted to do, but it was on the way to it. So much, she informed me, she particularly perceived in the light of a critical study which I put forth in a little magazine; which the publisher in his advertisements quoted from profusely; and as to which there sprang up some absurd story that Limbert himself had written it. I remember that on my asking some one why such an idiotic thing had been said my interlocutor replied: "Oh, because, you know, it's just the way he *would* have written!" My spirit sank a little perhaps as I reflected that with such analogies in our manner there might prove to be some in our fate.

It was during the next four or five years that our eyes were open to what, unless something could be done, that fate, at least on Limbert's part, might be. The thing to be done was of course to write the book, the book that would make the difference, really justify the burden he had accepted and consummately express his power. For the works that followed upon *The Major Key* he had inevitably to accept conditions the reverse of brilliant, at a time too when the strain upon his resources had begun to show sharpness. With three babies in due course, an ailing wife and a complication still greater than these, it became highly important that a man should do only his best. Whatever Limbert did was his best; so at least each time I thought and so I unfailingly said somewhere, though it was not my saying it, heaven knows, that made the desired difference. Every one else indeed said it, and there was among multiplied worries always the comfort that his position was quite assured. The two books that followed *The Major Key* did more than anything else to assure it, and Jane Highmore was always crying out: "You stand alone, dear Ray; you stand absolutely alone!" Dear Ray used to tell me that he felt the truth of this in feebly attempted discussions with his bookseller. His sister-in-law gave him good advice into the bargain; she was a repository of knowing hints, of esoteric learning. These things were doubtless not the less valuable to him for bearing wholly on the question of how a reputation might be with a little gumption, as Mrs. Highmore said, "worked." Save when she occasionally bore testimony to her desire to do, as Limbert did, something some day for her own very self, I never heard her speak of the literary motive as if it were distinguishable from the pecuniary. She cocked up his hat, she pricked up his prudence for him, reminding him that as one seemed to take one's self so the silly world was ready to take one. It was a fatal mistake to be too candid even with those who were all right—not to look and to talk prosperous, not at least to pretend that one had beautiful sales. To listen to her you would have thought the profession of letters a wonderful game of bluff. Wherever one's idea began it ended somehow in inspired paragraphs in the newspapers. "*I* pretend, I assure you, that you are going off like wildfire—I can at least do that for you!" she often declared, prevented as she was from doing much else by Mr. Highmore's insurmountable objection to *their* taking Mrs. Stannace.

I couldn't help regarding the presence of this latter lady in Limbert's life as the major complication: whatever he attempted it appeared given to him to achieve as best he could in the mere margin of the space in which she swung her petticoats. I may err in the belief that she practically lived on him, for though it was not in him to follow adequately Mrs. Highmore's counsel there were exasperated confessions he never made, scanty domestic curtains he rattled on their rings. I may exaggerate in the retrospect his apparent anxieties, for these after all were the years when his talent was freshest and when as a writer he most laid down his line. It wasn't of Mrs. Stannace nor even as time went on of Mrs. Limbert that we mainly talked when I got at longer intervals a smokier hour in the little grey den from which we could step out, as we used to say, to the lawn. The lawn was the back-garden, and Limbert's study was behind the dining-room, with folding doors not impervious to the clatter of the children's tea. We sometimes took refuge from it in the depths—a bush and a half deep—of the shrubbery, where was a bench that gave us a view while we gossiped of Mrs. Stannace's tiara-like headdress nodding at an upper window. Within doors and without Limbert's life was overhung by an awful region that figured in his conversation, comprehensively and with unpremeditated art, as Upstairs. It was Upstairs that the thunder gathered, that Mrs. Stannace kept her accounts and her state, that Mrs. Limbert had her babies and her headaches, that the bells for ever jangled at the maids, that everything imperative in short took place—everything that he had somehow, pen in hand, to meet and dispose of in the little room on the garden-level. I don't think he liked to go Upstairs, but no special burst of confidence was needed to make me feel that a terrible deal of service went. It was the habit of the ladies of the Stannace family to be extremely waited on, and I've never been in a house where three maids and a nursery-governess gave such an impression of a retinue. "Oh, they're so deucedly, so hereditarily fine!"—I remember how that dropped from him in some worried hour. Well, it was because Maud was so universally fine that we had both been in love with her. It was not an air moreover for the plaintive note: no private inconvenience could long outweigh for him the great happiness of these years—the happiness that sat with us when we talked and that made it always amusing to talk, the sense of his being on the heels of success, coming closer and closer, touching it at last, knowing that he should touch it again and hold it fast and hold it high. Of course when we said success we didn't mean exactly what Mrs. Highmore for instance meant. He used to quote at me as a definition something from a nameless page of my own, some stray dictum to the effect that the man of his craft had achieved it when of a beautiful subject his expression was complete. Well, wasn't Limbert's in all conscience complete?

III

It was bang upon this completeness all the same that the turn arrived, the turn I can't say of his fortune—for what was that?—but of his confidence, of his spirits and, what was more to the point, of his system. The whole occasion on which the first symptom flared out is before me as I write. I had met them both at dinner: they were diners who had reached the penultimate stage—the stage which in theory is a rigid selection and in practice a wan submission. It was late in the season and stronger spirits than theirs were broken; the night was close and the air of the banquet such as to restrict conversation to the refusal of dishes and consumption to the sniffing of a flower. It struck me all the more that Mrs. Limbert was flying her flag. As vivid as a page of her husband's prose, she had one of those flickers of freshness that are the miracle of her sex and one of those expensive dresses that are the miracle of ours. She had also a neat brougham in which she had offered to rescue an old lady from the possibilities of a queer cab-horse; so that when she had rolled away with her charge I proposed a walk home with her husband, whom I had overtaken on the doorstep. Before I had gone far with him he told me he had news for me—he had accepted, of all people and of all things, an "editorial position." It had come to pass that very day, from one hour to another, without time for appeals or ponderations: Mr. Bousefield, the proprietor of a "high-class monthly," making, as they said, a sudden change, had dropped on him heavily out of the blue. It was all right—there was a salary and an idea, and both of them, as such things went, rather high. We took our way slowly through the vacant streets, and in the explanations and revelations that as we lingered under lamp-posts I drew from him I found with an apprehension that I tried to gulp down a foretaste of the bitter end. He told me more than he had ever told me yet. He couldn't balance accounts—that was the trouble: his expenses were too rising a tide. It was absolutely necessary that he should at last make money, and now he must work only for that. The need this last year had gathered the force of a crusher: it had rolled over him and laid him on his back. He had his scheme; this time he knew what he was about; on some good occasion, with leisure to talk it over, he would tell me the blessed whole. His editorship would help him, and for the rest he must help himself. If he couldn't they would have to do something fundamental—change their life altogether, give up London, move into the country, take a house at thirty pounds a year, send their children to the Board-school. I saw that he was excited, and he admitted that he was: he had waked out of

411

a trance. He had been on the wrong tack; he had piled mistake on mistake. It was the vision of his remedy that now excited him: ineffably, grotesquely simple, it had yet come to him only within a day or two. No, he wouldn't tell me what it was; he would give me the night to guess, and if I shouldn't guess it would be because I was as big an ass as himself. However, a lone man might be an ass: he had room in his life for his ears. Ray had a burden that demanded a back: the back must therefore now be properly instituted. As to the editorship, it was simply heaven-sent, being not at all another case of *The Blackport Beacon* but a case of the very opposite. The proprietor, the great Mr. Bousefield, had approached him precisely because his name, which was to be on the cover, *didn't* represent the chatty. The whole thing was to be—oh, on fiddling little lines of course—a protest against the chatty. Bousefield wanted him to be himself; it was for himself Bousefield had picked him out. Wasn't it beautiful and brave of Bousefield? He wanted literature, he saw the great reaction coming, the way the cat was going to jump. "Where will you get literature?" I wofully asked; to which he replied with a laugh that what he had to get was not literature but only what Bousefield would take for it.

In that single phrase without more ado I discovered his famous remedy. What was before him for the future was not to do his work but to do what somebody else would take for it. I had the question out with him on the next opportunity, and of all the lively discussions into which we had been destined to drift it lingers in my mind as the liveliest. This was not, I hasten to add, because I disputed his conclusions: it was an effect of the very force with which, when I had fathomed his wretched premises, I took them to my soul. It was very well to talk with Jane Highmore about his standing alone: the eminent relief of this position had brought him to the verge of ruin. Several persons admired his books—nothing was less contestable; but they appeared to have a mortal objection to acquiring them by subscription or by purchase: they begged or borrowed or stole, they delegated one of the party perhaps to commit the volumes to memory and repeat them, like the bards of old, to listening multitudes. Some ingenious theory was required at any rate to account for the inexorable limits of his circulation. It wasn't a thing for five people to live on; therefore either the objects circulated must change their nature or the organisms to be nourished must. The former change was perhaps the easier to consider first. Limbert considered it with extraordinary ingenuity from that time on, and the ingenuity, greater even than any I had yet had occasion to admire in him, made the whole next stage of his career rich in curiosity and suspense.

"I have been butting my skull against a wall," he had said in those hours of confidence; "and, to be as sublime a blockhead, if you'll allow me the word, you, my dear fellow, have kept sounding the charge. We've sat prating here of 'success,' heaven help us, like chanting monks in a cloister, hugging the sweet delusion that it lies somewhere in the work itself, in the expression, as you said, of one's subject or the intensification, as somebody else somewhere says, of one's note. One has been going on in short as if the only thing to do were to accept the law of one's talent and thinking that if certain consequences didn't follow it was only because one wasn't logical enough. My disaster has served me right—I mean for using that ignoble word at all. It's a mere distributor's, a mere hawker's word. What *is* 'success' anyhow? When a book's right, it's right—shame to it surely if it isn't. When it sells it sells—it brings money like potatoes or beer. If there's dishonour one way and inconvenience the other, it certainly is comfortable, but it as certainly isn't glorious to have escaped them. People of delicacy don't brag either about their probity or about their luck. Success be hanged!—I want to sell. It's a question of life and death. I must study the way. I've studied too much the other way—I know the other way now, every inch of it. I must cultivate the market—it's a science like another. I must go in for an infernal cunning. It will be very amusing, I foresee that; I shall lead a dashing life and drive a roaring trade. I haven't been obvious—I must *be* obvious. I haven't been popular—I must *be* popular. It's another art—or perhaps it isn't an art at all. It's something else; one must find out what it is. Is it something awfully queer?—you blush!—something barely decent? All the greater incentive to curiosity! Curiosity's an immense motive; we shall have tremendous sport. They all do it; it's only a question of how. Of course I've everything to unlearn; but what is life, as Jane Highmore says, but a lesson? I must get all I can, all she can give me, from Jane. She can't explain herself much; she's all intuition; her processes are obscure; it's the spirit that swoops down and catches her up. But I must study her reverently in her works. Yes, you've defied me before, but now my loins are girded: I declare I'll read one of them—I really will: I'll put it through if I perish!"

I won't pretend that he made all these remarks at once; but there wasn't one that he didn't make at one time or another, for suggestion and occasion were plentiful enough, his life being now given up altogether to his new necessity. It wasn't a question of his having or not having, as they say, my intellectual sympathy: the brute force of the pressure left no room for judgment; it made all emotion a mere recourse to the spyglass. I watched him as I should have watched a long race or a long chase, irresistibly siding with him but much occupied with the calculation of odds. I confess indeed that my heart, for the endless stretch that he covered so fast, was often in my throat. I saw him peg away over the sun-dappled plain, I saw him double and wind and gain and lose; and all the while I secretly entertained a conviction. I wanted him to feed his many mouths, but at the bottom of all things was my sense that if he should succeed in doing so in this particular way I should think less well of him. Now I had an absolute terror of that. Meanwhile so far as I could I backed him up, I helped him: all the more that I had warned him immensely at first, smiled with a compassion it was very good of him not to have found exasperating over the complacency of his assumption that a man could escape from himself. Ray Limbert at all events would certainly never escape; but one could make believe for him, make believe very hard—an undertaking in which at first Mr. Bousefield was visibly a blessing. Limbert was delightful on the business of this being at last my chance too—my chance, so miraculously vouchsafed, to appear with a certain luxurance. He didn't care how often he printed me, for wasn't it exactly in my direction Mr. Bousefield held that the cat was going to jump? This was the least he could do for me. I might write on anything I liked—on anything at least but Mr. Limbert's second manner. He didn't wish attention strikingly called to his second manner; it was to operate insidiously; people were to be left to believe they had discovered it long ago. "Ralph Limbert? Why, when did we ever live without him?"—that's what he wanted them to say. Besides, they hated manners—let sleeping dogs lie. His understanding with Mr. Bousefield—on which he had had not at all to insist; it was the excellent man who insisted—was that he should run one of his beautiful stories in the magazine. As to the beauty of his story however Limbert was going to be less admirably straight than as to the beauty of everything else. That was another reason why I mustn't write about his new line: Mr. Bousefield was not to be too definitely warned that such a periodical was exposed to prostitution. By the time he should find it out for himself the public—*le gros public*—would have bitten, and then perhaps he would be conciliated and forgive. Everything else would be literary in short, and above all *I* would be; only Ralph Limbert wouldn't—he'd chuck up the whole thing sooner. He'd be vulgar, he'd be rudimentary, he'd be atrocious: he'd be elaborately what he hadn't been before. I duly noticed that he had more trouble in making "everything else" literary than he had at first allowed for; but this was largely counteracted by the ease with which he was able to obtain that his mark should not be overshot. He had taken well to heart the old lesson of the *Beacon*; he remembered that he was after all there to keep his contributors down much rather than to keep them up. I thought at times that he kept them down a trifle too far, but he assured me that I needn't be nervous: he had his limit—his limit was inexorable. He would reserve pure vulgarity for his serial, over which he was sweating blood and water; elsewhere it should be qualified by the prime qualification, the mediocrity that attaches, that endears. Bousefield, he allowed, was proud, was difficult: nothing was really good enough for him but the middling good; but he himself was prepared for adverse comment, resolute for his noble course. Hadn't Limbert moreover in the event of a charge of laxity from headquarters the great strength of being able to point to my contributions? Therefore I must let myself go, I must abound in my peculiar sense, I must be a resource in case of accidents. Limbert's vision of accidents hovered mainly over the sudden awakening of Mr. Bousefield to the stuff that in the department of fiction his editor was palming off. He would then have to confess in all humility that this was not what the good old man wanted, but I should be all the more there as a salutary specimen. I would cross the scent with something showily impossible, splendidly unpopular—I must be sure to have something on hand. I always had plenty on hand—poor Limbert needn't have worried: the magazine was forearmed each month by my care with a retort to any possible accusation of trifling with Mr. Bousefield's standard. He had admitted to Limbert, after much consideration indeed, that he was prepared to be perfectly human; but he had added that he was not prepared for an abuse of this admission. The thing in the world I think I least felt myself was an abuse, even though (as I had never mentioned to my friendly editor) I too had my project for a bigger reverberation. I daresay I trusted mine more than I trusted Limbert's; at all events the golden mean in which in the special case he saw his salvation as an editor was something I should be most sure of if I were to exhibit it myself. I exhibited it month after month in the form of a monstrous levity, only praying heaven that my editor might now not tell me, as he had so often told me, that my result was awfully good. I knew what that would signify—it would signify, sketchily speaking, disaster. What he did tell me heartily was that it was just what his game required: his new line had brought with it an earnest assumption—earnest save when we privately laughed about it—of the locutions proper to real bold enterprise. If I tried to keep him in the dark even as he kept Mr. Bousefield there was nothing to show that I was not tolerably successful: each case therefore presented a promising analogy for the other. He never noticed my descent, and it was accordingly possible that Mr. Bousefield would never notice his.

But would nobody notice it at all?—that was a question that added a prospective zest to one's possession of a critical sense. So much depended upon it that I was rather relieved than otherwise not to know the answer too soon. I waited in fact a year—the year for which Limbert had cannily engaged on trial with Mr. Bousefield; the year as to which through the same sharpened shrewdness it had been conveyed in the agreement between them that Mr. Bousefield was not to intermeddle. It had been Limbert's general prayer that we would during this period let him quite alone. His terror of my direct rays was a droll, dreadful force that always operated: he explained it by the fact that I understood him too well, expressed too much of his intention, saved him too little from himself. The less he was saved the more he didn't sell: I literally interpreted, and that was simply fatal.

I held my breath accordingly; I did more—I closed my eyes, I guarded my treacherous ears. He induced several of us to do that (of such devotions we were capable) so that not even glancing at the thing from month to month, and having nothing but his shamed, anxious silence to go by, I participated only vaguely in the little hum that surrounded his act of sacrifice. It was blown about the town that the public would be surprised; it was hinted, it was printed that he was making a desperate bid. His new work was spoken of as "more calculated for general acceptance." These tidings produced in some quarters much reprobation, and nowhere more, I think, than on the part of certain persons who had never read a word of him, or assuredly had never spent a shilling on him, and who hung for hours over the other attractions of the newspaper that announced his abasement. So much asperity cheered me a little—seemed to signify that he might really be doing something. On the other hand I had a distinct alarm; some one sent me for some alien reason an American journal (containing frankly more than that source of affliction) in which was quoted a passage from our friend's last instalment. The passage—I couldn't for my life help reading it—was simply superb. Ah, he *would* have to move to the country if that was the worst he could do! It gave me a pang to see how little after all he had improved since the days of his competition with Pat Moyle. There was nothing in the passage quoted in the American paper that Pat would for a moment have owned. During the last weeks, as the opportunity of reading the complete thing drew near, one's suspense was barely endurable, and I shall never forget the July evening on which I put it to rout. Coming home to dinner I found the two volumes on my table, and I sat up with them half the night, dazed, bewildered, rubbing my eyes, wondering at the monstrous joke. *Was* it a monstrous joke, his second manner—was *this* the new line, the desperate bid, the scheme for more general acceptance and the remedy for material failure? Had he made a fool of all his following, or had he most injuriously made a still bigger fool of himself? Obvious?—where the deuce was it obvious? Popular?—how on earth could it be popular? The thing was charming with all his charm and powerful with all his power: it was an unscrupulous, an unsparing, a shameless, merciless masterpiece. It was, no doubt, like the old letters to the *Beacon*, the worst he could do; but the perversity of the effort, even though heroic, had been frustrated by the purity of the gift. Under what illusion had he laboured, with what wavering, treacherous compass had he steered? His honour was inviolable, his measurements were all wrong. I was thrilled with the whole impression and with all that came crowding in its train. It was too grand a collapse—it was too hideous a triumph; I exalted almost with tears—I lamented with a strange delight. Indeed as the short night waned and, threshing about in my emotion, I fidgeted to my high-perched window for a glimpse of the summer dawn, I became at last aware that I was staring at it out of eyes that had compassionately and admiringly filled. The eastern sky, over the London housetops, had a wonderful tragic crimson. That was the colour of his magnificent mistake.

IV

If something less had depended on my impression I daresay I should have communicated it as soon as I had swallowed my breakfast; but the case was so embarrassing that I spent the first half of the day in reconsidering it, dipping into the book again, almost feverishly turning its leaves and trying to extract from them, for my friend's benefit, some symptom of reassurance, some ground for felicitation. This rash challenge had consequences merely dreadful; the wretched volumes, imperturbable and impeccable, with their shyer secrets and their second line of defence, were like a beautiful woman more denuded or a great symphony on a new hearing. There was something quite sinister in the way they stood up to me. I couldn't however be dumb—that was to give the wrong tinge to my disappointment; so that later in the afternoon, taking my courage in both hands, I approached with a vain tortuosity poor Limbert's door. A smart victoria waited before it in which from the bottom of the street I saw that a lady who had apparently just issued from the house was settling herself. I recognised Jane Highmore and instantly paused till she should drive down to me. She presently met me half-way and as soon as she saw me stopped her carriage in agitation. This was a relief—it postponed a moment the sight of that pale, fine face of our friend's fronting me for the right verdict. I gathered from the flushed eagerness with which Mrs. Highmore asked me if I had heard the news that a verdict of some sort had already been rendered.

"What news?—about the book?"

"About that horrid magazine. They're shockingly upset. He has lost his position—he has had a fearful flare-up with Mr. Bousefield."

I stood there blank, but not unaware in my blankness of how history repeats itself. There came to me across the years Maud's announcement of their ejection from the *Beacon*, and dimly, confusedly the same explanation was in the air. This time however I had been on my guard; I had had my suspicion. "He has made it too flippant?" I found breath after an instant to inquire.

Mrs. Highmore's vacuity exceeded my own. "Too 'flippant'? He has made it too oracular. Mr. Bousefield says he has killed it." Then perceiving my stupefaction: "Don't you know what has happened?" she pursued; "isn't it because in his trouble, poor love, he has sent for you that you've come? You've heard nothing at all? Then you had better know before you see them. Get in here with me—I'll take you a turn and tell you." We were close to the Park, the Regent's, and when with extreme alacrity I had placed myself beside her and the carriage had begun to enter it she went on: "It was what I feared, you know. It reeked with culture. He keyed it up too high."

I felt myself sinking in the general collapse. "What are you talking about?"

"Why, about that beastly magazine. They're all on the streets. I shall have to take mamma."

I pulled myself together. "What on earth then did Bousefield want? He said he wanted intellectual power."

"Yes, but Ray overdid it."

"Why, Bousefield said it was a thing he *couldn't* overdo."

"Well, Ray managed: he took Mr. Bousefield too literally. It appears the thing has been doing dreadfully, but the proprietor couldn't say anything, because he had covenanted to leave the editor quite free. He describes himself as having stood there in a fever and seen his ship go down. A day or two ago the year was up, so he could at last break out. Maud says he did break out quite fearfully; he came to the house and let poor Ray have it. Ray gave it to him back; he reminded him of his own idea of the way the cat was going to jump."

I gasped with dismay. "Has Bousefield abandoned that idea? Isn't the cat going to jump?"

Mrs. Highmore hesitated. "It appears that she doesn't seem in a hurry. Ray at any rate has jumped too far ahead of her. He should have temporised a little, Mr. Bousefield says; but I'm beginning to think, you know," said my companion, "that Ray *can't* temporise." Fresh from my emotions of the previous twenty-four hours I was scarcely in a position to disagree with her. "He published too much pure thought."

"Pure thought?" I cried. "Why, it struck me so often—certainly in a due proportion of cases—as pure drivel!"

"Oh, you're more keyed up than he! Mr. Bousefield says that of course he wanted things that were suggestive and clever, things that he could point to with pride. But he contends that Ray didn't allow for human weakness. He gave everything in too stiff doses."

Sensibly, I fear, to my neighbour I winced at her words; I felt a prick that made me meditate. Then I said: "Is that, by chance, the way he gave *me?*" Mrs. Highmore remained silent so long that I had somehow the sense of a fresh pang; and after a minute, turning in my seat, I laid my hand on her arm, fixed my eyes upon her face and pursued pressingly: "Do you suppose it to be to my 'Occasional Remarks' that Mr. Bousefield refers?"

At last she met my look. "Can you bear to hear it?"

"I think I can bear anything now."

"Well then, it was really what I wanted to give you an inkling of. It's largely over you that they've quarrelled. Mr. Bousefield wants him to chuck you."

I grabbed her arm again. "And Limbert *won't?*"

"He seems to cling to you. Mr. Bousefield says no magazine can afford you."

I gave a laugh that agitated the very coachman. "Why, my dear lady, has he any idea of my price?"

"It isn't your price—he says you're dear at any price; you do so much to sink the ship. Your 'Remarks' are called 'Occasional,' but nothing could be more deadly regular: you're there month after month and you're never anywhere else. And you supply no public want."

"I supply the most delicious irony."

"So Ray appears to have declared. Mr. Bousefield says that's not in the least a public want. No one can make out what you're talking about and no one would care if he could. I'm only quoting *him*, mind."

"Quote, quote—if Limbert holds out. I think I must leave you now, please: I must rush back to express to him what I feel."

"I'll drive you to his door. That isn't all," said Mrs. Highmore. And on the way, when the carriage had turned, she communicated the rest. "Mr. Bousefield really arrived with an ultimatum: it had the form of something or other by Minnie Meadows."

"Minnie Meadows?" I was stupefied.

"The new lady-humourist every one is talking about. It's the first of a series of screaming sketches for which poor Ray was to find a place."

"Is *that* Mr. Bousefield's idea of literature?"

"No, but he says it's the public's, and you've got to take *some* account of the public. *Aux grands maux les grands remèdes.* They had a tremendous lot of ground to make up, and no one would make it up like Minnie. She would be the best concession they could make to human weakness; she would strike at least this note of showing that it was not going to be quite all—well, all *you*. Now Ray draws the line at Minnie; he won't stoop to Minnie; he declines to touch, to look at Minnie. When Mr. Bousefield—rather imperiously, I believe—made Minnie a *sine quâ non* of his retention of his post he said something rather violent, told him to go to some unmentionable place and take Minnie with him. That of course put the fat on the fire. They had really a considerable scene."

"So had he with the *Beacon* man," I musingly replied. "Poor dear, he seems born for considerable scenes! It's on Minnie, then, that they've really split?" Mrs. Highmore exhaled her despair in a sound which I took for an assent, and when we had rolled a little further I rather in-consequently and to her visible surprise broke out of my reverie. "It will never do in the world—he *must* stoop to Minnie!"

"It's too late—and what I've told you still isn't all. Mr. Bousefield raises another objection."

"What other, pray?"

"Can't you guess?"

I wondered. "No more of Ray's fiction?"

"Not a line. That's something else no magazine can stand. Now that his novel has run its course Mr. Bousefield is distinctly disappointed."

I fairly bounded in my place. "Then it may do?"

Mrs. Highmore looked bewildered. "Why so, if he finds it too dull?"

"Dull? Ralph Limbert? He's as fine as a needle!"

"It comes to the same thing—he won't penetrate leather. Mr. Bousefield had counted on something that *would*, on something that would have a wide acceptance. Ray says he wants iron pegs." I collapsed again; my flicker of elation dropped to a throb of quieter comfort; and after a moment's silence I asked my neighbour if she had herself read the work our friend had just put forth. "No," she replied, "I gave him my word at the beginning, on his urgent request, that I wouldn't."

"Not even as a book?"

"He begged me never to look at it at all. He said he was trying a low experiment. Of course I knew what he meant and I entreated him to let me just for curiosity take a peep. But he was firm, he declared he couldn't bear the thought that a woman like me should see him in the depths."

"He's only, thank God, in the depths of distress," I replied. "His experiment's nothing worse than a failure."

"Then Bousefield *is* right—his circulation won't budge?"

"It won't move one, as they say in Fleet Street. The book has extraordinary beauty."

"Poor duck—after trying so hard!" Jane Highmore sighed with real tenderness. "What *will* then become of them?"

I was silent an instant. "You must take your mother."

She was silent too. "I must speak of it to Cecil!" she presently said. Cecil is Mr. Highmore, who then entertained, I knew, strong views on the inadjustability of circumstances in general to the idiosyncrasies of Mrs. Stannace. He held it supremely happy that in an important relation she should have met her match. Her match was Ray Limbert—not much of a writer but a practical man. "The dear things still think, you know," my companion continued, "that the book will be the beginning of their fortune. Their illusion, if you're right, will be rudely dispelled."

"That's what makes me dread to face them. I've just spent with his volumes an unforgettable night. His illusion has lasted because so many of us have been pledged till this moment to turn our faces the other way. We haven't known the truth and have therefore had nothing to say. Now that we do know it indeed we have practically quite as little. I hang back from the threshold. How can I follow up with a burst of enthusiasm such a catastrophe as Mr. Bousefield's visit?"

As I turned uneasily about my neighbour more comfortably snuggled. "Well, I'm glad then I haven't read him and have nothing unpleasant to say!" We had come back to Limbert's door, and I made the coachman stop short of it. "But he'll try again, with that determination of his: he'll build his hopes on the next time."

"On what else has he built them from the very first? It's never the present for him that bears the fruit; that's always postponed and for somebody else:

there has always to be another try. I admit that his idea of a 'new line' has made him try harder than ever. It makes no difference," I brooded, still timorously lingering; "his achievement of his necessity, his hope of a market will continue to attach themselves to the future. But the next time will disappoint him as each last time has done—and then the next and the next and the next!"

I found myself seeing it all with a clearness almost inspired: it evidently cast a chill on Mrs. Highmore. "Then what on earth will become of him?" she plaintively asked.

"I don't think I particularly care what may become of *him*," I returned with a conscious, reckless increase of my exaltation; "I feel it almost enough to be concerned with what may become of one's enjoyment of him. I don't know in short what will become of his circulation; I am only quite at my ease as to what will become of his work. It will simply keep all its quality. He'll try again for the common with what he'll believe to be a still more infernal cunning, and again the common will fatally elude him, for his infernal cunning will have been only his genius in an ineffectual disguise." We sat drawn up by the pavement, facing poor Limbert's future as I saw it. It relieved me in a manner to know the worst, and I prophesied with an assurance which as I look back upon it strikes me as rather remarkable. "*Que voulez-vous?*" I went on; "you can't make a sow's ear of a silk purse! It's grievous indeed if you like—there are people who can't be vulgar for trying. *He* can't—it wouldn't come off, I promise you, even once. It takes more than trying—it comes by grace. It happens not to be given to Limbert to fall. He belongs to the heights— he breathes there, he lives there, and it's accordingly to the heights I must ascend," I said as I took leave of my conductress, "to carry him this wretched news from where *we* move!"

V

A few months were sufficient to show how right I had been about his circulation. It didn't move one, as I had said; it stopped short in the same place, fell off in a sheer descent, like some precipice gaped up at by tourists. The public in other words drew the line for him as sharply as he had drawn it for Minnie Meadows. Minnie has skipped with a flouncing caper over his line, however; whereas the mark traced by a lustier cudgel has been a barrier insurmountable to Limbert. Those next times I had spoken of to Jane Highmore, I see them simplified by retrocession. Again and again he made his desperate bid—again and again he tried to. His rupture with Mr. Bousefield caused him, I fear, in professional circles to be thought impracticable, and I am perfectly aware, to speak candidly, that no sordid advantage ever accrued to him from such public patronage of my performances as he had occasionally been in a position to offer. I reflect for my comfort that any injury I may have done him by untimely application of a faculty of analysis which could point to no converts gained by honourable exercise was at least equalled by the injury he did himself. More than once, as I have hinted, I held my tongue at his request, but my frequent plea that such favours weren't politic never found him, when in other connections there was an opportunity to give me a lift, anything but indifferent to the danger of the association. He let them have me in a word whenever he could; sometimes in periodicals in which he had credit, sometimes only at dinner. He talked about me when he couldn't get me in, but it was always part of the bargain that I shouldn't make him a topic. "How can I successfully serve you if you do?" he used to ask: he was more afraid than I thought he ought to have been of the charge of tit for tat. I didn't care, for I never could distinguish tat from tit; but as I have intimated I dropped into silence really more than anything else because there was a certain fascinated observation of his course which was quite testimony enough and to which in this huddled conclusion of it he practically reduced me.

I see it all foreshortened, his wonderful remainder—see it from the end backward, with the direction widening toward me as if on a level with the eye. The migration to the country promised him at first great things—smaller expenses, larger leisure, conditions eminently conducive on each occasion to the possible triumph of the next time. Mrs. Stannace, who altogether disapproved of it, gave as one of her reasons that her son-in-law, living mainly in a village on the edge of a goose-green, would be deprived of that contact with the great world which was indispensable to the painter of manners. She had the showiest arguments for keeping him in touch, as she called it, with good society; wishing to know with some force where, from the moment he ceased to represent it from observation, the novelist could be said to be. In London fortunately a clever man was just a clever man; there were charming houses in which a person of Ray's undoubted ability, even though without the knack of making the best use of it, could always be sure of a quiet corner for watching decorously the social kaleidoscope. But the kaleidoscope of the goose-green, what in the world was that, and what such delusive thrift as drives about the land (with a fearful account for flys from the inn) to leave cards on the country magnates? This solicitude for Limbert's subject-matter was the specious colour with which, deeply determined not to affront mere tolerance in a cottage, Mrs. Stannace overlaid her indisposition to place herself under the heel of Cecil Highmore. She knew that he ruled Upstairs as well as down, and she clung to the fable of the association of interests in the north of London. The Highmores had a better address—they lived now in Stanhope Gardens; but Cecil was fearfully artful—he wouldn't hear of an association of interests nor treat with his mother-in-law save as a visitor. She didn't like false positions; but on the other hand she didn't like the sacrifice of everything she was accustomed to. Her universe at all events was a universe full of card-leavings and charming houses, and it was fortunate that she couldn't Upstairs catch the sound of the doom to which, in his little grey den, describing to me his diplomacy, Limbert consigned alike the country magnates and the opportunities of London. Despoiled of every guarantee she went to Stanhope Gardens like a mere maidservant, with restrictions on her very luggage, while during the year that followed this upheaval Limbert, strolling with me on the goose-green, to which I often ran down, played extravagantly over the theme that with what he was now going in for it was a positive comfort not to have the social kaleidoscope. With a cold-blooded trick in view what had life or manners or the best society or flys from the inn to say to the question? It was as good a place as another to play his new game. He had found a quieter corner than any corner of the great world, and a damp old house at sixpence a year, which, beside leaving him all his margin to educate his children, would allow of the supreme luxury of his frankly presenting himself as a poor man. This was a convenience that *ces dames*, as he called them, had never yet fully permitted him.

It rankled in me at first to see his reward so meagre, his conquest so mean; but the simplification effected had a charm that I finally felt; it was a forcing-house for the three or four other fine miscarriages to which his scheme was evidently condemned. I limited him to three or four, having had my sharp impression, in spite of the perpetual broad joke of the thing, that a spring had really snapped in him on the occasion of that deeply disconcerting sequel to the episode of his editorship. He never lost his sense of the grotesque want, in the difference made, of adequate relation to the effort that had been the intensest of his life. He had from that moment a charge of shot in him, and it slowly worked its way to a vital part. As he met his embarrassments each year with his punctual false remedy I wondered periodically where he found the energy to return to the attack. He did it every time with a rage more blanched, but it was clear to me that the tension must finally snap the cord. We got again and again the irrepressible work of art, but what did *he* get, poor man, who wanted something so different? There were likewise odder questions than this in the matter, phenomena more curious and mysteries more puzzling, which often for sympathy if not for illumination I intimately discussed with Mrs. Limbert. She had her burdens, dear lady: after the removal from London and a considerable interval she twice again became a mother. Mrs. Stannace too, in a more restricted sense, exhibited afresh, in relation to the home she had abandoned, the same exemplary character. In her poverty of guarantees at Stanhope Gardens there had been least of all, it appeared, a proviso that she shouldn't resentfully revert again from Goneril to Regan. She came down to the goose-green like Lear himself, with fewer knights, or at least baronets, and the joint household was at last patched up. It fell to pieces and was put together on various occasions before Ray Limbert died. He was ridden to the end by the superstition that he had broken up Mrs. Stannace's original home on pretences that had proved hollow and that if he hadn't given Maud what she might have had he could at least give her back her mother. I was always sure that a sense of the compensations he owed was half the motive of the dogged pride with which he tried to wake up the libraries. I believed Mrs. Stannace still had money, though she pretended that, called upon at every turn to retrieve deficits, she had long since poured it into the general fund. This conviction haunted me; I suspected her of secret hoards, and I said to myself that she couldn't be so infamous as not some day on her deathbed to leave everything to her less opulent daughter. My compassion for the Limberts led me to hover perhaps indiscreetly round that closing scene, to dream of some happy time when such an accession of means would make up a little for their present penury.

This however was crude comfort, as in the first place I had nothing definite to go by and in the second I held it for more and more indicated that Ray wouldn't outlive her. I never ventured to sound him as to what in this particular he hoped or feared, for after the crisis marked by his leaving London I had new scruples about suffering him to be reminded of where he fell short. The poor man was in truth humiliated, and there were things as to which that kept us both silent. In proportion as he tried more fiercely for the market the old plaintiff arithmetic, fertile in jokes, dropped from our conversation. We joked immensely still about the process, but our treatment of the results became sparing and superficial. He talked as much as ever, with monstrous arts and borrowed hints, of the traps he kept setting, but we all agreed to take merely for granted that the animal was caught. This propriety had really dawned upon me the day that after Mr. Bousefield's visit Mrs. Highmore put me down at his door. Mr. Bousefield in that juncture had been served up to me anew, but after we had disposed of him we came to the book, which I was obliged to confess I had already rushed through. It was from this moment—the moment at which my terrible impression of it had blinked out at his anxious query—that the image of his scared face was to abide with me. I couldn't attenuate then—the cat was out of the bag; but later, each of the next times, I did, I acknowledge, attenuate. We all did religiously, so far as was possible; we cast ingenious ambiguities over the strong places, the beauties that betrayed him most, and found ourselves in the queer position of admirers banded to mislead a confiding artist. If we stifled our cheers however and dissimulated our joy our fond hypocrisy accomplished little, for Limbert's finger was on a pulse that told a plainer story. It was a satisfaction to have secured a greater freedom with his wife, who at last, much to her honour, entered into the conspiracy and whose sense of responsibility was flattered by the frequency of our united appeal to her for some answer to the marvellous riddle. We had all turned it over till we were tired of it, threshing out the question why the note he strained every chord to pitch for common ears should invariably insist on addressing itself to the angels. Being, as it were, ourselves the angels we had only a limited quarrel in each case with the event; but its inconsequent character, given the forces set in motion, was peculiarly baffling. It was like an interminable sum that wouldn't come straight; nobody had the time to handle so many figures. Limbert gathered, to make his pudding, dry bones and dead husks; how then was one to formulate the law that made the dish prove a feast? What was the cerebral treachery that defied his own vigilance? There was some obscure interference of taste, some obsession of the exquisite. All one could say was that genius was a fatal disturber or that the unhappy man had no effectual *flair*. When he went abroad to gather garlic he came home with heliotrope.

I hasten to add that if Mrs. Limbert was not directly illuminating she was yet rich in anecdote and example, having found a refuge from mystification exactly where the rest of us had found it, in a more devoted embrace and the sense of a finer glory. Her disappointments and eventually her privations had been many, her discipline severe; but she had ended by accepting the long grind of life and was now quite willing to take her turn at the mill. She was essentially one of us—she always understood. Touching and admirable at the last, when through the unmistakable change in Limbert's health her troubles were thickest, was the spectacle of the particular pride that she wouldn't have exchanged for prosperity. She had said to me once—only once, in a gloomy hour in London days when things were not going at all—that one really had to think him a very great man because if one didn't one would be rather ashamed of him. She had distinctly felt it at first—and in a very tender place—that almost every one passed him on the road; but I believe that in these final years she would almost have been ashamed of him if he had suddenly gone into editions. It is certain indeed that her complacency was not subjected to that shock. She would have liked the money immensely, but she would have missed something she had taught herself to regard as rather rare. There is another remark I remember her making, a remark to the effect that of course if she could have chosen she would have liked him to be Shakespeare or Scott, but that failing this she was very glad he wasn't—well, she named the two gentlemen, but I won't. I daresay she sometimes laughed out to escape an alternative. She contributed passionately to the capture of the second manner, foraging for him further afield than he could conveniently go, gleaning in the barest stubble, picking up shreds to build the nest and in particular in the study of the great secret of how, as we always said, they all did it laying waste the circulating libraries. If Limbert had a weakness he rather broke down in his reading. It was fortunately not till after the appearance of *The Hidden Heart* that he broke down in everything else. He had had rheumatic fever in the spring, when the book was but half finished, and this ordeal in addition to interrupting his work had enfeebled his powers of resistance and greatly reduced his vitality. He recovered from the fever and was able to take up the book again, but the organ of life was pronounced ominously weak and it was enjoined upon him with some sharpness that he should lend himself to no worries. It might have struck me as on the cards that his worries would now be surmountable, for when he began to mend he expressed to me a conviction almost contagious that he had never yet made so adroit a bid as in the idea of *The Hidden Heart*. It is grimly droll to reflect that this superb little composition, the shortest of his novels but perhaps the loveliest, was planned from the first as an "adventure-story" on approved lines. It was the way they all did the adventure-story that he tried most dauntlessly to emulate. I wonder how many readers ever divined to which of their bookshelves *The Hidden Heart* was so exclusively addressed. High medical advice early in the summer had been quite viciously clear as to the inconvenience that might ensue to him should he neglect to spend the winter in Egypt. He was not a man to neglect anything; but Egypt seemed to us all then as unattainable as a second edition. He finished *The Hidden Heart* with the energy of apprehension and desire, for if the book should happen to do what "books of that class," as the publisher said, sometimes did he might well have a fund to draw on. As soon as I read the deep and delicate thing I knew, as I had known in each case before, exactly how well it would do. Poor Limbert in this long business always figured to me an undiscourageable parent to whom only girls kept being born. A bouncing boy, a son and heir was devoutly prayed for and almanacks and old wives consulted; but the spell was inveterate, incurable, and *The Hidden Heart* proved, so to speak, but another female child. When the winter arrived accordingly Egypt was out of the question. Jane Highmore, to my knowledge, wanted to lend him money, and there were even greater devotees who did their best to induce him to lean on them. There was so marked a "movement" among his friends that a very considerable sum would have been at his disposal; but his stiffness was invincible: it had its root, I think, in his sense, on his own side, of sacrifices already made. He had sacrificed honour and pride, and he had sacrificed them precisely to the question of money. He would evidently, should he be able to go on, have to continue to sacrifice them, but it must be all in the way to which he had now, as he considered, hardened himself. He had spent years in plotting for favour, and since on favour he must live it could only be as a bargain and a price.

He got through the early part of the season better than we feared, and I went down in great elation to spend Christmas on the goose-green.

He told me late on Christmas eve, after our simple domestic revels had sunk to rest and we sat together by the fire, that he had been visited the night before in wakeful hours by the finest fancy for a really good thing that he had ever felt descend in the darkness. "It's just the vision of a situation that contains, upon my honour, everything," he said, "and I wonder that I've never thought of it before." He didn't describe it further, contrary to his common practice, and I only knew later, by Mrs. Limbert, that he had begun *Derogation* and that he was completely full of his subject. It was a subject however that he was not to live to treat. The work went on for a couple of months in happy mystery, without revelations even to his wife. He had not invited her to help him to get up his case—she had not taken the field with him as on his previous campaigns. We only knew he was at it again but that less even than ever had been said about the impression to be made on the market. I saw him in February and thought him sufficiently at ease. The great thing was that he was immensely interested and was pleased with the omens. I got a strange, stirring sense that he had not consulted the usual ones and indeed that he had floated away into a grand indifference, into a reckless consciousness of art. The voice of the market had suddenly grown faint and far: he had come back at the last, as people so often do, to one of the moods, the sincerities of his prime. Was he really with a blurred sense of the urgent doing something now only for himself? We wondered and waited— we felt that he was a little confused. What had happened, I was afterwards satisfied, was that he had quite forgotten whether he generally sold or not. He had merely waked up one morning again in the country of the blue and had stayed there with a good conscience and a great idea. He stayed till death knocked at the gate, for the pen dropped from his hand only at the moment when from sudden failure of the heart his eyes, as he sank back in his chair, closed for ever. *Derogation* is a splendid fragment; it evidently would have been one of his high successes. I am not prepared to say it would have waked up the libraries.

THE WAY IT CAME

I find, as you prophesied, much that's interesting, but little that helps the delicate question—the possibility of publication. Her diaries are less systematic than I hoped; she only had a blessed habit of noting and narrating. She summarised, she saved; she appears seldom indeed to have let a good story pass without catching it on the wing. I allude of course not so much to things she heard as to things she saw and felt. She writes sometimes of herself, sometimes of others, sometimes of the combination. It's under this last rubric that she's usually most vivid. But it's not, you will understand, when she's most vivid that she's always most publish-able. To tell the truth she's fearfully indiscreet, or has at least all the material for making me so. Take as an instance the fragment I send you, after dividing it for your convenience into several small chapters. It is the contents of a thin blank-book which I have had copied out and which has the merit of being nearly enough a rounded thing, an intelligible whole. These pages evidently date from years ago. I've read with the liveliest wonder the statement they so circumstantially make and done my best to swallow the prodigy they leave to be inferred. These things would be striking, wouldn't they? to any reader; but can you imagine for a moment my placing such a document before the world, even though, as if she herself had desired the world should have the benefit of it, she has given her friends neither name nor initials? Have you any sort of clue to their identity? I leave her the floor.

I

I know perfectly of course that I brought it upon myself; but that doesn't make it any better. I was the first to speak of her to him—he had never even heard her mentioned. Even if I had happened not to speak some one else would have made up for it: I tried afterwards to find comfort in that reflection. But the comfort of reflections is thin: the only comfort that counts in life is not to have been a fool. That's a beatitude I shall doubtless never enjoy. "Why, you ought to meet her and talk it over," is what I immediately said. "Birds of a feather flock together." I told him who she was and that they were birds of a feather because if he had had in youth a strange adventure she had had about the same time just such another. It was well known to her friends—an incident she was constantly called on to describe. She was charming, clever, pretty, unhappy; but it was none the less the thing to which she had originally owed her reputation.

Being at the age of eighteen somewhere abroad with an aunt she had had a vision of one of her parents at the moment of death. The parent was in England, hundreds of miles away and so far as she knew neither dying nor dead. It was by day, in the museum of some great foreign town. She had passed alone, in advance of her companions, into a small room containing some famous work of art and occupied at that moment by two other persons. One of these was an old custodian; the second, before observing him, she took for a stranger, a tourist. She was merely conscious that he was bareheaded and seated on a bench. The instant her eyes rested on him however she beheld to her amazement her father, who, as if he had long waited for her, looked at her in singular distress, with an impatience that was akin to reproach. She rushed to him with a bewildered cry, "Papa, what *is* it?" but this was followed by an exhibition of still livelier feeling when on her movement he simply vanished, leaving the custodian and her relations, who were at her heels, to gather round her in dismay. These persons, the official, the aunt, the cousins were therefore in a manner witnesses of the fact—the fact at least of the impression made on her; and there was the further testimony of a doctor who was attending one of the party and to whom it was immediately afterwards communicated. He gave her a remedy for hysterics but said to the aunt privately: "Wait and see if something doesn't happen at home." Something *had* happened—the poor father, suddenly and violently seized, had died that morning. The aunt, the mother's sister, received before the day was out a telegram announcing the event and requesting her to prepare her niece for it. Her niece was already prepared, and the girl's sense of this visitation remained of course indelible. We had all as her friends had it conveyed to us and had conveyed it creepily to each other. Twelve years had elapsed and as a woman who had made an unhappy marriage and lived apart from her husband she had become interesting from other sources; but since the name she now bore was a name frequently borne, and since moreover her judicial separation, as things were going, could hardly count as a distinction, it was usual to qualify her as "the one, you know, who saw her father's ghost."

As for him, dear man, he had seen his mother's. I had never heard of that till this occasion on which our closer, our pleasanter acquaintance led him, through some turn of the subject of our talk, to mention it and to inspire me in so doing with the impulse to let him know that he had a rival in the field—a person with whom he could compare notes. Later on his story became for him, perhaps because of my unduly repeating it, likewise a convenient wordly label; but it had not a year before been the ground on which he was introduced to me. He had other merits, just as she, poor thing! had others. I can honestly say that I was quite aware of them from the first—I discovered them sooner than he discovered mine. I remember how it struck me even at the time that his sense of mine was quickened by my having been able to match, though not indeed straight from my own experience, his curious anecdote. It dated, this anecdote, as hers did, from some dozen years before—a year in which, at Oxford, he had for some reason of his own been staying on into the "Long." He had been in the August afternoon on the river. Coming back into his room while it was still distinct daylight he found his mother standing there as if her eyes had been fixed on the door. He had had a letter from her that morning out of Wales, where she was staying with her father. At the sight of him she smiled with extraordinary radiance and extended her arms to him, and then as he sprang forward and joyfully opened his own she vanished from the place. He wrote to her that night, telling her what had happened; the letter had been carefully preserved. The next morning he heard of her death. He was through this chance of our talk extremely struck with the little prodigy I was able to produce for him. He had never encountered another case. Certainly they ought to meet, my friend and he; certainly they would have something in common. I would arrange this, wouldn't I?—if *she* didn't mind; for himself he didn't mind in the least. I had promised to speak to her of the matter as soon as possible, and within the week I was able to do so. She "minded" as little as he; she was perfectly willing to see him. And yet no meeting was to occur—as meetings are commonly understood.

II

That's just half my tale—the extraordinary way it was hindered. This was the fault of a series of accidents; but the accidents continued for years and became, for me and for others, a subject of hilarity with either party. They were droll enough at first; then they grew rather a bore. The odd thing was that both parties were amenable: it wasn't a case of their being indifferent, much less of their being indisposed. It was one of the caprices of chance, aided I suppose by some opposition of their interests and habits. His were centred in his office, his eternal inspectorship, which left him small leisure, constantly calling him away and making him break engagements. He liked society, but he found it everywhere and took it at a run. I never knew at a given moment where he was, and there were times when for months together I never saw him. She was on her side practically suburban: she lived at Richmond and never went "out." She was a woman of distinction, but not of fashion, and felt, as people said, her situation. Decidedly proud and rather whimsical she lived her life as she had planned it. There were things one could do with her, but one couldn't make her come to one's parties. One went indeed a little more than seemed quite convenient to hers, which consisted of her cousin, a cup of tea and the view. The tea was good; but the view was familiar, though perhaps not, like the cousin—a disagreeable old maid who had been of the group at the museum and with whom she now lived—offensively so. This connection with an inferior relative, which had partly an economical motive—she proclaimed her companion a marvellous manager—was one of the little perversities we had to forgive her. Another was her estimate of the proprieties created by her rupture with her husband. That was extreme—many persons called it even morbid. She made no advances; she cultivated scruples; she suspected, or I should perhaps rather say she remembered slights: she was one of the few women I have known whom that particular predicament had rendered modest rather than bold. Dear thing! she had some delicacy.

Especially marked were the limits she had set to possible attentions from men: it was always her thought that her husband was waiting to pounce on her. She discouraged if she didn't forbid the visits of male persons not senile: she said she could never be too careful.

When I first mentioned to her that I had a friend whom fate had distinguished in the same weird way as herself I put her quite at liberty to say "Oh, bring him out to see me!" I should probably have been able to bring him, and a situation perfectly innocent or at any rate comparatively simple would have been created. But she uttered no such word; she only said: "I must meet him certainly; yes, I shall look out for him!" That caused the first delay, and meanwhile various things happened. One of them was that as time went on she made, charming as she was, more and more friends, and that it regularly befell that these friends were sufficiently also friends of his to bring him up in conversation. It was odd that without belonging, as it were, to the same world or, according to the horrid term, the same set, my baffled pair should have happened in so many cases to fall in with the same people and make them join in the funny chorus. She had friends who didn't know each other but who inevitably and punctually recommended *him*. She had also the sort of originality, the intrinsic interest that led her to be kept by each of us as a kind of private resource, cultivated jealously, more or less in secret, as a person whom one didn't meet in society, whom it was not for every one—whom it was not for the vulgar—to approach, and with whom therefore acquaintance was particularly difficult and particularly precious. We saw her separately, with appointments and conditions, and found it made on the whole for harmony not to tell each other. Somebody had always had a note from her still later than somebody else. There was some silly woman who for a long time, among the unprivileged, owed to three simple visits to Richmond a reputation for being intimate with "lots of awfully clever out-of-the-way people."

Every one has had friends it has seemed a happy thought to bring together, and every one remembers that his happiest thoughts have not been his greatest successes; but I doubt if there was ever a case in which the failure was in such direct proportion to the quantity of influence set in motion. It is really perhaps here the quantity of influence that was most remarkable. My lady and gentleman each declared to me and others that it was like the subject of a roaring farce. The reason first given had with time dropped-out of sight and fifty better ones flourished on top of it. They were so awfully alike: they had the same ideas and tricks and tastes, the same prejudices and superstitions and heresies; they said the same things and sometimes did them; they liked and disliked the same persons and places, the same books, authors and styles; any one could see a certain identity even in their looks and their features. It established much of a propriety that they were in common parlance equally "nice" and almost equally handsome. But the great sameness, for wonder and chatter, was their rare perversity in regard to being photographed. They were the only persons ever heard of who had never been "taken" and who had a passionate objection to it. They just *wouldn't* be, for anything any one could say. I had loudly complained of this; him in particular I had so vainly desired to be able to show on my drawing-room chimney-piece in a Bond Street frame. It was at any rate the very liveliest of all the reasons why they ought to know each other—all the lively reasons reduced to naught by the strange law that had made them bang so many doors in each other's face, made them the buckets in the well, the two ends of the see-saw, the two parties in the state, so that when one was up the other was down, when one was out the other was in; neither by any possibility entering a house till the other had left it, or leaving it, all unawares, till the other was at hand. They only arrived when they had been given up, which was precisely also when they departed. They were in a word alternate and incompatible; they missed each other with an inveteracy that could be explained only by its being preconcerted. It was however so far from preconcerted that it had ended—literally after several years—by disappointing and annoying them. I don't think their curiosity was lively till it had been proved utterly vain. A great deal was of course done to help them, but it merely laid wires for them to trip. To give examples I should have to have taken notes; but I happen to remember that neither had ever been able to dine on the right occasion. The right occasion for each was the occasion that would be wrong for the other. On the wrong one they were most punctual, and there were never any but wrong ones. The very elements conspired and the constitution of man reinforced them. A cold, a headache, a bereavement, a storm, a fog, an earthquake, a cataclysm infallibly intervened. The whole business was beyond a joke.

Yet as a joke it had still to be taken, though one couldn't help feeling that the joke had made the situation serious, had produced on the part of each a consciousness, an awkwardness, a positive dread of the last accident of all, the only one with any freshness left, the accident that would bring them face to face. The final effect of its predecessors had been to kindle this instinct. They were quite ashamed—perhaps even a little of each other. So much preparation, so much frustration: what indeed could be good enough for it all to lead up to? A mere meeting would be mere flatness. Did I see them at the end of years, they often asked, just stupidly confronted? If they were bored by the joke they might be worse bored by something else. They made exactly the same reflections, and each in some manner was sure to hear of the other's.

I really think it was this peculiar diffidence that finally controlled the situation. I mean that if they had failed for the first year or two because they couldn't help it they kept up the habit because they had—what shall I call it?—grown nervous. It really took some lurking volition to account for anything so absurd

III

When to crown our long acquaintance I accepted his renewed offer of marriage it was humorously said, I know, that I had made the gift of his photograph a condition. This was so far true that I had refused to give him mine without it. At any rate I had him at last, in his high distinction, on the chimney-piece, where the day she called to congratulate me she came nearer than she had ever done to seeing him. He had set her in being taken an example which I invited her to follow; he had sacrificed his perversity—wouldn't she sacrifice hers? She too must give me something on my engagement—wouldn't she give me the companion-piece? She laughed and shook her head; she had headshakes whose impulse seemed to come from as far away as the breeze that stirs a flower. The companion-piece to the portrait of my future husband was the portrait of his future wife. She had taken her stand—she could depart from it as little as she could explain it. It was a prejudice, an *entêtement*, a vow—she would live and die unphotographed. Now too she was alone in that state: this was what she liked; it made her so much more original. She rejoiced in the fall of her late associate and looked a long time at his picture, about which she made no memorable remark, though she even turned it over to see the back. About our engagement she was charming—full of cordiality and sympathy. "You've known him even longer than I've *not?*" she said, "and that seems a very long time." She understood how we had jogged together over hill and dale and how inevitable it was that we should now rest together. I'm definite about all this because what followed is so strange that it's a kind of relief to me to mark the point up to which our relations were as natural as ever. It was I myself who in a sudden madness altered and destroyed them. I see now that she gave me no pretext and that I only found one in the way she looked at the fine face in the Bond Street frame. How then would I have had her look at it? What I had wanted from the first was to make her care for him. Well, that was what I still wanted—up to the moment of her having promised me that he would on this occasion really aid me to break the silly spell that had kept them asunder. I had arranged with him to do his part if she would as triumphantly do hers. I was on a different footing now—I was on a footing to answer for him. I would positively engage that at five on the following Saturday he would be on that spot. He was out of town on pressing business; but pledged to keep his promise to the letter he would return on purpose and in abundant time. "Are you perfectly sure?" I remember she asked, looking grave and considering: I thought she had turned a little pale. She was tired, she was indisposed: it was a pity he was to see her after all at so poor a moment. If he only *could* have seen her five years before! However, I replied that this time I was sure and that success therefore depended simply on herself. At five o'clock on the Saturday she would find him in a particular chair I pointed out, the one in which he usually sat and in which—though this I didn't mention—he had been sitting when, the week before, he put the question of our future to me in the way that had brought me round. She looked at it in silence, just as she had looked at the photograph, while

I repeated for the twentieth time that it was too preposterous it shouldn't somehow be feasible to introduce to one's dearest friend one's second self. "*Am* I your dearest friend?" she asked with a smile that for a moment brought back her beauty. I replied by pressing her to my bosom; after which she said: "Well, I'll come. I'm extraordinarily afraid, but you may count on me."

When she had left me I began to wonder what she was afraid of, for she had spoken as if she fully meant it. The next day, late in the afternoon, I had three lines from her: she had found on getting home the announcement of her husband's death. She had not seen him for seven years, but she wished me to know it in this way before I should hear of it in another. It made however in her life, strange and sad to say, so little difference that she would scrupulously keep her appointment. I rejoiced for her—I supposed it would make at least the difference of her having more money; but even in this diversion, far from forgetting that she had said she was afraid, I seemed to catch sight of a reason for her being so. Her fear as the evening went on became contagious, and the contagion took in my breast the form of a sudden panic. It wasn't jealousy—it was the dread of jealousy. I called myself a fool for not having been quiet till we were man and wife. After that I should somehow feel secure. It was only a question of waiting another month—a trifle surely for people who had waited so long. It had been plain enough she was nervous, and now that she was free she naturally wouldn't be less so. What was her nervousness therefore but a presentiment? She had been hitherto the victim of interference, but it was quite possible she would henceforth be the source of it. The victim in that case would be my simple self. What had the interference been but the finger of providence pointing out a danger? The danger was of course for poor *me*. It had been kept at bay by a series of accidents unexampled in their frequency; but the reign of accident was now visibly at an end. I had an intimate conviction that both parties would keep the tryst. It was more and more impressed upon me that they were approaching, converging. We had talked about breaking the spell; well, it would be effectually broken—unless indeed it should merely take another form and overdo their encounters as it had overdone their escapes.

This was something I couldn't sit still for thinking of; it kept me awake—at midnight I was full of unrest. At last I felt there was only one way of laying the ghost. If the reign of accident was over I must just take up the succession. I sat down and wrote a hurried note which would meet him on his return and which as the servants had gone to bed I sallied forth bareheaded into the empty, gusty street to drop into the nearest pillar-box. It was to tell him that I shouldn't be able to be at home in the afternoon as I had hoped and that he must postpone his visit till dinner-time. This was an implication that he would find me alone.

IV

When accordingly at five she presented herself I naturally felt false and base. My act had been a momentary madness, but I had at least to be consistent. She remained an hour; he of course never came; and I could only persist in my perfidy. I had thought it best to let her come; singular as this now seems to me I thought it diminished my guilt. Yet as she sat there so visibly white and weary, stricken with a sense of everything her husband's death had opened up, I felt an almost intolerable pang of pity and remorse. If I didn't tell her on the spot what I had done it was because I was too ashamed. I feigned astonishment—I feigned it to the end; I protested that if ever I had had confidence I had had it that day. I blush as I tell my story—I take it as my penance. There was nothing indignant I didn't say about him; I invented suppositions, attenuations; I admitted in stupefaction, as the hands of the clock travelled, that their luck hadn't turned. She smiled at this vision of their "luck," but she looked anxious—she looked unusual: the only thing that kept me up was the fact that, oddly enough, she wore mourning—no great depths of crape, but simple and scrupulous black. She had in her bonnet three small black feathers. She carried a little muff of astrachan. This put me by the aid of some acute reflection a little in the right. She had written to me that the sudden event made no difference for her, but apparently it made as much difference as that. If she was inclined to the usual forms why didn't she observe that of not going the first day or two out to tea? There was some one she wanted so much to see that she couldn't wait till her husband was buried. Such a betrayal of eagerness made me hard and cruel enough to practise my odious deceit, though at the same time, as the hour waxed and waned, I suspected in her something deeper still than disappointment and somewhat less successfully concealed. I mean a strange underlying relief, the soft, low emission of the breath that comes when a danger is past. What happened as she spent her barren hour with me was that at last she gave him up. She let him go for ever. She made the most graceful joke of it that I've ever seen made of anything; but it was for all that a great date in her life. She spoke with her mild gaiety of all the other vain times, the long game of hide-and-seek, the unprecedented queerness of such a relation. For it was, or had been, a relation, wasn't it, hadn't it? That was just the absurd part of it. When she got up to go I said to her that it was more a relation than ever, but that I hadn't the face after what had occurred to propose to her for the present another opportunity. It was plain that the only valid opportunity would be my accomplished marriage. Of course she would be at my wedding? It was even to be hoped that *he* would.

"If *I* am, he won't be!" she declared with a laugh. I admitted there might be something in that. The thing was therefore to get us safely married first. "That won't help us. Nothing will help us!" she said as she kissed me farewell. "I shall never, never see him!" It was with those words she left me.

I could bear her disappointment as I've called it; but when a couple of hours later I received him at dinner I found that I couldn't bear his. The way my manoeuvre might have affected him had not been particularly present to me; but the result of it was the first word of reproach that had ever yet dropped from him. I say "reproach" because that expression is scarcely too strong for the terms in which he conveyed to me his surprise that under the extraordinary circumstances I should not have found some means not to deprive him of such an occasion. I might really have managed either not to be obliged to go out or to let their meeting take place all the same. They would probably have got on in my drawing-room without me. At this I quite broke down—I confessed my iniquity and the miserable reason of it. I had not put her off and I had not gone out; she had been there and after waiting for him an hour had departed in the belief that he had been absent by his own fault.

"She must think me a precious brute!" he exclaimed. "Did she say of me—what she had a right to say?"

"I assure you she said nothing that showed the least feeling. She looked at your photograph, she even turned round the back of it, on which your address happens to be inscribed. Yet it provoked her to no demonstration. She doesn't care so much as all that."

"Then why are you afraid of her?"

"It was not of her I was afraid. It was of you."

"Did you think I would fall in love with her? You never alluded to such a possibility before," he went on as I remained silent. "Admirable person as you pronounced her, that wasn't the light in which you showed her to me."

"Do you mean that if it *had* been you would have managed by this time to catch a glimpse of her? I didn't fear things then," I added. "I hadn't the same reason."

He kissed me at this, and when I remembered that she had done so an hour or two before I felt for an instant as if he were taking from my lips the very pressure of hers. In spite of kisses the incident had shed a certain chill, and I suffered horribly from the sense that he had seen me guilty of a fraud. He had seen it only through my frank avowal, but I was as unhappy as if I had a stain to efface. I couldn't get over the manner of his looking at me when I spoke of her apparent indifference to his not having come.

For the first time since I had known him he seemed to have expressed a doubt of my word. Before we parted I told him that I would undeceive her start the first thing in the morning for Richmond and there let her know that he had been blameless. At this he kissed me again. I would expiate my sin, I said; I would humble myself in the dust; I would confess and ask to be forgiven. At this he kissed me once more.

V

In the train the next day this struck me as a good deal for him to have consented to; but my purpose was firm enough to carry me on. I mounted the long hill to where the view begins, and then I knocked at her door. I was a trifle mystified by the fact that her blinds were still drawn, reflecting that if in the stress of my compunction I had come early I had certainly yet allowed people time to get up.

"At home, mum? She has left home for ever."

I was extraordinarily startled by this announcement of the elderly parlour-maid. "She has gone away?"

"She's dead, mum, please." Then as I gasped at the horrible word: "She died last night."

The loud cry that escaped me sounded even in my own ears like some harsh violation of the hour. I felt for the moment as if I had killed her; I turned faint and saw through a vagueness the woman hold out her arms to me. Of what next happened I have no recollection, nor of anything but my friend's poor stupid cousin, in a darkened room, after an interval that I suppose very brief, sobbing at me in a smothered accusatory way. I can't say how long it took me to understand, to believe and then to press back with an immense effort that pang of responsibility which, superstitiously, insanely had been at first almost all I was conscious of. The doctor, after the fact, had been superlatively wise and clear: he was satisfied of a long-latent weakness of the heart, determined probably years before by the agitations and terrors to which her marriage had introduced her. She had had in those days cruel scenes with her husband, she had been in fear of her life. All emotion, everything in the nature of anxiety and suspense had been after that to be strongly deprecated, as in her marked cultivation of a quiet life she was evidently well aware; but who could say that any one, especially a "real lady," could be successfully protected from every little rub? She had had one a day or two before in the news of her husband's death; for there were shocks of all kinds, not only those of grief and surprise. For that matter she had never dreamed of so near a release; it had looked uncommonly as if he would live as long as herself. Then in the evening, in town, she had manifestly had another: something must have happened there which it would be indispensable to clear up. She had come back very late—it was past eleven o'clock, and on being met in the hall by her cousin, who was extremely anxious, had said that she was tired and must rest a moment before mounting the stairs. They had passed together into the dining-room, her companion proposing a glass of wine and bustling to the sideboard to pour it out. This took but a moment, and when my informant turned round our poor friend had not had time to seat herself. Suddenly, with a little moan that was barely audible, she dropped upon the sofa. She was dead. What unknown "little rub" had dealt her the blow? What shock, in the name of wonder, *had* she had in town? I mentioned immediately the only one I could imagine—her having failed to meet at my house, to which by invitation for the purpose she had come at five o'clock, the gentleman I was to be married to, who had been accidentally kept away and with whom she had no acquaintance whatever. This obviously counted for little; but something else might easily have occurred; nothing in the London streets was more possible than an accident, especially an accident in those desperate cabs. What had she done, where had she gone on leaving my house? I had taken for granted she had gone straight home. We both presently remembered that in her excursions to town she sometimes, for convenience, for refreshment spent an hour or two at the "Gentlewomen," the quiet little ladies' club and I promised that it should be my first care to make at that establishment thorough inquiry. Then we entered the dim and dreadful chamber where she lay locked up in death and where, asking after a little to be left alone with her, I remained for half an hour. Death had made her, had kept her beautiful but I felt above all, as I knelt at her bed, that it had made her, had kept her silent. It had turned the key on something I was concerned to know.

On my return from Richmond and after another duty had been performed I drove to his chambers. It was the first time, but I had often wanted to see them. On the staircase, which, as the house contained twenty sets of rooms, was unrestrictedly public, I met his servant, who went back with me and ushered me in. At the sound of my entrance he appeared in the doorway of a further room, and the instant we were alone I produced my news: "She's dead!"

"Dead?"

He was tremendously struck, and I observed that he had no need to ask whom, in this abruptness, I meant.

"She died last evening—just after leaving me."

He stared with the strangest expression, his eyes searching mine as if they were looking for a trap. "Last evening—after leaving you?" He repeated my words in stupefaction. Then he brought out so that it was in stupefaction I heard: "Impossible! I saw her."

"You 'saw' her?"

"On that spot—where you stand."

This brought back to me after an instant, as if to help me to take it in, the memory of the strange warning of his youth. "In the hour of death—I understand: as you so beautifully saw your mother."

"Ah! *not* as I saw my mother—not that way, not that way!" He was deeply moved by my news—far more moved, I perceived, than he would have been the day before: it gave me a vivid sense that, as I had then said to myself, there was indeed a relation between them and that he had actually been face to face with her. Such an idea, by its reassertion of his extraordinary privilege, would have suddenly presented him as painfully abnormal had he not so vehemently insisted on the difference. "I saw her living—I saw her to speak to her—I saw her as I see you now!"

It is remarkable that for a moment, though only for a moment, I found relief in the more personal, as it were, but also the more natural of the two phenomena. The next, as I embraced this image of her having come to him on leaving me and of just what it accounted for in the disposal of her time, I demanded with a shade of harshness of which I was aware—"What on earth did she come for?" He had now had a minute to think—to recover himself and judge of effects, so that if it was still with excited eyes he spoke he showed a conscious redness and made an inconsequent attempt to smile away the gravity of his words.

"She came just to see me. She came—after what had passed at your house—so that we *should*, after all, at last meet. The impulse seemed to me exquisite, and that was the way I took it."

I looked round the room where she had been—where she had been and I never had been.

"And was the way you took it the way she expressed it?"

"She only expressed it by being here and by letting me look at her. That was enough!" he exclaimed with a singular laugh.

I wondered more and more. "You mean she didn't speak to you?"

"She said nothing. She only looked at me as I looked at her."

"And *you* didn't speak either?"

He gave me again his painful smile. "I thought of *you*. The situation was every way delicate. I used the finest tact. But she saw she had pleased me." He even repeated his dissonant laugh.

"She evidently pleased you!" Then I thought a moment. "How long did she stay?"

"How can I say? It seemed twenty minutes, but it was probably a good deal less."

"Twenty minutes of silence!" I began to have my definite view and now in fact quite to clutch at it. "Do you know you're telling me a story positively monstrous?"

He had been standing with his back to the fire; at this, with a pleading look, he came to me. "I beseech you, dearest, to take it kindly."

I could take it kindly, and I signified as much; but I couldn't somehow, as he rather awkwardly opened his arms, let him draw me to him. So there fell between us for an appreciable time the discomfort of a great silence.

VI

He broke it presently by saying: "There's absolutely no doubt of her death?"

"Unfortunately none. I've just risen from my knees by the bed where they've laid her out."

He fixed his eyes hard on the floor; then he raised them to mine. "How does she look?"

"She looks—at peace."

He turned away again, while I watched him; but after a moment he began: "At what hour, then——?"

"It must have been near midnight. She dropped as she reached her house—from an affection of the heart which she knew herself and her physician knew her to have, but of which, patiently, bravely she had never spoken to me."

He listened intently and for a minute he was unable to speak. At last he broke out with an accent of which the almost boyish confidence, the really sublime simplicity rings in my ears as I write: "Wasn't she *wonderful!*" Even at the time I was able to do it justice enough to remark in reply that I had always told him so; but the next minute, as if after speaking he had caught a glimpse of what he might have made me feel, he went on quickly: "You see that if she didn't get home till midnight——"

I instantly took him up. "There was plenty of time for you to have seen her? How so," I inquired, "when you didn't leave my house till late? I don't remember the very moment—I was preoccupied. But you know that though you said you had lots to do you sat for some time after dinner. She, on her side, was all the evening at the 'Gentlewomen.' I've just come from there—I've ascertained. She had tea there; she remained a long, long time."

"What was she doing all the long, long time?" I saw that he was eager to challenge at every step my account of the matter; and the more he showed this the more I found myself disposed to insist on that account, to prefer, with apparent perversity, an explanation which only deepened the marvel and the mystery, but which, of the two prodigies it had to choose from, my reviving jealousy found easiest to accept. He stood there pleading with a candour that now seems to me beautiful for the privilege of having in spite of supreme defeat known the living woman; while I, with a passion I wonder at to-day, though it still smoulders in a manner in its ashes, could only reply that, through a strange gift shared by her with his mother and on her own side likewise hereditary, the miracle of his youth had been renewed for him, the miracle of hers for her. She had been to him—yes, and by an impulse as charming as he liked; but oh! she had not been in the body. It was a simple question of evidence. I had had, I assured him, a definite statement of what she had done—most of the time—at the little club. The place was almost empty, but the servants had noticed her. She had sat motionless in a deep chair by the drawing-room fire; she had leaned back her head, she had closed her eyes, she had seemed softly to sleep.

"I see. But till what o'clock?"

"There," I was obliged to answer, "the servants fail me a little. The portress in particular is unfortunately a fool, though even she too is supposed to be a Gentlewoman. She was evidently at that period of the evening, without a substitute and, against regulations, absent for some little time from the cage in which it's her business to watch the comings and goings. She's muddled, she palpably prevaricates; so I can't positively, from her observation, give you an hour. But it was remarked toward half-past ten that our poor friend was no longer in the club."

"She came straight here; and from here she went straight to the train."

"She couldn't have run it so close," I declared. "That was a thing she particularly never did."

"There was no need of running it close, my dear—she had plenty of time. Your memory is at fault about my having left you late: I left you, as it happens, unusually early. I'm sorry my stay with you seemed long; for I was back here by ten."

"To put yourself into your slippers," I rejoined, "and fall asleep in your chair. You slept till morning—you saw her in a dream!" He looked at me in silence and with sombre eyes—eyes that showed me he had some irritation to repress. Presently I went on: "You had a visit, at an extraordinary hour, from a lady—*soit*: nothing in the world is more probable. But there are ladies and ladies. How in the name of goodness, if she was unannounced and dumb and you had into the bargain never seen the least portrait of her—how could you identify the person we're talking of?"

"Haven't I to absolute satiety heard her described? I'll describe her for you in every particular."

"Don't!" I exclaimed with a promptness that made him laugh once more. I coloured at this, but I continued: "Did your servant introduce her?"

"He wasn't here—he's always away when he's wanted. One of the features of this big house is that from the street-door the different floors are accessible practically without challenge. My servant makes love to a young person employed in the rooms above these, and he had a long bout of it last evening. When he's out on that job he leaves my outer door, on the staircase, so much ajar as to enable him to slip back without a sound. The door then only requires a push. She pushed it—that simply took a little courage."

"A little? It took tons! And it took all sorts of impossible calculations."

"Well, she had them—she made them. Mind you, I don't deny for a moment," he added, "that it was very, very wonderful!"

Something in his tone prevented me for a while from trusting myself to speak. At last I said: "How did she come to know where you live?"

"By remembering the address on the little label the shop-people happily left sticking to the frame I had had made for my photograph."

"And how was she dressed?"

"In mourning, my own dear. No great depths of crape, but simple and scrupulous black. She had in her bonnet three small black feathers. She carried a little muff of astrachan. She has near the left eye," he continued, "a tiny vertical scar—"

I stopped him short. "The mark of a caress from her husband." Then I added: "How close you must have been to her!" He made no answer to this, and I thought he blushed, observing which I broke straight off. "Well, goodbye."

"You won't stay a little?" He came to me again tenderly, and this time I suffered him. "Her visit had its beauty," he murmured as he held me, "but yours has a greater one."

I let him kiss me, but I remembered, as I had remembered the day before, that the last kiss she had given, as I supposed, in this world had been for the lips he touched.

"I'm life, you see," I answered. "What you saw last night was death."

"It was life—it was life!"

He spoke with a kind of soft stubbornness, and I disengaged myself. We stood looking at each other hard.

"You describe the scene—so far as you describe it at all—in terms that are incomprehensible. She was in the room before you knew it?"

"I looked up from my letter-writing—at that table under the lamp, I had been wholly absorbed in it—and she stood before me."

"Then what did you do?"

"I sprang up with an ejaculation, and she, with a smile, laid her finger, ever so warningly, yet with a sort of delicate dignity, to her lips. I knew it meant silence, but the strange thing was that it seemed immediately to explain and to justify her. We, at any rate, stood for a time that, as I've told you, I can't calculate, face to face. It was just as you and I stand now."

"Simply staring?"

He impatiently protested. "Ah! *we're* not staring!"

"Yes, but we're talking."

"Well, *we* were—after a fashion." He lost himself in the memory of it. "It was as friendly as this." I had it on my tongue's end to ask if that were saying much for it, but I remarked instead that what they had evidently done was to gaze in mutual admiration. Then I inquired whether his recognition of her had been immediate. "Not quite," he replied, "for, of course, I didn't expect her; but it came to me long before she went who she was—who she could only be."

I thought a little. "And how did she at last go?"

"Just as she arrived. The door was open behind her, and she passed out."

"Was she rapid—slow?"

"Rather quick. But looking behind her," he added, with a smile. "I let her go, for I perfectly understood that I was to take it as she wished."

I was conscious of exhaling a long, vague sigh. "Well, you must take it now as *I* wish—you must let *me* go."

At this he drew near me again, detaining and persuading me, declaring with all due gallantry that I was a very different matter. I would have given anything to have been able to ask him if he had touched her, but the words refused to form themselves: I knew well enough how horrid and vulgar they would sound. I said something else—I forget exactly what; it was feebly tortuous, and intended to make him tell me without my putting the question. But he didn't tell me; he only repeated, as if from a glimpse of the propriety of soothing and consoling me, the sense of his declaration of some minutes before—the assurance that she was indeed exquisite, as I had always insisted, but that I was his "real" friend and his very own for ever. This led me to reassert, in the spirit of my previous rejoinder, that I had at least the merit of being alive; which in turn drew from him again the flash of contradiction I dreaded. "Oh, *she* was alive! she was, she was!"

"She was dead! she was dead!" I asseverated with an energy, a determination that it should be so, which comes back to me now almost as grotesque. But the sound of the word, as it rang out, filled me suddenly with horror, and all the natural emotion the meaning of it might have evoked in other conditions gathered and broke in a flood. It rolled over me that here was a great affection quenched, and how much I had loved and trusted her. I had a vision at the same time of the lonely beauty of her end. "She's gone—she's lost to us for ever!" I burst into sobs.

"That's exactly what I feel," he exclaimed, speaking with extreme kindness and pressing me to him for comfort. "She's gone; she's lost to us for ever: so what does it matter now?" He bent over me, and when his face had touched mine I scarcely knew if it were wet with my tears or with his own.

VII

It was my theory, my conviction, it became, as I may say, my attitude, that they had still never "met;" and it was just on this ground that I said to myself it would be generous to ask him to stand with me beside her grave. He did so, very modestly and tenderly, and I assumed, though he himself clearly cared nothing for the danger, that the solemnity of the occasion, largely made up of persons who had known them both and had a sense of the long joke, would sufficiently deprive his presence of all light association. On the question of what had happened the evening of her death little more passed between us; I had been overtaken by a horror of the element of evidence. It seemed gross and prying on either hypothesis. He, on his side, had none to produce, none at least but a statement of his house-porter—on his own admission a most casual and intermittent personage—that between the hours of ten o'clock and midnight no less than three ladies in deep black had flitted in and out of the place. This proved far too much; we had neither of us any use for three. He knew that I considered I had accounted for every fragment of her time and we dropped the matter as settled; we abstained from further discussion. What I knew however was that he abstained to please me rather than because he yielded to my reasons. He didn't yield—he was only indulgent; he clung to his interpretation because he liked it better. He liked it better, I held, because it had more to say to his vanity. That, in a similar position, would not have been its effect on me, though I had doubtless quite as much; but these are things of individual humour, as to which no person can judge for another. I should have supposed it more gratifying to be the subject of one of those inexplicable occurrences that are chronicled in thrilling books and disputed about at learned meetings; I could conceive, on the part of a being just engulfed in the infinite and still vibrating with human emotion, of nothing more fine and pure, more high and august than such an impulse of reparation, of admonition or even of curiosity. *That* was beautiful, if one would, and I should in his place have thought more of myself for being so distinguished. It was public that he had already, that he had long been distinguished, and what was this in itself but almost a proof? Each of the strange visitations contributed to establish the other. He had a different feeling; but he had also, I hasten to add, an unmistakable desire not to make a stand or, as they say, a fuss about it. I might believe what I liked—the more so that the whole thing was in a manner a mystery of my producing. It was an event of my history, a puzzle of my consciousness, not of his; therefore he would take about it any tone that struck me as convenient. We had both at all events other business on hand; we were pressed with preparations for our marriage.

Mine were assuredly urgent, but I found as the days went on that to believe what I "liked" was to believe what I was more and more intimately convinced of. I found also that I didn't like it so much as that came to, or that the pleasure at all events was far from being the cause of my conviction. My obsession, as I may really call it and as I began to perceive, refused to be elbowed away, as I had hoped, by my sense of paramount duties. If I had a great deal to do I had still more to think about, and the moment came when my occupations were gravely menaced by my thoughts. I see it all now, I feel it, I live it over. It's terribly void of joy, it's full indeed to overflowing of bitterness; and yet I must do myself justice—I couldn't possibly be other than I was. The same strange impressions, had I to meet them again, would produce the same deep anguish, the same sharp doubts, the same still sharper certainties. Oh, it's all easier to remember than to write, but even if I could retrace the business hour by hour, could find terms for the inexpressible, the ugliness and the pain would quickly stay my hand. Let me then note very simply and briefly that a week before our wedding-day, three weeks after her death, I became fully aware that I had something very serious to look in the face, and that if I was to make this effort I must make it on the spot and before another hour should elapse. My unextinguished jealousy—*that* was the Medusa-mask. It hadn't died with her death, it had lividly survived, and it was fed by suspicions unspeakable. They *would* be unspeakable to-day, that is, if I hadn't felt the sharp need of uttering them at the time.

This need took possession of me—to save me, as it appeared, from my fate. When once it had done so I saw—in the urgency of the case, the diminishing hours and shrinking interval—only one issue, that of absolute promptness and frankness. I could at least not do him the wrong of delaying another day, I could at least treat my difficulty as too fine for a subterfuge. Therefore very quietly, but none the less abruptly and hideously, I put it before him on a certain evening that we must reconsider our situation and recognise that it had completely altered.

He stared bravely. "How has it altered?"

"Another person has come between us."

He hesitated a moment. "I won't pretend not to know whom you mean." He smiled in pity for my aberration, but he meant to be kind. "A woman dead and buried!"

"She's buried, but she's not dead. She's dead for the world—she's dead for me. But she's not dead for *you*."

"You hark back to the different construction we put on her appearance that evening?"

"No," I answered, "I hark back to nothing. I've no need of it. I've more than enough with what's before me."

"And pray, darling, what is that?"

"You're completely changed."

"By that absurdity?" he laughed.

"Not so much by that one as by other absurdities that have followed it."

"And what may they have been?"

We had faced each other fairly, with eyes that didn't flinch; but his had a dim, strange light, and my certitude triumphed in his perceptible paleness. "Do you really pretend," I asked, "not to know what they are?"

"My dear child," he replied, "you describe them too sketchily!"

I considered a moment. "One may well be embarrassed to finish the picture! But from that point of view—and from the beginning—what was ever more embarrassing than your idiosyncrasy?"

He was extremely vague. "My idiosyncrasy?"

"Your notorious, your peculiar power."

He gave a great shrug of impatience, a groan of overdone disdain. "Oh, my peculiar power!"

"Your accessibility to forms of life," I coldly went on, "your command of impressions, appearances, contacts closed—for our gain or our loss—to the rest of us. That was originally a part of the deep interest with which you inspired me—one of the reasons I was amused, I was indeed positively proud to know you. It was a magnificent distinction; it's a magnificent distinction still. But of course I had no prevision then of the way it would operate now; and even had that been the case I should have had none of the extraordinary way in which its action would affect me."

"To what in the name of goodness," he pleadingly inquired, "are you fantastically alluding?" Then as I remained silent, gathering a tone for my charge, "How in the world *does* it operate?" he went on; "and how in the world are you affected?"

"She missed you for five years," I said, "but she never misses you now. You're making it up!"

"Making it up?" He had begun to turn from white to red.

"You see her—you see her: you see her every night!" He gave a loud sound of derision, but it was not a genuine one. "She comes to you as she came that evening," I declared; "having tried it she found she liked it!" I was able, with God's help, to speak without blind passion or vulgar violence; but those were the exact words—and far from "sketchy" they then appeared to me—that I uttered. He had turned away in his laughter, clapping his hands at my folly, but in an instant he faced me again, with a change of expression that struck me. "Do you dare to deny," I asked, "that you habitually see her?"

He had taken the line of indulgence, of meeting me halfway and kindly humouring me. At all events, to my astonishment, he suddenly said: "Well, my dear, what if I do?"

"It's your natural right; it belongs to your constitution and to your wonderful, if not perhaps quite enviable fortune. But you will easily understand that it separates us. I unconditionally release you."

"Release me?"

"You must choose between me and her."

He looked at me hard. "I see." Then he walked away a little, as if grasping what I had said and thinking how he had best treat it. At last he turned upon me afresh. "How on earth do you know such an awfully private thing?"

"You mean because you've tried so hard to hide it? It *is* awfully private, and you may believe I shall never betray you. You've done your best, you've acted your part, you've behaved, poor dear! loyally and admirably. Therefore I've watched you in silence, playing my part too; I've noted every drop in your voice, every absence in your eyes, every effort in your indifferent hand: I've waited till I was utterly sure and miserably unhappy. How *can* you hide it when you're abjectly in love with her, when you're sick almost to death with the joy of what she gives you?" I checked his quick protest with a quicker gesture. "You love her as you've *never* loved, and, passion for passion, she gives it straight back! She rules you, she holds you, she has you all! A woman, in such a case as mine, divines and feels and sees; she's not an idiot who has to

458

be credibly informed. You come to me mechanically, compunctiously, with the dregs of your tenderness and the remnant of your life. I can renounce you, but I can't share you; the best of you is hers; I know what it is and I freely give you up to her for ever!"

He made a gallant fight, but it couldn't be patched up; he repeated his denial, he retracted his admission, he ridiculed my charge, of which I freely granted him moreover the indefensible extravagance. I didn't pretend for a moment that we were talking of common things; I didn't pretend for a moment that he and she were common people. Pray, if they *had* been, how should I ever have cared for them? They had enjoyed a rare extension of being and they had caught me up in their flight; only I couldn't breathe in such an air and I promptly asked to be set down. Everything in the facts was monstrous, and most of all my lucid perception of them; the only thing allied to nature and truth was my having to act on that perception. I felt after I had spoken in this sense that my assurance was complete; nothing had been wanting to it but the sight of my effect on him. He disguised indeed the effect in a cloud of chaff, a diversion that gained him time and covered his retreat. He challenged my sincerity, my sanity, almost my humanity, and that of course widened our breach and confirmed our rupture. He did everything in short but convince me either that I was wrong or that he was unhappy; we separated, and I left him to his inconceivable communion.

He never married, any more than I've done. When six years later, in solitude and silence, I heard of his death I hailed it as a direct contribution to my theory. It was sudden, it was never properly accounted for, it was surrounded by circumstances in which—for oh, I took them to pieces!—I distinctly read an intention, the mark of his own hidden hand. It was the result of a long necessity, of an unquenchable desire. To say exactly what I mean, it was a response to an irresistible call.

THE END

About Author

Henry James OM (15 April 1843 – 28 February 1916) was an American-British author regarded as a key transitional figure between literary realism and literary modernism, and is considered by many to be among the greatest novelists in the English language. He was the son of Henry James Sr. and the brother of renowned philosopher and psychologist William James and diarist Alice James.

He is best known for a number of novels dealing with the social and marital interplay between émigré Americans, English people, and continental Europeans. Examples of such novels include The Portrait of a Lady, The Ambassadors, and The Wings of the Dove. His later works were increasingly experimental. In describing the internal states of mind and social dynamics of his characters, James often made use of a style in which ambiguous or contradictory motives and impressions were overlaid or juxtaposed in the discussion of a character's psyche. For their unique ambiguity, as well as for other aspects of their composition, his late works have been compared to impressionist painting.

His novella The Turn of the Screw has garnered a reputation as the most analysed and ambiguous ghost story in the English language and remains his most widely adapted work in other media. He also wrote a number of other highly regarded ghost stories and is considered one of the greatest masters of the field.

James published articles and books of criticism, travel, biography, autobiography, and plays. Born in the United States, James largely relocated to Europe as a young man and eventually settled in England, becoming a British subject in 1915, one year before his death. James was nominated for the Nobel Prize in Literature in 1911, 1912 and 1916.

Life

Early years, 1843–1883

James was born at 2 Washington Place in New York City on 15 April 1843. His parents were Mary Walsh and Henry James Sr. His father was intelligent and steadfastly congenial. He was a lecturer and philosopher who had inherited independent means from his father, an Albany banker and investor. Mary came from a wealthy family long settled in New York City. Her sister Katherine lived with her adult family for an extended period of time. Henry Jr. had three brothers, William, who was one year his senior, and younger brothers Wilkinson (Wilkie) and Robertson. His younger sister was Alice. Both of his parents were of Irish and Scottish descent.

The family first lived in Albany, at 70 N. Pearl St., and then moved to Fourteenth Street in New York City when James was still a young boy. His education was calculated by his father to expose him to many influences, primarily scientific and philosophical; it was described by Percy Lubbock, the editor of his selected letters, as "extraordinarily haphazard and promiscuous." James did not share the usual education in Latin and Greek classics. Between 1855 and 1860, the James' household traveled to London, Paris, Geneva, Boulogne-sur-Mer and Newport, Rhode Island, according to the father's current interests and publishing ventures, retreating to the United States when funds were low. Henry studied primarily with tutors and briefly attended schools while the family traveled in Europe. Their longest stays were in France, where Henry began to feel at home and became fluent in French. He was afflicted with a stutter, which seems to have manifested itself only when he spoke English; in French, he did not stutter.

In 1860 the family returned to Newport. There Henry became a friend of the painter John La Farge, who introduced him to French literature, and in particular, to Balzac. James later called Balzac his "greatest master," and said that he had learned more about the craft of fiction from him than from anyone else.

In the autumn of 1861 Henry received an injury, probably to his back, while fighting a fire. This injury, which resurfaced at times throughout his life, made him unfit for military service in the American Civil War.

In 1864 the James family moved to Boston, Massachusetts to be near William, who had enrolled first in the Lawrence Scientific School at Harvard and then in the medical school. In 1862 Henry attended Harvard Law School, but realised that he was not interested in studying law. He pursued his interest in literature and associated with authors and critics William Dean Howells and Charles Eliot Norton in Boston and Cambridge, formed lifelong friendships with Oliver Wendell Holmes Jr., the future Supreme Court Justice, and with James and Annie Fields, his first professional mentors.

His first published work was a review of a stage performance, "Miss Maggie Mitchell in Fanchon the Cricket," published in 1863. About a year later, A Tragedy of Error, his first short story, was published anonymously. James's first payment was for an appreciation of Sir Walter Scott's novels, written for the North American Review. He wrote fiction and non-fiction pieces for The Nation and Atlantic Monthly, where Fields was editor. In 1871 he published his first novel, Watch and Ward, in serial form in the Atlantic Monthly. The novel was later published in book form in 1878.

During a 14-month trip through Europe in 1869–70 he met Ruskin, Dickens, Matthew Arnold, William Morris, and George Eliot. Rome impressed him profoundly. "Here I am then in the Eternal City," he wrote to his brother William. "At last—for the first time—I live!" He attempted to support himself as a freelance writer in Rome, then secured a position as Paris correspondent for the New York Tribune, through the influence of its editor John Hay. When these efforts failed he returned to New York City. During 1874 and 1875 he published Transatlantic Sketches, A Passionate Pilgrim, and Roderick Hudson. During this early period in his career he was influenced by Nathaniel Hawthorne.

In 1869 he settled in London. There he established relationships with Macmillan and other publishers, who paid for serial installments that they would later publish in book form. The audience for these serialized novels was largely made up of middle-class women, and James struggled to fashion serious literary work within the strictures imposed by editors' and publishers' notions of what was suitable for young women to read. He lived in rented rooms but was able to join gentlemen's clubs that had libraries and where he could entertain male friends. He was introduced to English society by Henry Adams and Charles Milnes Gaskell, the latter introducing him to the Travellers' and the Reform Clubs.

In the fall of 1875 he moved to the Latin Quarter of Paris. Aside from two trips to America, he spent the next three decades—the rest of his life—in Europe. In Paris he met Zola, Alphonse Daudet, Maupassant, Turgenev, and others. He stayed in Paris only a year before moving to London.

In England he met the leading figures of politics and culture. He continued to be a prolific writer, producing The American (1877), The Europeans (1878), a revision of Watch and Ward (1878), French Poets and Novelists (1878), Hawthorne (1879), and several shorter works of fiction. In 1878 Daisy Miller established his fame on both sides of the Atlantic. It drew notice perhaps mostly because it depicted a woman whose behavior is outside the social norms of Europe. He also began his first masterpiece, The Portrait of a Lady, which would appear in 1881.

In 1877 he first visited Wenlock Abbey in Shropshire, home of his friend Charles Milnes Gaskell whom he had met through Henry Adams. He was much inspired by the darkly romantic Abbey and the surrounding countryside, which features in his essay Abbeys and Castles. In particular the gloomy monastic fishponds behind the Abbey are said to have inspired the lake in The Turn of the Screw.

While living in London, James continued to follow the careers of the "French realists", Émile Zola in particular. Their stylistic methods influenced his own work in the years to come. Hawthorne's influence on him faded during this period, replaced by George Eliot and Ivan Turgenev. 1879–1882 saw the publication of The Europeans, Washington Square, Confidence, and The Portrait of a Lady. He visited America in 1882–1883, then returned to London.

The period from 1881 to 1883 was marked by several losses. His mother died in 1881, followed by his father a few months later, and then by his brother Wilkie. Emerson, an old family friend, died in 1882. His friend Turgenev died in 1883.

Middle years, 1884–1897

In 1884 James made another visit to Paris. There he met again with Zola, Daudet, and Goncourt. He had been following the careers of the French "realist" or "naturalist" writers, and was increasingly influenced by them. In 1886, he published The Bostonians and The Princess Casamassima, both influenced by the French writers he'd studied assiduously. Critical reaction and sales were poor. He wrote to Howells that the books had hurt his career rather than helped because they had "reduced the desire, and demand, for my productions to zero". During this time he became friends with Robert Louis Stevenson, John Singer Sargent, Edmund Gosse, George du Maurier, Paul Bourget, and Constance Fenimore Woolson. His third novel from the 1880s was The Tragic Muse. Although he was following the precepts of Zola in his novels of the '80s, their tone and attitude are closer to the fiction of Alphonse Daudet. The lack of critical and financial success for his novels during this period led him to try writing for the theatre. (His dramatic works and his experiences with theatre are discussed below.)

In the last quarter of 1889, he started translating "for pure and copious lucre" Port Tarascon, the third volume of Alphonse Daudet adventures of Tartarin de Tarascon. Serialized in Harper's Monthly Magazine from June 1890, this translation praised as "clever" by The Spectator was published in January 1891 by Sampson Low, Marston, Searle & Rivington.

After the stage failure of Guy Domville in 1895, James was near despair and thoughts of death plagued him. The years spent on dramatic works were not entirely a loss. As he moved into the last phase of his career he found ways to adapt dramatic techniques into the novel form.

In the late 1880s and throughout the 1890s James made several trips through Europe. He spent a long stay in Italy in 1887. In that year the short novel The Aspern Papers and The Reverberator were published.

Late years, 1898–1916

In 1897–1898 he moved to Rye, Sussex, and wrote The Turn of the Screw. 1899–1900 saw the publication of The Awkward Age and The Sacred

Fount. During 1902–1904 he wrote The Ambassadors, The Wings of the Dove, and The Golden Bowl.

In 1904 he revisited America and lectured on Balzac. In 1906–1910 he published The American Scene and edited the "New York Edition", a 24-volume collection of his works. In 1910 his brother William died; Henry had just joined William from an unsuccessful search for relief in Europe on what then turned out to be his (Henry's) last visit to the United States (from summer 1910 to July 1911), and was near him, according to a letter he wrote, when he died.

In 1913 he wrote his autobiographies, A Small Boy and Others, and Notes of a Son and Brother. After the outbreak of the First World War in 1914 he did war work. In 1915 he became a British subject and was awarded the Order of Merit the following year. He died on 28 February 1916, in Chelsea, London. As he requested, his ashes were buried in Cambridge Cemetery in Massachusetts.

Biographers

James regularly rejected suggestions that he should marry, and after settling in London proclaimed himself "a bachelor". F. W. Dupee, in several volumes on the James family, originated the theory that he had been in love with his cousin Mary ("Minnie") Temple, but that a neurotic fear of sex kept him from admitting such affections: "James's invalidism ... was itself the symptom of some fear of or scruple against sexual love on his part." Dupee used an episode from James's memoir A Small Boy and Others, recounting a dream of a Napoleonic image in the Louvre, to exemplify James's romanticism about Europe, a Napoleonic fantasy into which he fled.

Dupee had not had access to the James family papers and worked principally from James's published memoir of his older brother, William, and the limited collection of letters edited by Percy Lubbock, heavily weighted toward James's last years. His account therefore moved directly from James's childhood, when he trailed after his older brother, to elderly invalidism. As more material became available to scholars, including the diaries of contemporaries and hundreds of affectionate and sometimes erotic letters written by James to younger men, the picture of neurotic celibacy gave way to a portrait of a closeted homosexual.

Between 1953 and 1972, Leon Edel authored a major five-volume biography of James, which accessed unpublished letters and documents after Edel gained the permission of James's family. Edel's portrayal of James included the suggestion he was celibate. It was a view first propounded by critic Saul Rosenzweig in 1943. In 1996 Sheldon M. Novick published Henry James: The Young Master, followed by Henry James: The Mature Master (2007). The first book "caused something of an uproar in Jamesian circles" as it challenged the previous received notion of celibacy, a once-familiar paradigm in biographies of homosexuals when direct evidence was non-existent. Novick also criticised Edel for following the discounted Freudian interpretation of homosexuality "as a kind of failure." The difference of opinion erupted in a series of exchanges between Edel and Novick which were published by the online magazine Slate, with the latter arguing that even the suggestion of celibacy went against James's own injunction "live!"—not "fantasize!"

A letter James wrote in old age to Hugh Walpole has been cited as an explicit statement of this. Walpole confessed to him of indulging in "high jinks", and James wrote a reply endorsing it: "We must know, as much as possible, in our beautiful art, yours & mine, what we are talking about — & the only way to know it is to have lived & loved & cursed & floundered & enjoyed & suffered — I don't think I regret a single 'excess' of my responsive youth".

The interpretation of James as living a less austere emotional life has been subsequently explored by other scholars. The often intense politics of Jamesian scholarship has also been the subject of studies. Author Colm Tóibín has said that Eve Kosofsky Sedgwick's Epistemology of the Closet made a landmark difference to Jamesian scholarship by arguing that he be read as a homosexual writer whose desire to keep his sexuality a secret shaped his layered style and dramatic artistry. According to Tóibín such a reading "removed James from the realm of dead white males who wrote about posh people. He became our contemporary."

James's letters to expatriate American sculptor Hendrik Christian Andersen have attracted particular attention. James met the 27-year-old Andersen in Rome in 1899, when James was 56, and wrote letters to Andersen that are intensely emotional: "I hold you, dearest boy, in my innermost love, & count on your feeling me—in every throb of your soul". In a letter of 6 May 1904, to his brother William, James referred to himself as "always your hopelessly celibate even though sexagenarian Henry". How accurate that description might have been is the subject of contention among James's biographers,   but the letters to Andersen were occasionally quasi-erotic: "I put, my dear boy, my arm around you, & feel the pulsation, thereby, as it were, of our excellent future & your admirable endowment." To his homosexual friend Howard Sturgis, James could write: "I repeat, almost to indiscretion, that I could live with you. Meanwhile I can only try to live without you."

His numerous letters to the many young gay men among his close male friends are more forthcoming. In a letter to Howard Sturgis, following a long visit, James refers jocularly to their "happy little congress of two" and in letters to Hugh Walpole he pursues convoluted jokes and puns about their relationship, referring to himself as an elephant who "paws you oh so benevolently" and winds about Walpole his "well meaning old trunk". His letters to Walter Berry printed by the Black Sun Press have long been celebrated for their lightly veiled eroticism.

He corresponded in almost equally extravagant language with his many female friends, writing, for example, to fellow novelist Lucy Clifford: "Dearest Lucy! What shall I say? when I love you so very, very much, and see you nine times for once that I see Others! Therefore I think that—if you want it made clear to the meanest intelligence—I love you more than I love Others." To his New York friend Mary Cadwalader Jones: "Dearest Mary Cadwalader. I yearn over you, but I yearn in vain; & your long silence really breaks my heart, mystifies, depresses, almost alarms me, to the point even of making me wonder if poor unconscious & doting old Célimare [Jones's pet name for James] has 'done' anything, in some dark somnambulism of the spirit, which has ... given you a bad moment, or a wrong impression, or a 'colourable pretext' ... However these things may be, he loves you as tenderly as ever;

othing, to the end of time, will ever detach him from you, & he remembers
hose Eleventh St. matutinal intimes hours, those telephonic matinées, as
he most romantic of his life ..." His long friendship with American novelist
Constance Fenimore Woolson, in whose house he lived for a number of
weeks in Italy in 1887, and his shock and grief over her suicide in 1894, are
discussed in detail in Edel's biography and play a central role in a study by
Lyndall Gordon. (Edel conjectured that Woolson was in love with James and
killed herself in part because of his coldness, but Woolson's biographers have
objected to Edel's account.)

Works

Style and themes

James is one of the major figures of trans-Atlantic literature. His works
frequently juxtapose characters from the Old World (Europe), embodying
a feudal civilisation that is beautiful, often corrupt, and alluring, and from
the New World (United States), where people are often brash, open, and
assertive and embody the virtues—freedom and a more highly evolved
moral character—of the new American society. James explores this clash
of personalities and cultures, in stories of personal relationships in which
power is exercised well or badly. His protagonists were often young American
women facing oppression or abuse, and as his secretary Theodora Bosanquet
remarked in her monograph Henry James at Work:

> When he walked out of the refuge of his study and into the world
> and looked around him, he saw a place of torment, where creatures of
> prey perpetually thrust their claws into the quivering flesh of doomed,
> defenseless children of light ... His novels are a repeated exposure of this
> wickedness, a reiterated and passionate plea for the fullest freedom of
> development, unimperiled by reckless and barbarous stupidity.

Critics have jokingly described three phases in the development of
James's prose: "James I, James II, and The Old Pretender." He wrote short
stories and plays. Finally, in his third and last period he returned to the long,
serialised novel. Beginning in the second period, but most noticeably in
the third, he increasingly abandoned direct statement in favour of frequent

double negatives, and complex descriptive imagery. Single paragraphs began to run for page after page, in which an initial noun would be succeeded by pronouns surrounded by clouds of adjectives and prepositional clauses, far from their original referents, and verbs would be deferred and then preceded by a series of adverbs. The overall effect could be a vivid evocation of a scene as perceived by a sensitive observer. It has been debated whether this change of style was engendered by James's shifting from writing to dictating to a typist, a change made during the composition of What Maisie Knew.

In its intense focus on the consciousness of his major characters, James's later work foreshadows extensive developments in 20th century fiction. Indeed, he might have influenced stream-of-consciousness writers such as Virginia Woolf, who not only read some of his novels but also wrote essays about them. Both contemporary and modern readers have found the late style difficult and unnecessary; his friend Edith Wharton, who admired him greatly, said that there were passages in his work that were all but incomprehensible. James was harshly portrayed by H. G. Wells as a hippopotamus laboriously attempting to pick up a pea that had got into a corner of its cage. The "late James" style was ably parodied by Max Beerbohm in "The Mote in the Middle Distance".

More important for his work overall may have been his position as an expatriate, and in other ways an outsider, living in Europe. While he came from middle-class and provincial beginnings (seen from the perspective of European polite society) he worked very hard to gain access to all levels of society, and the settings of his fiction range from working class to aristocratic, and often describe the efforts of middle-class Americans to make their way in European capitals. He confessed he got some of his best story ideas from gossip at the dinner table or at country house weekends. He worked for a living, however, and lacked the experiences of select schools, university, and army service, the common bonds of masculine society. He was furthermore a man whose tastes and interests were, according to the prevailing standards of Victorian era Anglo-American culture, rather feminine, and who was shadowed by the cloud of prejudice that then and later accompanied suspicions of his homosexuality. Edmund Wilson famously compared James's objectivity to Shakespeare's:

One would be in a position to appreciate James better if one compared him with the dramatists of the seventeenth century—Racine and Molière, whom he resembles in form as well as in point of view, and even Shakespeare, when allowances are made for the most extreme differences in subject and form. These poets are not, like Dickens and Hardy, writers of melodrama—either humorous or pessimistic, nor secretaries of society like Balzac, nor prophets like Tolstoy: they are occupied simply with the presentation of conflicts of moral character, which they do not concern themselves about softening or averting. They do not indict society for these situations: they regard them as universal and inevitable. They do not even blame God for allowing them: they accept them as the conditions of life.

It is also possible to see many of James's stories as psychological thought-experiments. In his preface to the New York edition of The American he describes the development of the story in his mind as exactly such: the "situation" of an American, "some robust but insidiously beguiled and betrayed, some cruelly wronged, compatriot..." with the focus of the story being on the response of this wronged man. The Portrait of a Lady may be an experiment to see what happens when an idealistic young woman suddenly becomes very rich. In many of his tales, characters seem to exemplify alternative futures and possibilities, as most markedly in "The Jolly Corner", in which the protagonist and a ghost-doppelganger live alternative American and European lives; and in others, like The Ambassadors, an older James seems fondly to regard his own younger self facing a crucial moment.

Major novels

The first period of James's fiction, usually considered to have culminated in The Portrait of a Lady, concentrated on the contrast between Europe and America. The style of these novels is generally straightforward and, though personally characteristic, well within the norms of 19th-century fiction. Roderick Hudson (1875) is a Künstlerroman that traces the development of the title character, an extremely talented sculptor. Although the book shows some signs of immaturity—this was James's first serious attempt at a full-length novel—it has attracted favourable comment due to the vivid realisation of the three major characters: Roderick Hudson, superbly gifted but unstable and unreliable; Rowland Mallet, Roderick's limited but much more mature friend and patron; and Christina Light, one of James's most enchanting and maddening femmes fatales. The pair of Hudson and Mallet has been seen as representing the two sides of James's own nature: the wildly imaginative artist and the brooding conscientious mentor.

In The Portrait of a Lady (1881) James concluded the first phase of his career with a novel that remains his most popular piece of long fiction. The story is of a spirited young American woman, Isabel Archer, who "affronts her destiny" and finds it overwhelming. She inherits a large amount of money and subsequently becomes the victim of Machiavellian scheming by two American expatriates. The narrative is set mainly in Europe, especially in England and Italy. Generally regarded as the masterpiece of his early phase, The Portrait of a Lady is described as a psychological novel, exploring the minds of his characters, and almost a work of social science, exploring the differences between Europeans and Americans, the old and the new worlds.

The second period of James's career, which extends from the publication of The Portrait of a Lady through the end of the nineteenth century, features less popular novels including The Princess Casamassima, published serially in The Atlantic Monthly in 1885–1886, and The Bostonians, published serially in The Century Magazine during the same period. This period also featured James's celebrated Gothic novella, The Turn of the Screw.

The third period of James's career reached its most significant achievement in three novels published just around the start of the 20th century: The Wings of the Dove (1902), The Ambassadors (1903), and The Golden Bowl (1904). Critic F. O. Matthiessen called this "trilogy" James's major phase, and these novels have certainly received intense critical study. It was the second-written of the books, The Wings of the Dove (1902) that was the first published because it attracted no serialization. This novel tells the story of Milly Theale, an American heiress stricken with a serious disease, and her impact on the people around her. Some of these people befriend Milly with honourable motives, while others are more self-interested. James stated in his autobiographical books that Milly was based on Minny Temple, his beloved cousin who died at an early age of tuberculosis. He said that he attempted in the novel to wrap her memory in the "beauty and dignity of art".

Shorter narratives

James was particularly interested in what he called the "beautiful and blest nouvelle", or the longer form of short narrative. Still, he produced a number of very short stories in which he achieved notable compression of sometimes complex subjects. The following narratives are representative of James's achievement in the shorter forms of fiction.

- "A Tragedy of Error" (1864), short story
- "The Story of a Year" (1865), short story
- A Passionate Pilgrim (1871), novella
- Madame de Mauves (1874), novella
- Daisy Miller (1878), novella
- The Aspern Papers (1888), novella
- The Lesson of the Master (1888), novella
- The Pupil (1891), short story
- "The Figure in the Carpet" (1896), short story
- The Beast in the Jungle (1903), novella
- An International Episode (1878)
- Picture and Text
- Four Meetings (1885)
- A London Life, and Other Tales (1889)
- The Spoils of Poynton (1896)

- Embarrassments (1896)

- The Two Magics: The Turn of the Screw, Covering End (1898)

- A Little Tour of France (1900)

- The Sacred Fount (1901)

- Views and Reviews (1908)

- The Wings of the Dove, Volume I (1902)

- The Wings of the Dove, Volume II (1909)

- The Finer Grain (1910)

- The Outcry (1911)

- Lady Barbarina: The Siege of London, An International Episode and Other Tales (1922)

- The Birthplace (1922)

Plays

At several points in his career James wrote plays, beginning with one-act plays written for periodicals in 1869 and 1871 and a dramatisation of his popular novella Daisy Miller in 1882. From 1890 to 1892, having received a bequest that freed him from magazine publication, he made a strenuous effort to succeed on the London stage, writing a half-dozen plays of which only one, a dramatisation of his novel The American, was produced. This play was performed for several years by a touring repertory company and had a respectable run in London, but did not earn very much money for James. His other plays written at this time were not produced.

In 1893, however, he responded to a request from actor-manager George Alexander for a serious play for the opening of his renovated St. James's Theatre, and wrote a long drama, Guy Domville, which Alexander produced. There was a noisy uproar on the opening night, 5 January 1895, with hissing from the gallery when James took his bow after the final curtain, and the author was upset. The play received moderately good reviews and had a modest run of four weeks before being taken off to make way for Oscar Wilde's The Importance of Being Earnest, which Alexander thought would have better prospects for the coming season.

After the stresses and disappointment of these efforts James insisted that he would write no more for the theatre, but within weeks had agreed to write a curtain-raiser for Ellen Terry. This became the one-act "Summersoft", which he later rewrote into a short story, "Covering End", and then expanded into a full-length play, The High Bid, which had a brief run in London in 1907, when James made another concerted effort to write for the stage. He wrote three new plays, two of which were in production when the death of Edward VII on 6 May 1910 plunged London into mourning and theatres closed. Discouraged by failing health and the stresses of theatrical work, James did not renew his efforts in the theatre, but recycled his plays as successful novels. The Outcry was a best-seller in the United States when it was published in 1911. During the years 1890–1893 when he was most engaged with the theatre, James wrote a good deal of theatrical criticism and assisted Elizabeth Robins and others in translating and producing Henrik Ibsen for the first time in London.

Leon Edel argued in his psychoanalytic biography that James was traumatised by the opening night uproar that greeted Guy Domville, and that it plunged him into a prolonged depression. The successful later novels, in Edel's view, were the result of a kind of self-analysis, expressed in fiction, which partly freed him from his fears. Other biographers and scholars have not accepted this account, however; the more common view being that of F.O. Matthiessen, who wrote: "Instead of being crushed by the collapse of his hopes [for the theatre]... he felt a resurgence of new energy."

Non-fiction

Beyond his fiction, James was one of the more important literary critics in the history of the novel. In his classic essay The Art of Fiction (1884), he argued against rigid prescriptions on the novelist's choice of subject and method of treatment. He maintained that the widest possible freedom in content and approach would help ensure narrative fiction's continued vitality.

James wrote many valuable critical articles on other novelists; typical is his book-length study of Nathaniel Hawthorne, which has been the subject of critical debate. Richard Brodhead has suggested that the study was emblematic of James's struggle with Hawthorne's influence, and constituted an effort to place the elder writer "at a disadvantage." Gordon Fraser, meanwhile, has suggested that the study was part of a more commercial effort by James to introduce himself to British readers as Hawthorne's natural successor.

When James assembled the New York Edition of his fiction in his final years, he wrote a series of prefaces that subjected his own work to searching, occasionally harsh criticism.

At 22 James wrote The Noble School of Fiction for The Nation's first issue in 1865. He would write, in all, over 200 essays and book, art, and theatre reviews for the magazine.

For most of his life James harboured ambitions for success as a playwright. He converted his novel The American into a play that enjoyed modest returns in the early 1890s. In all he wrote about a dozen plays, most of which went unproduced. His costume drama Guy Domville failed disastrously on its opening night in 1895. James then largely abandoned his efforts to conquer the stage and returned to his fiction. In his Notebooks he maintained that his theatrical experiment benefited his novels and tales by helping him dramatise his characters' thoughts and emotions. James produced a small but valuable amount of theatrical criticism, including perceptive appreciations of Henrik Ibsen.

With his wide-ranging artistic interests, James occasionally wrote on the visual arts. Perhaps his most valuable contribution was his favourable assessment of fellow expatriate John Singer Sargent, a painter whose critical status has improved markedly in recent decades. James also wrote sometimes charming, sometimes brooding articles about various places he visited and lived in. His most famous books of travel writing include Italian Hours (an example of the charming approach) and The American Scene (most definitely on the brooding side).

James was one of the great letter-writers of any era. More than ten thousand of his personal letters are extant, and over three thousand have been published in a large number of collections. A complete edition of James's letters began publication in 2006, edited by Pierre Walker and Greg Zacharias. As of 2014, eight volumes have been published, covering the period from 1855 to 1880. James's correspondents included celebrated contemporaries like Robert Louis Stevenson, Edith Wharton and Joseph Conrad, along with many others in his wide circle of friends and acquaintances. The letters range from the "mere twaddle of graciousness" to serious discussions of artistic, social and personal issues.

Very late in life James began a series of autobiographical works: A Small Boy and Others, Notes of a Son and Brother, and the unfinished The Middle Years. These books portray the development of a classic observer who was passionately interested in artistic creation but was somewhat reticent about participating fully in the life around him.

Reception

Criticism, biographies and fictional treatments

James's work has remained steadily popular with the limited audience of educated readers to whom he spoke during his lifetime, and has remained firmly in the canon, but, after his death, some American critics, such as Van Wyck Brooks, expressed hostility towards James for his long expatriation and eventual naturalisation as a British subject. Other critics such as E. M. Forster complained about what they saw as James's squeamishness in the treatment of sex and other possibly controversial material, or dismissed his late style as difficult and obscure, relying heavily on extremely long sentences and excessively latinate language. Similarly Oscar Wilde criticised him for writing "fiction as if it were a painful duty". Vernon Parrington, composing a canon of American literature, condemned James for having cut himself off from America. Jorge Luis Borges wrote about him, "Despite the scruples and delicate complexities of James, his work suffers from a major defect: the absence of life." And Virginia Woolf, writing to Lytton Strachey, asked, "Please tell me what you find in Henry James. ... we have his works here, and

I read, and I can't find anything but faintly tinged rose water, urbane and sleek, but vulgar and pale as Walter Lamb. Is there really any sense in it?" The novelist W. Somerset Maugham wrote, "He did not know the English as an Englishman instinctively knows them and so his English characters never to my mind quite ring true," and argued "The great novelists, even in seclusion, have lived life passionately. Henry James was content to observe it from a window." Maugham nevertheless wrote, "The fact remains that those last novels of his, notwithstanding their unreality, make all other novels, except the very best, unreadable." Colm Tóibín observed that James "never really wrote about the English very well. His English characters don't work for me."

Despite these criticisms, James is now valued for his psychological and moral realism, his masterful creation of character, his low-key but playful humour, and his assured command of the language. In his 1983 book, The Novels of Henry James, Edward Wagenknecht offers an assessment that echoes Theodora Bosanquet's:

> "To be completely great," Henry James wrote in an early review, "a work of art must lift up the heart," and his own novels do this to an outstanding degree ... More than sixty years after his death, the great novelist who sometimes professed to have no opinions stands foursquare in the great Christian humanistic and democratic tradition. The men and women who, at the height of World War II, raided the secondhand shops for his out-of-print books knew what they were about. For no writer ever raised a braver banner to which all who love freedom might adhere.

William Dean Howells saw James as a representative of a new realist school of literary art which broke with the English romantic tradition epitomised by the works of Charles Dickens and William Makepeace Thackeray. Howells wrote that realism found "its chief exemplar in Mr. James... A novelist he is not, after the old fashion, or after any fashion but his own." F.R. Leavis championed Henry James as a novelist of "established pre-eminence" in The Great Tradition (1948), asserting that The Portrait of a Lady and The Bostonians were "the two most brilliant novels in the language." James is now prized as a master of point of view who moved literary fiction forward by insisting in showing, not telling, his stories to the reader. (Source: Wikipedia)

NOTABLE WORKS

NOVELS

Watch and Ward (1871)

Roderick Hudson (1875)

The American (1877)

The Europeans (1878)

Confidence (1879)

Washington Square (1880)

The Portrait of a Lady (1881)

The Bostonians (1886)

The Princess Casamassima (1886)

The Reverberator (1888)

The Tragic Muse (1890)

The Other House (1896)

The Spoils of Poynton (1897)

What Maisie Knew (1897)

The Awkward Age (1899)

The Sacred Fount (1901)

The Wings of the Dove (1902)

The Ambassadors (1903)

The Golden Bowl (1904)

The Whole Family (collaborative novel with eleven other authors, 1908)

The Outcry (1911)

The Ivory Tower (unfinished, published posthumously 1917)

The Sense of the Past (unfinished, published posthumously 1917)

SHORT STORIES AND NOVELLAS

A Tragedy of Error (1864)

The Story of a Year (1865)

A Landscape Painter (1866)

A Day of Days (1866)

My Friend Bingham (1867)

Poor Richard (1867)

The Story of a Masterpiece (1868)

A Most Extraordinary Case (1868)

A Problem (1868)

De Grey: A Romance (1868)

Osborne's Revenge (1868)

The Romance of Certain Old Clothes (1868)

A Light Man (1869)

Gabrielle de Bergerac (1869)

Travelling Companions (1870)

A Passionate Pilgrim (1871)

At Isella (1871)

Master Eustace (1871)

Guest's Confession (1872)

The Madonna of the Future (1873)

The Sweetheart of M. Briseux (1873)

The Last of the Valerii (1874)

Madame de Mauves (1874)

Adina (1874)

Professor Fargo (1874)

Eugene Pickering (1874)

Benvolio (1875)

Crawford's Consistency (1876)

The Ghostly Rental (1876)

Four Meetings (1877)

Rose-Agathe (1878, as Théodolinde)

Daisy Miller (1878)

Longstaff's Marriage (1878)

An International Episode (1878)

The Pension Beaurepas (1879)

A Diary of a Man of Fifty (1879)

A Bundle of Letters (1879)

The Point of View (1882)

The Siege of London (1883)

Impressions of a Cousin (1883)

Lady Barberina (1884)

Pandora (1884)

The Author of Beltraffio (1884)

Georgina's Reasons (1884)

A New England Winter (1884)

The Path of Duty (1884)

Mrs. Temperly (1887)

Louisa Pallant (1888)

The Aspern Papers (1888)

The Liar (1888)

The Modern Warning (1888, originally published as The Two Countries)

A London Life (1888)

The Patagonia (1888)

The Lesson of the Master (1888)

The Solution (1888)

The Pupil (1891)

Brooksmith (1891)

The Marriages (1891)

The Chaperon (1891)

Sir Edmund Orme (1891)

Nona Vincent (1892)

The Real Thing (1892)

The Private Life (1892)

Lord Beaupré (1892)

The Visits (1892)

Sir Dominick Ferrand (1892)

Greville Fane (1892)

Collaboration (1892)

Owen Wingrave (1892)

The Wheel of Time (1892)

The Middle Years (1893)

The Death of the Lion (1894)

The Coxon Fund (1894)

The Next Time (1895)

Glasses (1896)

The Altar of the Dead (1895)

The Figure in the Carpet (1896)

The Way It Came (1896, also published as The Friends of the Friends)

The Turn of the Screw (1898)

Covering End (1898)

In the Cage (1898)

John Delavoy (1898)

The Given Case (1898)

Europe (1899)

The Great Condition (1899)

The Real Right Thing (1899)

Paste (1899)

The Great Good Place (1900)

Maud-Evelyn (1900)

Miss Gunton of Poughkeepsie (1900)

The Tree of Knowledge (1900)

The Abasement of the Northmores (1900)

The Third Person (1900)

The Special Type (1900)

The Tone of Time (1900)

Broken Wings (1900)

The Two Faces (1900)

Mrs. Medwin (1901)

The Beldonald Holbein (1901)

The Story in It (1902)

Flickerbridge (1902)

The Birthplace (1903)

The Beast in the Jungle (1903)

The Papers (1903)

Fordham Castle (1904)

Julia Bride (1908)

The Jolly Corner (1908)

The Velvet Glove (1909)

Mora Montravers (1909)

Crapy Cornelia (1909)

The Bench of Desolation (1909)

A Round of Visits (1910)

OTHER

Transatlantic Sketches (1875)

French Poets and Novelists (1878)

Hawthorne (1879)

Portraits of Places (1883)

A Little Tour in France (1884)

Partial Portraits (1888)

Essays in London and Elsewhere (1893)

Picture and Text (1893)

Terminations (1893)

Theatricals (1894)

Theatricals: Second Series (1895)

Guy Domville (1895)

The Soft Side (1900)

William Wetmore Story and His Friends (1903)

The Better Sort (1903)

English Hours (1905)

The Question of our Speech; The Lesson of Balzac. Two Lectures (1905)

The American Scene (1907)

Views and Reviews (1908)

Italian Hours (1909)

A Small Boy and Others (1913)

Notes on Novelists (1914)

Notes of a Son and Brother (1914)

Within the Rim (1918)

Travelling Companions (1919)

Notebooks (various, published posthumously)

The Middle Years (unfinished, published posthumously 1917)

A Most Unholy Trade (1925, published posthumously)

The Art of the Novel : Critical Prefaces (1934)